THE APPARATUS

JASON TRAPP BOOK 5

JACK SLATER

 Created with Vellum

PROLOGUE

Colonel Marion Spratt was too old for his present rank, and he knew it. From time to time he suspected the only reason he remained in uniform was because the Army's Human Resources Command had forgotten he existed at all. The thought might have brought a smile to his lips, if he had been prone to humor, which he was not. After all, he had spent his entire career attempting to blend into the background hum of military life. It seemed he had succeeded beyond his wildest dreams.

In his right hand he held a brown paper bag which contained a sandwich brought in from home. He had no wife to make his lunches, and was unlikely to have trusted one with the task even if he had.

Spratt was a man of fastidious routine. The sandwich contained a half inch of pastrami, a scraping of Dijon mustard on the lower slice of rye, a pickle sliced six ways and placed evenly underneath two twists of black pepper and a large pinch of salt, before the final slice of rye finished the job. It was a meal designed to keep his cardiologist up at night, though his last physical had given him a clean bill of health. His exercise routine was positively fanatical, keeping his triathlete's frame taut and devoid of body fat.

He walked straight-backed through Lyndon B. Johnson Memorial Park on the edge of the Potomac, searching for a free bench as he did most days, regardless of the weather. It was only noon, so most of the area's office workers—military and civilian alike—were yet to spill out into the small but pleasant park.

Routine was the enemy for the men at the tip of the spear. Routine got you killed. But Colonel Spratt had never been at the tip of the spear. He had been deployed on occasion, but never placed a single toe past the wire. That wasn't his role, and nobody had ever trained him to do so anyway. It was easy to find men who could pull a trigger. Harder to identify those who could tell them why.

Finding the park bench he'd eaten at yesterday empty, Spratt sat down and reached inside the paper bag. The sandwich inside was wrapped in aluminum foil, which he folded back neatly. No sense tearing it.

Another man in his position might have allowed the silence in this tiny haven in his nation's capital to pray on his thoughts. He was nearing fifty, his days wearing his country's uniform numbered, and nobody to go home to at night. He'd spent his entire career behind a desk, writing words that were classified before the ink was dry. Files that he'd slaved over for weeks wouldn't see the light of day for another seventy years, and the Army was unlikely to make them public even then.

Had he achieved anything? It was difficult to say. He'd done his job. He gave his superiors options, some of which were acted upon, and many of which were filed away, never to be seen again.

And besides, it wasn't silent. Not really, not with the drone of traffic from the nearby George Washington Memorial Parkway, or the groan of the horns of boats chugging up and down the Potomac, or the sound of distant footsteps – now closer, in an easy rhythm until they stopped just a few feet away.

Spratt looked up and saw the face of a man he hadn't ever expected to cross paths with again. After all, he was supposed to be dead.

"What are you doing here?" he asked, his face displaying neither emotion nor any obvious sign of recognition even as he quickly scanned the tree line in search of danger.

He picked out half a dozen figures in the distance: two mothers pushing strollers, several more office workers, and a runner. Nobody who obviously presented as a threat.

No one else.

"Good to see you too, Colonel," the man said calmly. He was wearing a dark Carhart work jacket and gray jeans, his height and weight unremarkable, though he was clearly physically fit. He had his hands thrust into his pockets. "It's been a while."

Spratt glanced back down at the sandwich in his hands. He hadn't even taken a bite. He placed it on the aluminum foil, his hands shaking slightly as he did so. His analytical mind raced to make sense of the facts even as a cold chill spread throughout his body. Several bystanders were still visible in the distance, but nobody within fifty yards. The hum of traffic would dull the sound of violence. If it came to that.

Which he was increasingly sure it would.

"What are you doing here?" he repeated. He gritted his teeth, frustrated with the quaver of unease that he heard.

"An old friend sends his regards," the man said. He stood with exquisite poise with his weight tilted toward the balls of his feet, almost like a ballet dancer. Despite his own exquisite physical fitness, Spratt's thighs would have been burning by now in his place.

Spratt knew without asking who he was referring to. "He couldn't be here himself?"

His interlocutor shook his head slowly. "Unfortunately he's otherwise engaged."

"He's really going to do it," Spratt said, shaking his head in a state of stunned disbelief. "It's madness."

The man observed him with amusement on his lips. "Operation Redwood was your idea, was it not?"

"There's a reason I never filed it." Spratt said. He felt the urge to rise, to shake some sense into this man and explain to him the folly of his course of action. But his legs were jelly. He was stuck with fear. "It's doomed to fail."

"And you told no-one else?" his companion asked, observing his response intently.

"Of course not."

"Then you have a choice," the killer said, taking a step toward him and extending his left hand. "Come with me, now, and stay with us until it's done. Redwood is your baby, after all. You know it better than any of us. See it through. You might find that you enjoy it."

"Or what?" Spratt whispered, knowing that the man's left hand was not the dominant one, and understanding what that meant. The choice wasn't real. His fate was pre-determined. This man was simply here to execute it. He knew he should run, but couldn't. Perhaps this was the end he deserved.

A tear leaked down his cheek as the blade cut through his skin, driving up and underneath the rib cage until the tip severed the left coronary artery. Spratt's powerful heart kept beating for several more seconds, not yet understanding what his brain already did.

It was over.

1

The Fashion Center Mall in Pentagon City was already humming with the morning rush as Jason Trapp stepped inside. The throngs of tourists that flocked to Washington DC every summer and fall hadn't yet roused themselves, so the shopping mall mostly contained locals, soldiers, sailors, Marines, and airmen who staffed the US military's massive bureaucracy on the Potomac.

And civilians, Trapp thought idly as his eyes picked their way through a sea of uniforms, alighting on as many business suits.

He was dressed in an unremarkable fashion. A plain white T-shirt covered his scarred, muscular torso, though it too was concealed beneath a dark navy sport coat. Both sat astride a pair of black jeans purchased from a Goodwill store the day before, aged over years to a more indistinct gray. The look was neither eye-catching nor disagreeable. It was just...

Gray.

And that was the way that Trapp liked it.

He moved through the mall, the flow of human traffic carrying him downstream, his uneven eyes always moving, cataloging every face and outfit for future reference. Someone might be watching. Maybe some*ones*. Someone was always watching, whether they knew it yet or not.

But it was his job to remain unseen, unnoticed, to slink through a crowd without drawing a second glance, to remain alert without attracting attention. It was an infinitely difficult skill to acquire, and one that eroded through lack of use. Thankfully, it was one he called upon frequently.

In fact, his task today wasn't just to remain hidden; it was to be the hunter. He was doing a favor for a friend, FBI Supervisory Special Agent Nick Pope, one of the Bureau's premier counter-intelligence agents—a fact that Trapp knew from personal experience. Pope was currently putting on a training course to introduce newly minted Special Agents to the world of counterintelligence, one of the FBIs lesser known but vitally important functions.

Trapp—an infrequent visiting training officer at the Farm, the CIAs own training facility—had agreed to help share his experience with the Bureau's fresh recruits, mainly because he was bored and growing itchy. Today's mission was to get the new agents to think like spies. Their job was to conduct a brush past—a clandestine technique for handing off secrets from one operative to another—on a specific Metro line at a specific time. His was to see if he could catch them doing it.

Easy.

He rode the stream of warm bodies to its edge, then stepped out of its way and knelt in front of a glass-windowed storefront to tie his shoelace. No one in the crowd behind him paid him a second glance as he scanned the reflection for the flash of eyes passing over his frame.

Only an amateur would allow themselves to be fooled by such an obvious ploy. A trained surveillance operative would walk right on past without ever glancing down, knowing that another member of the team would seamlessly pick up the trail.

But they weren't always so professional. And maybe one in a hundred times, or five hundred, or a thousand, a trailing agent's gaze might be attracted for a fraction of a second too long – just enough time to be noticed.

However, not this time. As far as Trapp could tell, the flow of humanity carried on without a lull.

He tightened the loop of his shoelace, then rode the glass-walled elevator to the mall's second floor. Few of the stores were open yet, so he browsed a concession booth manned by a teenager with puffy, tired eyes who was staring aimlessly into the flashing screen of an enormous silver cell phone. The outlet sold mostly trinkets: baseball caps, keychains, phone covers, and the like, but the diversion gave him the opportunity to run a secondary tail check.

Trapp purchased a souvenir keychain that bore the logo of DC United, the local soccer franchise. He made a show of pulling a set of keys from his pocket, loosening the existing chain, and tossing it in a trashcan before fixing his keys to the new purchase. As he did so, he occasionally glanced at the display mirror in the concession booth.

Still nothing.

With nothing much open at this hour, this floor of the mall was mostly empty. Certain now that he was indeed alone, Trapp circled it, keeping away from the balcony that looked down into the central courtyard under the pretense of occasionally glancing into a still-closed storefront.

"This is Hangman," he muttered into his lapel mic. "You're going to lose me."

"Copy," Pope replied swiftly. "Training exercise is live. Good hunting."

Trapp called an elevator, which arrived swiftly and just as speedily carried him back down. This time, he fought against the river of office workers, a trick that would have made it easy to spot anyone following directly behind, which no one was, and walked through the tunnel that led to the Pentagon City Metro station.

A pair of screeching escalators ran down into the Metro station itself, causing Trapp to wince as he gently pressed his fingers into his ears for protection. Though the stairway to his side was packed two abreast with uniforms and suits, there was only one other lady traveling downward, a Latina who looked to be in her mid-fifties, hair pulled back into a graying bun and wearing the uniform of a local cleaning contractor.

Trapp passed through the ticket barriers and made his way down to the trains. Belowground the tracks had a cinematic feel to them, a dim back-lighting glowing from behind vaulted concrete rectangles. The space between the platforms was dark, giving up only the occasional glimpse of the gleaming metal of the worn tracks. Neither platform was busy, though a few trailing commuters from the last train to stop at the station were still making their way up to the ticket area.

The display above the platform indicated the next train would arrive in under two minutes. Then a gap of only a minute before the one after that.

A minute ticked away as Trapp waited alone on the platform, barring the cleaner from earlier. Two men waited on the opposite side, both wearing Army fatigues. The camo looked almost black in the gloom. One was leaning against the station's back wall, his eyes seemingly closed. The other had his eyes locked onto a glowing cell phone screen. Trapp casually glanced across, under the guise of pretending to check when the next train was due.

One minute.

A woman bounded down the escalator wearing short heels and a blue and white striped blouse. She had platinum blond hair that was cut just above her shoulders. She didn't appear to be paying attention to the steps beneath her, which she took two at a time, her attention focused on the handbag currently clutched against her chest with her right hand buried inside.

She looked up, and a wave of relief washed over her face as she saw that she still had time. Trapp watched out of the corner of his eye as she rushed past him, settling the handbag back on her shoulder, a small black disc in her fingers.

The woman stopped to his left, flicked open the small makeup case, and began hurriedly touching up her eyeliner. To Trapp's right, he saw a small, bronze-coated cylinder rotating slowly on the platform, rolling inch by inch toward the platform's edge. It was only a foot away from him, so he leaned down and picked it up an instant before it toppled toward the tracks. He lifted it to his eyes and peered curiously.

Lipstick.

"I'm sorry, ma'am," Trapp said, walking over and gently tapping her on the shoulder. "You dropped this."

"My God," she gasped, looking up from the mirror in her left hand. "You made me jump!"

He smiled and proffered her tube of lipstick. "Sorry about that."

He wasn't really. She was more chaff for anyone watching to deal with. More admin. Another crumb of due diligence for somebody to run down. No-one was hunting him, at least not today. But it didn't hurt to hone his skills.

"Thank you so much!"

Trapp stepped back and waved his hands magnanimously. "Forget about it."

The squeal of metal against metal echoed down the platform as a distant rumble of thunder warned of the approach of a Metro train. The sound attracted both their attention.

Just before it arrived, a large group of young men and women spilled onto the platform, all wearing casual clothes and laughing. There were perhaps a dozen of them in total. Maybe fifteen. They were probably students, Trapp guessed.

He casually glanced at them, long since having mastered the technique of appearing completely uninterested while actually studying them carefully. Had someone followed in their wake, using the distraction to lose themselves in the crowd and fool anyone watching?

There was a blonde girl. Short and plain, but not unattractive. She was physically fit, which matched the profile, and seemed a couple of years older than the students. That caught his attention also.

Maybe it's you, he thought. He stepped onto the train.

2

"Good morning, Papi."

Hector Alvarez León smiled at the sight of his young daughter's face, already smeared red with a streak of tomato juice from the breakfast plate in front of her. He reached for a paper towel, tore off a strip, and wiped away the mess before running his fingers through her hair.

"Morning, bella," he said, using the family nickname for Gabriella León , his only child. Bella for beautiful. A beautiful accident. "Are you excited for school today?"

Gabriella frowned, crossing her little arms over an equally delicate chest. "Can't I go to work with you?"

Looking up, Hector caught his dark-haired wife's eyes roll with amusement. Every morning was the same. He blew her an affectionate air kiss, then pulled a wooden stool up to the breakfast bar. It was the rickety one, he realized as he sat down on it. The one he'd been meaning to fix every weekend for the last month.

"You know you can't, Gabby." He smiled, glancing meaningfully at the half-eaten plate of baked tomato and eggs in front of his daughter. "But Papi will make you pancakes this weekend if you like?"

"Hey!" his wife exclaimed as she set down a steaming plate of his own in front of him. "What's wrong with my huevos?"

He winked lasciviously at María León , raking his gaze up and down his wife's perfect body in plain view of Gabriella. At only five years old, she was still too young to comprehend what her parents were up to. Yet somehow her childhood would disappear in an instant, and she would be all grown up.

The thought pained him. In her school uniform, a dark navy skirt topped with a tiny white polo shirt emblazoned with the icon of a fifteenth century Catholic saint, Gabriella looked almost too pure to comprehend. Too innocent for this world. The image allowed Hector – if only with painful brevity – to pretend that he could protect her from the chaos of the world outside these four walls.

But that was a lie.

Gabriella's school uniform was proof enough of that. Every morning, she was driven to school in an unmarked bus that was trailed by a pair of equally plain police vehicles. The school itself was attended mainly by children just like Gabby. The sons and daughters of police officers and local politicians and military types like him.

Ordinarily, on a captain's salary, Hector León would be unable to afford even a semester of Gabriella's school fees. But in Mexico, few enough were willing to go to war with the forces of darkness. Fewer still would run the risk if their families weren't offered at least a fig leaf of security.

"Are you listening, Hector?" his wife María chided as Gabriella looked on with dark, soulful, disappointed eyes that echoed her mother's words.

He grimaced and gave a slight shake of his head. "What did you say?"

"I cleaned your uniform," she said, jerking her head at a

duffel bag sitting by the front door. Her nose wrinkled. "The smell..."

Hector shrugged, remembering the plate of food in front of him for the first time. He began to shovel the now slightly cooler eggs into his mouth, speaking through the maelstrom. "It's natural. And we do a lot of running, remember?"

"Oh, I remember," María said, shooting her husband a look of her own. "And I thought we agreed you would learn to use the washing machine?"

The chime of Hector's fork meeting the now-empty plate in front of him scythed through the moment's mild tension just in time to prevent Gabriella becoming alarmed. He threw up his hands in apology and communicated the same message by fixing his gaze directly on his wife's eyes. "I'm sorry. Yesterday was busy. But that's not an excuse."

"Every day's busy," María remarked with a raised eyebrow, though her expression had by now softened. "For me as well."

"Papi," Gabriella yelped, pushing away her still-full plate so that it slid a few inches from her. "Will you drive me to school?"

Hector allowed his gaze to linger on his wife's eyes for a few more breaths to check she understood that he'd received her message loud and clear. María León was no pushover. That's what he liked so much about her.

"You know I can't," he said, standing and reaching across the table. He lifted Gabriella by her armpits and swooped her tiny frame through the air until she giggled, forgetting at least the immediacy of her request as he set her back down to earth. "Your friends would miss you."

Gabriella nodded to herself, her lips set in agreement, convinced in that way young children often are of their own centrality to the universe. "But you'll be home this weekend?"

He crouched down in front of his daughter, squeezing her cheeks, his eyes briefly catching the position of the clock's hands before they snapped back to her face. "For you, of course, hija."

With Gabriella mollified, he stood and kissed his wife goodbye. As always, he wondered if today might be his last opportunity. As always, he kissed his wife like he meant it, and she responded in kind.

"I'll check your car," he said softly as his lips pulled away from hers, and instantly, the shine in María's eyes died. Back to earth.

He winced as he applied the coup de grâce. "And I won't be back tonight. I'm on duty until tomorrow. I'll sleep at the base. Okay?"

María nodded, knowing not to make any overt show of concern in front of their daughter, but the worry in her dark brown eyes told that story regardless. He held her arms for a few seconds longer, communicating silently.

I'll be fine. I always am.

Hector ruffled Gabby's hair on his way out and drank in one last glimpse of his family as he hauled the battered Nike duffel bag over his shoulder. Like the rest of his public life, the bag was camouflage. He stepped out of the front door, and his eyes scanned the small, neat driveway outside his suburban house. The garage was detached from the main building but had its own security system, connected to the state police's switchboard. Still, Hector did not trust modern technology alone to keep him safe.

After all, technology was built and watched over by people. And in Mexico, everyone had their price.

This morning, nothing was visibly out of place. The chest-high gate that crowned the driveway was still closed and padlocked and bore no signs of any attempt to alter that equation. Flowerbeds ringed the inside of the fence, planted lushly with a riot of delicate, colorful flowers with barely an inch between them. They smoothed and beautified the appearance of the concrete driveway itself, but that was not their prime purpose.

There wasn't even a petal out of place.

Satisfied that his home was secure, Hector turned to the garage and unlocked the side entrance. The chime of the security system warned him that he had 30 seconds to input his code before the sirens would start pealing. It had happened once before to María in a moment of forgetfulness, and he still hadn't heard the last of it.

Both his own vehicle and María's were nondescript Ford sedans in dark, drab colors and usually covered in a thin layer of dust. He always picked the same models from the rental shops to avoid attracting attention from any of his more curious neighbors but switched out the vehicles themselves every few months.

Just in case.

The two cars were parked side by side, and he walked a figure eight between and around the two vehicles, checking for anything that looked out of place. A scratch in the paintwork, or a smudge in the dust coating that he didn't remember from the night before. It was difficult to replicate the way a road's filth coated a car. Even more so at night, and in the dark.

Hector took his time, his pulse beating slowly and evenly as he performed what was to him almost a meditative ritual. He checked every window, every door seam, beneath the wipers and under the hood of both sedans. The check didn't take long, but it was nevertheless thorough.

To complete it, he reached for a device that rested against the garage's wall. It looked a little like a golf club, a small rectangular mirror attached to a long handle. He twisted it in his grip, then fed the mirror underneath the chassis of first his vehicle, then María's. He walked slowly around both vehicles until he was certain beyond all doubt that no barnacle had been attached overnight.

Finally satisfied, he set the mirror aside and tapped the button that opened the garage door. The mechanism cranked into life overhead, its chain creaking grumpily in search of oil.

And as the morning sun crept beneath the rising door, Hector Alvarez León breathed a sigh of relief.

3

The Metro train was somewhat busy, but not unusually so for the hour. Trapp managed to snag one of the few remaining seats, about halfway down the carriage, chosen for the fact that unlike many, it faced into the walkway, rather than simply forward or back, allowing him to surveil both sides.

A little above head height and directly in Trapp's eye line was an electronic screen, which ordinarily would have displayed a map of the Metro system and warned commuting passengers when the next stop was approaching. That was the plan, anyway.

As so often with the new Kawasaki 7000 series carriages that had recently been introduced – accompanied by much fanfare in the local press – the screen wasn't working. It was encased in a glass box for additional protection, and a combination of the black backdrop and the reflective glass acted almost as a mirror, allowing Trapp both to stare directly ahead and for his attention to wander.

A homeless man was seated to Trapp's right, which perhaps explained why his seat wasn't already taken. The man smelled quite pungently of urine, a particularly acrid fragrance that suggested this was not the first time for either man or garment.

But Trapp didn't mind all that much. He'd worn such clothes before, though always out of choice rather than either necessity or the cruel hand of fate. He had visited a lot of countries over the course of his career, and some time ago realized that many countries treated the homeless better than America. In Japan and Korea, it was rare to ever lay eyes on one. In fact, few nations were so callous as his own.

It was not a fact that troubled Trapp all that much. Failure came hand in hand with opportunity, and his homeland offered much of the latter. Maybe it had something to do with the American Dream – in that nobody wanted to be reminded too much of the consequences of their own lives veering off the tracks. It wasn't so much a meanness of spirit as a desire not to think too hard. And so, few did. To be homeless in a major American city was the next best thing to being invisible.

And so if Trapp had happened to be a counterintelligence agent in the employ of the Federal Bureau of Investigation, perhaps he might have considered that fact an opportunity in itself.

The trick to detecting a tail was no secret – but that did not mean it wasn't fiendishly difficult to achieve. All that was required was for you to suspect everyone, at all times. The entire name of the game for the surveillance operative was to be *gray*. Seeing, yet unseen. The same went for the spies that counter-intelligence agents hunted.

Trapp consciously wrinkled his nose and glanced to his right at the exact moment that the homeless man started retching, grabbing his stomach and letting out a pained moan. A woman opposite him dressed in a sharp pantsuit and probably destined for the office of one of the many thinktanks that ringed the Beltway frowned and stood, moving a few yards down the carriage.

The bum's skin was caked yellow, though Trapp suspected that underneath the filth they shared a similar ancestry. His nails were impregnated with dirt, and age had carved deep furrows into his cheeks and brow.

If it was makeup, Trapp judged, then the artist should be working in Hollywood, not the espionage business. He knew from experience that masks, molded out of silicon and glued to multiple points on the wearer's face, could be hyper-realistic these days. But this was not one of those. Trapp decided that the man was exactly what he seemed. Hiding in plain sight not because he wanted to, but simply because the world had passed him by.

Trapp cocked his head to the side as if out of concern for the hobo beside him, but his eyes focused elsewhere, scanning the carriage quickly enough that even a seasoned observer would probably conclude it was a casual glance.

The train slowed and jerked to a halt at the Arlington Cemetery station. It was the second such stop, and already the carriage's original inhabitants had faded and been refreshed. Only half a dozen or so of those who had stepped onto the carriage at the same time as him were still aboard.

One was a mother with two children, and since he felt sure that an American agency was unlikely to use kids, he felt free to discard all three. Which left an obese man with big can headphones pumping tinny music into the carriage, an elderly woman with a cane, and the blonde woman.

He thought it was her. No reason really, just a suspicion. Perhaps she really was a simple office worker, after all. She seemed completely relaxed. Bored even, staring down at her phone and paying attention to no-one. But then, that was as good a cover as any in the modern age.

It probably wasn't the obese guy. Not definite, but it would be a surprise. As with the elderly woman. Infirmity wasn't an impossible trait to emulate, but she too would be giving an award-worthy performance. And besides, this was a simple training exercise, not the real thing.

Trapp chided himself for allowing that thought to drift into his mind. It was no way to operate. A long time ago, an Army drill instructor had repeated the phrase "train hard, fight easy" so many times during a single PT session the words had temporarily lost all meaning. But the man was right. The intelligence game was a hard, dangerous one. Operatives who allowed their standards to drop even once usually ended up paying with their lives.

The doors slid open, and a scattering of veterans and tourists entered, the latter immediately identifiable either from their loud, overexcited tones, or by merchandise branded with the names of one of the city's many landmarks that had barely had time to crease.

As the doors began to close, a man dressed in dark clothing and a baseball cap stepped onto the carriage, turning his shoulder just in time to avoid being clipped. He was a little above average height, and evidently muscular. He had a figure that was sculpted by work rather than hours in the gym, extraneous show muscles filed away by long hard yards of cardiovascular exercise. His fitness was functional, not so he could look good in front of a mirror.

Trapp observed the new arrival without making his interest obvious. It was immediately clear to him that the man's clothing had been chosen to gently disguise his form rather than flatter it – hiding his frame instead of flaunting it.

Or maybe he just isn't a fan of sucking in his gut, Trapp thought as he scratched the side of his nose, then yawned slightly. Tired people weren't threats.

That was the difficult part of the job, he knew. The same detail could be entirely innocent, or perfectly executed tradecraft. Half the carriage was wearing clothes that hung that same way. In every single case, the reason was either that they paid little attention to their fashion choices, or they were attempting to cover up a perceived physical defect.

And yet Trapp's attention was pulled back to the man a second time. He had never understood what it was in his subconscious that identified somebody as a threat, but those instincts were screaming now, as they had in so many countries and continents over the years. He felt the hairs rise on the back of his arms, and knew it had nothing to do with the carriage's air conditioning system kicking back in as the train began to move.

Not the girl, Trapp thought, bringing his hand up to cover his mouth as he yawned a second time, now more ostentatiously.

He was certain now that the man was a player. Trapp's practiced eye picked up on the way he was scanning his surroundings without being seen to do so. Some of his weight was distributed through the balls of his feet so that he could spring into action at any moment.

In fact, Trapp observed, he seemed to be practically vibrating with adrenaline.

It's only an exercise, buddy, he thought.

Or was it?

The subject was in his late thirties or early forties, though it was difficult to be more precise. That was a little old for an FBI agent, especially one joining one of the bureau's counter-intelligence teams fresh out of Quantico. It wasn't unknown – the FBI picked up plenty of recruits who didn't find civilian life to their liking and decided on a late in the day career change. Some came out of the military, others from one or other of the many thousands of police forces across America.

But the thing was, Trapp wasn't getting police vibes from this guy. He smelled like an operator. A player.

Or he was just nervous, Trapp conceded.

Special Agent Nick Pope's training exercises were notorious. He only picked the best of the best for his counterintelligence team. The agents going through the training course knew that their boss was looking for any reason to cut them – as brutal as any NFL coach. That was as good a reason for nerves as any.

Though their cousins at Langley didn't like to admit it – some institutional rivalries died hard – the FBI's counter-intel boys and girls were good. It had to be that way. Without their never-seen, endless efforts to uncover foreign intelligence operations on American soil, none of America's secrets would be safe.

Trapp watched the man through a reflection on the carriage's window as the Metro train pulled into then rolled out of the station at Stadium Armory. Was he armed? Maybe. It was impossible to make a judgment either way. There might have been a weapon in his right jacket pocket, but it could as easily be a cell phone.

He scanned the carriage again, wondering if the man might be a decoy for another operative. That would be a smart play. Was somebody trying to pull the wool over his eyes?

No, he decided, checking out the girl he'd initially suspected once again. She'd pulled out a well-thumbed paperback novel with a decidedly raunchy front cover featuring a male model in a state of undress. She was either a natural intelligence agent, or she was completely uninvolved.

His subject's posture altered as the train slowed for its arrival at Benning Road, causing a neuron to fire in Trapp's brain. He stood up and checked the Blue Line map printed above the carriage's window, still tracking the man's movement out of the corner of his eye. Was it a ploy? Did the man really intend to get off the train, or was he simply trying to smoke out a tail?

The train stopped and the doors hissed open again. The subject hadn't yet moved, but something about the way he held himself suggested he intended to. Trapp had to make a decision. He went with his gut and walked toward the door.

He walked past the subject, still seated by the door, internally cursing himself for making the wrong choice. But seconds before the doors closed, he felt as much as saw the man stand up and follow him out.

Trapp walked slowly, looking left and right as if searching for signage that pointed the way out of the station. His subject – for that was the way he had categorized the man – moved faster, quickly overtaking him. The movement told Trapp that his subject didn't believe he was being followed. Or it was another ploy. Was he looking for Trapp to speed up and confirm a suspicion?

You could go mad second-guessing yourself in this line of work. Sometimes you had to go with your instincts. And right now Trapp didn't think his subject had spotted the tail. He matched the man's pace through the subterranean tunnels, then the escalator that led up to ground level, making himself invisible in the crowd of commuters.

As he emerged above ground, Trapp squeezed a button fed through his left jacket cuff and spoke quietly into a mic. "Pope, I'm topside on Central Avenue NE. Following a male, about five foot eleven, late thirties or early forties. Am I on the right track?"

The digital radio set up was the same one used by the FBI on actual counterintelligence surveillance operations. The encrypted line was crystal clear through most of DC. It carried Pope's chuckle without a scratch, though the noise of a passing truck did its best to block out his words.

"You know I can't answer that. No cheating, remember?"

"Yeah, yeah," Trapp groused.

He let the subject pick up a few yards of distance, waiting until he passed a small, gated dog park on the left before resuming his tail. The man moved purposefully, walking a couple of miles an hour faster than most of the other people on the pavement, darting through the sparse traffic made up mostly of workers returning to their home offices after getting lunch and delivery personnel. The neighborhood was a mix of convenience stores and two- and three-storey red brick townhouses. It wasn't busy, but a handful of people were out and about.

Trapp cursed internally. A real surveillance operation would involve an orchestra of trailing agents – at least half a dozen or more, depending on the perceived importance of the case. Some required dozens of trained agents wearing a variety of disguises, some driving vehicles as well as those on foot. Surveillance operatives would pick up the tail for a couple of minutes, then hand off to another.

But this, as he kept reminding himself, was a training exercise. It was just him and his subject. And the man he was following was either simply in a rush – or doing his best to detect a tail.

"Subject is turning onto 46th Place NE.," he radioed, hanging back as the man walked past a white building on the right-hand side of the street and out of Trapp's sight. He paused for several breaths, then followed.

The instant he turned onto the street – a one-way road, given the orientation of the vehicles that were all facing toward him – he realized something was wrong. The subject he was trailing was gone. Though the entrances to a couple of houses were within ten or twenty yards, Trapp didn't think the man had disappeared into any of them.

"Lost visual," he reported to Pope in his makeshift control role. In a real operation, his friend would be vectoring aerial assets and guiding other surveillance personnel to the scene. Instead, Trapp was on his own.

Worse, his subject was taking evasive action. That could mean one of two things: either he was performing a surveillance detection routine as a matter of course, or he knew he was being tailed and was trying to shake it. Either way, he was definitely a player.

"Okay," Pope laughed over the radio in his ear. "I'll come clean. I have no idea who you've been following, but the woman I assigned to dodge you is about five foot five and blonde."

Trapp walked slowly down the street, his face screwed up as he tried to work out where the man had gone. Behind the white building to his right was the entrance to a small parking lot big enough to contain a half dozen or so cars. It was fenced in on either side, and at the far end sat a number of dumpsters.

He turned into the lot, wondering if the building had a rear entrance. The hair was standing up on the back of his arms, like it usually did when he was in danger. But more than anything, he was just confused. To his right was a Harley-Davidson that hadn't seen better days in a long time. The engine was rusted, and its tires sagged against the concrete ground. Behind that was a large white trailer similar to a horse box.

"I guess you do need a vacation," he muttered, shaking his head. He made a face and began turning back to the road.

As he did so, his peripheral vision caught a flash of movement. He reacted, but not quickly enough. A shape appeared from behind a parked car to his left and drove toward him. Before he knew what was happening, he found himself rammed up against the side of the trailer, his subject's forearm pressed against his throat.

The man breathed hard. "Who the fuck are you?"

4

Drug Enforcement Agency Administrator Mark Engel relaxed into the leather seat of his government-issue Chevrolet SUV as the short motorcade entered fast-moving traffic on the 395. For all that the head of his security detail was sitting in the front passenger seat, with another close protection agent behind the wheel and several more split between the chase and lead vehicles, he never felt safe in traffic.

Leo Conway, his chief of staff, glanced over knowingly. "Carsick, huh?"

"You could call it that, I guess," Engel grunted as the SUV vibrated gently as the tires passed over a set of road markings. "Never liked these damn things."

There was nothing rational about it, he knew that. No one had ever attacked a secretary at the DEA's Arlington headquarters before, let alone the administrator. And his close protection detail had enough quasi-military hardware between them to settle most any argument. But it was precisely *because*, not in spite of their presence that he felt the way he did. Just seeing them every day was a reminder of why they were needed. He was grateful, of course. But that didn't mean he had to like it.

Engel shook his head and pulled his gaze away from the window, and the glimpse of the rear window of the lead SUV was replaced by Leo's face. "Where are we, then?"

Leo nodded and dived straight into the detail. Engel liked that about him. No messing around. They spent about 15 minutes going through the previous night's developments in Colombia, Mexico, and everywhere else in the world where a DEA agent was stationed, which meant most of it.

It was always the same, Engel reflected. A drug seizure here, a bust there. Millions of dollars in cash found, and half a dozen more pushers and smugglers in American jail cells. Information from an informant on the one hand, and the news that a separate lead entirely hadn't quite panned out. Sometimes he wondered why they even bothered. Every time they took down one of the bad guys, a half dozen more popped up to take their place.

"Where are we with Carreon's extradition?" he asked, despite the fact the cartel chief was just another name on the carousel. "The president will want an update."

"It's going smoothly," Leo replied, rolling his eyes, which Engel understood to mean that the Mexicans were jamming things up, as usual. They didn't like handing over their citizens, even those as despicable as Fernando Carreon. "Could be any year now."

"Great," his boss sighed.

"Oh, and there's one last thing," Leo added as he snapped his customary leather binder closed. "Jennifer Reyes is on our patch. Shopping trip."

Engel frowned, trying to place the name. The most-wanted list was constantly changing, and by the time he was halfway caught up, it had usually changed entirely. It was unusual, though, for a woman's name to grace it. "Reyes... The Crusaders Cartel chief?"

"His wife," Leo confirmed. "She's down in LA with some

girlfriends. Sounds like they've rented a second hotel suite just to keep the shopping bags. We've got a team watching her. But..."

Engel raised his eyebrows. "But what?"

"I don't expect we'll learn much of anything. The head honchos don't tend to slip up. Same goes for their families. The smart ones, anyway. And we haven't heard anything yet."

The DEA administrator leaned forward as the SUV began slowing on its approach to the White House, excited despite himself. Ramon Reyes, Jennifer's husband, held the joint honor of gracing the top slot of the agency's most wanted list, and being the one they knew the least about. They didn't even have a photo. "Any chance we can pick her up, ask a few questions? Maybe there's a visa issue she doesn't know about."

Leo shook his head. "Not likely. She's represented by Solomon Day. The firm already sent a high-priced suit over as a courtesy call."

"Sure," Engel snorted. "Off limits, then. Dammit."

"Unfortunately so," Leo agreed as the SUV rolled to a halt. The agent behind the wheel jumped out, and a second later Engel's door opened.

The director hung back. "Keep an eye on her, anyway. You learn anything, you come straight to me, okay?"

"You got it, boss."

"REAL BIG FOXTROT, AIN'T HE?" Stan Butcher grunted as he pulled the nondescript Ford sedan into the curb at the head of Rodeo Drive, the high-end shopping street in Los Angeles.

His partner, Rex Haskell, turned to him and squinted before returning his gaze to the subject in question – a Latino male around 6 foot in height, wearing a black suit that attempted to mimic a tailored cut, but fell short when confronted with his mammoth frame. The man, a bodyguard, was staring right back at them as he opened the rear door of the matching black Range Rover, an insouciant smile on his face.

"Foxtrot?" Rex muttered with a hint of confusion before his face un-creased. "Right. A real big foxtrot."

"You think he's got a record?" Stan asked, killing the Ford's engine. He was parked on a red line but didn't figure anyone would pick him up on it. Not with the government plates, and especially not once they got close enough to see the stylish navy-blue windbreakers, complete with DEA lettering in yellow. It wasn't exactly subtle.

That was kind of the point.

"No way, José," Rex replied with an irritable shake of the head. More of a twitch, really. "Reyes wouldn't send anyone on our books. And he'd know, right?"

"Guess so," came Stan's reply.

He settled back into the driver's seat. With the engine off, and the AC with it, the heat of the noon sun was already building inside the car. He grimaced as a fold of skin got pinched between his belt and the holster of his service weapon and readjusted his frame to compensate. "But it's a shame."

"You got that right," Rex agreed.

The two agents were of similar height and build, and both had recently requalified at the range. No one was expecting trouble, but then again, no one ever did. The local cops knew something was going on down here and were on call if needed. But Stan doubted they would be.

He let out a whistle. "She's easy on the eye, huh?"

Rex's gaze dropped to a folder on his lap. "That's the wife?"

"Think so."

"She's what, 23?"

"Not even. Birthday's next month."

His partner shook his head as he watched a lithe woman wearing stiletto heels reach back into the Range Rover and retrieve a purse that probably cost half a month's worth of his salary. "I wonder what he sees in her."

That caused Stan to chuckle. He nodded in knowing agreement, watching Jennifer Reyes out of the corner of his eye but focusing the bulk of his attention on the three body-guards accompanying the Real Big Foxtrot. They were barely more diminutive in size, and each moved with a kind of casual arrogance that suggested they thought they owned these streets.

"Real shame," he murmured again underneath his breath, not knowing quite why he said it.

The wife was accompanied by a couple of girlfriends, one in leather pants and another in a miniskirt that didn't go very far south of her waist, and neither left much to the imagination. The two agents watched as another bodyguard exited the marble archway entrance to the Versace store and nodded to the RBF, who in turn ushered the three women inside.

Between the slightly darkened window glass and the sun reflecting overhead, it was difficult to make out precisely what was going on inside, but Stan thought he saw a trio of cham-pagne flutes suddenly appear in the women's hands before they disappeared between the clothes racks.

"Reckon you could take him?" Rex murmured, uncon-sciously drumming the middle and index fingers of his right hand against his own holster. "The big one, I mean."

"That doesn't narrow it down much," Stan grunted. "You want the truth?"

"I'm asking."

"I wouldn't go near him if you doubled my salary. Not unless I had a company of Marines backing me up. And even then, I don't know. I got a kid at home now, man. Priorities."

"You new parents are all the same." Rex grinned. "Believe me, you get five years in, you'll be hoping someone takes a swing at you and lands you a week in a hospital bed with some sexy nurse feeding you dinner through a straw. Better than changing diapers and taking out the trash, I'll tell you."

Stan murmured his agreement but never took his eyes off the four men flanking the store's exit.

Don't tempt fate.

JENNIFER REYES still didn't really believe that this was real life. She leaned against a pillar and smiled as her two best friends, Silvia and Adriana, danced through a fashion store that was for the time set aside as their own personal fitting room, and cackled with unbridled glee.

They would do this half a dozen more times today, she knew, switching the fashion label every time. She wondered whether it would get old.

Not today.

It wasn't healthy – couldn't be healthy – to withdraw so frequently into these bouts of reflective solipsism. Jennifer knew that. And yet she couldn't help it. Her station in life had risen so far so fast that sometimes it gave her whiplash. Only two years earlier, she'd still lived under her parents' roof in Culiacán, a building with far fewer rooms than offspring to occupy them. She'd worked through the night, from dusk till dawn, as a dancer in one of the city's more exclusive clubs.

It was hard work, and the pay was unimpressive, but the tips more than made up for that shortcoming. The other girls made more, but only by working smarter. Jennifer Diaz, at the time, was proud of her legs but had far too much pride to make a living on her back. The rest of them laughed at her, but she had a plan for how the rest of her life would unfold and no intention of compromising herself for the sake of a little easy cash.

The path she was on already would get her to where she

wanted to be. A better life for her parents. Then college. Maybe it would get her there a little slower, but that was a price worth paying.

And then she'd met Ramon.

Well, *met* wasn't exactly the operative word. She was delivered to him by one of his men, a sicario who understood well his master's tastes. And Jennifer knew better than to refuse a request from a man like Ramon Reyes. In Culiacán, the word of the cartels was law. You didn't make an enemy of a man like that.

Just two years. And a marriage. And maybe even a child, in a future that wasn't too far away.

She was too young for childbirth. Not physically, of course, nor even by the standards of most women in her country. But the idea of so prematurely embracing motherhood did not align with her chosen path.

But now you have no choice.

"Jennifer!"

She looked up and saw Silvia beckoning her over, pale droplets of champagne spilling free of her flute and sailing through the air like tiny glittering fireflies.

"I'm coming." She smiled. "I just needed a moment. It's going to be a long day."

And though she could not yet know it, Jennifer Reyes was right.

"Who's that?" Stan said, squinting and shielding his eyes from the sun as a dark figure resolved at the far end of Rodeo Drive, bracketed by two thin strips of shadow thrown off by para-palm trees towering overhead.

"A real Beverly Hills cop," Rex chuckled before his expression darkened. "I guess he didn't get the memo."

"It's fine, I guess." Stan shrugged. "Not like the druggies don't know we are watching them."

"I guess," Rex replied, echoing his partner's words, if not his certainty.

"You reckon he's itching to give us a parking ticket?" Stan said, lowering the sun shield so he could see better.

"I figure he clocks the government plates and walks right on by." Rex shrugged, returning his attention to the Versace storefront. "If he knows what's good for him, anyway. Doesn't look like no rookie, so I'm betting we're fine."

"You're probably right," Stan agreed. "I'll keep an eye on him, anyway."

He did so as Rex grunted an amiable response. The cop walked slowly down the street toward them, his right hand resting casually on his gun belt. He stopped a couple times in the shadow of a storefront, taking advantage of the shelter from the sun. Stan began to relax. The police officer – Rex was right, he looked to be in his mid-thirties – couldn't have failed to notice the presence of their sedan, and yet he'd made no beeline toward them. He was probably just walking his ordinary beat. Maybe he'd missed the morning's briefing on their surveillance op.

Must be that, he figured.

Still, he kept his eye on the man as he closed within 20 feet, then 10, then just five. Until the very last moment, it appeared as though he was just going to stroll right on by.

And then he turned, frowning beneath a BHPD baseball cap that shielded his face from the sun, and motioned at Stan to lower his window.

"Dammit," Stan hissed.

"What is it?" Rex said, turning back. "Ah. Want me to call it in, get his boss on the line?"

"Don't worry, I'll get rid of him," Stan grumbled, reaching

for the window button with one hand and his credentials with the other.

"You two gentlemen know you can't park here, right?" the cop said as the window lowered. He was looking down at the ground now, and Stan saw that he was pointing at it, also. "That line means no parking. I don't care who you're waiting for."

"Look up, Officer," Stan said curtly, holding up his credentials in full view.

"What you got there?" the cop replied amiably. He started reaching for the badge.

Did someone drop you on your head as a baby? Stan thought, though he resisted the urge to say it. Instead he bottled up the emotion, holding on to it for later, when he would be able to write up a satisfying complaint about the officer's behavior.

Still, his attention was drawn toward the hand reaching in through the window – the officer's left. Not what was happening with his right.

"I'm a federal agent, Officer," Stan said tautly, "and if you have any desire to hold on to your job, I suggest you get –"

"I don't give a fuck who you are," said the cop. "Put your hands on the dash where I can see them."

"What the hell's going on?" Rex said, turning and half reaching for his holstered weapon before he stopped dead, noticing for the first time the officer's weapon.

"You know how it goes. Don't do anything stupid. I don't got no desire to see either of you die today. We're not here to kill Americans. You just keep nice and quiet, and this will be over before you know it."

Stan gulped, his throat suddenly bone dry. "What will?"

And that's when the gunfire started.

〜

JENNIFER HAD her eyes on Adriana when the first round splintered through the designer store's plate glass windows. Her friend had her arm looped around the upright pole of a display rack and was demonstrating a slightly alcohol-impaired balletic spin as she and Silvia raised their flutes in a show of admiration.

So when the sheet glass cracked, then collapsed in a waterfall of glittering shards, her mind started filling in the dots and drew a separate picture entirely. For a full second she thought that Adriana had somehow brought the rail toppling down with her. Her brain was so committed to the accidental self-deception that she was already bending over in preparation to help her up when the store assistants began screaming in terror.

It was only then that Jennifer turned and watched as all four of the men who Ramon had sent to protect her fell, one by one, under a hail of gunfire. She was not scared, at least not yet, but only because this could not be happening. It simply did not compute.

In Mexico, maybe – but not in America. That was the unwritten rule, everybody knew that. Ramon had assured her that she would be safe here. That the men he'd assigned to protect her were simply there as a precaution.

Her assailants—there were four of them, at least that she could see—began approaching the store. The two on the flanks remained upright to cover their partners as the other two bent to check pulses and kick away fallen weapons. A knife appeared in the gloved hand of one of the crouching men, and swiftly filleted the neck of one of her former protectors. A pump of blood gushed out, and then a second, but already the flow was weaker, and then it stopped entirely.

The killer wiped the knife on her bodyguard's suit and then returned it to a khaki sheath attached to his belt. It seemed that the rest of Ramon's men were already dead, for the act was not repeated.

"Policia!" Jennifer started to scream, her mind surfacing a memory of her bodyguards pointing out the car sent by the DEA as they'd parked. She'd laughed then. Not now.

"Police, help!"

But no one came.

Are they already dead? Jennifer wondered abstractly. That did not compute either. No one killed DEA agents. Local cops, maybe. Both sides treated that as a cost of doing business. But federal agents were off limits. Killing them brought too much political heat, and political heat was usually doused in fire and blood.

It struck her as strangely discordant that while one of the gunmen walked through the space that the shattered glass had previously occupied, his boots crunching against the broken shards, the rest came through the door. The first held it open as the others entered. She thought she even heard a murmur of thanks.

Jennifer called out for the police one last time, more in vain hope than any sense of expectation. But her voice died even in the safety of her own throat.

She thought she saw one of the men smirk at her screams as he walked toward her, some form of rifle in his hands. His finger was off the trigger, resting on the side of the gun. Not like Ramon's sicarios. But a balaclava obscured his features.

"What do you want?" Jennifer said, mustering the strength to speak for the first time. She glanced behind her and saw that both Silvia and Adriana were white with fear. She beckoned them to shelter behind her.

You can save them, she knew. These men were here for her, not them.

The store assistants were sheltering behind the cash registers, she saw as she returned her attention to the man approaching her. She took a half step to the left, toward them, and held her breath in the hope that her friends would follow her lead.

Jennifer swallowed and tried again. "Whatever it is, you will get it. I promise you. Just don't hurt anyone else."

The man remained silent. His weapon did not waver. She noticed that, too. It was entirely still, as though his frame was carved from marble. It just hovered in midair, aimed at a spot half a foot to her side.

But not at her.

You don't point your gun at something unless you're prepared to kill it.

Ramon's words echoed in her head. He'd told her that. The thought emboldened Jennifer. These men were professionals; that much was evident by the mere fact that all four of her bodyguards had been gunned down without firing so much as a shot in return.

And professionals didn't kill for fun. They didn't slaughter innocent women.

Did they?

The gunman lowered his weapon slightly and pointed a gloved finger from his free hand at Jennifer's chest. The appendage rotated slowly in midair, and just as deliberately, he beckoned her toward him.

Jennifer released a breath she wasn't aware she'd been holding. Okay. This was a start. They were communicating, at least, and that was better than shooting. This was business. They would hold her for a few days, and then Ramon would pay a ransom, and it would all be a bad memory.

So she complied. Only with a single step at first, and then another, as the man opposite her did not react, and she slowly grew in confidence until they were face to face. So close that she could reach out and touch him if she so chose.

Though she did not.

The man spoke quietly. "Señorita Reyes. I need you to come with us."

Jennifer didn't notice the man behind him raising his weapon. She didn't see his finger sliding from the side of the rifle onto its trigger. But she heard the weapon's retort. Her head spun, and she saw Silvia's body on the floor, unmoving.

The weapon fired again.

And Jennifer Reyes screamed.

5

Trapp's eyes widened. For once in his life, his instincts failed him. No, that wasn't true, was it? His instincts had been right. His subconscious had told him that there was something off about the man. That was why he had decided to follow him. But he'd misinterpreted the message his brain was sending.

"Relax," he said, as much to himself as the other man. "It's over."

The man didn't respond. With his forearm still pressed up against Trapp's throat, partially cutting off the flow of air to his lungs, Trapp was unable to move his head and follow his adversary's actions. He didn't notice the knife until he felt the unmistakable sensation of sharp steel pressing into his abdomen.

"Jesus, buddy," Trapp said, adrenaline flooding his veins. "It's just a drill."

But it wasn't. Not for the man with the knife. Whoever this guy was, he was a killer, that much was plain. There was no emotion in his eyes. No anger. No hatred. None of the bloodshot glassiness of an addict or alcoholic. Just cold professionalism.

"Who sent you?" the man asked in unplaceable American English. He could have been from anywhere.

Trapp didn't answer the question. His mind was still turning at only half its usual speed. The adrenaline was beginning to rev up his pace of thought, but the training exercise had lulled him into a false sense of security. He was coming from a standing start.

"Easy, buddy," he said in an even tone of voice. The turn of events had startled him, but he was experienced enough to know that if he allowed himself to succumb to the panic that was beginning to tickle the edge of his consciousness, then this was already over. He needed the man with the knife to remain as calm as he was. Allowing the emotional intensity of the moment to spin out of control would only make his adversary jumpy. And jumpy men tended to stab first and ask questions later.

"Tell me who you are, and who sent you," his opponent said in the same emotionless tone. "Or I'll finish you right now."

Trapp's mind didn't have to be running at its usual speed to weigh up his chances of survival and find them wanting. He had no idea who his adversary was, or why the man had a weapon pressed into his side. The fact that only half the usual airflow was making its way to his lungs wasn't helping his decision-making process, either. He felt slow and sluggish in both body and thought.

Even so, one thing was clear. He was dealing with a pro. He didn't know who this man was, where he was coming from or going, or why he was so amped up.

Trapp sensed as much as felt the man's shift in posture. He wasn't going to wait for an answer. He was planning to end this here and now, against this abandoned trailer's wall. But he had made two crucial mistakes. First, his face was about three inches too close to Trapp's own, and second, his forearm was closer to his collarbone than the underside of his chin.

Closing his eyes, Trapp drove his head forward with all the strength that his neck and upper back could muster, twisting his rib cage to the left and away from the blade pressed up against his shirt. He felt the upper part of his forehead impact the bridge of his opponent's nose, then the telltale crunch of cartilage disintegrating from the force of the impact.

The pressure against his throat relented enough for Trapp to spin away from his adversary's unwanted embrace. His left hand came up to his throat and massaged it as stars bloomed at the edges of his vision from the lack of oxygen.

Still dulled by the surprise of the sudden and unexpected belt of combat, and perhaps expecting him to be licking his own wounds, Trapp was slow to anticipate his opponent's response.

It was a mistake.

He looked up to see the man now holding the knife in a reverse grip. The lower half of his face was bloodied, and fresh rivulets streamed from his smashed nose. But instead of reeling backward, he came out fighting, twisting to one side and lashing out with a heel kick that carried stunning force.

Trapp backed away from the incoming blow, still unprepared to bring the fight to his attacker. He wasn't fast enough. The kick caught him on the left-hand side of the torso, driving the oxygen from his lungs and spinning him around. The only saving grace was that he was off balance at the moment of impact, instead of braced against the ground. At least half of the kick's force was spent rotating his body around and throwing him back instead of snapping his ribs.

Grunting from the force of the blow, Trapp stumbled backward, his enormous frame doubled over with pain. The muscles in his diaphragm were temporarily paralyzed from the kick, and try as he might he found it impossible to breathe in.

What the hell is happening?

Even as Trapp's mind strained for answers, he knew now

was no time to go looking for them. Right now he was both a step behind and a second slower than his opponent, who was setting the terms of their engagement, not letting up for even a moment so that Trapp could formulate a response. All he could do was retreat, trading space for time so that his body could recover from the shock.

He looked up warily to see that his attacker held the combat knife in his right hand. The left was raised to guard against incoming blows from that direction. He moved with exquisite poise, light on his feet despite his compact, muscular frame. He seemed to ghost toward Trapp, eating up space faster than he could generate it.

Squeezing the button in his jacket cuff, Trapp radioed, "Mayday, Mayday, Mayday, I need immediate backup at my current location. Not a drill."

His adversary's eyes narrowed as the man took in the call for help. Trapp waited for a response, but none came. He glanced down as he prepared to try again, wondering whether the high walls of the buildings around him were blocking out the signal. His stomach sank as he saw the loose wire dangling below his waistband. The demands of hand-to-hand combat must have pulled it free of the radio handset.

"Shit," he muttered, understanding now that he was on his own.

The concern that had nibbled at the edges of his consciousness a few moments earlier now returned with renewed force. His opponent was faster than him. He couldn't blame it on the element of surprise, not now. The man could only be a handful of years younger, but Trapp felt like an ox going up against an Arabian racehorse. For the first time in a very long while, he had come up against somebody who wasn't just stronger or fitter than him – but better.

Trapp scanned left and right, quickly taking in his surroundings. The course of the fight had driven him deeper into the fenced plot. Loose pieces of trash flitted around his feet, perhaps blown by the wind into the forgotten space off the main street. A set of rusted iron railings was built around a stairwell into a basement level to his left. One of them was loose – bent and twisted from some unknown impact, completely rusted through at the top, and only barely holding at the bottom.

He drove forward, feinting with his right, driving his adversary back a couple of inches, buying himself just long enough to spin to his left, grab the top of the rusted iron bar with his right hand, and drive a forceful kick against its corroded lower half.

The bar came away from the railings with surprising ease. Trapp threw it up in the air and caught the bottom edge, his fingers instantly growing filthy from rust. Flakes of corroded metal fell like dust from both ends, but the painted center of the bar – several feet long – was reassuringly solid in his grasp.

"Come on, asshole," he said, wincing from the pain of the first kick at an entirely inopportune moment. His opponent looked like something out of a horror movie, with blood still streaming freely from his nose, and dark smears over most of his face. The blow from Trapp's forehead had knocked the baseball cap askew, but it still clung onto his head.

The man said nothing as he approached, more warily now that Trapp was also armed – and with a weapon that had greater reach. It was his eyes that worried Trapp the most. They were cold and calculating rather than panicked. He must have been feeling the strain of the fight as much as Trapp was, but if he was, he wasn't showing it.

Trapp hefted the bar, taking a step forward and sending it biting forward like a stab from a longsword, using the point rather than the sides of his makeshift staff. The last thing he needed was for his opponent to block and catch his weapon.

His adversary easily sidestepped the strike, driving forward with his own knife and surging inside the radius of Trapp's iron bar – a move that he hadn't anticipated. As Trapp drew his right elbow back and prepared to deliver a second blow, the man drew within a couple of feet of his torso.

Knife fighting range.

God, he was quick. Trapp was barely able to process the speed and violence of his decisions. He was playing offense, knowing that to be on the defense in a fight like this was a risk in itself.

The man stepped sideways, and Trapp twisted out of range, almost losing his grip on the iron bar. He only had a few yards behind him before the plot ended with a waist-high fence. Before that, the space behind him compressed further with a couple of large dumpsters blocking the way.

Not good.

Trapp attempted to regain the initiative, surging forward with a series of vicious, short stabbing strikes, any one of which could have broken his opponent's ribs. The man dodged each one, stepping back just far enough each time for the strike to die just a couple of inches from his torso. Trapp was sweating now, his lungs still straining from the initial kick, and he felt his strength fading.

He took a step back, watched as his opponent drove forward with his blade slashing downward, aimed toward his belly. Just as his adversary was fully outstretched, Trapp brought the iron bar down with all his remaining strength. The weapon cracked against the man's right forearm, instantly causing the knife to drop from his grip. The five-inch metal blade tinkled against the concrete below.

Vaguely, Trapp became aware of excitable voices from the street at the far end of the plot. The fight had attracted an audience. Not exactly surprising in a major American city. But the last thing he needed was for somebody to film the event and put it up on the Internet. What a way to blow his cover.

The distraction of the thought – and the belief that he had greatly wounded his opponent – slowed him just long enough for the man to spin around and lash out with another kick, clutching his right forearm with a grimace on his face even as he delivered it. This time his heel caught Trapp right in the gut, driving him onto his knees. A wave of nausea rose up his throat, and he felt the iron bar drop unbidden from his grasp.

Both men gasped with pain, separated by only a couple of feet. For the moment, neither could muster the strength to continue the fight. Trapp attempted to rise to his feet, but the combination of pain and a renewed lack of oxygen stopped him in his tracks. He watched as his opponent searched the ground for the knife. It was a few feet to his right. He backpedaled and reached out with his left – clearly not his dominant hand.

The man cast one last look at Trapp, then another at the growing crowd on the street. He seemed torn between wanting to finish the job, and his desire to escape.

"Somebody call 911," Trapp heard a worried voice say.

That seemed to make up the man's mind. He thrust the blade into a jacket pocket and sprinted for the street, leaving Trapp – mind spinning from the insanity of what had just happened – in his wake.

6

The intercom on the Resolute Desk buzzed, jolting
President Charles Nash from a momentary daydream
as he gazed out onto the South Lawn of the White
House.

"Administrator Engel is here for your 11 o'clock, Mr.
President."

Nash shook himself awake, turned, and pressed his finger
on the intercom's transmit button. "Thanks, Karen. You can
send him in."

The president had long ago ceased his previously frequent
attempts to get his office gatekeeper to refer to him by his given
name, rather than the title of his office. He still wasn't sure how
he felt about it. There were, of course, advantages to the pomp
and pageantry of the Oval Office. You couldn't underestimate
the effect the trappings of power had on those who came to
him, hands outstretched.

It wasn't any one piece of the picture, not the bust of
Winston Churchill, the Secret Service detail or the Marine
sergeant standing on the patio in full dress uniform, but the

way each blended together, in the process producing an effect that on rare occasions could even still a visitor's tongue.

Even for those less overtly affected by the pomp and ceremony and history, the impact tended to give the man in his chair the upper hand in negotiations, which the man in his chair was expected to undertake frequently.

A side door opened silently, and the imposing frame of a member of his detail briefly hove into view before Administrator Engel strode into the room, attaché case in his right hand. Nash couldn't help thinking that the man looked impossibly young. He was in his late forties, not that much younger than the president himself, when it came down to brass tacks. But age and stress had not yet wearied him.

That'll come, he thought dryly.

Nash watched as Engel's eyes pirouetted around the Oval Office in search of him, first passing across the windows that overlooked the greenery outside and seeming to slow before they alighted upon him.

"You like the view?"

"I could get used to it," Engel replied as he walked toward the desk before blanching as he realized precisely what he'd said. "Not, of course, that I intend to."

"Be my guest," Nash laughed. "I could use a nice long vacation, anyway. And maybe you would do a better job. Most people think they can."

"I doubt that, sir," Engel said, taking his boss' lead and smiling, though a hint of anxiety remained. "I have my hands full as it is."

Nash nodded to indicate he understood. "How's business, Mark?"

"The job title's accurate, that's all I'll say," Engel replied, his nerves visibly fading as the two men returned to safer ground. "Paperwork keeps building up, and all I seem to do these days is administrate."

"It'd make a better name for a wrestler, wouldn't it?" Nash mused, wondering indeed why it was that the DEA didn't rate a director. Probably politics back in the seventies, he figured. Herbert Hoover was nothing if not a jealous man, covetous of his fiefdom, and those who succeeded him were made in the same mold, if not quite so obvious about it. Though Rutger wasn't too bad. As these things went.

"That it might, sir," Engel agreed.

He gestured his guest toward the two sofas on the opposite side of the office. "And the kids?"

Engel's face lit up, and he did a delicate dance to switch his briefcase to his free hand so that he could retrieve a cell phone, which he waggled in the president's direction. "Doing real well, sir. Only thing is they grow up too fast. I'd show you some pics, but the security pukes locked this thing down harder than Fort Knox."

"Maybe next time." Nash smiled, hiding a pang of regret of his own as he remembered George at that age before the world caught up and then passed his son by. He followed the administrator to the sofa and sat down, rightly guessing that his subordinate was waiting for him to do just that.

"Can I get you anything to drink?"

"No sir," Engel said with a quick shake of the head. "I know you're busy, so I'll keep this quick. We've basically got two major items on the agenda. I figured you'd want to know about both."

"Carreon's extradition?"

"Yes sir," the administrator agreed. "That's one of them. Leo, my chief of staff, just filled me in on the latest. Sounds like the Mexicans are giving Justice a hard time, but that's the ballgame. We'll get it done. It's just a matter of trade-offs now: who gets what, when, where. And how, of course. Can't forget the paperwork."

Nash grimaced. "Fine. Keep me posted. Whatever it costs, I

want it done. The American people deserve to see this guy in the dock, and I intend to see that happen. So what's the other thing?"

"Understood, Mr. President," came the reply as Engel looked away, searching inside his case for a pair of identical manila folders which he pulled out. "I don't think it'll be too long now, anyway."

He handed one of the files to the president and kept the other for himself. "This is Operation Wishbone. I don't pick the names. That's the computer's job."

Nash rolled his eyes knowingly. With over a year of the job under his belt, he'd come to learn that the more banal the name choice, the more interesting the activity – and this one was positively stultifying. "Excuses, excuses... So what is it?"

The administrator opened his copy of the file and revealed a glossy full-page image of a Hispanic male whom the president did not recognize. It was a grainy shot and looked as though it had been taken mid-stride as the subject was looking down at the ground. He still had a full head of hair, though it was beginning to gray.

"This is Ramon Reyes, Mr. President," Engel remarked, tapping the page. "Otherwise known as El Toro."

"Who came up with that, I wonder?" Nash muttered, glancing back up. "El Toro," he repeated, rolling the R on his tongue in piratical fashion. "The bull. I like that. Real masculine. Better than mine, anyway. You know, my detail has taken to calling me *Gaslamp*. Never asked why."

"Has a ring to it, I guess."

Nash waved his hand. "Anyway, go on. This is your rodeo."

"No problem. Anyway, Reyes – he's the leader of the Crusaders cartel. Cruzados, in Spanish. They control most of the southern half of Mexico. Used to be at war with the Federation up in Sinaloa, but that's calmed down over the last couple of years."

"Why do they call him the bull?"

"Far as we know, he was a novillero, a trainee bullfighter. Went to a training academy three days a week from the age of six."

Nash squinted. "Hold on – we're talking about bullfighting here, right? Matadors, rings, the whole circus?"

"That's right."

"Six years old, huh?" The president whistled. "Guess they do things different down there."

"I sure wouldn't sign the permission slip for one of mine," Engel agreed. "Especially not since it seems he took the stomp to his temple when he was eleven. Nearly killed him."

"And he survived?" Nash asked, forehead crinkling with mild disbelief. "Must be made different, too."

"He *survived*," Engel agreed, his tone measured. "But by all accounts it changed the kid. And I stress, what we know about this guy is mainly gossip, so who knows how much of this is true? His organization is locked down pretty tight. We just feed on scraps."

"Changed him how?"

"Mood swings. A tendency toward the use of violence. A lack of remorse. Not exactly out of left field for these guys, but he matched it with ambition. Started as a runner for some local cartel, carrying product between safehouses. We don't have any records of him from back then. Nor do the Mexicans. But what we know is he became a sicario. A contract killer. And these guys follow a *might is right* kind of code."

"So he worked his way up?"

"Yes, sir. Real American dream. Well, Mexican dream, anyway. He's been running the Crusaders for the past three years."

"So why am I looking at a picture of this Reyes character, Mark?"

Engel flicked the page in his file, causing the president to do the same. "Sir, last month we received a tipoff. Names and locations for dozens of Crusaders operating inside the United States. Mainly logistics types. They don't tend to do much killing north of the border. That stuff's restricted for Mexico. They know it brings too much heat."

"Logistics?" Nash grunted, frowning.

"That's right, Mr. President. Doesn't sound like much, but we think they move about $20 billion of cocaine and opiates into the country each year. That's street value. They have a network of distribution routes, safehouses, and runners that rivals FedEx. We've just never gotten such a granular look at it before."

"The tipoff – where did it come from?"

Engel shifted uneasily in place. "Through our anonymous tip line, Mr. President."

"Doesn't sound like you're telling me the whole story, Administrator. I wonder why that might be. If you're protecting me for some reason, don't."

"The cartels aren't like they used to be. They grew up and got professional," Engel said. "Hired mercenaries to teach them how to shoot, and espionage professionals to learn how not to get caught."

"And you're saying we did the same?"

Engel bit his lip, clearly unwilling to say the quiet part out loud until Nash's expression made it clear that it was less an ask, and more a demand. "Sir, when we get information like this, it often comes from our side."

"You mean CIA?"

"Could be," Engel agreed. "Or NSA. There's a whole alphabet soup of agencies out there running around, sometimes hearing things they aren't meant to hear. The information doesn't come to us as marked *property of the Central Intelligence Agency*, but that's part of the game. This has that kind of feel."

"Is it legal?"

"It's a gray area," Engel replied. "We can't use it in court. So we have to catch them in the act. That's what we've spent the last three weeks doing. In this file are the names of almost three dozen senior Crusaders, along with the locations of twice that many safehouses. My people have observed the movement of what looks like hundreds of millions of dollars of narcotics over the past two weeks. It's time to bring these individuals into custody."

"So what's the play here, Mark?" Nash asked. He closed the folder and set it conspicuously between the two men, then tapped it. "You take these boys off the streets and what then? Two more come from nowhere to take their place."

"The way I see it, sir, we've got a window. Carreon's organization, the Federación, it's on the ropes with him behind bars. As far as we can make out, they've moved 30 percent less product this quarter than last, and it's dropping every week. We have an opportunity to take out the other major player – or at least, their distribution arm. It would be irresponsible not to."

Nash closed his eyes and began rubbing his sockets. An image of his son flashed in the kaleidoscope that erupted on his retinas as he did so. The way he was in that picture the detectives had shown him. A needle sticking out of his arm. His lips blue. A trail of vomit dried on the side of his cheek.

"What's the point, Mark?" he said in a voice that was little more than a whisper as a moment of doubt assailed him. "Where does this all end?"

"That's not my job, Mr. President," Engel said frankly, though his tone was soft. The younger Nash's fate was no secret in Washington. "All I know is you take this much supply out of the market, it takes them at least six months to replace it. Maybe longer. That's fewer new addictions, fewer families ripped apart, maybe a few less kids ending up in the morgue. But beyond that, sir, that's –"

"– My job," Nash finished, finally looking up. "Maybe it's time I twisted some arms on the Hill about my narcotics bill, after all. It's been dead in committee since before Christmas. Perhaps this gives me the political capital I need to bring it back to life."

Engel just nodded.

"Okay, Mark. You have my permission. When will you start picking them up?"

The DEA administrator grinned and glanced performatively at his watch. "Oh, I'd say in about an hour, sir. Now I've got the greenlight, I don't want to give them any more warning than we have to."

7

A black Suburban slowed just long enough for Trapp to climb inside. The black SUV merged smoothly back into traffic as he clipped the seatbelt into place, silencing the irritating reminder that had already begun to chime. He winced as the effort provoked a twinge of pain from his bruised stomach.

"You okay?" Pope asked from behind the wheel. His face was lined with worry.

"What the fuck was that, Nick?" Trapp asked without pausing for formalities. "Were you in on it?"

"Huh?" Pope said, looking genuinely surprised. "No way, man. I'm as in the dark as you are."

"Tell me you have an ID on the guy I just tangled with," Trapp said, grimacing as he probed his torso to gauge the seriousness of the damage it had sustained.

His ribs felt bruised, his stomach was going to be black and blue by the time he woke up the following morning, and his forehead ached from its cameo role as a sledgehammer. He really had to stop doing that. He didn't want to wake up one day at fifty to realize he was already forgetting his name.

"I pulled everybody into the office. They're already on the street pulling security footage from every camera you passed to see if any of them picked up a facial shot we can work with."

Trapp leaned gingerly back against the seat. Every muscle in his body was tense from the aftereffects of the adrenaline that had flowed through his veins. He finished checking over his injuries. Nothing serious. A few scrapes and bruises, maybe a cracked rib or two. Nothing that wouldn't heal up in time.

They hit a red light and Pope twisted in his seat. He studied Trapp carefully, searching for any sign of injury.

"I'm serious, buddy," he said. "I had no idea things were going to go down that way. I figured your antennae were just bent out of joint. I was going to let you follow some civilian and razz you over it after. I don't know who the hell you just came up against."

"He was a pro, Nick," Trapp said, admitting in those four words what he was only just beginning to realize himself. "He was good. He came this close to punching my ticket for good."

Trapp pinched his thumb and forefinger together for effect. It wasn't necessary. He saw from the look on his friend's face that the FBI agent understood how serious his brush with danger had been.

At this level of the game, there were no amateurs. Pope knew that Trapp was for real, and that he wasn't just crying wolf. The day might have started out as a training op, but it sure as hell wasn't ending that way.

The two men maintained eye contact until Trapp noticed traffic beginning to move on the other side of the intersection.

"Green means go," he said, jerking his chin up at the traffic light and instant before the driver of the car behind pummeled the horn.

"Geez," Pope said, shaking his head as he pushed down on the gas pedal. "You look like shit."

Glancing down at himself, Trapp noticed with some

surprise that his shirt was speckled with blood. He checked himself over one more time before concluding that it belonged to his assailant rather than him. He slipped his jacket off, then pulled the item over his head and tossed it onto the back seat, before shrugging his jacket back on and doing it up.

"Bag it and run a DNA check," he said.

"You got it. What else can you tell me?"

Trapp exhaled, pushing the air out slowly through his lips. As he'd waited for Pope to show up, he'd made sure to catalog his memories from the pursuit and fight.

"Like I said, he was definitely a pro. Probably American. Five foot eleven, maybe six foot. I'm guessing special forces training, or some other black outfit. He knew how to fight, that's for damn sure."

"He was good?" Pope said. Trapp knew what his friend was asking.

As good as you?

"Young. Late twenties, maybe. Extremely physically fit. Carried a knife and was quick to use it. He wanted to get away more than he wanted to finish me off. I guess I got lucky." Trapp answered. "But yeah, he was good."

"Did he say anything?"

Trapp shook his head. "Nothing that would identify him. He wanted to know who sent me. Like he was expecting somebody else."

Pope grimaced. "That's not a lot to go on."

"You're telling me," Trapp said. He doubted the FBI agents now trawling footage of the putative training operation would get a clear image of his assailant's face. Their only hope of identifying him was that the man's DNA was on file somewhere.

But he had a gut feeling that it wouldn't be. Whether he was special forces trained or not, there were ways of making information like that disappear.

"You said he carried a knife?"

"That's right. Why?"

"Metropolitan PD just called in a dead body in Lyndon B. Johnson Memorial Park. That's pretty close to the Metro station at Arlington Cemetery."

"You think there's a link?"

"You know what they say about coincidences," Pope shrugged.

"Who's the vic?"

"No idea. I've got a guy heading to the coroner's office now. If it's connected, we'll get to the bottom of it."

"It's connected, all right," Trapp thought aloud, feeling a familiar telltale sensation in his gut. He might not know what the hell had happened today, or why, but he sensed that it was somehow important even so.

"Yeah. But to what?"

"Beats me," he admitted, subconsciously rubbing his bruised ribs. He winced at the memory of the fight.

"It was really that close, huh?" Pope asked quietly, his eyes fixed to the road.

The Suburban turned uncannily quiet, almost like the crypt of a church. The thought was unsettling. Trapp briefly wondered whether he would end up in a place like that one day.

"Maybe I'm losing my edge," he said ruefully. "But yeah. It really was."

8

"Long day, honey?" Eliza Ikeda grinned.

Trapp stopped dead in the doorway and looked his girlfriend up and down. She looked better than the day they'd first met, though since she'd been in the process of being kidnapped by a team of psychopathic North Korean terrorists, that wasn't exactly difficult. He whistled and ostentatiously drank in her frame one last time, now down and up. She was wearing well-fitted hiking pants colored a rusty maroon, of the type that unzip to become shorts. Not exactly the epitome of modern fashion, but well suited for the week in the woods they had planned.

Instead of replying, he reached out, grabbed her hand, and dragged her toward him, ignoring half a dozen twinges of pain from all over his body as he planted his lips on hers and stole a long, deep kiss.

She pulled away, panting. "I'll take that as a no..."

"It's a long story. You all set?"

Ikeda gestured at the hiking pack by the door. "Left yours there in case you needed to add anything. Car's packed."

The car, like the small, isolated cottage in the Virginia countryside, was rented. Someone at Langley had handled both, which was the way Trapp liked it. Better than paying for a mortgage on a place you only got to enjoy three months of the year. The government took enough of his paycheck in taxes. He figured it was only right they gave a little back. Besides, it was safer to keep moving around. The bad guys only had to guess right once.

"Okay," Trapp muttered, removing his jacket and throwing it onto the couch just long enough for Ikeda to pick it up and shoot him a reproving look. "Let me shower, then we can go."

Ikeda's eyebrow danced upward. "Want any company?"

Her expression changed in an instant as she took in the yellowing bruises that covered his torso. "What the hell happened to you? You look like you took on a semi-truck. And lost."

"Ouch," Trapp said. "I told you—long story."

"You're going to need to give me more than that," Ikeda said archly.

Trapp sighed and explained what little he knew about what had happened earlier that day. The story sounded pitifully incomplete even in its second telling.

"You seriously don't know who came at you?" Ikeda asked skeptically. "That's a hell of a case of wrong place, wrong time."

"If I knew, I'd tell you," Trapp shrugged. "But I don't. Maybe I picked up a nemesis somewhere. But if I did, he didn't tell me why. So your guess is as good as mine."

They were on the road ten minutes later, which was just long enough for Trapp to shower and change. The car was nondescript but spacious enough to ingest all their camping gear without blocking the view out the back. It was Japanese, which meant it handled well, but when the hybrid motor kicked in, you sometimes forgot you were driving at all.

Several hours passed as they chased the sun across the horizon, and suburbia gave way to the raw beauty of the Allegheny

Mountains, their home for the next few days. They pulled into a parking lot just east of Cheat Bridge, right before the tugging at the bottom of Trapp's eyelids began to worry him.

They hiked about ten minutes into the forest before he grimaced, reaching down to tap his pocket. "You bring a cell phone?"

"Like hell I did!" Ikeda replied hotly, spinning around so that he could see more of her than the back of her pack. "The world can handle a few days without you, Jason. It managed before you came along, and I'm sure it will do just fine after."

"You know, if you weren't so damn good-looking," he grumbled, "you wouldn't get away with half the stuff you do. Anyway, it's not about that. I haven't spoken to Mike for weeks. I get the sense he's putting me out to pasture."

And after today, he reflected silently. *Maybe he's right.*

"Then what?" Ikeda asked, relaxing a little.

Trapp looked pointedly down at his hiking boot-clad ankles. "How far you figure you could carry me if I broke my leg?"

Ikeda's dark pigtail danced in the fading light as she cocked her head to one side. "Are you planning to?"

"Not presently," he replied mildly. "But you know what they say, fail to prepare –"

"Prepare to fail," she replied, reaching into her half-zipped gilet and removing a dark plastic rectangle attached to a lanyard around her neck.

"You've thought of everything, huh?"

"You bet your ass." She grinned, making a show of placing her hands on her hips. "And you know something?"

"I'm guessing you're about to tell me," he said dryly.

"You really need to up your self-help game. I mean c'mon, Jason, *fail to prepare*? What are you reading right now, a 1940s Boy Scouts of America handbook?"

The sound Trapp made in response was more of an indistinct grumble emanating deep inside his throat than anything that could truthfully be said to resemble diction.

It took a little over an hour to hike to their chosen campsite, by which time the luminous tips of the hands of Trapp's watch were dimly visible every time his arms swung at his sides. Beams from the flashlights strapped to both his and Ikeda's foreheads lit up about twenty yards of forest in whichever direction they chose to look. The rest was swallowed by darkness.

"Satellite or star?" Ikeda said, stopping so suddenly that he crunched into the back of her and had to reach out and grab the straps on her pack to save her from tumbling over.

"Space station, I'm guessing," Trapp said, glancing up once her boots were settled firmly back on the ground. "Though I guess it could be one of those new satellite constellations. It's a real free-for-all up there right now, I hear."

"You hear? Where do you hear?"

"The news."

"You don't read the news."

"I'm like Chuck Norris. The news reads me."

She rolled her eyes. "Try saying that with a straight face."

"You got me." Trapp grinned, dumping his pack onto the turf with a sigh of relief. "It was some briefing at Langley. They make me sit through them from time to time. Guess maybe they're trying to transition me to a desk job."

"You want that?"

Trapp shrugged. "Not really. Truth be told, I'm not really sure what I want. This training gig with the Bureau ain't so bad. But –"

"It doesn't feel the same?"

"Not really."

Ikeda arched her eyebrow. "What about today? That was real, right?"

"What are you saying?"

"Maybe it's a good thing," Ikeda mused. "You're not getting any younger."

"Thanks."

"You know what I mean... Besides, now you've got more to lose. We both do."

"Yeah," he replied, rubbing his aching torso. "I guess I do."

"Sore subject?"

"Sore everything," he said, sidestepping the question.

"Well, maybe a break is as good as a change," Ikeda said brightly, pulling the tent pack from her backpack. "And we've got all week to find out."

9

ederal Social Rehabilitation Center no. 1 Almoloya Estado de Mexico.

THE CONVOY ROLLED through the first, then the second of the two military checkpoints that guarded the final approaches to Altiplano prison without incident. It was, after all, expected. The man in the fifth vehicle, the waiting warden knew, was a senior lieutenant to the leader of the Crusaders Cartel. Not important enough to merit a helicopter transfer to the helipad to the west of the prison, but sufficiently valuable to demand an escort of twenty heavily armed paramilitaries. Though it looked like more.

It was almost midnight, but that was not in itself unusual – high-value inmates were often transported early in the morning or last thing at night because the roads were empty and thus quick. More than one such motorcade had been ambushed by cartel gunmen over the years, and the authorities had learned to adapt. It was an arms race. The police purchased ballistic vests, and the cartels bought bigger guns. The Army acquired tanks, so the gunmen returned with rockets.

On and on the wheel turned, tallying up with every revolution an endless list of the names of the dead.

Red and blue lights flashed on top of the armored vehicles, which were emblazoned in white lettering with the words *GUARDIA NACIONAL*. Their sirens did not sound, which gave the procession a funereal quality when viewed from a distance.

They slowed for a third time at the main gateway into the prison, which was flanked on either side by a pair of light tanks belonging to the Mexican army – a brash but highly effective deterrent to anyone foolish enough to contemplate attacking the prison itself.

Such a thing had never happened before. But this was Mexico, in the second decade of a brutal war against the narcotics cartels—a war which the government wasn't losing, but certainly was not winning.

And that, as far as anyone who thought about it knew, meant only that *such a thing had not happened yet*.

Altiplano, after all, was the prison in which the famed Joaquin Guzman had once been incarcerated.

Which meant that it was the prison from which the drug kingpin known as El Chapo had subsequently escaped, courtesy of a 1.5 mile-long tunnel that exited directly into the cartel leader's cell.

Security had been beefed up since then, of course. Not just the two tanks at the gate, or the military checkpoints. No one was allowed within 500 yards of the prison, and every structure or plant taller than a blade of grass had been leveled to ensure clear fields of fire for the snipers in the guard towers that dotted the now-dark walls, blazing like torches in the night.

And there were other, less visible additions too. Delicate instruments buried deep beneath the ground, capable of detecting even the burrowing of a small rodent. Jamming devices that blanketed the airwaves with static, so that inmates could no longer communicate with their compatriots on the outside.

No, the planners in Mexico City were certain that nothing short of a frontal assault on the prison would be successful, and preparations had even been made to counter that infinitely unlikely scenario. As long as the hundreds of armed prison guards inside the walls could hold out for twenty minutes, Air Force helicopters would blanket the skies overhead, closing off all routes out.

Another twenty would bring the Naval Infantry Corps.

The Marines.

The convoy sped through two sets of internal chain-link fences before coming to a halt in the exercise yard just behind the prison walls. For a few seconds, silence reigned, and all that could be heard was the clinking and groaning of heated metal as the armored vehicles settled on the dirt.

Then the crunch of boots as the warden walked halfway to the unmoving procession, flanked forward and behind by a pair of armed prison guards. He was a shorter man than the four around him and wore only thin-soled leather shoes rather than boots, which didn't help. The disparity meant that he only caught occasional glimpses of the stopped vehicles as he made the journey toward them, occasionally squinting against the glow of the prison's floodlights as he wondered why nobody was getting out.

His small group came to a halt, and two guards flanked him on either side. And then they all waited. Ten seconds passed. Then another ten.

The warden coughed nervously, drawing a side-glance from one of the prison guards to his right. "Everything okay, boss?"

The small man smoothed his suit jacket against his torso in an act that was meant to convey calm but produced an effect that was quite the opposite. In truth, he hated nights like tonight. They reminded him of the danger that came holding hands with the job.

Of course, a little voice reminded him, tinged with shame, *there is no danger really.*

Not for him.

After all, he accepted the payments and kept the inmates comfortable. The ones who mattered, anyway. The cartels knew where the line lay, and they toed it exactly. A bottle of whiskey slipped into a cell after dusk. The occasional visit by a woman of the night. He rationalized his transgressions to himself by reasoning that he wasn't doing anything truly wrong. This way, he stayed alive, the prisoners stayed behind bars, and no one caused any trouble.

He'd heard about this particular transfer twice in the space of the same hour. First from the independent broker who handled such matters for the cartels, and only then from the prison department. The first payment was already in his retirement account.

Finally there was movement. As though the action was coordinated, every door on four of the five armored vehicles swung open, and armed gunmen in dark blue fatigues jumped onto the dirt with easy grace. They fanned out, forming a loose ring around the stopped convoy.

One of the warden's guards reflexively reached for his weapon.

"Easy, Luis," the warden murmured, gesturing at the most junior of the guards who accompanied him. "It's always the same. They like to make a show."

"Sorry, boss," the guard replied shamefacedly.

The warden watched as the armed men came to a halt, some dropping to their knees and bringing their rifles to their shoulders, searching for targets on the walls and in the guard towers. A chill swept down his neck, belying the heat.

But a second later, a command rang out ordering the newcomers to stand easy, and as one, they relaxed. The same man from whom the command had emanated lifted a radio to his lips and issued a second order, which seconds later prompted the doors of the final armored vehicle to swing open.

Four men climbed out. One wore the same light-brown prison uniform worn by the inmates of his own institution. The prisoner had a black bag over his head and was shackled at the ankles and wrists, which themselves were chained to a thick leather strap around his waist. He jangled as his guards lowered him to the ground.

The chiming stopped briefly, then restarted as the four-man procession began walking toward the welcoming committee. The three receiving guards were armed only with bright yellow tasers, but the warden noticed that the eyes of the masked men all around never missed a step.

"They're getting more competent," he muttered. The Mexican National Guard was a relatively new organization, first constituted only a year earlier. It was nominally both led and staffed by civilians, though it hadn't escaped notice that the bulk of its equipment and manpower had been provided by the military.

And they hadn't sent their best.

But maybe that was changing, he reflected. This squad appeared well drilled.

The small formation stopped in front of him, and he watched as two of the guards grabbed their prisoner's upper arms and pushed him to the floor. He collapsed with a grunt, and would have toppled over, had they not retained their hold.

"Prisoner Emmanuel Garcia," the front most of the man's escorts barked in strange, clipped Spanish. "To be held for pre-trial detention."

"You have the papers?" the warden inquired softly, reaching out his arm.

The man nodded and reached inside one of the pockets on his ballistic vest, pulling out a sheaf of forms which he handed over. Other than that, he did not give a name, or even show his face. That was not entirely unusual, however.

"Can I ask you a favor, warden?"

He looked up from perusing the documentation, satisfied that all seemed in order. "Of course..."

His opposite number adopted a soft, almost wistful tone, leaning forward so that the words were for the warden's ears only. "Do you mind if I bring a couple of my men to the control room to watch as Garcia is taken to his cell? We've been hunting this rat for a long, long time. My men, they have lost friends. *Brothers.* It would do them good to see the fruits of that sacrifice."

The warden paused to consider the request. It was unorthodox, but impossible to refuse.

"It won't be that interesting..." he warned. "But if that's what you want, I have no problem with it."

"My friend," the masked man breathed, visibly satisfied, "believe me when I tell you, it will be fascinating for us."

10

The Guardia Nacional officer was breathing heavily, the warden thought, as the two men watched the new inmate being led through the prison's gray concrete hallways. He was headed for the maximum-security section, where the majority of the high-value cartel detainees were kept, both those awaiting trial and those for whom their cell's bare walls would prove the limits of their universe for the rest of their lives.

It was a strange quirk of the prison's setup that the high-security wing required the fewest guards to man it. The hallway gates were electronically operated, unlike most in the jail, and required the presentation of both a physical key card and confirmation from an operator inside the control room that he currently occupied.

The warden did not kid himself that the system was failsafe, but it was at least fail *resistant*. As secure as any human-controlled system could be.

Half a dozen of his guards were assigned to precisely that task, and the warden allowed himself a small smile of satisfaction as he watched the small procession come to a halt at the final gate that governed entry into the maximum-security wing. The Guardia Nacional troops stopped and physically secured their charge with a hand on each shoulder as the prison guard leading them reached for the card attached to his belt by a section of elasticated cord. He leaned and held it against the corresponding reader before shooting a thumbs-up toward the nearest camera.

He's not going anywhere, the warden thought, amused at the extra precaution. *But whatever makes you happy.*

"Do we meet your expectations, señor...?" he said out loud, trailing off as he realized he didn't know the soldier's name.

"César," the man replied with a strange inflection. He seemed to exhale slightly as his men led their prisoner through the gate, and he turned toward the warden. "And very much so. Thank you for allowing me to watch this, sir. You have made me very happy indeed."

"I'm glad you got what you needed," the warden replied with an easy smile. He didn't pretend to understand the officer's needs, but they had proved easy to accommodate. "Will that be all?"

His counterpart nodded and peeled his mask off his head. It dropped to the ground, and the warden thought the man looked familiar. But from where?

César smiled. "For you, yes..."

The warden blinked at the reply, puzzled at its meaning. He wasn't left hanging for long. The Guardia Nacional officer drew his weapon from the holster at his right side and raised it to a point between the warden's eyes.

And fired.

"Captain!"

Hector León froze with his rear end approximately two

inches from the seat of his office chair, a steaming plastic container containing leftovers of his wife's cooking the previous night in his hands. His chin dipped slightly toward his chest as he realized what was coming.

He sighed and placed his lunch on the desk in front of him, sensing from the urgency in his second-in-command's voice that it would be stone cold by the time he was able to return to it. "Lieutenant?"

The young man was out of breath as he barged through Captain León's office door – and Hector knew that it was not a result of physical exertion. His men were far too fit for that. Even the officers.

Especially the officers.

He grimaced to conceal a smile at the untruth as he reflected that he ought to spend more time with the PT instructors. The problem with command was the same the world over: too much paperwork. He hadn't signed up to ride a desk, and even though he was an officer in the Marines, he found himself doing altogether too much of that.

"What is it, Ramirez?"

"Shots fired at Altiplano Prison, sir," Lieutenant Ramirez said, regaining control over his breath.

Hector glanced automatically at the alarm strobe just above the young man's head.

"It didn't come through the hard line, sir. A guard called it in by phone. They are taking heavy fire from unknown attackers who have penetrated the prison's outer walls."

"Great," he muttered, opening his desk drawer and pulling out his side-arm. "That's all you got?"

"For now, sir. The Air Force has been notified, that's all I know. The alert squadron is lifting off now."

"The men?"

"Forming up as we speak."

"Good job, Ramirez," León said, already jogging as he

passed the younger man, a spike of adrenaline constricting his throat and slightly altering his usual deep timbre. "Let's go."

CÉSAR CHECKED HIS WATCH. The timer on the screen told him that nine minutes had elapsed since he'd shot the jail's warden and his men had begun their assault.

The prison's thick concrete walls smothered the sound of gunfire, but the rhythmic reverberation of the heavier caliber weapons was impossible to ignore. Every couple of minutes a louder crash echoed, signaling that his men were using explosives to deal with the heavier pockets of resistance from the prison's guards.

César had no last name, or at least not one he advertised. It had been so long since anyone had said it out loud, even he had mostly forgotten.

He frowned as he noticed several glistening patches on his adopted uniform. He'd only discharged his weapon once, which meant that the brain matter and viscera belonged to the prison's erstwhile warden. The liquid had already seeped into the material, so he didn't bother attempting to wipe it away.

"Okay," he said out loud, raising his voice to address the entire control room. "We're done here. Is the package ready?"

One of his men, crouched over a computer terminal that connected to the prison's central control system, flashed a thumbs-up at him. "It's all queued up."

César glanced around the bloodied control room one last time. There was no satisfaction on his face. He felt nothing for the bodies of the dead guards that now littered the space. They had posed an obstacle to the successful conclusion of his mission, and now they did not. He felt no more compunction at eliminating their resistance then he might at excising a particularly intrusive infestation of rodents.

"Good. Stay with me."

The technician nodded and grabbed a tablet computer that sat beside him. He shoved it into a backpack and joined his master, who let out a loud whistle to warn the rest of his men that it was time to go.

They responded immediately and followed him out, not ducking as a particularly violent crash from somewhere in the giant prison caused dust to fall like a light covering of snow from the ceiling. The last one out closed the heavy steel door gingerly.

It was for the best, César knew, since the same man had earlier attached a pound of heavy explosives to a desk on the opposite side of the doorway and packed the plastic explosive with ball bearings. Unless they were careful, whoever opened that door would meet a very sticky ending.

The team's digital radio system beeped, and a crystal-clear voice reported, "Target is secure. Moving now."

César glanced at his watch. The number 11 now blinked into life onto its face. He grimaced. They were behind schedule. The target wasn't where he was supposed to be. When his men had entered the cell, they'd found it empty.

Several frantic minutes of searching had ensued before the target was discovered face-down in the caged exercise yard, dust coating his face and the front of his prison uniform, and a guard's weapon aimed directly at his back. The guard in question, César presumed, was now dead.

Another explosion reverberated through the prison, and he frowned. He hadn't expected the prison's guards to put up such stiff resistance, though of course it was never entirely out of the question. Men have a habit of stiffening their spine when their backs are up against the wall.

He keyed his radio. "Report."

The updates came in from each of the teams scattered around the prison. Alfa squad was in the courtyard just inside the prison's main entrance, defending the infiltration team's vehicles. César did not intend to exit the prison on four wheels, but he was too experienced an operator not to maintain a backup plan just in case.

"We're pinned down," Alfa's squad leader reported, tension clipping his voice, but without panic. "They have sharpshooters in turrets five and seven. We've taken the rest out already. One walking casualty."

"Help's on its way," César replied as he jogged through the prison's corridors. "Bravo?"

A new voice reported, "We have the target. On the move."

César's small procession came to a halt at a steel door, and he momentarily pulled his attention away from the radio. "What's the holdup?"

One of his men was fumbling with a bunch of keys. This was an older part of the prison, and unlike the high-security wing from which they were extracting their target, it wasn't wired up with the electronically operated doors they had observed earlier from the control room. His technician didn't bother removing the tablet computer from his backpack, but César shot a warning look at his demolitions expert.

"I'm good," the man with the keys said, trying a third and being rewarded with a heavy mechanical click as the locking mechanism swung open, and he yanked the door after it. "Let's _"

Whatever he was about to say was cruelly curtailed in his throat, courtesy of a flurry of gunfire. For a moment, César watched as the mercenary's body seemed to hang in midair, jerking slightly as a second and a third round impacted the plates in his armor carrier before one final round pierced his skull and tugged his head back like it was being yanked by a string.

César reacted immediately, first pressing himself against the wall, then dropping his chest to the ground. "Someone close that fucking door," he yelled over the roar of small arms fire.

Rounds cracked overhead and chewed chunks out of the concrete walls. A ricochet glanced off one wall and bounced against the other before the brass came to a halt in front of his face. He withdrew his pistol and from his position on the floor fired blind through the doorway.

"Contact, contact," he said into his radio handset once one of his men finally pushed the steel doorway into its frame, and the crackling wildfire of gunshots was momentarily dimmed, only to be replaced by the occasional metallic clunk as a bullet impacted the thick door. Whoever was on the other side appeared anxious to remind them they were there. "Report."

Each of his units checked in in turn and confirmed that either they were not currently in contact, or if they were it was in another sector of the prison entirely.

César reloaded and heard his men doing the same. There was a clarity in knowing that the resistance in the next hallway was one of malice, not ignorance. It meant that whatever action he took to squash it was justified. That was important, since even in a military unit as handsomely remunerated as this one, friendly fire was frowned upon.

"Grenades," he said in a voice loud enough to be heard but not so powerful as to carry through the doorway.

"Ready," one of his men indicated, brandishing a pair of dark green orbs about the size of baseballs and decorated with a few lines of spidery yellow text. César grunted with approval.

He pointed at another of his men and gestured at him to move toward the side of the doorway. Another gunshot impact echoed from the other side, though they were becoming more infrequent now. Perhaps the defenders on the other side were running out of ammunition.

It didn't matter.

César held up three fingers and made sure that both men

saw them. Then he checked to ensure the rest of his team was ready.

This was the way he'd fought in Mosul, and in Basra, and every place in which he had made war since. Stun grenades were for amateurs, in his view. Fighting was about survival and beating the other guy – not honor.

He glanced at his watch. Nineteen minutes. This was taking too long. He dropped a finger.

The last finger fell, and César watched as the man to the left of the doorway pulled it back, prompting the man to its right to unleash the barrel of his submachine gun on full automatic. The full thirty round magazine clicked dry in a couple of seconds, but it was plenty long enough to allow the man right in the middle to pull the fuses from both grenades and toss them into the hallway behind.

César counted in his head, pressing himself to the ground as his man hastily swung the door closed once again. The grenades had a five-second fuse.

Three.

Four.

The blood pumping in his eardrums sounded like waves crashing against a shoreline, and he heard two swells breaking in his mind as the final second stretched away.

The explosion shook the floor and was followed half a second later by a second. A hail of metal fragments rattled against the door, and a plume of dust erupted from beneath it, surfing along the floor and coating the nearest men in its folds.

César launched himself to his feet faster than any of his men. He sprinted toward the door with his weapon drawn and was the first man through. The hallway beyond it was thick with dust and smoke and the acrid stink of detonated explosives. It was almost impossible to make out detail, so he fired blindly at anything that looked like it might be a figure – human or otherwise.

When the dust began to settle, he saw three men in the hallway, each shredded by the grenade's fragments. Unlike his own men, they were not wearing body armor. There was little need for it behind the safety of the prison wall. After all, inmates rarely came equipped with any firepower greater than a sharpened toothbrush handle.

Until today.

A fourth individual was slumped against a wall five yards farther down the corridor. The blast had shredded his blue uniform pants, which had the added effect of making it quite evident that he was bleeding profusely. He wasn't armed, though a handgun lay a few feet to his side. César strode toward him, and the sound of movement somehow penetrated the fortress of shock that must surely have encompassed the man's entire existence.

The mortally wounded guard looked up at César, then turned for the weapon, but succeeded only in toppling onto the floor and forcing a mournful, even pitiful yelp of pain from his lips.

César kicked the weapon away dispassionately and leveled his own at the injured man's skull. He leaned down, pressing the muzzle of his weapon against the man's bloodied temple. "Are there more of you?"

The man only moaned once more. Even now, the life was fading from his eyes, measured in the units of blood leaking from his shattered, useless leg. Yet somehow he seemed to derive strength from somewhere deep inside and levered himself upward with a grunt only of effort, not agony – though his whitened lips and face gave the lie to the act.

With a force of effort, the dying guard raised his face to César's and whispered, "Screw you!"

Flecks of bloodied spittle rained from his lips and landed on his adversary's proffered cheek.

César nodded, and though it might have appeared

surprising to an onlooker, it was entirely without malice. The pistol in his hand fired once, and the wounded guard's head was no more.

In the confines of the hallway, the weapon's report was almost unimaginably loud, and though it was not a sound he was unaccustomed to, César winced nonetheless. He stood up and enjoyed the brief moment of silence that often follows the taking of a man's life. A space of calm and reflection.

His men were waiting for him when he turned, and he was pleased to note that the team's weapons were spaced out to cover every possible angle of attack. The computer technician was the only man who wasn't armed, and even he was crouched low, head swiveling as he scanned from side to side in search of anyone approaching.

César exhaled. But the moment of peace did not last. The radio earpiece blared in his ear, and it was evident from the body language of his men that they heard the transmission also.

"Boss, it's Alfa. They found a heavy machine gun. We could use some help."

\

11

Captain León's ragged convoy sped down the Carreterra Federal 55. Ordinarily the journey from their base at the headquarters of the 22nd Military Zone in Toluca to Altiplano prison would have taken a hair under 40 minutes. More with traffic.

But today there would be no traffic. Pickup trucks and SUVs marked POLICIA ESTATAL had sealed off every entrance to the highway between Toluca and San Antonio Bonixi, and even more units streaked alongside and ahead of the Marine convoy, corralling any hapless commuter that strayed into their path.

The captain's command vehicle was a souped-up Ford F-250, outfitted with a full complement of communications equipment. It was one of eight similar vehicles, along with five Scorpion armored personnel carriers. All told, he had a full company of 80 men with him. All practiced shooters.

"Do we have eyes over the prison yet?" León said without turning to face Lieutenant Ramirez. Instead, he nervously checked his carbine for what seemed like the hundredth time.

"Thirty seconds," Ramirez replied, not tearing his attention away from the rapid stream of communication emanating from his radio handset. "1st Air Group out of Santa Lucia AFB has two flights of choppers en route. The first group should be blades over any moment now."

León nodded curtly and craned his neck to peer into the sky. He was grateful for the presence of the air support. The primary role for which his unit trained as the designated Rapid Reaction Force for Altiplano Prison was to put down an inmate riot. This – whatever *this* was – was a different kettle of fish entirely. Almost to a man, his Marines were combat veterans. It was hard to be anything else in the Mexican Naval Infantry, which had been at the tip of the spear of its country's war against the cartels for almost a decade.

But even so, his boys were trained and equipped to put down small-scale unrest. Perhaps to subdue a wing that had fallen under the control of its inmates and commandeered a small number of weapons from captured guards. But put down a full-scale assault?

I need more men.

"We're three minutes out, Captain," the driver reported from up front as he pulled a hard left and exited the highway, following directly behind a pair of Scorpion APCs driving abreast. There was some traffic left on this road, but the second their drivers noticed the Marine vehicles in the rearview mirrors, they quickly made themselves scarce.

"Where's my air support, Ramirez?" Hector muttered, his voice clipped. He needed to know what was going on inside that prison.

The lieutenant held up a finger to pre-empt his commanding officer's question and listened intently to the flow of chatter over the radio. He answered something else entirely.

"The guards inside got to a radio," he reported. "They have control of towers five and seven, and isolated units are spread out throughout the prison. Whoever's behind this attack is well armed. They have about forty men, wearing National Guard uniforms."

He fell silent and returned his attention to the radio.

And a moment later, the thump-thump-thump of helicopter rotors in the skies overhead answered Hector's question anyway. He angled his neck once more and searched for the telltale black dots in the sky.

Twisting entirely around in his seat, he saw them at last through the SUV's rear window. Four light helicopters, banking from the east and racing low over the road toward his convoy. They were only a hundred feet or so from the ground.

"Look like Defenders," a sergeant muttered from the back.

"Ramirez," Hector ordered. "Find out if they've got sharpshooters on board. Then tell them to find out what the hell the bad guys are up to."

"Yes, sir."

The roar from the engines of the four McDonnell Douglas MD 500 Defenders grew as they got closer. The small helicopters sounded more like amped-up lawnmowers than their heavier cousins, but they were quick and endlessly maneuvrable. The Americans had used a very similar bird in Vietnam, Hector knew, and they were perfect for this type of reconnaissance work.

The helicopters closed the last few yards, and for a short breath they disappeared from sight, blocked by the Ford's roof, before soaring through the air as they emerged through the glass of the vehicle's windshield. If anything, they now seemed even lower than they had before. In the distance behind them, and just to the left of the road, the hulking form of Altiplano Prison hove into view.

"Two minutes out, Captain," the driver reported.

Hector nodded, his eyes drawn to the helicopters overhead. They were each equipped with a pair of gun pods, he saw— 7.62mm miniguns capable of putting several thousand rounds a minute onto a target. A small exhalation whistled free from his pursed lips as he noted their presence with approval.

His men were not technically outnumbered by the prison's attackers – at least what they knew of the numbers – but in urban combat a two-to-one ratio of attackers to defenders was extremely underweight. He would prefer to have at least four times as many men with him, and maybe even more. After all, Altiplano Prison contained several thousand hardened criminals, mostly cartel sicarios. It was possible – plausible, even – that the enemy had released some or all of these men to fight alongside them. Something not so dissimilar had occurred in Sinaloa only a year or so before.

And if that was true, then he and his men might be walking into a death trap.

"What the hell?"

The driver's outburst summoned Hector's attention back to the here and now. He squinted as, now several hundred yards ahead of his speeding convoy, the flight of helicopters broke left and right before spinning as neatly as a top and coming to a halt in the sky. They were now spread out in a square formation, one stacked upon the other, hovering dead over the road.

"I say again," Ramirez said, his voice rising in pitch. "Unknown flight of helicopters from 101 Air Squadron, you are directed to close on the prison and –"

A puff of what appeared to be steam or smoke appeared at the tip of one of the gun pods attached to the helicopter at the top right of the tight formation. Barely a second later, all four of the light attack choppers were firing down on his company of Marines. The minigun rounds spat vengefully from the mouths of the hovering aircraft, chewing up the asphalt ahead of the procession of vehicles. A storm of dust and chunks of debris was blown into life in an instant, swirling with greater intensity as the gunfire rattled overhead.

And then the first of Captain León's vehicles was swallowed by it.

"Dios mio," Hector León murmured, momentarily stunned into indecision by the sight of death raining down from the skies above. The cartels had never tried anything like this before. Nothing even close. He'd once faced down an eighteen-wheeler they'd up-armored into a makeshift tank, but even that deformed beast paled in comparison to these weapons of war.

"Break contact, break contact," Lieutenant Ramirez screamed into his handset. "I say again, break contact. You are firing on Marine vehicles. Break, break, break."

Hector understood what his subordinate as yet did not. This was no accident. Somehow the cartels had arranged this, either by stealing the choppers or convincing their crews to turn on the country that had birthed and trained them.

But whichever it was, it didn't matter right now. There were only two options: either keep on driving in the hope of escape or roll the dice and take the battle to them. It was fight or flight, as it ever was.

He turned and grabbed Ramirez by the shoulder, digging his fingertips in and squeezing tight until the man fell silent. He stared into his captain's eyes, his own black with terror, his chest heaving frantically.

"Order the convoy to stop," Hector said. "The men in the trucks need to dismount and get to cover."

"Yes sir. And the Scorpions?"

"Just give the order," Hector snapped. His own radio unit was in the footwell between his feet, and he cursed his lack of preparation.

Ramirez nodded and spoke hurriedly into his own handset. Immediately, the convoy began to slow, and the Minigun fire from overhead overshot the procession, forcing the helicopters to reposition and momentarily buying him and his men a few seconds' respite from the deadly hail overhead.

Hector raised his voice as he reached down between his legs and grabbed his radio. "Everybody out. Get to cover. Now!"

He tugged at the door handle, then shouldered it open, jumping to the ground and crouching behind the stopped Ford truck for a second to suck in a lungful of air. His heart was racing, and his shouldered carbine thumped painfully against his side.

"Ramirez," he yelled over the roar of screaming men and the returning rattle of gunfire from the choppers overhead. "Stick with me."

The lieutenant did as instructed, hugging his CO as Hector sprinted to the nearest building, a shanty-like structure made of corrugated iron and concrete bricks. It would do little to stop a 7.62 round if one was fired at it in anger, but it was all that was on offer. Around him, his Marines were doing the same. Overhead, the sound of helicopter rotors was as ominous as it was relentless. The four choppers were now firing independently, lining up targets and loosing off short bursts at will.

One of the Scorpions took a pummeling, rounds sparking off its armor chassis and leaving deep welts where the paint was sheared clean off, but the helicopters seemed to be concentrating their fire on the Fords. Though the MiniCommando pickups were specially modified for military operations, incorporating roll bars, gun points and communications equipment, they were not armored, and depleted uranium rounds ripped through them as though they were protected by nothing more than cotton candy. One by one the vehicles were destroyed, and with them the unit's mobility.

"Ramirez," Hector called out, not allowing himself a moment to think. "Get gunners on those Scorpions. We need to put some fire onto those choppers now."

The lieutenant relayed the order, and as he did so Hector cursed. They had antitank rockets in the trunks of most of the trucks. In his haste to get his men to safety, he hadn't even thought of them.

A few feet away, a Marine was pressed against the building, his rifle nestled against his chin, occasionally firing measured bursts into the sky. Hector knew that it was fruitless, and the Marine probably did too – but in combat, men prefer to feel in control of their fate, whether or not their actions truly have any chance of tipping the scales.

"Sergeant!" Hector yelled. "Take two men and get me some RPGs. Second you get a shot, take it. Understood?"

The Marine nodded curtly but didn't acknowledge the order verbally before grabbing two other men and sprinting into hell. Hector understood that. It could easily be a death sentence. And yet the man did it anyway.

He turned his attention to the armored personnel carriers, which were stretched messily down the road over about a hundred yards. Each one had a Browning M2 heavy machine gun mounted on top, accessed through a port in the vehicle's roof. In transit, and thus when his convoy was hit, the weapons were unmanned, but he now saw men scrambling into position, and the vehicles themselves maneuvering for better aim.

Hector understood that the weapons would be little use if the gunships came close in. The machine guns mounted to his armored personnel carriers were designed for an anti-personnel mission, not anti-air. Without removing them from the vehicles, it would only be possible to get so much elevation.

"Get some fire onto those choppers," he yelled out unnecessarily to the men around him, who were already taking the lead of the earlier Marine sergeant and unloading everything they had. "We need to hold them off to give the Scorpions a chance."

He raised his own carbine to his shoulder and fired several three-round bursts into the sky, targeting one of the Defenders as it began maneuvering into position for another gun run. He knew that unless a particularly unfortunate bird happened to get in the way, he had precious little chance of hitting anything. But the pilots were only human. They would see flashes and smoke and know not to get too close.

Dropping his eyes, he watched his three men running through the debris to the nearest of the pickups, the one he himself had abandoned just a couple of minutes earlier. It was now a smoking husk of shattered glass and rent metal. The front tire on the side he couldn't see must have been pierced right through, because even though they were run-flat, it was sitting at a funny, sunken angle.

The two men accompanying the sergeant crouched and provided covering fire as he jumped into the back of the pickup, though Hector judged that it might've proved a better course of action to simply hide. Trying to shoot one of these things with 5.62 mm ammunition was like a toddler tweaking the nose of a grizzly bear. It was only likely to get them mad.

On the road behind him, the heavier chatter of the 50 cal machine guns opened up, and for the first time the helicopters responded to something that was happening on the ground rather than the other way round. Each of them responded to the new threat immediately, breaking left or right and speeding away from the site of their ambush.

Hector pumped his fist with elation. They were doing exactly the wrong thing – at least from their point of view. They were running from the gunfire, instead of getting close and high and picking his troops off from directly above, where it would be difficult for his men to return fire.

They could still do that, of course, but it would cost time and airspeed. Which gave him a chance.

The gunners were in position on all five of the wheeled APCs now, even the one that had survived a drive-by from one of the choppers overhead. Most of their rubber tires were chewed up and blown out. They wouldn't be going anywhere.

But they were still in the fight – working together to herd the closest of the choppers with bursts of gunfire.

Now that he could do nothing but watch, Hector finally took the time to hook his radio unit into his headset, cursing the error of judgment that had caused him to fail to do so earlier. He'd expected to have time to get into position once he arrived at the walls of the prison. Instead, the mistake had left him deaf and dumb during the crucible of battle. Maybe some of his men had even died as a result of it.

You couldn't have predicted this.

"Move him west, move him west," a voice repeated hoarsely over the net. "I've got a shot."

Hector watched as four of the Scorpions concentrated their fire in the same place, to the left side of the rearmost chopper, which was a hundred yards or so away from the road. It started banking sharply to its right as a storm of lead and tracer rounds rattled through the air to its left.

And as it did so, it ran right into the aim of the fifth Scorpion, and a long burst from its M2 cut the little aircraft apart.

The chopper hung in the air for a few seconds, slowly losing its forward momentum as a thick cloud of choking black smoke billowed from its side. The speed of the main rotor began to slow, and whether it was too close to the ground to recover, or the pilot was already dead didn't seem to matter.

It fell to the ground, first slowly, then all at once. It didn't explode when it impacted the earth, but the smoke intensified, and flames started licking its chassis. Each of the Scorpions concentrated their fire into its crippled skeleton until Hector was certain that no one inside was left alive.

A roar of exaltation filled the air, then a woosh as a rocket trail scratched out across the sky, chasing the other three helicopters. The RPG – an old Soviet design manufactured locally – was not designed to hunt and kill a moving target, let alone one that traversed the skies rather than the ground, and so its exhaust traced a long, lonely chart line into the sky before hitting the ground somewhere far out of sight.

The rest of the choppers were out of effective machine gun range now. Technically the Browning could hit a target at a distance of over 8000 yards – but not one traveling that fast. Hector waited for them to turn, to learn a lesson from the sacrifice of their fallen comrades and close for the kill, but they did not.

Instead, they set a course for the prison, only a couple of miles distant.

Now that the gunfire had fallen silent, a brief, ethereal calm seemed to reign. One of his Marines, Hector could not even see where the sound was coming from, was weeping, but even that sound did not feel real, especially over the backing track of the ringing cry of cells in his ear dying.

Ramirez walked toward him, unbuckling his helmet and dropping it loosely to his side as the soles of his boots dragged along the dusty ground. His tongue was slow, expression shell-shocked. "What the hell just happened?"

Hector kept his eyes locked on the choppers, needing to be certain that they would not return. He wasn't sure his men could withstand another assault from the skies. But they did not turn. Instead, they buzzed around the prison like gnats, opening fire on its guard towers as they closed in.

"Casualties?" he asked.

"At least a dozen dead."

The captain swore and punched his thigh with a closed fist. How had this happened? He turned back to the lieutenant, attempting to wrestle his mind back to the matters pressing at this very moment. "Medevac?"

"I wasn't sure whether to request one," Ramirez admitted, his face hangdog. "In case –"

"If they are planning on hitting us again, they won't wait for us to call it in," Hector said. "Do it now."

"Yes, sir."

He turned and surveyed the damage as the lieutenant carried out his orders. Five of his eight pickups were smoldering wrecks, and one more was entirely boxed in by the carcasses of its brethren. Like the Scorpion armored personnel carriers, the tires on the remaining two trucks had been cut to pieces. His Marines were stuck where they were.

Hector sank to his haunches as he took in the totality of the horror for the first time. He had lost men before in his country's brutal war with the cartels. But always before it had been a fair fight.

Not like this.

And from his numbed shock grew a blistering anger. He didn't yet see the whole picture. But he didn't need to. Somebody had planned the day's prison break. That person had sacrificed his men's lives like pawns on a chessboard.

And whoever it was, they would pay.

12

F ernando Carreon emerged from the far end of a long, drab prison hallway with an entirely bewildered expression on his face. He was surrounded by a quartet of César's men, hemmed in at every angle. They had been instructed to take a bullet for him if necessary, and since it was unlikely that they would do such a thing without the prospect of a considerable financial reward, one commensurate with the risk had been offered.

The gunfire in the distance was now sparse. Occasional bursts from automatic weapons were rare, though more common was the sound of a single gunshot bouncing off the featureless gray walls. It was clear what the latter heralded: the settling of scores.

César whistled at his men to pick up the pace. They did so, and he was pleased to note that they did not forget their training, even now, so close to perceived safety, slowing every time they passed a closed doorway to either side of their route for a team member to provide cover.

As the small unit came to a halt in front of César's own

personal detail, the two men at its head parted. "Jefe, it's good to see you at long last. And looking so well."

Carreon had lost at least fifteen pounds since becoming acquainted with food behind bars. On his somewhat gaunt face was mixed suspicion and not a little fear. "Who are you? I recognize your face."

"A friend."

"What's happening?" Carreon demanded, a touch of imperiousness in his tone as he reacquainted himself with the memory of command.

César cocked his head to one side and smiled. "Why, jefe – did nobody tell you? You are escaping."

"Impossible!" the cartel boss scoffed, his face visibly draining of color. "We'll never get out of here alive. What have you done?"

"Maybe that would be better than being handed over to the Americans to spend the rest of your life in Supermax." César shrugged. "But that is a matter for the philosophers. I do not expect to have to find out. Come, we have a ride to catch."

The sicario turned without waiting for any further response and beckoned Carreon to follow. After a moment's hesitation, he did so, turning left at the end of the hallway and following it until they reached an exterior wall of the prison wing which led into an interior courtyard.

They emerged onto it, an exercise yard painted a faded blue, with netless basketball hoops at either end. Several of César's men were already there, and more joined every minute, some leading small columns of men dressed in similar fashion to Carreon's own light brown prison scrubs.

Already thirty men were lined against the courtyard's far wall, giving their names as César's men checked them off lists contained in ruggedized tablet computers. The door swung shut after the last of César's small group stepped out, and Carreon glanced over his shoulder in momentary alarm.

"Nothing to worry about, jefe." César grinned.

Carreon opened his mouth to say something in response before closing it as a flurry of excitement erupted on the other side of the exercise yard. César watched with interest as two of his men dragged an inmate from the group, pulling him away from a developing tussle. They threw the man against the ground, and one placed his boot on the inmate's chest, conspicuously brandishing his rifle to keep him in place.

"What's happening?" Carreon asked.

Again, César shrugged. "I couldn't say. Perhaps a case of mistaken identity."

The larger group of inmates started to bellow with rage, all aimed at the hapless man lying prostrate on the ground. The masked soldier holding him down turned his head toward César, who casually drew his fingers across his throat.

A gunshot rang out a second later, chased by echoes that bounced off all four walls. The courtyard momentarily fell silent, or near enough, a quiet that was only broken by the distant, heavy thump of helicopter rotors.

In the calm, the inmates' attention turned to César's small group of fighters. Instantly a murmur of intrigue, then outright excitement began bubbling among them. Then a cheer. A man beat the air with his fist.

Then singing.

Carreon turned to his mysterious rescuer, his face wrinkling. He looked partly in shock. "What are they saying?"

"They're chanting your name, jefe. Why don't you show them your appreciation? Tell them to fight. I suspect we may need their help."

César gave his supposed boss a discreet but forceful shove forward as the noise from the helicopters grew louder overhead. And as he watched Carreon nail his colors to their mast, an unseen grin stretched across his face.

13

The villa was modest in size but opulent in finish. It sat in the Sierra Madre mountains northeast of Culiacán, somewhere between the foothills of the range and its jagged rocky peaks.

The cartel chief didn't know whether he owned this particular villa, or whether it was presently under loan from one of his lieutenants, or any of the businessmen who straddled the gray line between the straight and narrow in this dangerous part of the world, a place that had been home to the cartels for decades, and their predecessors for hundreds more. Still, it would suffice for now.

He knew that if one was to take a helicopter into the skies, flashes of red would appear on the land below, denoting fields of poppies that flowered three times a year. The marijuana plantations were easier to hide, though much less profitable now that a chill wave of legalization had swept across much of Mexico's neighbor to the north.

Carreon looked down, his nose wrinkling as he spied the intentionally dirtied, foul-smelling sportswear he'd been forced to wear for the past eighteen hours, since his men had broken him free of the confines of Altiplano Prison.

This, at least, was something he could change.

He shrugged off first the zipped top, then the stained jogging bottoms, and left both in an untidy heap on the floor, correctly presuming that by the time he was done in the shower, both would be gone.

Standing naked in front of a floor-length mirror, he surveyed his frame with evident distaste. He shook his head. "What have they done to you, old man?"

Twenty-three hours a day in solitary confinement, with only forty minutes allotted daily to pace around a ten-by-ten foot concrete and steel cage for exercise had withered away what little muscle had survived into his fifth decade.

Times change, he mused.

Not too many years before, men like him lived little worse behind bars than they did outside. Prison cells could be made to look like high-end hotels, and there was little that was impossible to procure for an important prisoner, presuming of course that sufficient American dollars made their way to the correct bank accounts, and that a few scraps were left over for the guards themselves.

Perhaps $10,000 per month would have proved sufficient rent in those times to acquire a second suite of cells entirely, one that could be fitted with modern exercise equipment. Perhaps even a fitness instructor.

Still, at least some of the worst excesses of the past decade had melted free of his gut. Carreon wasn't a particularly vain individual, but no man eyes with pleasure the softening of his waistline, the sagging of his skin, or the drooping of his cheeks. Perhaps his enforced diet would not prove a bad thing after all. It might be a solid foundation to build on later.

"But not tonight," he grunted as he turned the shower on,

twisting the knob until jets of steam sizzled through the air. Tonight would be an occasion of excess. Perhaps Ortega would arrive later on and bring with him some women to enjoy after dinner. His long-time lieutenant knew his master's tastes very well.

There were women in the villa already, of course. He'd seen one or two of them, and they had seen him also, though they'd pretended not to. Old ones, aunts and grandmothers, dressed in black. There to cook and clean and keep their mouths shut. They would probably spend several days here, as long as he did, and then a few more, and if they kept their heads down then they would be driven away from this place with five thousand dollars in their pockets.

And if they didn't, the coyotes would make short work of their corpses.

Soap suds frosted Carreon's head and shoulders for a few seconds as he pulled them free of the stream of water flowing overhead as his fingers worked furiously to create a thick lather, then coursed down his body as he dived back under and flowed into the drain below, gray with the filth of days and the memory of many months more.

He lingered underneath the scalding flow for several minutes, his mind blank, his head resting against the tiled marble as the rain beat against the flesh of his back like the skin of a drum, a mellifluous gentle rhythm that became almost meditative.

Eventually he dragged himself from the shower, tilting his head to drain the water from it as he wrapped a heavy towel around his waist. He marveled at the luxury of such a small thing after so long without. All the bribes in the world couldn't conjure up a shower like that, not through prison pipes.

The filthy tracksuit was gone by the time he stepped back out into the master bedroom. He walked to the small bar and removed two ice cubes from a small silver cooler. He placed them into a crystal whiskey glass and poured over a hefty measure of Macallan 1956. The exact cost eluded him, but he knew the liquor had to be expensive, if only because otherwise he would not be drinking it.

The liquid singed his throat as he knocked back half the dram in a fashion its distillers never intended, and his eyes closed as his mouth formed an expression that was half a grimace, half satisfaction.

Suitably refreshed, he refilled his glass, then dressed in a pair of pressed wool trousers and a light silken shirt. He felt...

Human.

With his base needs attended to, his mind wandered. His lieutenants had kept him apprised of business throughout his incarceration, of course. He was still entitled to legal representation, and although the authorities never wavered in their attempts to frustrate his exercise of that right, he was equally unbending in thwarting them.

But there was only so much detail that could be covered in those two-hour meetings. Broad brush strokes, when he craved minute detail, as relentlessly focused on every aspect of his business as Steve Jobs in his pomp.

"What are they saying about you, I wonder?" he murmured, searching for a screen or a remote control.

No television. Strange.

And frustrating.

Though Carreon would not admit it, perhaps not even to himself, he was as vain a man as any in his position might be. Like most cartel bosses of his generation, he had never courted the limelight. Escobar had done so decades before and made himself a target. The man had mocked the Americans, and while Carreon admired the dead man's cojones, he was exactly that.

Dead.

No, there was no sense in tempting fate. The Americans were a simple people, when it came down to it. The truth was that they didn't want to eradicate the drug trade, not really. Not even if they could, which he doubted.

After all, drugs built fear, and fear built jobs.

Jobs for prosecutors who made their reputations by going toe to toe with men like him. Then jobs for those same lawyers as they became politicians, running on platforms that promised results they failed to achieve in the courts. Jobs in the Coast Guard, in shipyards, for police chiefs and cops on the beat.

And so for someone to entirely choke off the flow of drugs across America's southern border was also to put to an end the economic carousel that had spun faster every decade for over 50 years. They wouldn't do it. Sure, they would take a scalp or two, extradite men like him from Mexican jails and parade them in front of American courts. They would find one of his narco submarines and send a camera crew below decks before scuttling the vessel to the bottom of the ocean, just so the heartland voters watching the nightly news knew exactly how terrified they were supposed to be.

They would never actually dare stop it. So for a man in his position all that remained was to avoid becoming one of those scalps.

Yet for all of that, Carreon itched to see his face broadcast on the evening news. Notoriety was a currency all its own. You couldn't spend it. But it salved the soul.

"Yet why so obvious?" he murmured.

It wasn't like Ortega, his right-hand man, to court attention in this way. His lieutenant knew as well as he did the price of fame. Understood that however alluring the flame, it never paid to become the moth.

More to the point, where was he?

Carreon's fingers clenched around the crystal glass in his hand. He was not accustomed to being kept waiting.

But since he knew he would not find the answers he wanted inside the villa's master bedroom, he finished the second measure of whiskey and set the glass down on the nearest surface. The ice cubes rattled before settling, a thin sheen of melt water already visible at its base.

He descended to the villa's first floor, passing only a maid who bowed her head as he swept by. The possibility of questioning the woman about his present situation did not even cross his mind. She was no more important than the furniture, and as far as he was concerned, probably less informative.

Besides, he was taking the time to revel in his newfound freedom. Attired at long-last in clothing that didn't make his skin itch, it was at first difficult to focus on the concern which slowly but surely began surfacing at the base of his consciousness.

Carreon stepped out onto the villa's front terrace, an area the size of two tennis courts gored into the rocky mountainside and adorned with an Olympic length swimming lane that fell off the edge and glittered turquoise in the onrushing dusk. In addition to the glow emanating from lights embedded in the pool's tiles, clusters of flickering candles sat on the edge of the terrace, spaced out every few feet.

Where is everyone?

The concern that had previously flickered now built itself into a flame as Carreon confronted the realization that after so long in the shadows, he was now a target. The target. Even the crooks in the Mexican government would not be able to overlook the crimes of a man who had blasted his way out of one of their jails in such attention-grabbing fashion. It didn't matter how much he offered them now, they would have to come after him.

To encourage the others.

"Then why, Ortega?" Carreon breathed. Why greenlight such an operation – and more to the point, why do such a thing without at least consulting him first?

Could it be a play? Ortega making a move for control?

Carreon dismissed the thought almost immediately, but that it had occurred to him at all spoke to the wilderness of shadows into which he had now been thrust.

The whisky took the edge off the tide of anxiety sloshing in his gut, but he needed more. A table was set in the center of the terrace, and yet more candlelight reflected off the familiar shape of a silver champagne bucket. He looked around for someone to fetch him a glass, yet still there was no sight of company. Grimacing with irritation, he walked toward it, accompanied only by the sounds of his footsteps, and the cicadas in the distance.

He plucked a champagne flute that looked almost risibly delicate in his meaty hands and slowly poured from the ice-cold bottle, decreasing the angle of the glass until it was both full and level. He replaced the bottle in the ice water and walked toward the edge of the terrace, staring out into the mountains below. Flaming torches, spaced farther apart than the candles on the terrace, were set into the rocky earth throughout the villa's grounds, and he focused on one in particular, his eyes growing heavy as he stared into the flickering flame.

For an instant, it disappeared. The cartel chief's brow furrowed, and then a chill crept down his spine as he realized the cause. Someone was out there. Silent and close to invisible, save for the very second that he had passed in front of the fire.

Were they his?

Of course they are, Carreon chided himself, shaking his head. He was becoming an old woman well before his time. Perhaps that was a byproduct of spending time behind bars.

Before his arrest he'd thought himself invulnerable. Whether that was still the case, he could not yet say.

He raised the glass to his lips and kept it there for a long time as the bubbles coursed down his throat. He only stopped when the champagne was almost gone, and the sound of footsteps that were not his own met his ears.

Carreon twisted, squinting his eyes until a familiar face hove into sight.

"Jefe," the man said, pausing and bowing his head. "It is good to see you looking so well."

The cartel chief released the tension in his face. "Warren," he grunted, exhaling a not insignificant breath of relief. "I wasn't expecting *you*."

"My apologies, jefe," came the reply, the Spanish accented with a familiar Texan drawl, but perfectly understandable. "You'll understand, we were forced to take certain precautions. No one could know where we planned to spirit you. It's not safe. For now, at least."

Carreon nodded, mollified at last by the show of respect. He convinced himself that his prior worries were just figments of an overactive imagination. "How long?"

The American, Warren Grover, brushed the palm of his hand over his shaven head as he considered the question. "Until it is safe," he finally replied.

That was no answer at all, Carreon thought, his expression echoing his frustration. "And when will that be?"

Grover stretched out his arm and pointed toward the table at the center of the terrace, which his boss only now remembered was set for two. "You must be hungry."

"Answer the damn question," Carreon hissed. "Where is Ortega? I need to speak to him."

"Of course," Grover said, not waiting for his boss as he started toward the table. "We can talk about that."

Carreon began to follow before he recognized what his

subordinate had done. He stopped dead, fingers clenching the fragile champagne flute as his mind groped with the flagrant display of disrespect. It took him a few seconds to process the insult. Men simply did not speak to him this way. And if they did, they had to go, no matter that Grover was the head of his security wing. Insubordination could not be tolerated.

He dropped the champagne glass, and the tinkle of smashing glass rattling across the marble tiles caused Grover to stop, turn, and observe his boss with what appeared to be an amused upturn at the corners of his lips. He was close enough to the table that he could almost touch it.

"Is there a problem?" Grover asked, in English this time.

"Get me a phone," Carreon said, his tone laced with danger.

Grover paused a beat before delivering his answer, the amusement now plain on his face. He dragged back the nearest of the two chairs and took a seat. "I'm afraid that won't be possible. Security concerns. It's just too dangerous."

"I don't give a damn what you think," Carreon replied, stretching out his arm imperiously and jabbing his finger to accentuate his point.

"That's a shame," Grover murmured, reaching for a second flute as he poured himself a glass. "Unfortunately, jefe, things have changed since you were last with us."

He turned his head toward the villa and let out a loud whistle that momentarily startled his erstwhile master, still standing a few feet away in a state of stunned indecision. Then he gestured at the remaining seat and repeated his offer for Carreon to join him. The Mexican did so, because in that moment he didn't see any other option. It was plain that the plates were – or had already – shifting underneath his feet.

"Explain yourself, Warren," Carreon croaked once he had the comfort of a solid foundation beneath him. "Where is Ortega? What is –"

He almost said *happening* but caught himself just in time.

He had a very clear sense of what was probably occurring, even if he couldn't quite bring himself to believe that it really was. Yet saying it aloud seemed somehow wrong, as though it was crystallizing a situation that was still in flux.

"Ortega –" Grover started, stopping himself as a procession of servants neared the table, setting down platters of seafood and sushi. He waited until they departed before he resumed speaking.

"Unfortunately, Ortega is unable to join us," he finally replied, relaxing into his chair in a show of proprietorial comfort.

"Why?" Carreon asked, numb to the inevitable answer.

"You know why," Grover replied, casually filling a plate with sushi rolls. He looked up. "You gotta try the wasabi, jefe. I had it flown in from Japan to celebrate your release."

"What have you done?"

Grover cocked his head, set the plate down, and reached into his inside breast pocket. He pulled out a phone, and the light from the screen reflected off his face like a child recounting a ghost story. His thumb flicked up on the screen before he set it down on the table and flicked it toward Carreon.

"What –?"

The cartel chief's eyes fell toward the phone's glow. They focused, then bugged wide as the color drained from his skin. Ortega's face was as recognizable as the last time he'd seen his oldest, most loyal friend.

Nothing else was.

Blood splattered the white restaurant tablecloth, and Carreon stopped counting after he made it to seven entry wounds scattered across his lieutenant's back. The other man in the image he did not recognize. But they did not matter.

Nothing did now.

As tendrils of shock tugged against Carreon's tongue,

attempting to still his power of speech, he fought to raise his gaze back to Grover's smug face. "Why?"

His security chief – though that description no longer fit – shrugged, a piece of sushi suspended near his lips by a pair of chopsticks, which bit into the flesh rather than cradling it. "Nobody told you? There's been a change of management."

14

"I suggest you let me through, soldado," sneered Senadora Josefina Salazar, her lips curling as she spat out that final word.

Soldier.

The disdain in the woman's voice was evident. The cause, impossible to ignore. The acrid stench of the smoke still pouring out of Altiplano hung on the air, a thick, heavy blanket, a visible testament to the slow, inexorable failure of the hulking, tottering institution known as the Mexican state.

The soldier, a sergeant in his mid-twenties, stood his ground. "Senator, please, you cannot. This is a restricted –"

Salazar was too professional to look back at the huddle of press behind her, but she knew exactly where their lenses were pointed. After all, they were why she was here. And it was better not to look too concerned about people's opinions of you. They tended to be more positive that way.

"It wasn't so restricted when you failed to stop those monsters destroying this place, was it?" Salazar said, jabbing her finger angrily at the scorched prison walls a few hundred yards away, across the scrub. Each of the larger holes, those which a man could scramble through, was guarded by a military Jeep and several men. She had no doubt that the television cameras would linger on those areas. The shot was, after all, made for TV.

She might have allowed herself a small smile at the thought of the image the viewers would see. A small child thrusting his fingers into a dam, not understanding that a swollen river lay behind it. But of course, she did not. Fury came off her in crackling waves—whether she truly felt it or not.

The Mexican senator didn't stop. She was wearing a matching skirt and jacket combo, both in a dark blue. The heels on her feet were wholly unsuitable for the uneven terrain beneath her but gave her several inches of additional height, which never hurt.

"How many got out?" she demanded, not turning her head to face the NCO, who was now frozen in her wake. With no answer forthcoming, she finally turned, her arms spreading wide in a gesture of both Latin passion and in deliberate resemblance of a figure that could be found in every house in a country as religious as this.

A photographer's shutter clicked, and Josefina Salazar knew precisely what image would grace the front pages in the morning.

"Please, madam senator, I cannot allow you to –"

"I am a duly elected representative of the citizens of this country, young man," she said passionately, punctuating every word with a dancing fingertip. "And I shall go wherever I please. This government has failed us long enough. It is time that someone exposed the corruption of this so-called president and his cabinet. Are we really supposed to believe that all of this chaos was allowed to happen without his knowing about it?"

Salazar paused just long enough to allow the idea to sink in, but not so long that a reporter might take the opportunity to shout out a question and puncture her moment in the spotlight.

"Our president," she said with mocking derision dripping off her tongue like syrup, "truly expects us to swallow the idea that he could be somehow unaware that even our *Air Force* is riddled with corruption. How does he propose that we defend ourselves when the brave men and women who sign up to do that are led by cowards and crooks?

"And let us for just one moment humor the idea that he had nothing to do with it. No sense that something like this was barreling toward him. Well, if that is really true, then he has no business leading this great country. I'm sure that every single one of you sitting at home agrees with me."

By now, the hapless sergeant had given up attempting to cajole the senator and was instead attempting to make himself as small as possible. Salazar pointed at him, careful not to show her amusement. "This young man here," she said, "would do far better than our exalted president. Perhaps we should ask *him* to do the job?"

She looked expectantly at him, watching as the cameras swung into focus on his face. As shutters clacked and camera film rolled – or at least, saved to disk – she waited. Waited until slowly, hesitantly, the sergeant shook his head.

"I agree," she said pleasantly as a dozen lenses turned the focus back on her. "It's best that we leave brave men and women like you where you can do the most good.

"And that is why I, Senadora Josefina Maria Salazar, will be running for the presidency this year. I will take no money from the cartels. I will not allow my administration to be corrupted by crooks and criminals like the present regime. And I will not rest until the hard-working, honorable people of this country are led by someone who respects those values. And until the cancer of the cartels is burned from our body politic once and for all. Thank you."

15

Ramon "El Toro" Reyes didn't take the seat at the head of the long, polished hardwood conference table, though nobody else did either. He slumped halfway down his chair, not because he was beaten but because he was smoldering with rage. The events of the past few days had not unfolded to his satisfaction.

It was bad enough that a dozen of his best men had been slaughtered during the attack on Altiplano that had, it was rumored, also freed his arch-rival, Fernando Carreon. But now *this*. The norteamericanos had spent the past day systematically dismantling his distribution operation north of the border. He didn't care about the lost product. Cocaine was cheap.

Good people, however, were not.

He had lost a decade's worth of experience in the blink of an eye. Already, reliable lawyers were meeting their clients and advising them that their best course of action was to keep their mouths shut. That they would be well rewarded on the other side for doing so. But faced with the prospect of a decade or more behind bars, some of his men would flip. Reyes knew that. It was part of the calculation. And for every one that did, his organization would suffer still more.

"The Federation," he muttered, flexing his right hand against the cool wood in front of him. "Are they behind this?"

From opposite his seat, his cousin Carlos Guerra thumped his palm against the table like a petulant gorilla. "It's time we wiped Carreon out. We should have done it years ago. It can be no coincidence that Altiplano happens the same day as this disaster."

The announcement drew a few murmurs of agreement, but for the most part the more discerning of his lieutenants kept their mouths shut and their eyes on their principal.

Reyes opened and closed his fist several times more, stretching out the motion as he considered the events that had led them to this point. When he finally spoke, he did so quietly, so the others were forced to lean in to listen.

"I don't want war. War is bad for business. War puts all of our livelihoods at risk. If it comes to that, then so be it. But I will not provoke this fight."

Carlos didn't take the hint. "Provoke?" he said sardonically. "We are already in the foxhole, cousin. They came for us while we were taking a shit, while we had our pants around our ankles. And I'm glad they did."

El Toro was not the caricature that his nickname suggested, nor the character painted by more sensationalist news outlets. Though he was indeed a squat bull of a man, and a killer many times over, a keen mind resided within that less than delicate skull. That did not mean he was any stranger to the infliction of violence, nor timid in his skin, just that he was not a prisoner of the more sordid urges that afflict so many men of his ilk.

"Be quiet, Carlos."

His cousin ignored him for a second time, a claret tint of rage in his cheeks indicating that he probably hadn't heard. "We can't let it stand. Whoever did this, they need to pay. And the world needs to know what happened to them. Otherwise what are we: whores?"

"Enough!" Reyes grumbled, barely raising his voice but layering it with a crack of irritation that was sufficiently powerful to penetrate his cousin's thick skull. He slowly raised his head, allowing his gaze to fall first on his glowering, practically vibrating relative before examining the other half-dozen men in the room in turn. He spoke to them, though each knew the true target of his words.

"We will not move until we know what the hell is going on. Something about this doesn't smell right. Did our people inside the Federation give us any warning of this?"

Carlos, who shared some responsibility for running the Crusaders' informants, re-took his seat, the tint on his cheeks doubling. "None."

"None!" Reyes roared. "I pay millions in bribes every year, and none of them came forward? Not one?"

His cousin shook his head. Red was battling with black rage on his expression now, though he knew better than to test his cousin's commitment to familial loyalty at this present moment.

"Then before we blow our load like an over-excited virgin, I suggest you bring me something I can use. Understand?"

Carlos glowered back at him, but eventually buckled under the pressure and gave him a single, sharp nod. Reyes held his punishing gaze yet longer and broke away only when the sliding doors opened.

"Boss," Emiliano said, without apologizing for his tardiness. "There's something you need to see."

Reyes watched as Emiliano Mendoza, his right-hand man, entered the conference room, not stopping to close the doors after him. His aide walked around the table, stopping at the center on the opposite side, just next to Carlos. He leaned over and tapped a button on the console, a unit that doubled as both a telephone speaker and an audiovisual controller. Overhead, a digital projector blinked into life.

For a few seconds, only the Japanese manufacturer's logo was evident on the accompanying screen, moving in smooth arcs from the bottom right to left corners before jumping diagonally to the top and repeating the pattern in reverse.

"What is this, Mendoza?" Carlos scoffed. "This is important, or haven't you noticed?"

Reyes slammed his palm down on the conference table and shot his cousin a look that would have chilled the blood of any other man, and probably would do the same for Carlos, if he was intelligent enough to grasp the message.

"Shut the fuck up, cousin," he hissed.

He returned his attention to Mendoza, who was now flicking through television channels. Reyes might have shared Carlos' frustration if it wasn't for the fact that he knew that Emiliano would not do something like this without good reason. Even so, he sensed that he was losing control of his message, and in an organization infested by men with little loyalty and lots of ambition, that was a dangerous thing indeed.

He cleared his throat as Mendoza puffed out his cheeks with satisfaction and straightened his frame. "What am I watching, Emiliano?"

THE PRESS CONFERENCE was being carried live on WTN and would probably make the lead item on all that evening's news packages. Depending on how fast the media's relentless tornado spun over the next twenty-four hours, the talking heads might even have it on their minds tomorrow.

Administrator Engel accepted the proffered water bottle from Leo, took a swig, then handed it back. "How do I look?"

"A million bucks, boss. Tie's fine."

Engel grinned. "Sarah got to you too, huh?"

"Your wife has that effect on people." His chief of staff grinned.

"Don't I know it," he said with a rueful roll of his eyes.

Leo glanced at his watch, then made a beckoning motion toward a gaggle of half a dozen sharply suited men and women a few yards away. All were in their fifties or sixties and wore the focused expressions of top prosecutors. Each was a US Attorney, mostly drawn from districts near the border with Mexico.

The podium bore the crest of the Department of Justice, the DEA's parent organization, and that of each of the prosecutors now making their way toward Engel. Leo made himself scarce after muttering, "Live in five, boss. Give 'em hell."

Engel greeted each of the US Attorneys in turn, but didn't linger too long, as he wanted to review his notes one last time. Five minutes ticked away into four, and before he knew it, it was none.

The room hushed as if by some unheard signal, and then it was time. He strode out onto the platform and looked out at the cavernous space of a Houston hotel ballroom, decorated around the edges by huge gold-patterned hanging curtains that reminded him of tapestries from a time long in the past. About a dozen reporters were in attendance, seated on a tightly-packed cluster of dining chairs. To the left and right of the podium, out of shot for the cameras, two large television monitors faced him, displaying the live camera feed.

"Ladies and gentlemen," he said, musing to himself that the television viewers had no idea he was speaking only to a scarce handful of people live, and how funny a thing it was to have to pretend that was not the case. "Thank you for joining me today. I will keep my remarks short before handing over to the individuals behind me, who will each brief you on how events unfolded in their districts over the past 48 hours."

He glanced down at the podium, where he saw Leo had

placed a set of flashcards, each of which only bore a few words, written in thick Sharpie ink. He found his train of thought.

"The Mexican drug cartel known as the Crusaders is responsible for approximately 40 percent of the cocaine imported into the continental United States, along with 30 percent of the methamphetamines and a similar amount of heroin and other opioids. All told, they traffic narcotics whose worth extends into the tens of billions of dollars each year."

Engel paused for effect, though he knew better than to expect any reaction from the news reporters in front of him, all of them pros who were far too experienced to display anything so amateurish as emotion. He surreptitiously slid the topmost of the flashcards to one side.

"In addition to their operations south of the border, the Crusaders also operate a distribution network that we know to have a presence in at least 35 states, and most likely every single one. I am pleased to report today that agents of the Drug Enforcement Administration, acting alongside our colleagues in state, local and other federal agencies, moved on this network and – we believe –dealt it a crippling blow."

A loud bang echoed at the far end of the ballroom, though conscious that he was live on television, Engel knew better than to look toward the source of the sound. The camera mics were directional and might not have picked up the commotion. Even if they had, rule number one on camera was that the show must go on. He was sure that if there was a problem, Leo would even now be fixing it.

Where the hell is he?

Besides, it was probably just some slightly confused hotel guest who had stumbled into the wrong room at the wrong time after one too many. And even if he had wanted to find out what was going on in the far end of the room, the television lights trained on him were simply too dazzling.

"Overnight, we apprehended several dozen suspects, three

of whom are on the Administration's most wanted list. Each of these men are killers, and –"

Engel saw the blood before he heard the gunshot, his peripheral vision catching the sight of the US Attorney for the Eastern District of Texas dropping to the ground on one of the monitors in front of him. He turned his head, open-mouthed with horror as another of the prosecutors was cut down by a flurry of shots that seemed to bisect the man's chest.

A scream rent the air as a round passed through the bulb of the brightest of the television lights. There was no flurry of sparks, but the tripod structure toppled to the ground, clattering against a reporter frozen in place in her chair, fingertips still poised over the keypad of her iPad.

Engel too was frozen, his own hands locked against the sides of the podium. Just a few seconds before, it was a position designed to display a sense of strength, one of complete command of his abilities, and now a much greater liability. With the television light gone, he could see again, though he wished he could not. Still twisted in place, torso facing front, head turned toward the dead and dying who stood behind him, the administrator of the Drug Enforcement Agency watched as the rest of the gaggle of prosecutors behind him were cut to the ground one by one by short, measured bursts of gunfire.

Finally, Engel's grip on the podium released, though the loss of support only succeeded in allowing him to stagger backward, where his ankle caught against something warm and solid and...

Wet...

His gaze snapped up, his subconscious simply not allowing him to look down and register what his conscious mind knew was down there. This could not be happening. How was this happening? He had people with him every hour of every day precisely for this eventuality. Men with guns. Agents trained to use them.

Where are they?

Desperately, Engel searched for the cavalry, only for the answer to his question to come with surprising, horrifying rapidity. All three of the members of his protection detail who had entered the hotel with him were already dead. Only two had managed even to draw their weapons before being gunned down.

As he registered the sight of the bodies of three men who he knew, if not intimately, then at least well, a jolt of adrenaline hit the administrator. No one else was coming to help him. If he was to escape this horror, he was on his own.

RAMON REYES REALIZED that he was standing. He could not remember when that had happened, but he knew why. Even now, icy tendrils of shock were beginning to grip his gut. The scene unfolding on the projector screen in front of him was a slaughter. He could not understand why the WTN newsroom was allowing the feed to be broadcast. The Americans were a strange people, no less religious than his own, yet strangely fearful of allowing such a calamity as a swear word to be broadcast on live television. The cold-blooded, professional execution of some of the most senior officials in their Justice Department was, however, apparently okay.

The cartel chief was no stranger to bloodbaths like the one he was watching unfold, but he was rarely surprised by them, as he was now.

"Emiliano," he said hoarsely, jabbing at the sky. "Volume."

Mendoza did as he was instructed, and the gentle raindrop against windowpane rattle of gunfire through the speakers turned into a veritable hailstorm.

"Please, I beg you again," an unseen presenter said in a strangled yelp over the feed.

"If you have children with you, please turn off your set. Our crew has been taken hostage by whoever"—her voice broke before its strength reasserted itself—"whoever is doing this. We've been told that if they stop broadcasting..."

Again, her voice trailed away. The threat, though, was implicit.

Smart, Reyes thought coolly as he appraised the situation. *So that answers that.*

The television feed shook, went blurry, then refocused, all the time directed at the center of the small stage upon which the Justice Department's podium stood. Each of the prosecutors who had earlier stood behind it were now dead, or at least doing their best to appear so. Only one man was left alive.

Mark Engel.

He was frozen in place, looking somewhere off to the side of the stage, out of shot. The backs of the heads of several reporters were visible at the bottom of the projector feed, still seated in their original places. It was unclear whether they still lived or not. Reyes sensed that they did. Whoever the assailants were, you did not do something like this without wanting it to be talked about. And who better to do that for you than the reporters who watched it happen?

The question was: why?

The gunfire started to trail away and soon after fell silent, and still Engel did not move. He was caught like a rabbit in the headlights, not knowing whether to go left or right to forward or back and in the end doing nothing very much at all. He failed even to run when a man dressed all in black, from his boots to his balaclava, strode onto the stage, a similarly-hued pistol in his right hand.

The man grabbed Engel roughly and dragged him to the front of the stage, just beside the podium. Reyes was transfixed. He barely dared to breathe. It was plain that what was happening here was, in its own way, as momentous as the events of 9/11. If not for the whole of America, then at least for El Toro and his Crusaders.

The Americans would not forget this. They would want vengeance. And when they came looking, no matter how long it took, they were rarely denied.

"Please..." the DEA administrator said in a hoarse, whistling whisper. "I'll –"

Whatever exactly it was that Engel proposed to do or say in order to save his skin was, sadly for him, lost to posterity as a result of the impact of a 9 mm round entering the back of his head and exiting somewhere around his left temple, painting one of the last few sections of the stage that wasn't already covered in blood a dark red.

And finally, the television feed from the Hilton ballroom in downtown Houston went dead.

For a long few seconds, nobody spoke. Not the television presenters in their Atlanta studio, not the cartel barons in that conference room, not even Ramon Reyes himself. He let out a deep breath, one that he had been holding on to for far too long, then steepled his fingers on the table in front of him and slowly lowered himself back into his seat.

For the second time that day, he eyed each of his men in turn. Even Emiliano Mendoza, a man he trusted implicitly. His gaze bored into their souls, burning with such fierce intensity, but it was plain to each of them that only the truth would suffice.

"Did we have anything to do with this?"

16

Trapp rose not very long after dawn, when the sun was still hanging somewhere low beneath the horizon. A thin layer of condensation glistened on the interior of the tent, and there was a surprising chill in the air.

He rolled out of his sleeping bag, careful not to disturb Eliza, who was still snoring to his side, her face obscured beneath a shock of black hair. A smile toyed with the corner of his lips as he considered recording the sound to play back to her later, but he made the executive decision that it was probably best not to get on the wrong side of a woman who could kill him half a dozen different ways before she brushed her teeth in the morning. She wouldn't believe him anyway. She would just claim he'd recorded a fighter jet's exhaust – and it wasn't as if he could prove her wrong. That was a problem with snorers.

They only did it when they were asleep.

The tent's zipper was loud as he pulled it down, but gentle in comparison, so he didn't worry too much about waking her. He closed it after he was done.

The lake was bordered by a rocky beach about twenty yards

away from their campsite. They'd borrowed stones from it the night before to ring their campfire, the embers of which had smoldered through the early hours and were now nothing more than a thin covering of gray ash. It was the same color as a light mist that hung a couple of feet over the water's surface.

Trapp walked toward it, not bothering to pull on his boots, and peeled off his T-shirt instead. He folded it and placed it on a rounded boulder at the very edge of the lake. He glanced around, checking no one was watching. There was another campsite a couple of hundred yards down the lake – they'd met the couple staying there the night before – but a small copse of trees that had somehow colonized the stony earth blocked their view.

Besides, they would probably not be awake. Normal people weren't, not at this time.

His hiking pants joined the T-shirt, and shortly after, his boxers. Even they were folded neatly. Old habits didn't change.

Trapp stood entirely naked at the water's edge for a few seconds before he waded in. The lake was crystal clear and cold enough to steal his breath after he dunked his head beneath the surface. The world was silent and calm beneath the waterline, and he held himself beneath it for a few long seconds, luxuriating in the total absence of worry and stress, wondering if maybe he should simply move to the woods for good.

You'd probably live longer, he thought wryly.

The top of his head broke the water's surface, and he returned to the world of the living, though it wasn't much more frenetic than the space below. A bird of prey swooped out of the sky and skimmed the surface of the lake, perhaps mistaking Trapp's emergence for that of its normal sustenance before it just as suddenly resumed normal service and disappeared into the sky above.

A gentle breeze stirred the air, causing the mist to swirl

gently above the water, though it was thicker observed from afar rather than right up close.

Trapp twisted, picked a spot about halfway across the lake, and swam toward it with long, easy strokes, moving just fast enough to keep his body temperature up, but not exerting himself greatly. They had a long hike planned for the remainder of the day, and he was getting old enough to have to start worrying about tiring himself out too early.

When he pulled himself back out of the water fifteen minutes later, Eliza was standing there, wearing a towel as a shawl. She pouted as he ran his fingers through his hair and swept the water from his eyes. "You should've said you were going in. I would have joined you."

"And risk waking you up?" Trapp grinned, widening his eyes for effect. "I wouldn't dare."

He reached out for the towel, and Eliza spun around as she grudgingly relinquished it. He dried himself off gratefully and tied it around his waist. The smell of wood smoke was already in the air, and he glanced up at the campsite to see a small fire already blazing – only large enough to heat the coffee pot.

He bent over to retrieve his folded clothes, then offered Eliza his arm. "Breakfast?"

"You cooking?" she asked.

"You bet."

"Then put some damn clothes on," she laughed as they walked back up to the campsite. "I'll start a pot of coffee."

Some sixth sense alerted Trapp to the sound of the incoming helicopter at least a minute before it resolved itself more clearly, though he did not pay much attention to it – at least not while he finished drying himself down and getting dressed.

It was only when the chopper circled twice over the surface of the lake, appearing to check out first the other campsite, then their own, that Trapp realized something else was up. He pulled on his boots, then joined Eliza in watching the chopper come down for a landing.

"Hey, you remember the last time you took me on vacation?" Eliza murmured over the sound of the approaching aircraft.

"Uh huh."

"So I'm guessing you remember those guys who tried to kill us?"

"Kind of a hard thing to forget..." Trapp quipped.

"Anything I need to be worried about?"

The helicopter rotated in midair, opening up its side for full view as it slowed and began to hover, the rotor wash chasing away the last remnants of the mist from the lake's surface. Trapp's chin met his chest, carried there by a brief exhalation of dismay.

"Unless the bad guys have borrowed an FBI chopper, I'm guessing we don't have to worry about that," he said, shooting her a glance that said, *I'll make it up to you.*

The look he received in response was easy enough to interpret. It said: *You better.*

The chopper's pilot set the bird down gently on the lake's rocky shore, and though his skids kissed the ground gently, he couldn't do anything about the hurricane his rotors were whipping up, sending a flurry of dust and smaller stones in the direction of the campsite.

The tent's pins, mostly weighed down by blocks of stones, struggled manfully to resist the storm, but could only hang on so long. Trapp managed to unzip the doors on either side just in time, letting the air pass through to avoid the whole thing making like a sail and blowing away.

The bird's engine announced that it was powering down by emanating a low-pitched whine, and shortly after the rotors began to slow. An FBI agent, complete with the stenciled windbreaker they all seemed to wear, jumped out and ran toward where Trapp and Eliza were standing, hunched ostentatiously low to avoid the blades even when he was well out of their range.

"What do you want, agent?" Trapp called out.

"I'm sorry for disturbing you, sir. Are you –?"

Trapp nodded. "I am."

"You're needed back in Washington."

"Why?"

The agent, a kid who looked fresh out of Quantico, shrugged. "I don't know, sir. They don't tell me much."

"Me neither, buddy," Trapp grunted. He turned to Eliza and said, "I guess we're getting breakfast back home."

She laughed. "As long as you're paying."

Trapp glanced around the campsite and determined he wouldn't need any of his hiking gear for a meeting inside the Beltway, so he left it right where it was and started walking toward the chopper with Eliza in tow, only stooping to lift the coffee pot off the flame. He poured a cup for both of them and warmed his hands on it as he walked.

A few seconds later, it was evident the FBI agent was following a few steps behind. Trapp stopped, frowning, and turned back. "Where do you think you're going?"

The agent squinted. "Uh," he said uncertainly. "The *helicopter?*"

"Then who's going to return my car to the rental shop?" Trapp asked mischievously.

"That's gotta be, like, a five-hour drive," the agent protested, his gaze drifting to Eliza, who just shrugged and sipped her coffee.

"Six, long as you don't hit traffic," Trapp agreed amiably. "You ever pack up a tent? Properly, I mean."

"I'm from Glenville, West Virginia," the agent replied glumly, glancing over his shoulder at the campsite, now entirely askew from the effects of the rotor wash. "All we got to do down there is hills and kills."

"So that's a yes?"

Trapp grinned, collected Eliza's now empty coffee cup, and handed it over along with his own. "Good man. Thanks for the ride."

17

An FBI car was waiting at the helipad to whisk them through DC's light weekend traffic without being forced to resort to the lights behind the grille. They entered the Hoover building through the access ramp on the corner of Ninth and East. It led to a subterranean parking garage, where Nick Pope was waiting.

Trapp had suspected he would be.

"Sorry about this," the FBI agent said as Trapp climbed out of the SUV, Ikeda following just behind. He closed the passenger door behind them, then thumped the roof of the vehicle twice, at which it duly departed.

"I'm feeling a little underdressed," Ikeda commented, glancing at Pope's freshly pressed suit, then at Trapp's khaki hiking pants and her own flannel shirt. They were both wearing hiking boots that were more than just spotted with mud.

"Don't be," Pope said. He thrust out his hand. "Sorry for dragging you along. I'm guessing you're Eliza? Jason has told me a lot about you."

"Any of it good?" Ikeda laughed, surreptitiously smoothing her outfit as best she could once the greeting was done.

"All of it." Pope grinned, though Trapp noticed that the smile did not reach his eyes. The agent was carrying a hell of a lot of tension – far more than at their last meeting just a couple days earlier.

Trapp rolled his neck, ostentatiously eyeing the FBI's parking garage. "We even allowed in here?"

"J Edgar is probably turning in his grave," Pope remarked, handing each of them a security badge attached to a lanyard.

"I thought they crushed his bones and mixed them into the foundations, just to be sure," Trapp quipped as he ducked his neck to put it on. Unfortunately for him, he didn't also dodge Ikeda's unseen elbow.

"Very good," Pope replied, beckoning them to follow him.

"You don't mean that." Trapp grinned, winking at Ikeda.

"No, not really."

"So what's the fire?" Trapp asked as they reached the bank of elevators and waited for one to arrive. "You get an ID on that guy?"

The comment clearly stunned Pope. "You didn't hear?"

Trapp shrugged as the elevator dinged and its doors slid open. "Not really. I wasn't exactly glued to Twitter for all, oh, ten minutes my vacation lasted."

Pope winced. "My bad."

The elevator pinged, and they followed him inside, waiting in silence as Pope selected a destination. Once the doors slid closed, he sighed. "Cartels hit the administrator of the DEA and a bunch of US Attorneys at a press conference in Houston. Chewed them up real good."

Trapp winced. "How is he?"

"Dead."

"Seriously?"

"I'm not in a joking mood, Jason. We –" Pope dropped his

head, grimacing. "*I* fucked up. If your encounter had anything to do with this, then..."

"Any reason you think it did?"

"You'll see..."

As the elevator doors opened, Trapp reached out and squeezed Pope's shoulder. It didn't take a genius to work out how his friend was feeling right now. Trapp had shared the same dark pit many times before, and knew it never got any easier.

"You couldn't have known," he said.

"I could have worked harder," Pope replied, white-lipped. "If I did, maybe Mark Engel would be alive right now. Maybe they all would."

The corridor beyond was empty, and Pope strode into it without looking back, not stopping until they reached an empty breakout area which was equipped with a coffee machine, several comfortable chairs, and a few well-thumbed copies of security journals. Very on brand for the FBI, but not exactly easy reading.

Pope turned to Ikeda. "You can wait here. I don't know how long this will take. I'm sorry."

Trapp frowned. "Hold up, Nick. Why don't you tell me what the hell is going on?"

His friend's eyes flickered toward Ikeda's face before landing back on Trapp's. "I –"

"Give me a break, Nick," Trapp snorted, sensing the hold-up. "She's got a higher security clearance than either of us. They've got her running around in – well, it doesn't exactly matter where. I don't think she's going to run to the media on this one, if you know what I mean. Besides, it was her trip too."

Pope chewed his lower lip, his chin contorting into an angular shape as he worked over the problem in his head.

"Okay," he groaned. "I guess I can tell you. The president

asked for you directly, Jason. We're speaking to him in a moment. But I can't just –"

"Perfect," Trapp interrupted, slapping Pope on his upper arm. "President Nash and Eliza are firm friends. Well, they've spoken, at any rate. And he owes her one. Besides, it sounds like you could use all the help you can get."

To his side, Ikeda frowned, but Trapp wasn't done talking yet. "Listen, Nick. Before we go into that room you need to understand something. We all drop the ball from time to time. They make 'em too damn round and slippery. It's not your fault. And if you keep beating yourself up about it, you'll drop another and another, and that ain't no good for anybody. You understand?"

Pope stood opposite, anxiously running his fingers through his hair, seeming to linger on the patch of white strands above his temple. "Yeah, okay. I guess."

"Don't just guess, buddy. Scrunch it up inside you and bury it deep, I don't care. Just don't think about it for a bit. Not until the crisis is over. Because it will be, it always is. And when that happens, you and me we can get a beer, and if you want to carry the weight of the world on your shoulders then, that's your prerogative. But you're the expert in counterintelligence, not me. So let me ask you a question."

Pope waited expectantly for him to continue, and when it was evident that Trapp was doing the same, he grimaced and flicked his fingers irritably. "Well, go on."

"You ever hear of a real surveillance op getting spooled up over the course of the weekend? For that matter, did you even identify the guy I tangled with yet?"

The FBI agent shook his head. "Not exactly."

"Didn't think so. These things take time. And sometimes time's on the bad guys' side, not ours. That's just the way it goes. But we've got a lead, and that's important too. So stop beating yourself over the head, and let's go fix this thing. Okay?"

"Okay," Pope said closing his eyes for a second and letting out a breath. "Okay."

He straightened, seeming to take strength from what Trapp had said, then gestured the pair of them past the breakout area.

"This...isn't a *video* call, is it?" Ikeda inquired nervously as they walked behind. "I wasn't exactly expecting to visit the White House when I packed for a weekend away in the hills..."

"He's a real stickler for appearances, too..." Trapp commented ominously.

For a second time, Ikeda's elbow met his side. "Shut up. You've met him once."

"A couple of times." Trapp grinned. "He told me he hates flannel."

She rolled her eyes.

Pope stopped in front of a door that was secured by a card reader and had an impenetrably long room number on a panel mounted just to its right. He tapped his access card against it, and the light on the reader blinked from red to green, accompanied by a click from the locking mechanism.

On entry, Trapp noticed Kelly Andrews, the agent he'd been tasked to train on the fateful day in question. The freshly minted agent was seated at the conference table and barely even looked up as the party entered the room. She might as well have been rocking back and forth, so clearly preoccupied was she by her thoughts.

He nodded at her. "Kelly."

Nothing.

Trapp cleared his throat and tried again. "Kelly."

This time, she looked up, and a spark of recognition flared in her eyes at the sight of a familiar face, accompanied swiftly after by a slight, and quickly disguised, frown of surprise at Ikeda's presence.

"This is Eliza," he said in explanation. "My girlfriend."

Ikeda stifled a smile as the words escaped Trapp's lips and

stretched out a hand in greeting. He felt unaccountably embarrassed at the admission, though there was no good reason to do so, especially since Kelly took it in her stride.

The door clicked shut behind Pope, who leaned over the conference table and punched a series of digits into the keypad of the phone sitting in the center before lifting the handset to his ear. He paused for a second before saying, "This is Agent Nick Pope from the FBI. I understand that you're – yes. Okay."

He replaced the handset in the cradle, and the speakerphone played – well, a whole lot of nothing. Just a tiny rustle on the line to indicate that the phone call was active and hadn't dropped.

"No hold music, huh?" Trapp commented. "You think after everything we pay in taxes, they could at least afford that."

He fell silent after Pope shot him an irritable glance and thrust his fingers through his hair once more. Instead, his eyes met Ikeda's as he wondered what she was thinking right now. This wasn't the relaxing weekend away that he'd promised.

His thoughts drifted back to the case at hand. He frowned at Pope and said, "What did you mean when you said you didn't *exactly* get an ID on that guy? What do you have?"

"A partial facial match. We ran it against millions of hours of footage supplied by MPD and every federal building in town and got one hit—"

Before he could finish, a male voice emanated from the speaker and announced, "Mr. President, the FBI."

"Thank you," President Nash's booming voice replied, causing the speaker to crackle before Pope tapped the volume down button a couple of times. "I didn't keep you waiting, did I?"

"Not at all, Mr. President," he lied, leaning forward and resting on his elbows to get closer to the speaker.

Just a man, Trapp reminded himself. Though even he was forced to admit that the trappings of the office, and the history, and even the charisma of the individual who occupied it at this present moment meant that that wasn't entirely true.

"Is Jason there?" President Nash inquired.

"Yes sir. Along with Special Agent Kelly Andrews, and Eliza –" His eyes flickered to Kelly, and his voice momentarily trailed away.

"That's my doing, Mr. President," Trapp added, covering for him. "I thought she might be useful."

"A crack team," Nash agreed, not seeming particularly concerned by the news. "I'm sure you're wondering why I'm speaking to you like this, Agent Pope."

"The thought had crossed my mind, sir."

"First of all, let me be clear: I have cleared both this conversation and my proposed course of action with Director Rutger. We are of one mind on this."

"That's good to know, sir." Pope said, visibly relaxing.

"What I find myself needing to know – and doing so with considerable urgency – is not just why this happened, but why it happened *now*. Neither the FBI nor CIA had any inclination that an attack of this magnitude was coming. I read my daily brief religiously, Agent Pope, and to my recollection there was no indication that the cartels had any desire to so dramatically raise the table stakes. And yet in the past 48 hours, one cartel has gone to war with the United States, and another seems to be doing their best to tear Mexico apart."

Trapp frowned. What on earth was President Nash talking about? The US bit he understood. But what had happened in Mexico?

"I also have no intention of pre-empting the results of the inter-agency process. We will discover who killed the administrator, and I imagine the Justice Department will appreciate being let off the leash after the losses it sustained. But all that will take time, and I sense that the men we are up against might be quite practiced at covering their tracks. Especially..."

"If they know what we're thinking," Pope agreed, eyes flaring as he realized he'd just cut across his President.

Trapp ground his teeth together, frustrated that he didn't have the full picture. This clearly had something to do with the facial match that his friend had mentioned before the President dialled in. But participating in this conversation without knowing who or what the trawl had uncovered felt like scuba-diving blindfolded. He chose the safe course of action and kept his mouth shut.

"Precisely. I need to know if the incident you discovered this week is a once-off, or whether the cartels have more thoroughly penetrated our law enforcement and intelligence communities. And after the –" Nash said, pausing to clear his throat, "the situation a few months back, you're a man I know I can trust. I would appreciate it if you can assure me the same about the rest of my executive agencies. And *soon*."

"Yes sir," Pope agreed. "I'll do my best."

Trapp made a face. "Sir, not to be a stickler for the rules, but CIA can't operate on American soil. I'm not really sure what I'm doing here. I'm glad I could help Special Agent Pope a few days ago—but that was a lucky accident." *Or an unlucky one,* he didn't add. "Going any further could push the Agency onto thin ice."

Only silence greeted his statement, at least at first. Finally Nash cleared his throat and said, "Jason, you and I both know that you've operated on American soil before."

Trapp glanced uneasily around the room. Not even Ikeda knew the full details of his actions following Bloody Monday. Of course, the President had the authority to declassify any piece of information the intelligence community owned. But he had to actually say the words.

He played it safe. "Yes sir. But that was—"

"A special case?"

"That would about cover it, sir," Trapp agreed.

Nash's anger crackled down the line. "Well so is this, okay? I'm not in the business of losing the heads of my executive agencies. At least, I don't want to be. It's my job to keep them safe. And when I fail, I need to make damn sure that someone pays for it so that it doesn't happen again. The world respects America. But they need to fear us, too. Sometimes people forget that. And another thing, Jason."

"Yes, Mr President?"

"This one's not just business. It's personal," Nash said, his tone steadying. "You've heard about what happened to George, haven't you?"

George Nash, Trapp knew, had been the President's son. He'd died of a drug overdose before his father was inaugurated. The tragedy had cost the President his marriage. "Yes, sir."

"Addiction is a horrible disease, Jason," Nash said softly. "Believe me, I've watched it happen close up. It took my son's life as surely as if he'd been murdered. And in a way, he was."

Trapp met Ikeda's gaze but didn't reply. There was a terrible stillness to the room now.

"So maybe now I have the opportunity to get these bastards back for what they did to my family, along with so many others. And I trust you, Jason. I know what you're capable of. More than that, I know you'll do the right thing. If you're worried about blowback, don't be. I have broad shoulders. If this goes to shit, I'll take the slings and arrows. But I want you on the team. So—what do you say?"

"I'm at your service, Mr President."

"Good," Nash said, sounding coldly satisfied. "Any other questions?"

When there were none, he signed off.

"So what happened in Mexico?" Trapp asked after the line clicked.

"Where have you been the last couple of days, Jason – the bottom of a well?" Pope grunted, rocking back on the rear legs of his chair, evidently relieved that the call was now over. Some of the tension began to fade from the room, though Trapp couldn't dodge the sensation that he'd been given a personal mission by the President himself.

"Close enough."

"You heard the name Fernando Carreon?" Pope asked.

Trapp bit his lip, trying to place the name. "Carreon... Yeah. Cartel boss, right? The Mexicans picked him up a few months ago. He's awaiting trial. That's all I got."

"You're half right, anyway," Pope said with a grimace. "The Mexicans had him, all right. In Altiplano Prison. They were slow-walking his extradition, but they were sitting on him nice and tight."

"So..."

"So *were* is the operative word. At about the same time Administrator Engel was getting pumped full of lead in Houston, a bunch of sicarios took down the joint. Hell, they pulled it apart."

"What do you mean, took it down?" Trapp frowned as Ikeda leaned forward, eyes alive with interest.

"Exactly what I said, Jason. They came armed for bear. Trojan horsed their way inside, then flew off in hijacked Mexican Air Force choppers, chewing up a whole company of Marines on the way out. Well, not hijacked, exactly. The pilots and their families, they're all gone."

"Paid off," Trapp muttered.

"Sure feels like it," he agreed. "Put yourself in Carreon's shoes. Say it sets you back 5 million bucks for each of the crewmembers. Six choppers, that can't be more than eighty, maybe a hundred million. I'm not saying that's what he paid, but the guy's worth billions. In his shoes, I'd pull the trigger at ten times the price."

"Just a cost of doing business."

"That's about right."

"So what now?"

Pope shrugged. "You heard the president: We start digging. If these assholes want to start a war with us, that's their prerogative. But I don't figure they're the ones who will get to end it. Besides, we have a solid lead."

Trapp's eyebrows kinked up with interest. "Go on."

"I told you we got a facial recognition hit on your sparring partner. It's only a partial, and we don't have a name to add to it, but we got lucky. The same guy showed up on camera a couple of days earlier meeting a high value subject."

"Who?" Ikeda interjected.

"Leo Conway. He is—or was—Engel's chief of staff. He was one of a very short list of people who knew the administrator's exact schedule."

"It's a start. Let's get moving."

18

"You did well, my friend," Warren Grover observed, leaning back against a wheeled chair in his makeshift office. It promptly squeaked. "Carreon's people have their suspicions about what has taken place, but as long as we control the king, we have the board."

César said nothing.

"I understand you have a talent for extracting information," Grover said after enough time had elapsed in silence that he was sure that was all he was getting. "I may have some use of it over the coming weeks."

"I am at your service," César said, drawing out the words at such length that Grover began to wonder whether he was being mocked.

"Good," Grover said, steepling his fingers and pushing himself upright before glancing at the watch on his left wrist. "It's about time. Would you like to watch?"

"Why not?" César shrugged.

The sicario followed his present boss down the hallway in the basement of a nondescript warehouse situated in a nondescript part of Mexico City. It was not the kind of location one might expect to find a cartel leader, and not just because Mexico's capital was ordinarily an inhospitable environment for the drug gangs.

In the comfort of his own mind, Grover could admit that César unsettled him. There was something about the Mexican that prevented him from ever relaxing, and that was unusual indeed. After all, he had spent most of his career in the employ of the more hard-nosed of America's military and intelligence organizations – including an outfit whose very existence was known only to a battle-tested few as the Apparatus – and there was little that truly scared him anymore.

But César did.

He had met plenty of dangerous men over his life, and there were many who considered him to fit that bracket. But these cartel people, they were indisputably different, Grover knew. Where his people were professionals who mostly took no particular pleasure in the taking of human life, men like César were different.

They had neither souls, nor remorse. They were animals.

But sometimes animals had their uses.

Still, Grover was relieved when they entered the grandly titled control center, which was in truth little more than a conference room equipped with a fiber-optic Internet cable and enough screens and communications equipment to render the space a sweltering hellhole, despite the best efforts of the ancient air conditioning system.

Three separate television screens were set up on the room's long wall, each displaying an overhead video feed supplied by a loitering drone. The UAVs had been purchased commercially, and while they were equipped with thermal imaging cameras, the quality was not as clear as that provided by a USAF Reaper.

But they were also a hundredth of the price.

"Who are they?" César asked, walking to the wall and studying the television screen on the left.

"Reyes's men. The one you're looking at, that's Carlos Guerra, his cousin. The two buildings to the right are both owned by Emiliano Mendoza. We believe he's in one of them. We just don't know which."

"So you decided to hit both," César mused.

"Indeed," Grover agreed.

Did the Mexican sound impressed? It was hard to say; the man showed little if any emotion, even at the best of times. Perhaps that was what made him so effective. It also meant he was damned difficult to read.

César peered at the screen, the fingers of his right hand flickering. He was counting, Grover realized.

"I see seven," he said. "All yours?"

"That's right," Grover agreed. "There's an eighth on the building opposite. A sniper, you see?"

César's head turned slightly, and the American watched as he focused on the somewhat indistinct light gray dot on top of the compound opposite Guerra's villa. "I see him."

"Watch."

The Mexican nodded, and the two men lapsed back into silence once more. It was a little like watching a video game, and Grover marveled that a lifetime spent practicing the darker arts for his country had so perfectly prepared him for his present role.

The dots moved in unison, as he had trained them to do. They were mostly Mexican, drawn from Carreon's own sicarios, though he'd seeded many of the units with mercenaries. Mostly officers and NCOs who preferred the finer things in life and were prepared to lead a unit of cartel gunmen in exchange for sufficient payment. Two decades of a global war on terror had created a ready supply of such men.

There were even those for whom money wasn't the prime motivator. Men like César himself, who was driven not by the prospect of financial reward but by the aphrodisiac of power.

Not – or not *just* – power as Grover himself conceived it, but control over other men.

It made him a dangerous bedfellow, of course. But Grover had convinced himself that by understanding what drove César and others like him, he had the upper hand when it came to using them.

That was the theory, anyway.

There was a slight flash on the screen as the sniper fired several shots. A second later, the doorway flared, presumably as a result of a breaching charge removing the impediment. The dots that indicated Grover's strike force quickly piled into Carlos Guerra's villa.

"You don't want to listen?" César said.

"I trust them." Grover shrugged. "They've proven highly effective these past few nights."

"They haven't come up against anyone this senior yet. You think seven is enough?"

"Eight," he corrected. "And Carlos is a fool. Everyone knows that. He doesn't take his own personal security seriously. We've been watching the villa for a week. He has half a dozen guards. They are mostly drunk or high. At least, when he's home."

"Which he is tonight."

"Exactly. He's a weak link. I have no idea why Reyes keeps him around."

"Carlos is family," César said. "That means something down here."

Grover bristled. Was the sicario trying to say something? "Not to you."

"Not to me," he agreed, "but I'm not typical."

No, Grover thought. *No, you are not.*

At some point, he knew, César would prove a liability. And when that time came, he would have to be eliminated. The man was willing to subordinate himself for the present, but it would not last. It wasn't so much that he was ambitious, but that some psychological process within his mind drove him to test his boundaries. And once he found one, to not stop until it was crushed into rubble. Right now, there were other obstacles in his path.

But not for long.

And yet, for now at least, Grover needed him. Over the past two years, he had created dozens of special forces-type units inside the Federacion Cartel. Carreon hadn't needed much convincing even before he went behind bars. After, consumed by anger at his enemies, it was even easier.

But those men were tactical operators, not strategic minds. And except for the mercenaries stiffening their spines, they mostly followed Carreon himself, only listening to Warren Grover's instructions because they thought he still spoke for their boss.

César married both technical skill and strategic genius, and beyond that he commanded the respect of the Federacion's sicarios. The grunts didn't like him, but they feared him. And that was good enough.

"Forty seconds," César murmured approvingly, looking away from the screen. "Looks like they have a prisoner."

"Casualties?" Grover barked.

The communications operator held a hand against his headset, then shook his head. "None. They're bugging out now. They found a couple hard drives and a bunch of cell phones. Intel will go through it all the second it arrives."

"Good." Grover looked over at César, finding himself strangely hungry for the killer's approval. "So – what do you think?"

"As I said, very impressive. But it won't be enough."

Grover frowned. "Why not?"

"You need Reyes, or your plan will fail."

"We'll get him," Grover insisted.

"When?"

"Soon."

"That's not good enough." César shrugged. "You get one shot at this. If you miss, Reyes will burn this country to cinders just so you can't have it. Either the Mexican government will be stung into doing something about the aftermath, or the Americans will. Either way, unless you chop his head off right at the start, you're screwed. It'll be all-out war, and your toy soldiers will help, but they'll only get you so far."

"That's the plan," Grover snapped. "But it's not so easy to find a man like Ramon Reyes when he doesn't want to be found."

The communications operator winced, clearly unwilling to interrupt the intense conversation between the two men. "They hit the Mendoza place. It's empty."

"Which one?"

"Both of them."

Grover cursed, wishing that César hadn't heard. It gave credence to the man's view, whether he liked it or not. "Dammit. He was the key."

"Carlos might know something," César remarked.

"The cousin? I told you, he's a fool."

"Even fools have ears. And sometimes men can be most intemperate around those they do not respect. You're right when you say that Ramon has no trust in his cousin. Perhaps we might use that to our advantage."

"What are you suggesting?"

"Let me interrogate him when he arrives. If he knows something, I will tease it out."

Grover gritted his teeth, still furious that they'd missed Mendoza. Reyes' lieutenant was a slippery bastard, but the intelligence should still have been good. And losing him was a hell of a setback. Anything Reyes knew, so did Mendoza. With him in their clutches, finding Reyes would have been child's play.

But now he was in the wind, that would be a dozen times harder. And the worst of it was that Grover began to think that César was right. His plan only worked while he was on the front foot. The odds of success dropped precipitously if Reyes could bring this to the mat. And there was real danger of that happening.

"Fine. He's yours. But I want results."

César smiled, an evil thing. "You will get them."

19

"So what do we know about Leo Conway?"

Kelly looked up from the stack of files and print-outs scattered on her lap. She clearly had the particulars committed to memory, and Trapp suspected that she only referred to them to make everyone else more comfortable. Presently, though, she only had an audience of one, and her stage was the cramped, windowless and humid rear compartment of a purported telephone utility van, lit only by the glow of several large LCD screens.

"Father of two. Married."

Trapp's eyebrows kinked. "Happily?"

"Far as we know," she confirmed. "No easily identifiable profiles on dating websites or apps. And no evidence in his telephone or email records of any extramarital activity."

"But?"

"Gambling problem. For most of the last year he's been about $60,000 in the red across four credit cards. His wife's are paid off every month, so I'm guessing she doesn't know about his money troubles. The cards were zeroed out last week."

"That the extent of it?"

"Probably not. That's just the debt we know about. A 725 number calls him like clockwork every Monday morning, around eight-thirty."

"Just after he gets to work," Trapp observed. "Where's 725?"

A smile – or at least a faint echo of one – appeared on Kelly's face. It was some evidence, at least, that she wasn't simply a machine. "Vegas."

"Not so happy after all," Trapp mused, glancing up at one of the screens.

"Depends how long he keeps it from her, I guess..."

A nest of cameras sat on the roof of the surveillance van they currently occupied, disguised among the ladders and construction equipment the notional technician would require. Currently the only live feed in the van was of the front of Leo Conway's house, a four bed, two bath redbrick – currently painted light gray – not far from Grant Circle Park in North DC.

"Not bad, Kel," Trapp said, closing his eyes to give them a break from the glow of the computer screens. He knew better than to reward her with praise more fulsome than that – personalities like hers responded best to forms of encouragement that others might perceive as a near-reprimand.

But regardless, it was true. Pope had chosen well. This really was a good catch. Anyone could pick up on the credit card debt. The computer did most of the hard work for you. You just had to look. But that was table stakes. Recognizing the significance of that area code spoke volumes about her attention to detail – which boded well for her career. You couldn't teach gut instinct, and Kelly clearly had that in spades.

She didn't respond to his guarded compliment, not that he'd expected her to, saying instead, "Looks like we got movement."

"I see it," Trapp replied, focusing on the screen.

It was early in the morning, not quite first thing, but up and down New Hampshire Avenue, parents were getting their kids ready for the school run. The Conway family was no different. They watched as Rita Conway, the wife, exited with the two kids. Both were young enough to be attending pre-school, Trapp guessed.

"Come on," he murmured under his breath. "Go with her."

The couple had two vehicles registered in their name. Both purchased on credit, though there was nothing particularly unusual about that. It was difficult to buy a car any other way in America these days, and the financing was so cheap it was a no-brainer.

Not for you though, Leo. Not anymore.

Money was as good a reason as any to betray one's country, Trapp supposed. He'd never liked working with assets motivated by that incentive. They tended to sell you out once they found a higher bidder. Then again, he didn't really like working with anyone else at all.

The ones motivated by ideology were no better. They always measured you against what you could do to achieve their ends, always waiting for you to fall short or disappoint them. But at least they believed in something other than themselves.

They watched as Leo Conway stopped in the doorway and kissed his wife goodbye. His arm was in a Velcro sling. She lingered for a few seconds as she returned his affection, perhaps spooked by his brush with death a couple days before. He stooped and hugged each of his kids goodbye in turn.

"Damn."

Trapp glanced up at Kelly's face, mildly surprised by her use of the expletive. But only because he didn't think anything ruffled the young FBI agent.

"Just be patient," he murmured, looking back at the screen and watching as Rita Conway walked out of shot. "If he's our guy, he must be feeling the heat. He'll do something to screw up, and we'll be there to watch it. Assuming this isn't just a wild goose chase, of course."

"You really think it might be?" Kelly asked.

Trapp concealed a smile. *Not so cold after all, kid.*

"I think it's usually best not to get hung up on a hypothesis. We're all just dumb apes at the end of the day. Even the best of us look for evidence that supports our arguments, even at the expense of ignoring the bits that don't."

On the other hand, a man really had tried to kill Trapp. And that same man had met with Leo Conway just days before the murder of the man's boss. It wasn't proof. But it was getting there.

"Noted," Kelly replied without comment.

Up at the house, the camera watched without judgment as Leo Conway lingered for a few seconds longer, gripping the door frame with one hand for support as he waved with the other. The sound of his wife's car starting up and then driving away was audible even through the van's thin metal skin, which was a good reminder for them both to keep their voices low when they conversed.

Leo glanced down at his watch and then seemed to peer down the street, as if checking that his wife was really gone.

"I think we might have something," Trapp muttered.

They watched a little longer as their target disappeared from the doorway without closing it. He reappeared about forty seconds later, now wearing a thin jacket, and gingerly descended the stairs to ground level.

"I'll call it in," Kelly agreed, her eyes glued to the screen. She bowed her lips to a small microphone and depressed the transmit button before murmuring a few clipped words into it.

A second car engine started in the background, as the wife's had just done. It grumbled for a few seconds without really catching, then growled into life. Then it, too, departed.

Trapp hooked his earpiece in just in time to hear Ikeda's

voice confirming that she had eyes on the target. He grabbed an orange construction helmet from the hook on the van's wall, then grinned. "Go time."

ABOUT TWENTY HOUSES farther down the street, a Toyota Prius pulled out into traffic. The left rear passenger door bore the scrapes of some long-forgotten sideswipe, though nothing serious enough that it would be unusable for a ride-share driver. Dangling from the rearview mirror was a pair of novelty dice, prominently marked with the logo of one such company.

Ikeda was sitting in the back, concealed by a window tint that was a couple of shades darker than would ordinarily be allowed. She had a notebook computer open on her lap, which was in turn connected to a small mobile Internet router.

"CIA gets all the cool shit," Nick Pope remarked, momentarily looking at his supposed passenger through the mirror.

"We have a cheat code," she remarked, manipulating the mousepad without glancing up.

"What's that?" he asked, killing the indicator light.

"Strictly speaking, we don't have to play by the rules you guys do."

"Or at all."

"That too."

Pope grunted with amusement as the Prius slowed to a stop as they reached a set of traffic lights. "His cell phone moving?"

Ikeda looked up and shot Pope a thumbs-up. "Yep. You can hang back a bit. No point giving him a fair chance at spotting us."

"Just the way I like it."

TRAPP SHOULDERED his way through a set of hanging plastic fronds that shielded the business end of the surveillance van, Kelly in close pursuit. She closed and locked the doors behind them.

Together, they walked toward the nearest telephone pole, ostentatiously peering up at it before turning down the street and tracing an imaginary line in the air. It didn't mean anything, but it looked as though it plausibly might, and that was all that was important.

"How'd I look?" Trapp said, gesturing down at the bright orange hi-viz jacket draped over his shoulders and a khaki utility belt weighing down his waist. It was loaded with tools, but they were mostly for show. The important kit was in the pouches, hidden from view.

Kelly shrugged and deadpanned, "Guess it'll be comforting having this to fall back on. If the Bureau thing goes wrong."

Trapp grunted his amusement. He took one last, long look up and down the street, still tracing imaginary telephone lines in the sky but scanning for any sign that either Leo or Rita Conway were about to return.

Before executing, he keyed his radio's transmit button and murmured, "Location on the wife?"

Ikeda replied without missing a beat, her familiar voice clear in his earpiece. "Still driving. School's ten minutes away from the house, so you should have at least that much warning."

"Copy. Thanks."

"You got it."

A countdown began in Trapp's mind as they walked slowly from the van to their target. Though the street was busy at this time of the morning, if anything that worked to their advantage. In their company-issued – or at least company-adjacent – workwear, they might as well have been invisible to the professional classes that occupied this neighborhood. Both still scanned the windows and doorways all around for any sign that they were being observed, but they could have just as easily not bothered.

Only a wooden gate and fence separated the Conways' backyard from the street out front. Trapp often wondered what the point was in bothering to use locks like the one he was confronted with. Any junkie or criminal worth their salt could shoulder their way through the flimsy mechanism without breaking stride.

It took Kelly less than five seconds to defeat it the old-fashioned way. She was good, he saw, picking the lock without leaving so much as a scratch.

The yard behind was neatly maintained and scattered with abandoned toys and a wooden swing set, which hung entirely still in the morning's calm. The flowerbeds and foliage were pleasant enough but had the sense of sterility that came with hiring an expensive landscaping service. One last scan confirmed that many of the windows overlooking the yard were still obstructed by curtains, and those that weren't were empty.

Trapp inclined his head, and the pair of them walked quickly but deliberately to the back door of the house. Once under cover and shielded from any unwanted attention from nosy neighbors, they paused for breath – though not for too long.

They went to work like a well-oiled team, though they'd only met each other a few days before. Trapp pulled an electronic detection device from one of the pouches on his utility belt and turned it on before crouching down. He ran it along the base of the door frame, then up each side, then along the top. It detected all forms of semiconductor activity and would growl like a well-trained working dog if it came into contact with a system that could plausibly warn someone – whether Leo Conway or another player entirely – of a forced entry.

But the unit didn't make a sound. And when Trapp gave a

half-shrug, silently asking whether his partner had detected anything on the visual spectrum, she confirmed that she had not. As far as either of them could reasonably make out, the Conway house was clean. It was always possible that a passive system was in place: maybe a camera or an infrared device positioned somewhere out of sight or well-disguised, but you couldn't legislate for every possibility.

All you could do was play the odds. And Trapp was satisfied that they were, at least, in his favor. He nodded again, and Kelly beat the back door lock as well. It took her a few seconds longer, but the job was done just as cleanly.

This time he doled out a thumbs-up. He received no response.

Atta girl.

∿

"Looks like she's back in the car, Jason," Ikeda said into her lapel mic.

She could have probably gotten away with a radio handset in the relative safety of the back of the Toyota, but there was always the chance she would need to go on foot. It was better to be prepared.

"ETA?" Came the no-nonsense response.

"Twelve minutes in this traffic. Count on nine, just in case she steps on it." Ikeda squinted at the screen on her lap, her eyes focused on the red dot that was assigned to Rita Conway's cell phone signal. "Hold up. She's heading away from the house. Must be going grocery shopping or something. You've got plenty of time."

The acknowledgment of the update was equally terse. She smiled, having expected nothing less.

Pope spoke from up front. "And our boy?"

"Still a couple of hundred yards ahead of us. Looks like he's heading into the center. He's on Sherman Avenue now. I'll tell you if he turns."

"Got it," Pope said, briefly tapping the brakes as another rideshare car cut him off.

"Asshole," he muttered under his breath. "I should write you a fucking ticket."

Ikeda couldn't help herself laughing out loud, though she kept her eyes glued to the screen in front of her, alert to any sign that either their target —or the wife —was changing course. "That might give the game away a little, don't you think, Nick?"

The FBI agent mumbled something equally irreverent underneath his breath but fell silent as his evident irritation faded and concentrated on his driving instead.

Rita Conway's signal disappeared for a few seconds, a ghostly, pulsating dot superimposed on the map where it had been last spotted. Ikeda zoomed in and found that she was looking at an underground parking garage, which relieved her a little. She kept an eye on the signal until it reappeared about 90 seconds later as the cell phone reacquainted itself with its parent cell network. The device was moving slowly now, indicating that she was probably on foot. Unless the Conways were running a fairly sophisticated intelligence operation between each other and the wife had somehow handed the phone off to a runner, it was safe enough to assume that Rita was out of the picture for a while.

By this point, the tracker signal radiating from Leo Conway's car had passed through Columbia Heights, the FBI surveillance vehicle following at a sensible distance. He didn't appear to be slowing, so Ikeda settled in for the ride.

∽

TRAPP AND KELLY checked the entire Conway house for electronic surveillance and found nothing. It was a little more difficult to be certain that the place was clean than it had been to be confident that the doorway wasn't monitored. Two decades into the 21st century, almost anything could be a vector for electronic surveillance. Refrigerators were connected to the Internet. Computers weren't just on every desk, but in every pocket.

Hell, Trapp thought, shaking his head as he spied a home automation speaker from the rainforest company nestled on a side table. Millions of people all over the country had willingly brought into their homes devices that had the sole intention of spying on their owners. And paid for them!

The Conways were apparently no different.

When he had joined the Farm, the CIA's training school in Virginia, there were still a few instructors left on staff who'd been there through the dark days of the Cold War. Real relics, men – and all men – who barely knew how to operate a toaster, let alone a cell phone.

The world had moved on a long way since then. The espionage business had probably shifted even further. Trapp sometimes wondered whether he too was now a vestige of a bygone age. Was there still use for men like him in a world where bytes were a thousand times more deadly than bullets?

He shook his head to clear it and retrieved the first of the listening devices from his belt. It was the size of a little fingernail and almost transparent. The battery life could stretch to a couple of weeks if it limited its frequency of transmissions, though he didn't anticipate that this operation would take nearly that long. If they didn't have results in a couple of days, then it would probably be time to think about bringing Leo Conway in for questioning.

He knelt to the ground by a large, rectangular coffee table stacked with high-end fashion magazines, none of which appeared ever to have been opened, and a selection of three photo books of a type that were designed to be displayed rather than read.

In another room, he sensed Kelly's almost silent footsteps as she padded nearby, performing a very similar task. Neither of them spoke, just in case they'd missed a listening device that another interested party had already left behind. And besides, there was nothing much to say.

Trapp donned a latex glove for his working hand, leaving the other unencumbered for any more tactile work. He placed the listening device on the tip of his right index finger, then lowered his body to the ground before gently flipping onto his back, the underside of the table now occupying his vision. With his free hand, he reached for a penlight and searched for a spot to install it with its beam. He quickly found one, nestled in one of the joins at which the legs joined the tabletop.

He placed the flashlight between his teeth and peeled the adhesive back of the listening device off, sticking it to his lip for safekeeping while he worked. Actually installing the bug took only seconds, most of which was taken up by checking that the device actually did what it was supposed to. The old wooden floorboards beneath him creaked as he climbed back to his feet.

With the task done, he installed two more bugs in the room to cover all dead spots. One would probably have sufficed, but the devices were cheap – relatively speaking – and returning to install more could prove an expensive risk.

The bugs consumed extremely low levels of power, but all technological leaps come with trade-offs, and in this case low power meant short range. Because the house brick, it would be even shorter. But there was a fix for that, too.

Trapp scanned the living room as he extracted a needle-point drill from his belt. Unlike the outside, the building's interior walls were for the most part just plasterboard. He found a suitable spot behind the television and drilled a small hole into it. The drill produced only a tiny amount of dust, and a small vacuum within it meant that only a couple of flakes fell to the ground.

The mothership device was a combination receiver and burst transmitter, not much thicker than a strip of metal wire, with its own built-in battery as well as the ability to absorb waste power from nearby electrical wiring, of which there was plenty. It would suck up power all day long, compress all the files it received, then transmit them to another relay outside the house at random times. Unless someone was scanning for bugs all day long, the chances of such a transmission being detected were minimal.

He finished the installation, painted the installation hole with a brush not much bigger than a toothpick, then pulled back a little to check that the shades matched. They did. Unless someone really went looking, the addition was almost invisible to the naked eye.

All done.

He clicked his microphone three times to communicate this fact to his partner. She replied with one, which meant that she wasn't quite done wiring the upstairs. Trapp bent to vacuum the scattering of dust from the floor and started hooking the device back to his belt when he was finished.

The scrape of shoes at the front door warned him a second before the sound of a woman's voice calling out for Leo Conway's wife.

"Rita?"

The woman fell silent for a couple of seconds, waiting, then pulled out a second time. "Rita – you guys in there? Leo?"

Trapp froze the second he heard her voice, leaving his hand still half-extended, in the process of returning his tools to his belt. They were so damn close to being done. Who the hell was this? And why couldn't she have waited just a couple of minutes longer?

The doorbell rang a couple of times, its first rendition truncated halfway through by a second, which the woman at least had the decency to allow to fully play out. Trapp moved only his eyes, scanning the room to confirm what he already knew – that if he needed to escape, the backyard was his only option. But that meant crossing about ten feet of old flooring that would provide as much warning to an attentive listener that there was an intruder as any security alarm.

So a simple question lingered in Trapp's mind: was Rita's houseguest as innocent as she seemed, or was someone else coming to pay her husband a visit?

And if it was the latter – *were they here alone?*

"I brought you some food. I heard about what happened to Leo, so awful," the woman called out for half the neighborhood to hear. Trapp suspected that that part wasn't accidental. "I'll leave it out here, okay? It's Katie. Call me."

Trapp held his breath as he waited for the woman's footsteps to disappear. His hand was still in the exact same place as it had been when she'd first started talking.

"Looks like Rita Conway is on her way back home," Ikeda said through the radio, startling Trapp half to death. "You have about twenty minutes."

He still didn't move, instead waiting another couple of minutes until he was absolutely certain that the unwanted visitor was definitely gone. Kelly appeared to come to the same conclusion about the same time, descending the stairs and emerging into the living room. He shot her a thumbs-up, which she reciprocated with a sharp nod of her head.

Trapp brushed the button of his mic but didn't start transmitting until they re-emerged into the Conways' backyard. "We're done. Out."

"WHERE THE HECK do you think he's going?" Ikeda muttered, genuinely surprised by Leo Conway's route. He was heading right into the heart of DC.

"Beats me," Pope replied, glancing at her in the mirror. "We sure he didn't make plans?"

"None we know of," she replied, following Leo Conway's progress on the map. "Hold up, I think he's stopping."

"Want me to get closer?"

"A little bit. He must've come all this way for a reason."

They both fell silent for a few seconds as Pope guided the Toyota through a set of traffic lights, closing the distance between their vehicle and Conway's to just 20 or 30 yards. Close enough to get eyes on without exposing themselves to too much risk of being noticed.

The indicator light on his car was blinking, and Ikeda squinted, noticing a familiar blue sign. "Looks like –"

"Parking garage," Pope said at about the same time.

"Okay," Ikeda said, grabbing a purse from beside her and shouldering it. "Take me half a block further, then let me out."

Pope did as he was instructed without comment. Neither of them visibly looked to the side as they passed Conway's car turning into the entrance of an underground parking garage beneath a mid-budget DC hotel. Twenty seconds later, Ikeda climbed out of the Prius, then retrieved her cell phone from her purse as the car pulled away from the sidewalk.

She fiddled with it for a couple of seconds, turning it on and tapping with aimless purpose at the screen before returning the device to the purse. To anyone watching, it would have looked like she was leaving a rating for her driver.

"Can you hear me?" Pope said into her ear.

She clicked the transmit button hidden in her sleeve twice to confirm that he was coming through nice and clear.

"Signal hasn't moved. Which either means he's fiddling around down there, or he's left his phone in the car for a reason."

He's meeting someone, Ikeda thought. *Someone he's not supposed to.*

It was almost impossible to run a successful close surveillance operation with just two operatives, so Ikeda knew that if she was going to have any chance at pulling this off, she needed to keep her distance.

It wasn't really Leo Conway that Ikeda was worried about. It was possible that he'd had some counter-surveillance training at some point, but she was willing to wager that it would have been no more rigorous than a PowerPoint presentation by a contractor at a DEA off-site day. On the other hand, he was probably anxious, and cornered animals sometimes found they possessed a sixth sense they never knew they had.

But no matter how good he might inadvertently prove, Ikeda wagered she was better.

Her worry centered more around anyone her target might be here to meet, rather than Conway himself. She was on alert for the tall fighter whom Trapp had tangled with a few days earlier.

But as far as she could tell, he wasn't here.

"Wait," Pope said. "Conway is coming up to street level now. Not far from where you're standing."

"Got it," Ikeda murmured, momentarily making herself scarce. She watched as the target emerged from the parking garage. "He's walking up 11th St, toward the corner of East."

"It's like he wants us to catch him," Pope remarked over the radio.

Ikeda was careful to walk a few steps behind another – slightly plumper – woman, to obscure her from Conway's view if he happened to turn. "Why do you say that?"

"He's what – 150 yards from the Hoover building? It's like he's tempting fate."

"Yeah," Ikeda agreed, falling silent as Conway rounded the corner and headed right. He was, she reflected, doing nothing to dispel Pope's suspicion. But these moments were the hardest in any surveillance operation, particularly one as under-manned as this. A corner was a perfect opportunity to make a tail, since the surveillance operative always had to take it blind.

She held back just before East Street and waited until the rear window of a passing car briefly flashed an image of what she was about to face. Someone was walking toward her. A woman. Another figure walking away.

It was clear. She kept following.

"He looks antsy," she reported.

"How so?"

"I don't know. I just get that vibe. Something in the way he's walking, it's all jerky. Like he's real tense."

Conway was walking like someone had replaced the soles of his shoes with lead. Ikeda hung back to avoid being spotted, pretending to study the window of what she soon realized was a lingerie shop. Out of the corner of her eye, she could see the jutting concrete structure of the Hoover building, the guard post on the corner and the blast barriers on the edge of the sidewalk.

He stopped at the pedestrian crossing, even though the man was green. The light flicked red, waited thirty seconds, and then went green all over again before he made it across. And even after that all he did was stop and stare.

"I'm not kidding, Nick," she said softly, as a quizzical frown lifted from her forehead. "He's looking at that front door like it's a long-lost lover. I think he's considering turning himself in."

Leo Conway's heart was still racing almost an hour later. He found an empty parking spot about 10 houses up from his own and killed the engine. His fingers ached as he pulled them away from the steering wheel and realized exactly how hard he'd been gripping it.

"You should have just turned yourself in," he moaned, half out loud, half in his head. He dropped his forehead to the steering wheel, hard enough that the horn let out a single, mournful chirp. He stayed there for a few long, ragged breaths, sucking oxygen greedily into his lungs as he tried to figure out which option would allow him to chart the furthest course from disaster.

The passenger door opened, and a figure climbed in and closed it behind him before Leo was really aware of what was happening. He was slow to react, numb with fear and worry. All he saw of the man was a flash of blond hair in the rear mirror.

A familiar voice filled the car, but not one that brought Leo any comfort. "What were you doing, Leo?"

"What –?" he squeaked. "What are you talking about?"

"I was watching you," the man said without shame. "And I didn't like what I saw."

"And what was that?" Leo said with surprising vigor, turning his head and eyeing his contact, a man he knew only as Ethan, for the first time. "You people almost killed me!"

Ethan seemed entirely unaffected by Leo's rage, which only made it worse. He found that he was gripping the steering wheel again, white-knuckled, contemplating punching this man right in the face.

And what good would that do?

Perhaps sensing what Leo was thinking, his visitor smiled. He didn't say anything, but he didn't need to. Both men knew there would be only one outcome if their tussle turned physical.

Finally, his handler spoke. "You are a hero, Leo. Rita must have told you that. You survived the cartels. For the rest of your life, you'll always have that anecdote in your locker. If you're smart, you'll build a hell of a political career out of this."

"What career?" Leo snarled, gesturing wildly down the street, at his house, at his whole life. "I'm done. It's over. They didn't get me today, but they will. It's only a matter of time. And then I lose all this. Shit, what happens when Rita finds out? Her dad's a pastor, dammit. The first time she got screwed was our wedding night. You think she's going to bring the kids to visit me in prison? No chance."

"And what if it didn't have to be that way?"

"Why should I trust you?" Leo said dumbly, suddenly drained of energy. "You could have killed me. You probably meant to."

Ethan shrugged. "I won't lie to you. It would have been neater if you disappeared. Everyone makes mistakes."

"So why would you bother keeping me alive now? Why not just kill me and be done with it? No more loose ends. That's what you want, right?"

"We certainly could." Ethan nodded thoughtfully. "It would get messy, but it could certainly be arranged. A suicide, maybe."

He fell silent, and Leo found himself waiting impatiently for him to continue, the uncomfortable weight of a sword of judgment dangling over his neck. When the burden became overpowering, he broke, sick of himself for doing so yet unable to refrain. "But?"

"But what?"

"You haven't come here just to tell me you're going to kill me," Leo said desperately, mainly to convince himself that it was true. "So there must be one."

"You see, it's a question of priorities," Ethan said at last. "Trade-offs. We would of course prefer that you were dead. But to remove you from the board now would both attract unwanted attention and require resources that can be better employed elsewhere. So it's a trade-off between the value of keeping you alive and the cost of letting you die."

"Don't fucking sugarcoat it," Leo spat, desperation momentarily overriding his fear.

"You're a big boy. And you got yourself into this mess. So you're going to have to dig yourself out."

"And you're here to sell me the shovel, right?" Leo replied in a tone of voice that wasn't much removed from an animal's whine.

But even as he spoke, his quick mind was turning. Perhaps he really did have an opportunity to keep himself not just alive, but free. And hell, if he played his cards right, then maybe not just free – but rich. Still, he had no illusions about the bargain he was making. If once, when this nightmare began, he'd thought that he was simply trading nuggets of low-value information as a way of bailing himself out of debt, and at no personal risk, those scales of innocence had been torn from his eyes.

These people had already tried to kill him once. They'd

murdered his boss. His *friend*. And they would come after him again, he knew that just as well as night follows day. He swallowed hard as he realized that they might come after his family too.

"You see?" His handler smiled. "You're a quick learner."

"So what am I supposed to learn?" Leo asked. "They'll put me on medical leave. What if I don't have access to anything important? Hell, the cops might even want to talk to me again. I was there when it happened, you know?"

"I'm counting on it, Leo. You knew Engel well—correct?"

Leo's guts were ice as he nodded in reply. "You know this. Mark was a personal friend."

And I killed him, he didn't say. *As surely as if I was holding the gun.*

But that was in the past. It was a mistake. An awful, irreversible *mistake*. And surely Mark wouldn't want to condemn his friend for a little slip-up, would he?

"Will they pull your security clearance?"

Leo considered the question before answering. As he did so, he noticed for the first time that there was a purple bruise on his handler's face, as if he'd been in a fight. He trembled at the thought of a man scary enough to lay a finger on this monster. "Maybe. But probably not. But unless I give them a reason to suspect –"

"*Don't*," the man ordered coldly, holding his gaze without blinking. "Remember what's riding on this, Leo. It's not just your life, you understand?"

Leo nodded, fear for his family's safety freezing his vocal cords into uselessness. Not the kids. Surely they wouldn't touch the kids? They were still human, after all.

"Good. The FBI will interview you, I have no doubt about that. I want to know everything they ask. Everything."

"I can do that," Leo gasped, driving a ragged, jerky breath into his lungs. "Is that all?"

"Of course not. I want you to go into the office, whatever they tell you to do. Read everything that passes your desk. Make friends with whoever is running the investigation inside the DEA. And read everything that crosses *their* desk."

"And what do I get out of this?" Leo snapped as the gravity of what he was now compelled to do hit him. He would be placing himself at great risk by doing this. The FBI was sure to wonder why he was asking so many questions. What would happen if they started digging?

If the cartel learned about your debt, how long will it take the Bureau?

"Isn't your life enough? Your family's safety?"

"No!" Leo yelled, slapping his hand against the dashboard with enough force that it stung. "I mean, yes, *of course*. But if I do what you are asking, then at some point they'll work it out. And when they do, I need to be gone."

"*When* you do what I'm asking," the man growled.

"Sure, when," Leo said desperately. "I'll need money. Not much, maybe a couple of million. Enough to disappear somewhere cheap. And passports, for my wife and kids too."

His handler considered the request for a few seconds, leaving Leo to stew. Finally, he gave a curt nod. "I think this will be acceptable."

To who? Leo wondered. He sat there, not daring to speak.

"I will get you a down payment soon," the man said. "The remainder you will receive when I am satisfied."

"I need those passports," Leo pressed. "Until I get them, I'm not doing anything."

The man thought for a few seconds, as before, then nodded. He opened the car door a crack and spoke before leaving. "A fair trade. Better for both of us. Let's meet again soon."

He closed the car door after him.

21

Fernando Carreon scrunched his face in between a pair of goose down pillows, willing the darkness to return. He'd forgotten to close the blinds the previous night, and the mid-morning sun now streaming through the master bedroom drilled through his eyelids despite his best efforts to shield them from it.

He reached blindly for a glass of water but succeeded only in toppling a whisky tumbler that he'd abandoned on his bedside table some hours before. It shattered against the marble tiles, and shards careened across the floor with all the delicacy of nails scratching on a chalkboard.

"Hell!" he groaned, his voice rusty with disuse.

It wasn't just the result of a few hours in bed, but because there was no one in this place for him to talk to. The maids barely said a word beyond bowing their heads and scuttling out of sight the moment they had a chance. The guards were mostly unseen – though it wasn't as if he had any desire to communicate with them anyway.

Finally accepting that he couldn't linger in hungover squalor for the remainder of the day, Carreon rolled over, revealing a face like thunder, dotted with gentle lines indented into the skin courtesy of his bedsheets. His eyelashes came slowly unglued, revealing a world that was at first blurry and indistinct.

Water.

His body's command wasn't so much a desire as a necessity. The liquid might at least prevent his stomach, now gargling hot and spitting acid, from unloading itself in an attempt at finding respite.

The one-time narcotics magnate dragged himself upright, leaning gratefully against the wall as his vision slowly clarified. The worst of the night's excesses still remained: a bottle of champagne now tipped upside down in a silver bucket, smashed glasses, clothes scattered across the floor. He'd even found high-grade cocaine in one of the cabinets downstairs, finely ground and complete with a metal straw. It was probably his own product, too, which made the discovery all the more galling.

Water.

The command repeated itself, the sensation now urging irresistible haste. Carreon bolted out of bed, slowing his flight to the bathroom only enough to avoid the worst clusters of broken glass on the floor. A tiny shard cut him regardless, slicing into the side of his left heel, though not enough to draw more than a mild grunt of discomfort. He left a trail of single bloody footsteps all the way to the sink.

He buried his face in it, sluicing cold water against his face, into his mouth, and drinking greedily from the faucet until he had swallowed all that was physically possible. Only then did he pull the offending needle of glass from his flesh. He did not even particularly mind the pain it caused. It was, at least, a distraction from the vise crushing his skull and the magma threatening to erupt from his stomach.

He didn't bother showering before leaving the bedroom, only stopping to don a silk shirt and a pair of Bermuda shorts.

The breakfast table was set up in a corner of the terraced courtyard, not far from the pool. It was sheltered from the worst excesses of the sunshine by a canvas umbrella and contained every item he could reasonably desire. The croissants weren't half bad, he'd learned yesterday. The ham was well-aged, Iberian, and meticulously arranged on a platter with fresh-baked bread. Another contained a variety of fruits, all ripe and freshly cut.

He didn't touch any of it. Not yet, anyway. His stomach wouldn't wear it.

The OJ was good, though. Poured straight from a jug nestled in a bed of ice, with just enough bits in it to make it feel premium without getting stuck in his teeth. The way he liked it.

In fact, his drink-befuddled mind belatedly recognized, everything in this place was how he liked it. The wine, the food, the exact setting of the air conditioning, even the firmness of his mattress. It was as though someone had read his mind and attempted to re-create his idea of the perfect home.

Except this wasn't home.

The realization that someone had gone to the trouble of studying him this closely might have been more troubling if he wasn't so damned hungover. It still irked him, but in a more untethered way.

A thin glass of orange juice clutched in his meaty palm, Carreon walked into the sunshine for the first time and made his way to the edge of the pool. He closed his eyes and allowed the sun's rays to wash over his body. For a few seconds at least, he allowed himself to forget where he was, and why.

But not for long.

Because this place was just as much a prison as the one Grover had broken him from. Far more comfortable, there was no denying that, but just as restrictive. He had everything his heart could possibly desire—except the one thing it actually did.

And worse, Fernando Carreon was not a stupid man. He understood the facts of life better than most in Mexico. It was how he had ascended to the top of such a prodigiously dangerous industry. It didn't take a great leap of imagination to guess why he was being kept in this place.

For now, Grover needed him alive. How long that would last was anyone's guess. Probably only until his newfound position was secure. And that would be the end for him.

Carreon finished his drink and returned the glass to the breakfast table. He briefly cast his eye over the fare on display, but again decided against sampling any of it. The energy from the sugar was beginning to course into his system with quite positive effects, but he suspected that anything more substantial was likely to provoke a more adverse reaction.

He popped an ice cube into his mouth and sucked on it as a hedge against his mouth drying out as he walked around the gleaming patio. He walked to the very end, where a wall made of glass rose from the stone flooring, up to about waist height. Below that was just sections of brown grass, ripped through by jetting escarpments of stone, steep enough that if one fell while attempting to traverse them, it would probably be the last thing they ever did. It might be possible to pick out a path down the mountainside given enough time, but it would not be easy.

"And go where?" Carreon murmured. He knew as well as anyone how vast these mountains were. After all, so many of his operations were hidden within them. He was probably thirty miles from the nearest settlement, and even then it was likely to be nothing more substantial than a shack or two occupied by a few peasant shepherd families.

Movement naturally attracted his attention. He glanced toward its source, half expecting to see a bird of prey hovering on a thermal, but instead found himself staring at a person, probably two hundred yards down the mountainside, standing on an outcropping of rock.

"Where the hell did you come from?"

Covering his brow with one hand to block the sun from his eyes, Carreon squinted at the shape. It was a man, he decided. Impossible to say how old or tall at this distance, though there was one distinguishing feature.

He was armed. A man has a distinctive shape when he carries a rifle, and this one was no different. His right hand rested higher than the left, which cradled the weapon's barrel. His right foot was out at a slight angle, and most of his weight seemed to be resting on the other.

The guard stood there a few seconds longer, seeming to return the attention. The moment lasted long enough for the kingpin's heart to start hammering in his chest, reminding him how long it had been since he'd dared to breathe.

And then he disappeared, like a wraith vanishing into the night. Except whoever this guy was, he did it in broad daylight. One moment he was there, and the next he simply wasn't, as though he had simply melted into the rock.

Message received, Carreon thought grimly.

He closed his eyes for a second in order to wrestle back control over his nerves. It had been a long time since he was truly relaxed. Since before the Marines arrested him and incarcerated him in Altiplano. And definitely before armed men attacked the prison and brought him here.

Whoever was in control of his life now, it certainly wasn't him. That was plain. Attempting to escape from this place was a fool's errand. The villa was situated halfway up the mountain, on a small plateau carved directly out of the rock face. If he turned to his right, he could see the road that led to the bottom of the valley peeking out from behind the building.

Taking that way out was patently out of the question. It would be wired and guarded and watched, and as far as his vague recollections of the journey up the mountain allowed – damn, he wished he knew then what he knew now – it would take a man hours on foot to make it to the bottom. Far enough for his captors to allow him to tire himself out before they ever bothered to come pick him up.

Or you could go straight down the mountainside, trusting that you would find a safe route and not just fall to your death.

Except now Carreon knew that his captors were watching that, too.

And so it wasn't fear that Fernando Carreon felt in that moment.

It was abject hopelessness.

He was trapped in his very own Catch-22. If he stayed in this place, then at some point his captors would reach the moment at which he was no longer useful – and then he would die.

Or he could try and escape.

And sure, there was a tiny chance he'd make it out alive. But in reality no greater than that of winning the lottery. And he wouldn't stake his life on winning a scratch card, so how could he justify an attempt at escape?

Carreon swore and punched the air by his side, hard enough to jar his shoulder. He winced at the resulting jolt of pain and turned abruptly away from the terrace's edge, no longer wishing to view the endless expanse of freedom that he was unable to access.

He strode back into the villa and stopped dead as he passed by a bedroom doorway that had previously been closed. One of the maids had her cleaning cart pulled just inside the door and was making up the bed.

He stood and watched her for a few seconds, his mind turning faster than it had in some time. Perhaps it was as a result of the adrenaline caused by the glimpse of his watcher. Or maybe it was just his finely-tuned intelligence reasserting itself after several months of enforced inactivity.

Either way, it was immediately plain to him that something was afoot. He had been in this place for almost two full days, and this was the first sign of anything out of the ordinary. There was no reason for this woman to be preparing a second bedroom if he was to be the only guest.

Captive, he thought with a snort.

The woman finished with the sheets and leaned over the bed to plump up the pillows. Either she was short-sighted, or simply not paying attention to her surroundings, since she did not notice that she was being observed. It wasn't until she was finished with her tasks, her cleaning supplies returned to her cart, and she was halfway out the door before she stopped dead, eyes widening at the unexpected blockage in her way.

"What are you doing?" Carreon hissed.

The maid turned, startled, before bowing her head apprehensively. "Just following my instructions, jefe. I don't know anything more than that. Now please – I must go."

"You go when I say you can," he replied firmly, barring her exit with his forearm. "And I'm not done asking. So let's try that again. What were you doing here?"

"I think not," came a second voice from behind both of them, this time causing Carreon to flinch.

He spun in search of its source, breath scrabbling for purchase in his throat. "Who the hell are you?"

"Let the woman go," the voice said.

It belonged to a man dressed in a charcoal gray polo shirt tucked into a pair of khaki pants. As far as Carreon could tell, he wasn't armed, but judging by his physique, he didn't really need to be. There was little about his dress or appearance that would immediately occasion alarm if you passed him walking down a sidewalk.

Except that he was wearing a balaclava.

"Not till I get some damn answers," Carreon said hoarsely, anger for a moment beating back his fear. His arm had somehow come dislodged from the doorframe as he turned, and he shakily replaced it. "Who the hell are you people? And what do you want from me?"

"Let the woman go, and then we can talk. Like men."

The voice was mocking, but Carreon understood that he was lacking in other options. This man was plainly younger than him, far stronger, and if he had been watching, then so were others. Any defiance would be in vain, and while he could not abide being mocked, he was wise enough not to risk open confrontation when the odds were stacked so greatly against him.

Without turning, he growled, "Go."

The maid did as she was told, her white-knuckled hands clutching the handle of her cart as she pushed it past him and around the nearest corner. A squeaky wheel provided a backing track for her departure.

And then it was just the two of them.

"Why don't you take that mask off?" Carreon said. "And we can talk. *Like men.*"

The man leaned against a nearby wall with studied insouciance. He paused for a few seconds before he opened his mouth. And when he did, he didn't bother addressing Carreon's suggestion. "Don't talk to the staff again. Life could get much less comfortable for you."

"You need me," Carreon grunted, jutting out his chin.

The guard shrugged. "Maybe. Or maybe not. You're an option. As long as the costs of retaining you do not exceed the value of keeping you alive, then you remain profitable. But I suggest you don't do anything to raise those costs. If I were you, I wouldn't want to find out how low our tolerance for losses might be."

～

THE SOUND of the engine carried a long way in the mountains, though it periodically faded away entirely as it made its way up the steeply winding road, blocked by one outcropping of rock or another. For several minutes, as he lay on a lounge by the pool, condensation forming on a chilled bottle of beer that sat on a table beside him, Carreon thought that it might be coming from a light aircraft in the skies overhead.

Many of them plied their trade in these mountains, ferrying drugs from one remote airstrip to another. It took him several long minutes to recognize it for what it was: a car engine. And if that was the source, then he instantly understood that it had to be close.

Another change.

He almost didn't bother getting up, assuming they were simply ferrying in supplies. At the rate he was getting through the alcohol in this place, it wasn't unexpected.

But in the end, he did, his curiosity piqued. The sound of the engine built until it was sufficiently loud to confirm that the source could only be a motor vehicle of some sort – and that it was close.

Carreon followed it across the terrace to a small section of wall that overlooked the courtyard at the entrance to the villa where the road up the mountain ended. He waited there in the night's semi-darkness. It took another minute or so for the car to reach the villa's open gate.

It was traveling without lights, he noted immediately, as the tires navigated the gravel driveway with a low, grating crunch. Just one vehicle. But that illuminated little. It was unlikely to be a delivery vehicle, or a changing of the guard, for surely both would require greater strength in numbers.

Then – what?

The driver's door opened, and a dark silhouette exited. It was undoubtedly male. The shape walked to the back of the car and lingered for a couple of seconds before popping the trunk.

Carreon started to lose interest. He was almost turning away when a low, terrified moan echoed from down below as the silhouette leaned forward and disappeared behind the back of the vehicle.

He froze.

Deciding that it probably was not a good idea to be caught watching this – whatever *this* was – Fernando Carreon backed away. His heel brushed against a loose stone, which skittered behind him against the terrace. Down below, boots scraped on gravel, and without looking down to confirm whether that signified anything untoward, Carreon fled back to his lounge chair.

It took a few minutes after that, his heart still racing, before things became even fractionally clearer. The trunk thunked shut. Another low moan quivered on the night's still, humid air. A man's boots scraped on gravel dragging something, or someone, behind him. Then quiet thuds echoed from within the building. Footsteps that grew closer, and closer, until…

A guard emerged through the doors.

Like the others, he was dressed in khakis and a charcoal polo shirt. The balaclava, Carreon now understood, came standard. He wondered whether the uniformity of their outfits was intentional, to deprive him of anything familiar to hold on to, but the voice of this one at least sounded like the man who'd spoken to him earlier. The girl cowered behind him, not bound, but her hair drooping down the front and sides of her face.

"Brought you some company."

He pushed the woman forward, and though the momentum imputed was gentle enough, she toppled forward and landed heavily on the floor, breaking her fall only at the very last moment. The guard glanced down but appeared to lose interest once he determined that she wasn't badly hurt and returned to the villa.

The girl stayed where she was for several long seconds, and

the sound of her quiet weeping started to grate on Carreon's nerves. And so he spoke with a little more abruptness than he'd intended. "Who the hell are you?"

She looked up. Even in the darkness, her puffy eyes and the well-worn streaks of salt down her cheeks were well apparent. But even so, Fernando Carreon instantly recognized one thing. Whoever she was, his visitor was indecently attractive.

22

"You're sure?"

Kelly shrugged. "I saw what I saw. It was the same guy from the facial match."

Trapp let out a short burst of laughter. "You heard her, Nick. You wanna bet she's wrong?"

Pope shook his head and let out a long, slow breath. "Not really. But damn, who the hell is this guy? The balls on him, you know what I mean?"

He fell silent, and all four of their little group considered what he'd just said. Kelly had gotten lucky. After she and Trapp had bugged the Conway residence, they'd departed in the same truck in which they'd arrived. But shortly after, she'd returned on foot, white wireless headphones in her ears and her hair pulled back into a taut ponytail to allow her to blend in with the street's many yoga moms. She was only supposed to be checking the recording devices inside the house were transmitting correctly.

But she'd seen a whole lot more than that. Whoever Leo Conway's mysterious handler was, he had only contacted him when he arrived back home. Did the handler know that

Conway was being tailed that morning? It was unknowable, but it was the only thing that made sense.

"So what do we do?" Eliza asked, floating the question everyone was thinking.

"Let's start with what we know," Pope announced. "We know that Leo Conway is in way over his head. He's a problem gambler, and as far as we are aware, his wife has no idea. And we know that both before and after the attack, he's been passing information to a highly-skilled individual we suspect to be his handler. We don't know what data he's passed along, or to whom."

"Maybe he's having an affair," Trapp posited, not because he believed the proposition, but because he knew from long experience that it was better to test every hypothesis, no matter how far-fetched. "That would account for the cloak and dagger shit. DC's a liberal town, but he's got a wife and kids. We could be misreading this whole thing."

"It wasn't like that," Kelly immediately interjected. "The conversation was too...intense. Conway was scared."

"And you don't hang out outside the Hoover building like a lovesick teenager either," Eliza added. "Like you're waiting for someone to come out and arrest you. But Leo did. He feels guilty about something."

"Not guilty enough to turn himself in," Trapp remarked.

"That's nothing unusual," Pope said. "Most crooks aren't sociopaths. They feel remorse and shame just like everybody else. It's just not powerful enough to overcome their desire to save their own skins. Or live out their days in comfort. Especially guys like Conway. He's an Ivy League lobbyist type. Had his whole life mapped out from the day he was born. Fancy suits, nice cars, the right kind of parties. Going to prison doesn't fit with that mental model. He might feel real bad about what he's done. But he'll rationalize it in the end. And I'm guessing that since he didn't turn himself in this morning, he already has."

The room fell silent. "Then what?" Eliza said.

Another pause.

"He made his bed," Kelly intoned coldly. "He had a chance to turn himself in, and he clearly didn't take it. He's trying to save his own skin, fine. Let's make it happen on our terms."

Trapp raised an eyebrow at the unprepossessing yet entirely self-assured young FBI agent. She was quite impressive. He suspected she would go far.

"What do you suggest?" Pope asked.

"Conway will be a dead-end. He's a desperate man looking to line his own pockets, not a mastermind. His handler is our only link to the people who attacked the DOJ press conference. So let's squeeze Leo. Bring him in and give him a simple choice: his freedom for his handler's."

"We don't have enough for a warrant. And most of what we do have is circumstantial," Pope warned. "If he's smart, he'll know that. And we'll only blow our cover. Right now, that's all we've got going for us."

"Maybe there's a middle ground," Trapp murmured, his brow furrowed as he turned the problem over in his head. "A way to get him to come to us, rather than the other way around."

"Go on..."

"Kelly's right. We need to squeeze this guy, get him feeling the heat. But not to bring him in. We want him to run right to his handler to spill his guts. And when he does, we'll be watching."

"And then what?" Pope wondered aloud. "We follow the handler? Conway's no expert, but this guy definitely is. He'll notice a tail if it's only four of us, and the op will be just as blown. So how's your idea any different?"

"Well—" Trapp grinned. "What if we could put a tail on him without ever getting close?"

"What are you getting at? Hook into the camera network? We don't have the manpower for that. And he'll know better than to show his face. I'm surprised he screwed up once. It won't happen again, not now he knows he's being watched. It's a dead-end."

"That's part of it." Trapp nodded. "But back when I went through the Farm, years ago, I remember one of my instructors mentioning this trick the Soviets used to use, back in the Cold War days. Usually if they were tailing someone, they wanted them to know it. Not real subtle, the KGB. But not always. When they were trying to be coy about things, they'd dust a target's shoes with low-grade radioactive dust. It's invisible, bug detectors won't pick it up, and there's no physical tail to detect. But we would know everywhere this guy went, and everyone he saw."

"So what?" Pope asked, wrinkling his nose in a way that didn't indicate he was particularly impressed. "You want us to run around downtown DC with Geiger counters? That doesn't seem real subtle either."

"No need." Trapp smiled, evidently self-satisfied. "DARPA already did the hard work for us. There's a Geiger counter on every street corner in the District, remember? Part of the SIGMA program. They've been working on it ever since 9/11, and I guess a couple years ago they decided it was ready for prime time. Rolled it out to DC and the tri-state area first. So we're in luck."

Pope opened his mouth, looking like he wanted to object, then closed it. Then opened it again and went through the process several more times before finally settling on a response. "It won't work."

"Why not?"

"If it did, wouldn't someone have thought about it already?"

"This is the federal government, Nick," Trapp chuckled ruefully. "We don't get paid for good ideas. Look, I'm not saying this is going to lead us right to the guy's front door. But if we can squirt him with some nuke juice, we'll be able to narrow down our search grid to a couple blocks, maybe less. If he's got other sources, we'll find them. And he won't have a damn clue."

"It's an idea, I guess..." Pope finally muttered, though judging by the expression on his face, his doubts were at least beginning to fade away.

"Thanks accepted," Trapp said. "The radiation source won't need to be strong. I'm not real keen on glowing green, either. Just enough to trigger the sensors."

"How do we paint him?"

"That's where Leo comes in. We need to arrange a meeting on our terms. I'll leave that up to you."

23

Hector Alvarez León's forearms ached with exhaustion as he guided his sedan back home. He hadn't slept in thirty-six hours and hadn't showered in at least twelve more. He was wearing a fresh uniform shirt in Marine blue, sleeves rolled up to just below his elbows. The faint outline of a bloodstain still lingered on his knuckles.

His face, still youthful, looked significantly less so that afternoon. A day's thick black stubble decorated his chin and jaw line, though as usual entirely avoided the middle of his cheeks – a family trait.

He turned left on to his home street in a leafy suburb of Toluca, tired eyes still darting back and forth across the scene in front of him, as always searching for anything that looked out of place. Mostly, his neighbors' cars were parked in their driveways, but a few families owned more than one vehicle, and those were pulled up neatly by the curb.

He recognized each, cross-referencing their registrations with the list stored in his mind. All except one.

The vehicle in question was parked several houses down from his own. It was a nondescript white Ford sedan, recently washed, though already kissed by a thin layer of the yellow dust that was endemic to the region. The license plates began with the letters MEX, indicating that they had been issued by the State of Mexico—the region, not the country.

Had one of his neighbors purchased a new vehicle? It wasn't impossible. He lived in an area that was comfortably middle-class, and the car didn't look particularly expensive.

The license plate on his own vehicle began with the same three letters, as did pretty much every car on this street. The region wasn't known for significant cartel activity, though the previous day's events had demonstrated that wasn't nearly the whole story. And besides, even if a hired gun *was* here to kill him, they would hardly drive their own car.

Hector frowned. His paranoia wasn't worth the energy it drained from him. He indicated into his own driveway, and after glancing in the mirror to check that he was in no danger of colliding with any of the local youths who often played soccer in the street, he made his turn.

As he did so, in his peripheral vision he spotted a man seated in the driver's seat of the parked Ford. The revelation instantly put him on alert. His thoughts, dulled by lack of rest, entered a paranoiac spiral which only steepened as adrenaline spiked in his system.

María and Gabby, he thought. *Are they home?*

At this time of day, they would be. María would have just returned from the school run. His daughter would be inside, probably inhaling a snack as she did every day. The thought of his beautiful girl suffering because of him stiffened Hector's resolve and snapped him out of his panic.

He killed the engine of his sedan and casually leaned forward, pulling open the car's glove compartment. Inside was a pistol, along with two magazines. The weapon was unloaded – a concession to María, in case their child somehow came across it – but that was easily remedied. As was the safety.

Hector repositioned the rearview mirror using the tiny joystick in the center console. An electronic motor hummed for a few seconds as he manipulated the angle. The slight movement was essentially invisible from outside the vehicle, and as the sound from the motor decreased the image settled on the parked Ford now illuminated by the late afternoon sun.

A thump from outside confirmed what his eyes had already told him. The car's driver door, which just a few seconds ago was wide open, had just swung shut. The man previously sitting inside the vehicle was now walking toward his car.

Hector knew he had to move fast. If this guy was after him, he had no choice but to fire first. Any other course of action endangered his family.

In one smooth motion, he pulled his door open, stepped onto solid ground with his left foot, and twisted his torso, all as he brought his weapon up in a solid two-handed grip. His frame was at least partially shielded behind the chassis of his sedan, and his right elbow came to rest on its roof as he barked a command.

"Down!"

The man in the middle of the street looked strangely familiar, though with adrenaline running through his veins and the angle of the sun partly obscuring his vision, Hector couldn't be sure. Besides, familiarity meant nothing. Perhaps he'd even arrested this criminal before.

The oncoming shape stopped, hands rising above his head with a deliberate lack of haste as he descended to his knees. "Hey buddy, chill!"

"Face down on the asphalt, or I shoot," Hector growled in Spanish.

He frowned. Why the hell was that relevant? Something the guy had said?

Or how he said it.

"I'm DEA. Name's Raymond Burke."

"Stay down," Hector called out, switching to English. His brain seemed to be operating on half-speed, hearing what the man was saying but completely unable to actually process his meaning.

"That's what I tend to do when a guy pulls a gun on me," Agent Burke grumbled from the asphalt, his voice an octave higher with tense, wry humor. "My badge is in my back left pocket. I'm unarmed. I just want to talk."

Hector said nothing, but stepped fully out of the vehicle and walked slowly toward his captive. Although he was as physically exhausted as he was mentally, the barrel of his weapon stayed entirely level as he closed on the figure still prone on the street in front of him. As he got within a couple of feet, he issued another command. "Palms down flat, legs apart."

Agent Burke complied without attempting another witty rejoinder.

"Stay nice and still," Hector said, crouching down and retrieving the DEA agent's ID from his back pocket with a pickpocket's two-fingered grip. He took several steps back before looking at it and didn't take his eyes off the man on the ground before there was plenty of distance between them.

Only then did he open the leather case, which felt lighter than they looked in the movies. And cheaper. The badge looked legit, although he hadn't worked much with American federales in the past. The identification photo on the top right of the credential section, though, showed the man he knew as Raymond Burke. A little younger, a little paler in the flare of the flash, but undeniably him.

"What are you doing at my home?" Hector grunted without apology, dropping the weapon to his side and the ID to the ground. His arm felt heavy, and he cast an anxious glance over his shoulder to see whether María was watching. She wasn't, but he stuffed the weapon into his waistband anyway.

"Can I get up?" Burke asked.

"Yes."

The DEA agent did exactly that, pushing himself up onto his hands and knees first before resuming a vertical stance with a quiet groan. He rolled his eyes at Hector. "Not as young as I used to be..."

"How did you find me?" Hector demanded, no more amiable than he had been when holding the gun.

"I'll take that as an apology." Burke grinned without any evident display of offense on his affable face. "I asked around. Turns out the guys at the embassy know quite a lot."

Hector felt somewhat lightheaded as the adrenaline drained from his system, and he felt an unaccountable urge to take a swing at Burke. He gritted his teeth at the smiling American, and his intentions must have been written on his face.

"Look," Burke said, taking a half step back at the same time as he extended his hand in greeting. "I think we got off on the wrong foot. I just figured it might be worth catching up, that's all. After what happened yesterday in both our countries."

"By showing up at my house unannounced?" Hector replied curtly. "I could have shot you."

"Yeah." Burke grinned, ruefully shaking his head. He glanced down and started dusting off his front. "I see that now. You don't look like you've slept."

It wasn't phrased as a question, but Hector shook his head anyway, starting to regret the way he had treated his visitor. Not particularly the drawing his weapon part, just everything that came after. "Not much, no."

"You should try it," the American observed, ostentatiously eyeing Hector from head to toe. "I find it does me a world of good. So – how about that chat?"

Hector grimaced, still strangely reticent to give this man what he had come for. But he recognized that his reaction was mostly a chemical one, driven by some ancient evolutionary pathway. He bowed his head, sighed deeply, and gestured toward his house. "Outside. My wife is in there."

"I get that," Burke replied. "And no hard feelings, okay?"

He nodded, leading the American to the front step before muttering, "I'll be right out."

Hector unlocked his front door and slipped inside. He could hear his daughter's burbling laughter coming from upstairs, accompanied by the sound of splashing. She was in the bath, and María was singing her a lullaby.

Thank God she didn't see, he thought, briefly closing his eyes and resting his forehead on a cool interior wall. He only allowed himself a couple of seconds of self-pity before levering himself off and walking to the refrigerator. He pulled out two screwtop beers, dumped the caps, and walked back outside, offering one to his guest.

Burke nodded his thanks. "Only one. I gotta drive. But you look like you could use a beer."

Hector was halfway finished with his own by the time Burke lifted the bottle to his lips. He grunted with wry acknowledgment. After a few seconds of silence, he asked, "So why are you here, Agent Burke?"

"Looks like your neighbor saw the show," Burke remarked, gesturing at a man anxiously peering out of the window from across the street.

"I'll apologize later," Hector said, thrusting out his fist and shooting a tired thumbs-up.

"Sorry to make a rod for you."

"A rod?" Hector squinted.

"For your back. Causing you all this trouble," Burke added. "I assure you, it wasn't my intention."

"Oh, that... Not your fault. I was – how do you say it in English?"

Burke grinned. "Tense? On a hair trigger? Real fucking angry?"

"All three."

"I'm not surprised," Burke murmured, eyes scanning the street appraisingly. "Is this area safe? For your family, I mean."

Hector let out a bitter laugh. "Is anywhere? I'm sorry. I'm tired, and I shouldn't be unloading on you. I don't even know you. This place is as safe as any. A few officers from my unit live around here. It's only fifteen minutes from work, and the policia patrol frequently."

Burke raised his eyebrows at that, though he said nothing. Hector heard him anyway. *And is that safe?*

What a thing it was to live in a place where a man from another country's police judged your own. What a humiliation. And yet it was true, wasn't it?

Apparently the flood of emotion, of anger and shame showed on Hector's face, for the American agent gestured an apology, raising the palm of one hand and the bottle with the other. "I didn't mean that."

"You did. And it's not your fault. Very few of my countrymen can resist a bribe, not when the alternative is a bullet in the back of their head, or a car bomb taking out their children on the way to school. It doesn't matter if they are police or military or government. The cartels get to everyone in the end."

"But not you, Captain León," Burke grunted. "I've heard about you. The way your men follow you. You're no turncoat. You're a patriot."

"Maybe." Hector shrugged, draining his bottle of beer. "Why are you here, Agent Raymond Burke?"

The DEA agent paused before he answered, as a thoughtful look kindled first at the creased corners of his eyes. "Because it is my fault."

Hector squinted, somewhat confused.

"Not mine exactly, but my country's. Your people take bribes because mine take drugs. Without us, there is no market, and there is no cartel. No bribes, no violence, no death."

The Mexican said nothing. It was all true. His confirmation wouldn't change that.

Burke changed tack. "They killed my boss, did you hear? His name was Mark. I met him once. Real nice guy."

"You get used to it," Hector replied with a bitter laugh.

"I hope not. What about yours? What do you think of him?"

"Who—the colonel?"

"Your boss."

"Oh, Vicealmirante Abalos," Hector said, unable to conceal the sneer of disdain that crept onto his face at the mention of the man's name. "Is this between just us?"

"You have my word."

"Look around, Agent Burke, and tell me – do you see any ocean?"

The American, looking confused, confirmed that he did not.

"No. Toluca is a funny place to harbor an admiral, isn't it? The kind of place you might stow an officer who doesn't know very much about sailing. The problem is, he knows even less about soldiering."

"No arguments there," Burke murmured before falling silent for a few moments. "What do you know about him – Abalos?"

Something in the agent's tone raised Hector's suspicions, though Burke was staring studiously ahead. "He's new. Why?"

"This is off the record, correct?" Burke said, echoing Hector's own earlier caution. He continued after receiving a confirmatory nod. "His name came up a few months ago in an intercepted phone call. We were unable to determine who the remaining participants were. But the message was clear enough – the admiral has been on someone's payroll for quite some time."

Hector knocked his now empty beer bottle onto its side, after which it began to roll sonorously away. "Carreon," he spat.

"Perhaps."

"Why are you telling me this?" Hector asked. "Why not take it to someone more senior?"

Burke stood, prompting him to do the same. The American extended his hand and said, "Because I think I can trust you. I want to know who killed the administrator. And I suspect that this entire sequence of events, from Engel's murder to the abduction of Jennifer Reyes, and Carreon's prison break—is all connected. I just don't know how. But I intend to find out, and I think we might be useful to each other. Don't you agree?"

Hector glanced down at the agent's extended hand and considered the offer for a little time before responding. His instincts screamed a competing, argumentative chorus: that to protect his family he would be wise to run as far and fast away from this as his legs would carry him. And as it always did, a countervailing argument whispered back that safety was only illusory so long as his country was ruled from the shadows by men like Fernando Carreon, Ramon Reyes, and turncoats like Abalos.

He nodded curtly.

The two men shook hands.

24

The girl was awake. The one his guards had brought two nights earlier. Her eyes were puffy from tears, and she looked as though she hadn't slept in days, though he hadn't seen her leave her room until now.

Carreon crossed his arms and without hiding his interest examined her figure. "At last, you emerge."

"I'm hungry," she said simply.

"It's been two days," Carreon replied. "I'm not surprised."

He took a step forward, and the girl flinched. "Who are you?"

Carreon grinned. "You don't know?"

"You look familiar." She paused, biting her lip before continuing in a softer, more childish voice, "Why did you bring me here?"

"Why –?" Carreon said, surprised for the first time. He shook his head. "You misunderstand. I had nothing to do with your arrival."

"Then who did?" the girl exclaimed, her voice rising.

"That, my dear, is a very good question."

"Who are you?" she asked, voice harsh and accusatory now,

though without the confidence that came only from years of experience with wealth and power. "Stop playing games."

He considered his answer for a few seconds. Better to learn her name first, he decided. His own carried with it a somewhat checkered baggage. And he didn't want to scare her off. Not yet, at least. She was... intriguing. Or at least, her presence was. She was a captive too.

Which begged the question: Could she be useful?

"Why don't you go first?"

She glowered at him, fists curling into white-knuckled bunches like a little child.

"I'm sorry." Carreon smiled. "Another game."

Still, he did not make the first move, wary of scaring her off. He fell silent, but held her gaze without blinking, knowing that the human brain abhors such a vacuum.

"I'm Jennifer," she said, keeping her cards close to her chest. "Now you."

Carreon inclined his head, appreciating the subtle intelligence of her answer. So she did know how the game was played, after all. Perhaps not so ingenuous as she seemed. Curiouser and curiouser. "Nice to meet you, Jennifer."

He paused for a few seconds to test her resolve, but soon saw that she would not break so easily a second time. He stretched out his hand. "Fernando."

Jennifer's eyes flared in recognition. She took an involuntary step back, eyes flaring white. "You..."

"Have we met?"

"I know you. I've seen pictures of you. What do you *want* with me?"

"I want nothing from you," Carreon said smoothly. And then, remembering, he cocked his head and whispered, "Jennifer..."

The two fell silent, Jennifer Reyes backing away from him warily, prey unwilling to tempt the hunter into action, knowing that her efforts were fruitless all the same. Carreon decided to choose a different path. There was no sense knocking the girl further off balance. She would doubtless be useful.

"You said you were hungry," Carreon said in an airy tone of voice. "Come, let's eat."

He noticed that Jennifer's fists were still compressed into hard little gemstones. He walked alongside her, rather than toward, demonstrating an empathy for which he was not well known. Then again, it wasn't so much empathy as a tactic, one honed through personal experience of the difficulty of catching flies with vinegar.

Still she held back. He allayed her fears, at least of him. "Jennifer, you know who I am. And I suspect now I know who you are also. But you must know that you are not my captive. We are both prisoners in this place."

She didn't believe him. That much was evident. Neither did she move.

"Then I will eat," he said, walking inside. "You can join me if you wish."

Hunger and intrigue soon proved a more potent motivator than fear, and she joined him at the dining table – or at least near it. It was about eleven in the morning, and the customary breakfast feast had mostly been cleared away, leaving behind only a selection of fresh fruits and cakes.

Carreon selected an apple and a chocolate almond cake, not because he was hungry, but to allay the girl's anxiety. He took a seat and started eating. Jennifer remained a few feet away, though he noted that her hands had relaxed somewhat.

"What do you mean you're a prisoner?" she ventured after a long pause. Her tone was tinged with disbelief.

"Your husband is Ramon, correct?" Carreon said, glancing up from his plate.

Ramon Reyes was the most powerful cartel leader in Mexico other than Carreon himself. The two men were bitter rivals. And yet both he and his enemy's wife were, somehow, captives in this strange place.

But for what purpose?

"You know he is."

"Do you think that your husband *expected* people to take you?"

She flinched. "Don't talk about him like that."

"Answer the question."

"No. No, of course not. He –"

"– was taken by surprise. And so was I."

"But that's not possible," Jennifer exclaimed.

"And yet here we are..." Carreon shrugged.

"This is a trick. You, you..." She trailed away.

"There is no trick. No illusion. The same people who kidnapped you did the same to me. Look around. You've been here two days. Have you seen any visitors? You think I would rot here for so long just to hoodwink you?"

"I don't know, I –"

"You haven't left your room. I know that. But you have ears, don't you? And your room looks out onto the courtyard, and the only road in and out of this place. Or do I lie?"

Jennifer fell silent as she considered the question. Carreon studied her as her mind turned, studiously examining her expressions without appearing to do so. It was like leading an anxious oxen to a jungle watering hole. Pushing too hard would only undermine her trust in him. Better to let her take the first step. To build trust. What he would use that trust to achieve was as yet unclear. But he would find some value in it, he was sure of that.

She joined him at the table, nervously reaching for a plate and stacking it with food, which she proceeded to devour without modesty. It was a full ten minutes before she was done, during which time Carreon said nothing.

"I'm still hungry..."

"I'm surprised." Carreon grinned, gesturing at the half-emptied selection of delicacies on the table. "That's all they give us until morning."

Jennifer's eyes widened. "What?"

"I'm kidding... they'll bring lunch out soon."

"They," she repeated. "Who are *they*?"

"That," Carreon murmured, "is an excellent question. Why don't you ask them?"

Her forehead crinkled, and she looked around anxiously. "What are you talking about?"

"The walls have ears, Jennifer," Carreon said, gesturing around the room and leading her attention to the camera looking down on them. "They're listening anyway. Why not ask?"

Jennifer gulped and shook her head. Carreon nodded and stopped pushing. His message had been received. The girl now understood that she needed to watch what came out of her mouth, though it was precious little already.

"I wouldn't worry. I suspect we'll find out what they have planned soon enough. Though I doubt we'll like what they have to say..."

25

The administrator's office suite at the DEA's 700 Army-Navy Drive headquarters was cold and mostly empty when Leo Conway limped inside. Not in the physical sense, for office workers aimlessly wandered to and fro with nothing particular to do – the sun around which they orbited having so recently been extinguished – but in an emotional one. It seemed somehow grayer.

Conway stood in the entrance way, a satchel bag over his shoulder shielding his healing left arm. A cold lump of marble froze in his gut as he surveyed the scene. They were like him, but he was not like them. Not anymore. Not after what he had done.

"Leo," a familiar voice called out, high and tired and broken. "What are you doing here? You're supposed to be at home."

"Lisa..." Conway whispered, sighting Lisa Rushkoff for the first time. She'd been Engel's executive assistant for the past five years, going with him from job to job.

And now she was alone.

"You've been crying," he said for lack of anything else. And it was true. In her late forties, normally businesslike and efficient with a runner's frame, dark, heavy bags now clung to Lisa's eyes. She seemed somehow smaller, less alive, hunched with grief.

"You shouldn't be here," she said, and for a moment Leo was wracked with worry. Worry that she saw right through him. That she knew what he had done. And that everybody else did as well.

Pull yourself together, he told himself.

For now, at least, they would think he was grieving just like them. And he was, that much was true. But his was a tortured morass of emotion, for he was not solely a sufferer of grief but its cause. And that is a difficult position for any man to occupy.

Leo gulped.

"I had to get out of the house," he said, and that was also true. Mark Engel had been his friend. Their wives were close. And when his own wife now looked at him with genuine concern in her eyes, he saw only accusation in its place. Mark was dead, and it was his fault, and there was no changing that. There was only survival. And that was the real reason for his presence.

"I understand," Lisa said, nodding. But she didn't really. "I'm the same way. Of course it's different for you. You were there..."

"Maybe we can do lunch?" Leo offered weakly. "He'd like that, I think."

"Yeah," Lisa repeated. "Yes, I think he would. Oh, Mr. Engel..."

It was always Mr. Engel to her, wasn't it? Never Mark. A sign of respect, he supposed. Or just professional distance. Some people were like that, and maybe Lisa was one of them. Not anymore, though. All those barriers had been washed away.

"That's right. Lunch," he repeated and turned away, grateful for any excuse to escape this moment.

His own desk was mostly as he'd left it. A few papers had been moved, and he suspected the place had been photographed. Investigators were like that: they investigated things. It was in their DNA, he supposed. They left no stone unturned not because they had any particular desire to see what was on the other side, but because they were driven to do so.

Had they learned anything about him, he wondered, as he'd done every waking hour since waking from that living nightmare in Houston, spattered by his dead friend's blood? And if so, what did they know?

"Pull yourself together," he mumbled out loud through gritted teeth the second the door to his private office was closed. He banged his head against it, relishing the jolt of pain that surged through his skull.

He returned to his desk and set the satchel down next to it. A manila folder sat at the center of his desk. It wasn't one he recognized, but then he saw dozens like it every day. He had, at any rate. Though he suspected those days were long gone. He was a middling chief of staff who had once had the privilege of working for an excellent boss. But now Mark was dead, and he, Leo Conway, had the stink of death on him. It would be career kryptonite inside the Beltway. No one would hire him, not now.

And for what?

That was the shame of it. He'd valued Mark's life for the price of a bet on a three-year-old gelding at the Belmont Stakes – a horse that never stood a chance of winning anyway.

He opened the file, and his eyes instantly widened. All thoughts of Mark Engel fled. His handler would want to see this. Maybe it was even enough to buy his freedom.

～

"YOU THINK HE TOOK THE BAIT?" Trapp asked, watching on a grainy screen as Conway's car sped out of the underground parking lot and into traffic.

"Kinda looks like it, doesn't it?" Pope replied. "Kelly – we getting anything?"

Typically, the junior special agent's short-cut hair was impeccably turned out, though she'd had as little opportunity for personal care as any of the rest of them. It was difficult to see the precise details of what was on her screen, but it looked like a map of the DC area.

"The counter on the corner just buzzed. Not much more than a banana, though. I'm guessing he didn't read it the whole way through."

"Good," Pope mused.

Trapp remained silent. They had hoped for this outcome. The radioactive isotope was largely contained between several sheets of paper within the file that were slightly stuck together. The act of pulling them apart would release a thin sheen of dust – cesium 136. The dosage of radiation that would, if things went well, fall upon Conway's handler was equivalent to about a dozen x-rays. Just enough to tickle the DARPA radiation sensors, and no more.

Kelly's laptop was tied into a direct feed from the Metro police command center. The duty officers had been told that they were calibrating several of the sensors, and to ignore minor anomalies over the next few days. Their hesitation necessitated the lubrication of a call from the DARPA program manager, who in turn had required coaxing of her own.

A red icon superimposed onto a map of DC rendered on Kelly's screen showed where one of the radiation monitors had been triggered on the corner of Army Navy Drive and South Eads Street. Trapp watched for any further indication that the system was working, but still nothing.

"Where is he?" he asked.

"Cell phone has him…" Kelly murmured, switching tabs, "… on George Mason Memorial Bridge, crossing over the Potomac."

"Wonder where he's headed?"

Trapp's question prompted only a disinterested shrug from the young agent, and he quietly chided himself for vocalizing something quite so obvious. The truth was, he didn't really like counter-intelligence work. It was all shirt and no pants. Or was it the other way around? A whole lot of sitting around on your ass and waiting for something to happen. He didn't know how Pope did it.

He peered down at Kelly's laptop and watched as the blue dot that indicated Conway's sedan passed by the Thomas Jefferson Memorial, and then grinned, releasing an audible exhalation of breath.

Pope looked up. "What's so funny?"

Trapp pointed at the screen. "James Bond here just drove past the International Spy Museum."

"How about that."

Guess it was funnier in my head, Trapp mused.

He returned to his previous train of thought. He hadn't minded helping Nick out with his training program. Alternately catching and trying to avoid being caught by legions of hungry young counter-intelligence agents who'd just burst out of Quantico full of the Bureau's latest methods was good for his fieldcraft. And it was less dangerous than being shot at by the Russians or the Iranians. Not quite as fun, but a damn sight less hairy.

But deep down, he was getting itchy. Ikeda was right. All this sitting around on his ass stuff might be what got Nick going, but it was putting him to sleep. Blunting his edge. And what happened next, anyway? Once they identified Conway's handler, this would become even more fully an FBI matter. Up till now, his and Ikeda's presence could be easily explained away as inter-agency cooperation. But if Pope decided to bring the guy in, then the Agency's fingerprints couldn't be anywhere nearby.

So what, then? How much more of this waiting?

"Go for a walk, Jason," Pope said a couple of minutes later as Conway's car turned on to 6th Street. "You're looking antsy. You'll be the first to know if he does anything interesting."

"That obvious, huh?" Trapp flushed.

"I guess I know you too well."

"Um, sir..." Kelly ventured.

Pope turned, all signs of levity disappearing in an instant. "What is it?"

"He just stopped, short of Pennsylvania Avenue."

"Traffic?"

"Maybe..." She didn't sound convinced. "Or he could be parking."

"Parking where?" Pope wondered. "How's our access to the street level cameras?"

"Bringing them up right away," she said, typing a command into her laptop. All three of them huddled around the small screen, the two men watching as her dexterous fingers manipulated the flow of information in a way that both knew was well beyond the skills of their generation.

When it appeared on screen, the feed was from a traffic cam mounted on top of the lights at the intersection where 6th crossed Pennsylvania. Since the camera was only designed to give the city warning of traffic foul-ups, the quality was grainy. All three squinted at the screen, searching for Conway's vehicle.

Trapp spotted it first. As Kelly had thought, their target was parking, and not doing a very good job at it, either.

They watched as finally, laboriously, Leo Conway brought his car to a stop and stepped out. He glanced left and right, then started walking.

"Wondering if he's being followed?" Pope murmured.

"Probably. Like I said, a real James Bond type..." Trapp replied dryly.

Conway followed the sidewalk around the hairpin bend onto Pennsylvania Avenue, heading back toward the Potomac. Kelly was forced to switch camera feeds mid-stream, and they lost visual for about thirty seconds as she searched for one that might work inside the horror of an interface that looked like it was designed back in the eighties.

When the new feed appeared on the laptop screen, Conway was gone.

"Shit," Pope murmured. "Where is he?"

Three sets of eyes switched to the map. The cell phone signal was still strong and hovering inside building 611.

"What's that?" Trapp asked, gesturing at the screen.

Kelly, clearly of the same mind, queried the computer and came up with an answer no more than a couple of seconds later. "UPS store."

"Dead drop?" Trapp asked. "Could be a PO box. The handler and the mole both have keys. Not exactly the most sophisticated operation, but then we know Conway's no pro. He's a DEA suit, not a field operative. Nothing in his file suggests he has any tradecraft experience. And besides – he's DEA, not CIA or FBI. Who would bother surveilling him in the first place? I'm guessing this is it."

"Either that or he's mailing it somewhere." Pope shrugged. "Either way, it's a lead. And a damn sight more than we had a few moments ago."

26

An enormous flag of the Mexican Republic rippled in a crackling late-afternoon breeze in the center parade ground of the 22nd Military Zone, the lines running up the naval gray flagpole fizzing in the wind. Captain Hector León, now attired in a dark blue dress uniform, beret tucked into his shoulder straps, let his head sink to his chest and sucked in one last, greedy breath before entering the headquarters building.

Outside it was painted a palm tree green, faded and weathered by the sun. Inside was similar, except for medical linoleum, and equally worn. The place had the feel of a 1960s high school that had never found the budget for a renovation. The setting fit León's mood.

He found his way to the admiral's office suite for the third time in as many days and steeled himself for much the same conversation to take place as each time before. Conversation was not the right word for it, he thought. Chewing out was better. Rant fit. And all three times, he was on the receiving end of Abalos' anger.

The man's shrewish secretary gestured him inside without a word. He didn't know her name and only recognized her by sight. Her nose was permanently upturned, as though a speck of feces sat just beneath the nostrils. It was clear she didn't like him. Or maybe she was just like that with everyone.

Either way, he didn't bother to learn her name.

"Captain, sit," Vicealmirante Abalos grunted in a curiously hoarse, guttural voice.

Abalos' office was entirely unlike the functional nature of the rest of the military base and was mahogany-paneled and designed to impress. It had that curiously library-like ability to absorb and deaden sound and reminded Hector more of a temple than an office.

"Yes, sir," he said, his words fading away among the heavy padded leather furniture that dominated the remainder of the room and its thick, expensive carpets.

He understood the effect on him that the industrial design was intended to achieve – a sensation that he was small, meaningless, insignificant in comparison to the grand matters of state that occurred in this place. And although consciously he knew that it was all a façade, it was hard to ignore the results. After all, Vicealmirante Abalos had the power to crush his career on a whim.

Worse, that was precisely what the man was attempting to do.

"Are you a traitor, Captain?" Abalos started, not pulling any punches.

Hector blanched, his eyes opening wide the moment he processed the unfounded accusation. At the last meeting, the admiral had ranted for hours, leaving his polished hardwood desk flecked with spittle and loose papers messily swept aside scattered all over the floor. But then the accusations had pertained to his decisions in the heat of combat and a supposed ineptitude.

This was different. And more dangerous.

"What –?" León spluttered before quickly composing himself. He was on unsteady ground, and he knew it. One slip could be the end of him. "Sir, of course not. I am a Marine. We were up against an overwhelming force, under fire from the air and ground. With reinforcements, perhaps we could have prevented the escape. As it is, we did the best we could."

"Are you blaming me for that, Captain?" Abalos asked through thin lips, his voice husky with distaste.

"Sir, you must know that the operation never had a chance of –"

"I know no such thing, Captain. All I know is that you let Fernando Carreon slip through your fingers. And that leads me to wonder: why? Why would a loyal servant of the Mexican Republic do such a thing? Or are you not loyal after all, Captain León?"

"Admiral!" Hector shouted, standing up and pushing his chair back away from him. "You know that is not true. I am a loyal –"

The intercom on Abalos' desk chimed, a strangely melodic sound amidst the tension of the moment, and the man held up one finger to stifle León, who fell silent, taken by surprise even as he was bristling with anger.

"I have received evidence, Captain, that you have taken money from the Federación in exchange for permitting the escape of a wanted man."

"Who?" León choked through a rapidly closing throat, though he suspected he already knew what Abalos was going to say. His superior had his nuts in a vise, and he was beginning to apply pressure. It didn't matter that the man was the real crook; he would railroad him regardless. That was the cold logic of power. Abalos had it, and León did not.

Abalos smiled. "Fernando Carreon."

"But you know that isn't true," León protested. "Sir, you know who I am."

"I know who you have pretended to be, Captain," Abalos replied harshly. "I am ashamed to admit that you duped me and so many others."

León's cell phone chose that moment to warble a ring tone from inside his dress jacket. In particular, a nursery rhyme that had been chosen by his daughter. The incongruity of the sound in a moment of extreme tension, and in this environment, almost caused him to burst out laughing. Catching sight of the expression on the admiral's face, he steeled his own.

"Am I keeping you, Captain León?"

"I'm sorry, sir. It's a personal call. Perhaps my wife. I'll get rid of her."

Hector reached into his pocket, his fingers trembling from the adrenaline of the moment. He knew that his entire career was on the line – and perhaps even his freedom. Abalos' accusations were laughable and clearly intended to save his own skin – but that didn't mean they wouldn't be enough to bury him. It would be his word as a junior officer against that of a man with flag rank. It was a battle he couldn't win.

He turned the device in his hand to reveal the screen, expecting to see his wife's name. Instead, it read: *Burke, DEA.*

León froze. The American narcotics agent's warning echoed once again in his mind. The DEA believed Abalos to be in the pay of the cartels.

What should I do?

Recognizing the call for the lifeline it was, he made the only decision he could. "Sir, it's my contact at the DEA. I apologize, but I have to answer it."

Before Abalos had a chance to protest, León tapped the screen to accept the call and said, "Agent Burke, how can I help you? I'm sitting with Vicealmirante Abalos."

The admiral, for his part, dropped his fists to his desk with a meaty thud and leaned back in his executive chair. The mechanism creaked, drawing León's attention. His superior officer was glowering with frustration.

"Are you on speaker?" Burke asked without skipping a beat, his voice evenly measured.

"Not yet," León replied.

"I'll be quick. Hector, you and your family are in danger. I have reason to believe that your name and address have been leaked to Federación sicarios. I'm heading to your place now."

For a second time in as many minutes, Hector Alvarez León froze. He fancied that he could feel the muscle fibers in his heart grinding against each other instead of sliding easily past. For a moment, he found it entirely impossible to breathe.

He choked out a single word. "What?"

Opposite, Abalos was motioning at him to either end the call or place it on speaker. It wasn't precisely clear which he preferred. Hector stared dumbly at the man, and it was no act.

"Do you have anyone you trust? Anyone who will help you, no questions asked?"

"Some," León whispered, his brain finally catching up with the gravity of the situation. His heart released, thudding wildly in his chest, and blood started rushing into his limbs.

"I suggest you get them moving. I'll be there in under an hour. I was meeting a contact in Mexico City, or I'd be there sooner. I'm sorry."

"I'm going now," León said, taking an involuntary step back.

"Going where, Captain?" Abalos growled. "I insist you put the phone down. Now."

"Hector – this is urgent. The man who leaked your name. It's Abalos. I have proof. I'm sending it now."

León killed the phone call. His arm dropped numbly to his side. A thousand possibilities flashed through his mind, all involving the same nightmare that haunted him night and day, of failing to protect his wife and daughter.

"What did he want?" Abalos rasped hoarsely. "Who gave you leave to interact with the DEA?"

In León's numb fingers, his phone buzzed. He glanced at the screen and saw Burke's name flash up a second time, along with the icon that indicated he'd been sent an audio file.

For a second time, he asked himself desperately what course of action lay open to him. He was beset on all sides, fixed in the jaws of his decision by unknowns and hidden dangers. And the most dangerous of them all was the man still seated opposite him: Abalos.

Again, León acted on instinct, suspecting what he had without knowing for sure. He raised his arm, half offering up his phone while carefully keeping it out of the man's reach and said blandly, "He sent me this."

He tapped play on the audio file and brought it even closer to his body, just in case, under the guise of pretending to adjust the volume.

"Is that you?" asked a female voice, one that León was sure he recognized, without knowing whose it was.

Abalos frowned, his thick eyebrows joining a spiderweb of wrinkles on his lined forehead. It was as though his brain had recognized what this was before his ears were done telling him.

"It is," a hoarse voice replied.

This time León recognized it without even a scintilla of doubt. It was Abalos' own.

The woman's voice spoke again, and again León strained to identify her. "Our... mutual friends have been in contact with me. They say the situation is delicate. They want to shift the focus."

The vicealmirante rocked forward in his seat, the color draining from his face. He opened his mouth as if to speak, but before he could, his own disembodied voice echoed forth from León's phone.

"I have what you want," the recording of Abalos said. "A captain. The boy who failed to prevent Carreon escaping. I'm sending you his details now. I trust that will work?"

"Admirably, Admiral," the woman trilled. "He will need to be dealt with, of course. I don't like the idea of leaving loose strands for someone to pull."

"I'm sure our friends will be happy to oblige," the voice of Abalos said, followed by a short, humorless laugh. "You're the golden goose."

The recording ended, and for a long, hard moment there was only silence in the room.

"Where did you get that?" Abalos said, his customary growl momentarily truncated by a quiver of emotion that sounded perilously close to fear.

"I told you, sir. I was sent it. By the DEA."

Those three letters carried with them an almost religious power in León's mind, as though he were holding out some sacred artifact to ward off the dangers of the night. He recognized that he was still in deep peril, for there was nothing that Agent Burke, let alone his organization, could do for him inside the confines of a military base where Abalos' word was king.

But nevertheless, simply uttering them inarguably changed the dynamic in the room. They shattered the hierarchy, and the two men in that moment, on that topic, were equal.

"I think this meeting is over," León said, dispensing with the ordinary customs of rank and respect, for in his eyes this man deserved neither.

"Stay!" Abalos bellowed.

Strangely, though he was far from out of danger, León was somehow reassured by the man's overt display of anger. It indicated a level of fear.

"You know I can't do that," León said matter-of-factly, as

though the issue was already settled. "My family is in danger. I must be with them."

"I'll have you arrested!" Abalos said, lumbering to his feet and jabbing an accusatory finger. "You've taken bribes. Sold out your own men!"

By now, his voice was uneven and high-pitched, like that of a pubescent boy. Conversely, as he stood, his age and bulk caught up with him, and he was forced to grip his desk for support.

"We both know I've done nothing of the sort. You're projecting, vicealmirante. And you sold out my family. I will tell you now, if anything happens to my wife and child, I will hold you responsible. And nothing will stop me from repaying the favor. No matter who your friends are. No matter where you hide."

León shoved the phone into his pants pocket and began walking from the room without looking back.

"Captain León!" Abalos yelled again, his voice this time a choked moan. "You will –"

Hector paused with his fingers on the cool brass of the door handle.

"I'm leaving, Abalos," he said, intentionally disregarding the man's rank to illustrate to him exactly where he stood. "If you try and stop me, Burke will release the tape. I suspect you don't want that. Good day."

The second part, of course, was a lie. If he was arrested, or worse, Burke might very well release the tape, but there was no way to be sure. Perhaps it was even unlikely, given the explosive nature of the contents.

But, of course, there was no way that Abalos could know that.

And that was what León was counting on.

He didn't acknowledge the thin-lipped secretary as he strode out of her master's office, slamming the door behind him. She squawked a shrill complaint, but he didn't acknowledge that either.

His pace subconsciously quickened until by the time he was back on the parade ground he was running for his car, holding his phone in front of his eyes as he narrowly navigated around obstacles in his path, texting everyone he could think of, anyone he trusted, with one simple instruction.

Help.

27

The safe house was in a small neighborhood of Culiacán called Los Olivos, a place that was neither working class nor home to any of the major beneficiaries of the city's most lucrative industry: narcotics.

The building itself had two stories above ground and one below and was painted a faded pink. It sat on Calle Castizas, among many just like it. Most were roofed with terracotta tiles and painted pink or white or yellow, facing out at each other through barred windows.

A careful observer might have spotted other evidence of security precautions, but the bars were the most obvious to an untrained eye. Culiacán wasn't quite in the top 20 most deadly cities in the world, but it only missed out by one spot, and only then because fully half the list was comprised of other cities in Mexico.

But as far as Ramon Reyes could make out, standing on the inside and staring out, there were no observers – careful or otherwise – to be found.

"Boss," ventured a lanky, hazel-eyed sicario named Miguel,

who was cradling an automatic rifle against his chest. "Is it wise to stand there? Someone could see you."

Reyes sucked his teeth with irritation, not at the mild suggestion, nor even the milder way it was delivered, but at the position in which he now found himself. His key lieutenants were being taken out one after another. In only a few days of fighting, his organization had lost a month's worth of product after an archipelago of safehouses, trucks, and mules were hit by this invisible enemy. That was on top of the mess north of the border. Operation Wishbone, as the feds were calling it, had wiped out half his American distribution operation.

Only the night before, another convoy had been taken in Texas. Carreon's doing, he presumed. They'd taken every precaution, and still they'd lost the shipment. Another month of this, and the Crusaders Cartel would be a footnote in history.

Hell, another couple of weeks will probably do it.

"Boss –?" Miguel said again, raising his voice a little with obvious hesitance.

"I heard you the first time," Reyes said, turning on his heel and retreating from the window. "Where is Emiliano?"

"Cleaning his tail, boss," came the reply.

"Is he being followed?"

The sicario shrugged. "He thinks not. But it is better to be safe than sorry."

The Crusaders chief grunted in agreement and resumed pacing the confines of the safe house. About a dozen of his men were stationed with him for security. Fighters he knew he could trust, for they had either been with him since the beginning or were related to those who had.

Any more bodies might raise suspicion, even in a city like this where the residents knew better than to ask questions. He had sicarios stationed in other houses in the neighborhood, living with their usual owners. Emiliano had arranged that, as he did most things.

All of his men had been trained by the best: both the Israelis and former British special forces, just as his rival Fernando Carreon had hired the Americans for the same purpose. They were good shots, experienced under fire—and most importantly, loyal to a fault. A trait for which they were extremely well remunerated. To what extent that loyalty relied on financial recompense was a matter for debate, and one that Reyes was disinclined to engage in. When it came to his personal security, he preferred to pay over the odds than run the risks of cheaping out.

Reyes found a faded, creased faux-leather couch in the safe house's plain living room and settled onto it. A silver pistol lay on a dented coffee table a few feet away, among a small forest of upturned, gleaming brass rounds and several small stacks of dollar bills and pesos. There was no television, only a faded square on the whitewashed wall indicating where one had once sat. In the corner lay several black duffel bags, which contained money, clothes, and several flavors of false documents and weapons, all ready to be grabbed at a moment's notice.

He closed his eyes, but the moment's respite lasted just that. A mild commotion erupted nearby, coming from the front door, causing his lids to snap open and his eyes to dart around the room in search of the source. Miguel appeared barely a second later, quietly clicking his weapon's safety switch off and sticking to his principal like glue. The bodyguard said nothing but placed a finger over his lips to indicate they should both remain quiet.

The momentary tension deflated as his chief lieutenant, Emiliano Mendoza stepped into the living room. He was wearing an oversized black denim jacket and matching jeans. Perfect for blending into the night. He opened the jacket and shrugged it off, revealing a flak jacket lying underneath a pair of shoulder holsters fastened to a harness.

"Milo," Reyes exclaimed with relief, lengthening the first

syllable in his friend's childhood nickname so that it rhymed with me. "You made it."

"The bastards have Carlos," Emiliano announced without ceremony. "Took him last night. His wife's been shot. She's in intensive care. Might pull through. Probably won't."

Reyes absorbed the information without obvious concern, though his mind was roiling. Carlos was his cousin, and though it was putting it mildly to say that they didn't often meet eye to eye, he was family. The indignity couldn't be allowed to stand unanswered.

And they have Jennifer.

"Sit, Milo." He gestured tiredly. "Any information on my wife's whereabouts?"

Emiliano shook his head and settled into an adjoining armchair, resting his dusty tan boots on the coffee table, rattling the brass on top. One of the rounds toppled over, then rolled to the edge, where it rocked from side to side and briefly threatened to plunge to the floor. "Still nothing. No ransom demand. No communication. I'm sorry."

Reyes grasped his knee and massaged the joint, digging the base of his thumb into the bone and pressing down until his eyes began to water. Carlos was one thing, but Jennifer? She wasn't fair game. Family was off limits. That had always been the case.

"Who is behind this?" he spat. "The Federación?"

Emiliano shrugged. His face was heavily lined with exhaustion, and he rolled his neck from left to right with evident pleasure, reaching to his side to adjust the position of a pistol that was clearly digging into his ribs before he spoke. "Makes sense, no?"

"But why?" Reyes wondered aloud, mostly to himself. "What do they have to gain? The peace was prosperous for us all."

And why now?

Emiliano didn't answer. He pursed his lips with the look of a man who wants to say something but fears the consequences.

"Spit it out, Milo," Reyes muttered, waving with irritation. "Whatever it is, it will only burn your throat if you keep swallowing it."

"Miguel," Emiliano grunted at the sicario, who was already attempting to make himself scarce. "Outside."

He waited until the bodyguard closed the door behind him, leaving the two of them alone, before he spoke again. "What does your wife know?"

"Jennifer?" Reyes squinted.

"Do you have another you haven't told me about?" Emiliano said sardonically.

"Careful, Milo," Reyes said, his face darkening.

His friend threw his hands up in apology. "I'm sorry. You know I didn't mean it like that. Just a long day, that's all."

"A long week," Reyes agreed, forgiveness granted immediately. "She knows nothing. Nothing important."

"This place?"

Reyes shook his head. "I promise you, she... prefers not to look too deeply into what it is we do and where the money comes from. Perhaps in the future, but not now. She has never visited this place. Nor does she know anything about our operations. Maybe a few names, but nothing they couldn't get from Carlos or from any of the other capos."

"Whoever *they* are," Emiliano murmured.

"We need to find out," Reyes said, his face suddenly animated. He leaned forward, resting his elbows on his thighs in an inelegant, hunched pose. "Another week of this and there won't be any capos left."

"I'm trying," Emiliano said earnestly. "They're like ghosts. They leave nothing behind. Just bodies and empty cartridges. I've even had those forensically analyzed. It's a dead-end. Same stuff the Army uses. Could be a hundred different dealers for it."

Reyes jumped to his feet. The fake leather covering audibly crackled as he rose from it, though he paid it no attention. He strode forward and plucked the pistol from the coffee table. He released the magazine, checked it was loaded, and slammed it back in. The weapon felt reassuringly heavy in his hand. It was a reminder of precisely how much damage man was capable of inflicting on other men.

Something Ramon Reyes was no stranger to. Hundreds of men and women had died at his direct command. Thousands more had become collateral damage in fights over territory, over status, or just because they were in the way. Countless others had lost their lives to the product he pushed with indiscriminate abandon across an entire continent.

"Then we raise the stakes," he spat through gritted teeth. "Start hitting back. I don't care who, I don't care where. We start fucking them like they are fucking us."

Out of his peripheral vision, Reyes saw his friend stiffen, then lean forward, the wrinkles on his face creasing ever deeper.

Emiliano said, "Ramon."

"They need to learn the consequences of going up against the Crusaders," Reyes said, slapping his thigh excitedly. "See what happens –"

"Ramon!"

Reyes clenched his fist with unbridled irritation. "What?"

"Shut the hell up, hombre," Emiliano said softly, head slightly cocked. His eyes were darting around the room, and he had the hungered look of a hunting dog first catching a scent.

Even with the arousal rising within him, Reyes knew better than to argue with his oldest friend. Emiliano had a nose for danger. It had saved both their lives on more than one occasion.

"You hear that?" his friend whispered, rising to his feet as his right hand searched for the butt of his pistol. He unclipped the holster but didn't yet draw the weapon.

Reyes shook his head. He heard nothing. Sensed nothing. Or did he?

A muffled crack echoed in the street outside. It might have been nothing more than a car driving over a drainage grate, or the closing of a metal gate. It might have been.

But judging by the look on Emiliano's face, it was not.

"Miguel!" his lieutenant hissed.

After a hesitation of no more than a second, the sicario entered the room, concern and confusion inked on his face in equal measure. The man spoke in an outside voice. "What is it?"

Emiliano gestured him to hush. "Cameras – where are they?"

Suddenly alert, Miguel glanced around the room, unconsciously half-raising his weapon to his shoulder. Emiliano shook the sicario with impatience, and the man got the message. Miguel led them deeper into the safe house, into a room hastily converted into a security center. It had once been a child's bedroom, complete with a hand-drawn chart in blue crayon corresponding to a boy's height year by year. The entries were uneven. March one year, May the next. The trend was undeniable. The line always went up.

Until it didn't.

On an office desk pushed against the wall were four flatscreen monitors. Each was split into quadrants that contained a distinct surveillance feed. Only fourteen of the squares were active. Two just displayed blank tiles. A sicario was sitting behind the desk, and he looked up as the three men entered the room. He blanched as he saw Reyes.

"Move," Emiliano grunted.

The pistol now felt even heavier in Reyes' palm than it had

a few moments before. What was it that Milo had said? That they were *ghosts*.

No, not ghosts. Men, Reyes thought scornfully. And yet did that make things any better? Whoever was coming after his organization, they were professional killers—and exceptional at their trade. His cousin was gone. Probably dead. Jennifer, too, though at least she likely still lived.

Were they now coming for him?

"What do you see?" Reyes hissed, unable to bear the silence a moment longer.

Emiliano's gaze roved across the four monitors, settling on one camera feed in particular. It looked out over the street. He pointed at the sicario who, moments earlier, had been watching the security feeds and now had an embarrassed look on his face. "You – there's a man in that car, right?"

The sicario nodded and mumbled an agreement.

"Radio him. Tell him to flash the lights."

A fumble at the radio handset later, the order was carried out. All four men leaned forward and stared at the camera feeds. It was dark outside, and any flare of light would be immediately obvious in the high-resolution security feeds.

None came.

A weevil of concern squirmed down Reyes' spine. "Again," he said.

The sicario spoke louder into the radio, as though that would help. But no reply.

"Someone's jamming the radios," Emiliano said matter-of-factly. "Miguel, you're with us. You – make sure everyone knows we are about to be attacked. Do not allow this place to fall. You understand?"

"Yes, yes," the sicario mumbled, eyes now white with fear. He grabbed his rifle from where it was leaning against the wall and ran out of the room, almost tripping over his own feet in his haste to leave.

Strangely, Reyes now felt very little fear. Perhaps it was adrenaline, or perhaps just a reminder that he hadn't always been the boss. Once he was just like Miguel, or the sicario now running into battle.

"What's the plan?" Miguel asked.

"Follow me," Emiliano said without explanation.

He led the small procession down into the basement, bolting the wooden door at the top of the stairs behind them in three places. It wouldn't repel a determined attempt at entry but might at least buy a few seconds.

Reyes remained silent. Though he had never laid eyes on it himself, he knew what this place was. As Emiliano searched for the light switch, he turned to Miguel and placed one of his meaty palms on the young man's shoulder, pulling him forward and directly holding his gaze. He settled his bare hand on the stock of his rifle. "Are you with me, Miguel?"

"Sí, jefe." The kid nodded. "To the end."

He conjured a smile on to his face that he did not really feel and chuckled, "Let's hope it doesn't get that far. You see that door?"

A nod.

"Shoot anyone who comes through it."

Reyes held the look long enough to be sure the kid knew exactly what he truly meant. There was to be no retreat. Not for the sicarios above.

As they spoke, Emiliano holstered his pistol and pulled a moth-eaten wool rug from the floor. A thin layer of dust and grit fell off it, choking the basement's cool air like a coal pit. He tossed it aside and crouched down, sliding his palms slowly across the dusty concrete floor.

From outside the basement's door came the unmistakable, clattering sound of gunfire. It was close. It had begun.

Miguel glanced anxiously over his shoulder. "Is that –?"

"Eyes on the prize, kid," Reyes growled, voice devoid of empathy. "What's your job?"

"To... To shoot anyone –"

"To *kill* anyone who comes through that door."

Miguel's stance widened, yet a small but undeniable tremor which had early appeared slowly but clearly began to fade. He would do his duty.

"How you getting on, Milo?"

"One second..." Emiliano murmured, then he let out a guttural grunt of satisfaction. "Got it."

He pulled one of his pistols free, flipped it in his hand, and used the butt as a hammer, gently tapping at a barely visible indentation on the basement's concrete floor. The concrete – really ceramic – shattered. Emiliano swept it aside and revealed a metal circle, which he yanked upward. A length of metal chain came out, attached to what was evidently a hatch hidden in the concrete.

"Give me a hand, Toro," he said, raising his voice over the advancing rattle of gunfire above. It sounded only feet away. "Quick."

"They're coming!" Miguel yelled.

"Quiet!" Reyes hissed. Without pausing, he grabbed the middle of the chain. Turning to Emiliano, he said, "Ready?"

"Go!"

The two men yanked at the same moment, and with audible effort, the hatch came free, shattering a thin layer of painted plaster around the edges of the hatchway. It disintegrated into a thin gray dust. Emiliano tossed it back and jumped inside.

Miguel looked over his shoulder once more, an expression of relief lighting his face as he glimpsed a way out.

Reyes jumped into the tunnel after Emiliano. It was only a few feet tall, and so even though he was not a tall man, he found it necessary to crouch. Every few yards on the tunnel, glowing electric lamps lit the way, exposing strange shapes covered by blue tarps.

"Can I join you, jefe?" Miguel called, his voice taut as a fishing line. "They're coming..."

Above, only barely muffled by the basement's thick walls was the unmistakable sound of a helicopter hovering just feet over the safe house's flat roof. Reyes imagined the dropping of rappelling lines and the thudding of boots.

Behind him, Emiliano cast one tarp free, then another. The cartel boss gripped his weapon tightly, knowing that this was a moment of truth. No matter how loyal, no matter how well trained, all men are liable to snap when their backs are placed against a wall.

"No, you fool," Reyes hissed coldly. "Close the hatch and cover it. Do as I say."

"Quick, Toro," Emiliano muttered. "We have to get moving."

"Set the charges," Reyes replied.

"Please, jefe," Miguel said, peering down from above, his weapon now slack in his arms. His voice was barely audible. "If I do this –"

"I won't forget it, Miguel," Reyes said, imbuing his tone with a practiced manipulator's art. He focused his gaze on the sicario without blinking. "You will be richly rewarded. Now close the hatch."

Miguel moved jerkily, with the numbed, leaden limbs of a condemned man walking to the gallows. And yet he did it. Condemned himself to death. And the hatch thudded closed above Reyes, causing a thin shower of dust to coat his hair.

Bloodlessly, Reyes bolted the hatch shut. Perhaps it was imagined, but he thought he heard a moan of despair from above as he did so.

An explosion rocked the safe house's foundations, and Emiliano grabbed his arm a second later. "Time to go, boss."

"It's armed?"

Emiliano nodded.

Now exposed in the tunnel's dim lighting were two electric mopeds. Their keys were taped to them, and Reyes ripped his set free, quickly turning the motor on. On the dash in front of him, three green electric bars gleamed. Out of five.

That was an oversight. When were they last checked?

It doesn't matter. Not now.

Reyes led the way as the two men sped down the tunnel, crouched low over the front of their scooters to avoid outcroppings of rock and exposed support beams in the roughly hewn tunnel. It was mostly straight but curved gently to the left, so it was necessary to apply a slight touch to the controls to avoid scraping against one of the jagged walls. The air tasted stale.

Though they were making almost thirty miles an hour in the cramped tunnel, the electric motors below them let out only a low-pitched whine which gave the scene an almost science-fiction feel.

It took less than ninety seconds to travel the full length of the tunnel, a distance that had cost six months of relentless hacking and filling in the desert soil. Reyes braked sharply as a solid wall quickly consumed his vision, and behind him Emiliano only barely avoided a collision.

Reyes winced. Not exactly the way he wanted to go. He killed the moped's electric motor and leaned it against the wall gently, so as not to make a sound. Behind, Emiliano did the same.

The two men stood in a half-crouch, each now holding a weapon once more. They communicated with hand signals and quiet whispers as they stared up at a ladder that led either to salvation, or death...

Reyes shrugged. He was in God's hands. "I'll go first," he murmured.

Emiliano shook his head vehemently. "I go."

"Not this time, friend," Reyes replied, grabbing a rung and

pulling himself upward to forestall the argument. He paused halfway up the ladder. "You think they figured it out?"

Emiliano looked back down the tunnel. "I'm guessing any moment now."

Both men ducked from the faraway sound of an explosion. Seconds later, as Reyes climbed the ladder with renewed fervor, a rush of cool air bathed them. It was a breaching charge, he knew. Whoever was after him had figured out the escape route. Given how professional they appeared to be, it was only a surprise they hadn't already known.

Unless they were waiting on the other side of this hatch.

Reyes considered the prospect with equanimity. Gripping the pistol tightly in his hand, he quietly slid back the bolt. Blood rushed in his ears as he lifted it, moving in fractions of inches.

A crack of gloom emerged on the other side. Not quite lit, and not entirely dark.

He paused, listening for any sign that there was a party waiting. But he heard nothing. There was nothing for it. Reyes pushed, and the hatch clanged back against the concrete of the empty warehouse's floor.

The building was empty. They were safe.

And as Emiliano clambered out of the tunnel after him, his black denim coated with dust and dirt, a far louder explosion erupted from the far end of the tunnel.

28

The newly rented safe house now housing their operation was messily strewn with loose papers, empty candy wrappers and various bits of equipment, as was so often the case on counter-espionage operations. The long hours and intense focus needed to hunt a mole or identify their handler rarely allowed much time for cleaning or left anyone with either the desire or energy to do so.

All four members of Pope's ad hoc team were present. Trapp was half asleep, lying on the couch that had come with the place. It smelled of stale cigarette smoke, but he'd slept on worse. The aroma of coffee brewing in the kitchen battled with the more deeply ingrained scent and began to tug him toward wakefulness. Eliza was leaning against him.

The television in the living room was large, and the box it had arrived in was still leaning against a nearby wall. No one had thought to purchase either a stand or a wall mount, so it now sat on top of a dented coffee table, perilously balanced in such a way that it threatened to topple over at any moment. It was muted, though the kaleidoscopic image of ATN News' intro graphic was flashing in the dimly-lit room.

"Guys..." Ikeda called, reaching for the remote and stealing her warmth away. "I'm guessing we want to watch this."

Behind Trapp, Pope dropped a stack of paper onto the dining table and said, "What?"

The sound on the television barked into life as Ikeda keyed the remote, catching the ATN anchor halfway through her spiel. "– And we go right to our Washington correspondent, Ciara Olson for the latest. Ciara?"

Trapp levered himself into a vertical position on the sofa as the news producer switched the feed. He faintly recognized the reporter, a redhead with deeply freckled cheeks that almost looked like a tan until the camera zoomed in.

"Thank you, Amanda," Ciara said. "A brutal but until now limited war between Mexico's two largest drug cartels, the Crusaders and the Federación, last night spilled onto America's streets for a second time."

The image on the screen cut to a scene from a highway in Texas, California, or somewhere equally hot, dry, and dusty. A location flashed up a second later, confirming his suspicions. The feed showed a smashed-up Honda SUV, windshield riddled with bullets, and a spattering of what was unmistakably blood on the driver's cracked window.

"National security sources here in Washington say that a large shipment of drugs that came through the southern border was last night hijacked by a rival narcotics gang, resulting in at least six homicides that we are so far aware of, and perhaps several more. It is not yet known which of the rival factions the drugs initially belonged to, but as you can see, Amanda, this is a dramatic escalation in cartel behavior – and following the murder of Administrator Mark Engel along with several US Attorneys last week, a dark sign indeed."

"Thank you, Ciara. Is there any indication as to why this attack took place?"

"That's where it gets interesting, Amanda. Until last night, this was primarily a Mexican affair. Squabbles between the cartels are not uncommon, though the early indications are that this one is becoming extremely serious. We know that over the past week, several key figures in the Crusaders have been assassinated or gone missing. It's understood that last night there was also an attempt on the life of Ramon Reyes, the leader of this particular organization. The fight appears to be over territory within Mexico – the violence in the United States is an unfortunate side effect."

"How so?" the anchor asked.

"It seems that a network of Crusaders-operated safehouses and drug runners inside Mexico has been targeted by the Federación. Drug gangs affiliated with the Crusaders inside the United States have started running out of product, and it seems that they have begun resorting to extreme measures to acquire it. We don't yet know whether last night's violence was a result of Crusaders gangsters targeting a Federación shipment or the other way around – but the results are the same. Violence on American streets."

"Thank you, Ciara," the blond newsreader said, shifting her gaze to a different camera angle. "ATN is also able to reveal an exclusive recording from the cartel leader Ciara just mentioned, Ramon Reyes, that we believe was sent to his supporters last night. Please note, if you have minors in the room, this may not be suitable."

An image of a squat yet obviously muscular man appeared on the television screen. He had dark hair, and that was about all that could be made out from the grainy, long-distance photograph. A name appeared on screen to help those who hadn't been paying attention. The recording was in Spanish, but captions promptly appeared on-screen.

*"Guys, it's time to fight. They came after me, they came after our people. And we f****** killed them, okay? You know who I'm talking about. It's time to go to war. We never wanted this fight. But now*

we're in it, we will win it. You know that, okay? You are killers. So go kill. If you see a Federación cockroach, kill him. I will give $1000 for every sicario. Ten thousand for any capo. Ten million for the man who brings me Carreon's skull."

The anchor returned to the screen. "And in a disturbing development only just breaking in the state of Michoacán, deep in Federación territory, more than fifty bodies were dumped in the middle of the highway. ATN has also received unconfirmed reports of several similar atrocities. The question now is whether the Mexican authorities will be able to get a handle on this horrific wave of violence – and whether they will do so before we see more death and destruction on American streets."

The producer cut away to a new segment on soybean prices in Iowa, or some other topic that Trapp rationally understood must have importance, without being able to prompt any great personal interest one way or another.

"Okay..." Pope murmured, drumming his fingers against the flatpack table. "You guys are thinking what I'm thinking, right? This is all just one big coincidence. Right?"

"Right," Trapp snorted.

"Director Rutger's going to want results," Pope remarked. "Now that this thing has spilled over onto home soil, the press is going to be on this like a bitch in heat. The president's going to need to give them something."

"You can't tell him not to?" Ikeda asked, a smile dancing on her lips. "I thought that's all you counter-intel pukes did: just hide in a corner somewhere and tell everyone how hard you're working."

"We are!" Pope grinned back. "We just can't tell anyone about it. Problem is –"

"– it's not the Russians or the Chinese we're up against," Trapp cut in. "At least, I doubt it. I'm guessing the cartels finally figured they'd get further in life by hiring experts. Whoever

Conway's handler is, we know he's good. He's probably former intelligence. Whether ours, the Brits, someone else, who knows. It doesn't really matter. We won't get away with pulling the national security card on this one."

"Then what?"

"We need to accelerate the sting. Find out who the handler is and who he works for," Pope said.

"Do we?" Ikeda asked.

Pope frowned. "Do we what?"

"Need to find out who he's working for. Seems to me like the cartels are starting to tear themselves apart. Is that such a bad thing? Why don't we just let them do the hard work for us?"

"You really are CIA, aren't you?" Pope said, shaking his head wryly. "That sounds like something you guys would have pulled back in the eighties. Real Machiavellian shit. And you look so innocent, too..."

"It won't work," Trapp agreed.

"Why not?"

"What we just saw on the news is only the start. It's simple supply and demand. If the supply coming up through Mexico falls, then the price north of the border skyrockets. This thing's only gone hot in the last week, and gangbangers are already having it out right in the open. If it's this bad now, it'll be an inferno in a month's time. No way the politicians stand for it. They'll be clamoring for a solution – and looking to us to provide it."

Ikeda pouted, though he could tell she agreed with most of what he was saying. "That's why nothing ever gets done around here."

She wrinkled her nose and continued, "*Politicians.* If they just left it to us, maybe we'd actually get somewhere. Okay. Let's say you're right – where does that leave us? Counterintelligence is a slow business. Even if this mad-scientist idea of yours pays off, who's to say how long it'll take for us to figure out who he is – let alone who he works for?"

"I had an idea about that, too..."

Pope looked up. "What are you saying, Jason?"

"I think it's about time Eliza and I took a vacation. I hear Mexico's nice this time of year."

29

Fernando Carreon was enjoying a scotch by the pool at about seven that evening when he recognized the first sign that something strange was going on. Jennifer Reyes was in her room, where she'd spent most of the last few days. He couldn't work out whether she was more terrified of him or the guards.

A masked guard – the one with the mirrored Oakleys – strode onto the terrace, the heels of his boots reverberating against the stone with his own importance.

"Come with me," he grunted imperiously.

Carreon had enough alcohol in his veins both not to want to and also not to be concerned about the consequences of disobeying. He set the scotch glass down on the side table next to his lounger with a clink.

"Why?"

"Stand up," the guard grunted, drumming the tips of his fingers against a holstered pistol.

He wondered idly whether he could be quick enough to disarm the man but decided against it. He had always been more of a thinker than a fighter. Other people were better with their fists, and thankfully they spent their lives cheaply. For most of his life that awareness had carried him where he needed to go. And so Carreon came to the conclusion that now wasn't the time to change the habits of a lifetime.

"Now!" the guard intoned, though the added stress wasn't necessary. His prisoner was already rousing himself from his alcoholic half-slumber.

His muscles were pleasantly loose in the heat of the evening, and he pushed himself upright without too much effort. He shrugged insolently, resting most of his weight only on his rear leg and thrust the other forward with a nonchalance that was only half feigned. "What do you want?"

"Inside, now," the guard barked.

Carreon did as he was told, irritably shaking his arm loose of the guard's outstretched grasp. He could at least do things with dignity.

Within the villa, another guard reached for a bank of light switches and killed the pool lights. The turquoise glow died instantly, leaving only a lingering image in Fernando's retinas and the string of glimmering LEDs set into the flagstones that ringed the terrace still alight.

"Stop," the guard ordered the second they were back inside the villa.

"Why don't you tell me what the hell is going on?" Carreon said, grimacing with frustration. "What does it matter to you where I spend my evenings?"

He fell silent then, considering that very question. He'd been here for a week, maybe eight days now. He hadn't exactly been in a suitable mental state to commit his exact movements to memory those first two or three. And yet in all that time – barring Jennifer's arrival – the overall routine had not changed. Breakfast was set out on the table every morning by the time he arose. Lunch a few hours later. And dinner some time after that.

The guards had barely troubled him with their presence in all that time, other than as a subtle reminder that he was not in fact free. So what had changed?

He didn't expect an answer to his question, of course, so he wasn't surprised when he didn't receive one. The three men simply stood inside the villa.

Waiting.

But for what?

Because they were waiting, Carreon could see that now. His two guards were tense. It wasn't in what they said, it was the way they said it. Voices taut, muscles almost vibrating with energy. They hadn't been like this before.

And as he reached that conclusion, another thought struck him. Both were searching the sky with their eyes. They were expecting someone.

Could it be a rescue mission?

Carreon dismissed the prospect before hope had any opportunity to flare in his breast. He was not a sentimental man. That wasn't an appropriate character trait in a business like this. He cared only for the cold, hard facts, which were not in his favor. If his people had located him, and the guards knew about it, then the last thing they would allow him to do was stand here.

So a visitor, then.

Deciding that he had no intention of waiting at the door like a mother pining for her children, Carreon paced inside and made for the small bar area. The movement caught the attention of the guard with the Oakleys – now perching ostentatiously on the top of his head – but he was afforded no more than a cursory glance.

Carreon poured himself another drink. He idly wondered whether he was the one paying for all this. Probably. That piece of shit Grover had tricked him. He had to admire the balls on the man, and the skill of his execution, if not the outcome.

Definitely not the outcome.

He heard the chopper blades a few seconds later. There were none, and then they seemed to be right overhead, which meant the helicopter had to be flying low. In these mountains, the sound would be trapped inside a rocky valley with no way out. You could be a few hundred feet away and have no idea a chopper was anywhere nearby.

It would take a good pilot, though. Especially in the dark. And the only pilots with that kind of experience were military.

Like his guards. And like Warren Grover, too.

The helicopter was flying without running lights and set down on the terrace by the swimming pool like a wraith appearing from the darkness. Its sudden arrival startled even Carreon, who had been expecting it.

The second the skids touched down, the rest of the lights on the terrace died, leaving the whole place lit only by the glow from the villa's interior.

Two figures exited the helicopter while the blades were still turning. Carreon didn't bother putting a crick in his neck to find out who was coming to pay him a visit. They would be here soon enough. He sat down on the sofa opposite a pair of plush armchairs and waited.

He recognized both men as they entered the villa. One conjured a sense of seething, incandescent rage within him, the other a cold, quenching fear. Perhaps that was the effect they intended. A good cop/bad cop kind of deal.

"Fernando," Warren Grover said.

"You didn't used to call me that," Carreon observed. "Not so long ago you called me boss."

"Times change."

"Apparently so."

"How are you enjoying my hospitality?" Grover asked. This time he was unable to conceal the smugness in his eyes.

Carreon raised his glass of scotch and a mock salute. "And here I thought I was paying for all this."

"Times change."

We'll see, he thought, saying instead, "Can I offer you a drink?"

Grover shook his head. César said nothing. He remembered the man properly now. At Altiplano prison, when the sicario had broken him out, things had been muddled. But they were clearer now.

Carreon crossed his legs and took a sip of his whisky. Not much. Just enough to give the right impression. He had no doubt that his guards were sending Grover frequent updates about his behavior. It was important to play the part. He didn't like the American – how could he? – but he could admit that the man was meticulous. It was why he'd hired him in the first place.

And how did that turn out?

Grover took a seat opposite him. César remained standing.

Carreon raised his eyebrow. "So?"

"I need you to do something for me," Grover said without ceremony.

"I'm not particularly inclined to help you at the moment," he replied, schooling his expression to avoid displaying even a hint of interest. He was right after all: Grover wanted something.

But that wasn't entirely accurate. No – if he'd wanted something, he would have sent an underling.

Grover *needed* something from him. And that placed Fernando Carreon into a position of power. Sure, you had to squint to make it out, but it was there. And that was better.

"Perhaps César can convince you to help," Grover remarked offhand.

The prospect sent a shiver of apprehension up Carreon's spine. César was the kind of man you didn't do business with, just in case. A lot of bad men worked for the Federación Cartel. But none had so little empathy as the one standing opposite him. César was a sociopath. A man who did not just kill but delighted in the application of pain.

"Why don't you tell me what you need?" Carreon rejoined, stifling his fear. "I've never found your friend to be much of a conversationalist."

"He has his uses," Grover said. He reached into his pocket and retrieved a slim cell phone. The screen flashed into life, and the American quickly navigated to an audio file. He placed the phone between the two men and tapped play.

Carreon listened to the voice of Ramon Reyes with fascination. His rival was incandescent with rage. And the target of that anger was most curious indeed. He had to know more.

"It seems that you acquire enemies at quite a rate," Carreon said, his mind racing behind a blank façade that he consciously leavened with a self-conscious smile. "I can warn you from bitter experience that there are more fruitful paths to choose."

Grover flicked his fingers contemptuously. "You are not my enemy, Fernando," he said. "Just an obstacle. Had things worked out differently perhaps it would be Señor Reyes in your place and not the other way round."

Carreon understood then that this was not an accident. Grover had planned all this, and now the pieces of the jigsaw were tumbling into place. But to what end?

"Ramon wants your head," he said. "Well, mine, he just doesn't know who he's really fighting."

And nor do I.

"He was not supposed to survive," Grover admitted. "But he escaped. It was a mistake."

"You tried cutting the head off the snake," Carreon mused aloud. "Not a bad plan. As long as it works. Unfortunately for you, Reyes won't stop now. He can't, not without losing the respect of his men. And he won't risk that. I wouldn't."

"He's rallying them to fight," Grover snarled.

Carreon closed his eyes. He understood now. Grover had entered his service almost two years before and turned the Federación Cartel's security arm into a professional, deadly outfit. He'd sourced experts from Britain and Israel, guns from the United States and France, drones from Turkey, and a hundred other items from countries all around the world. For a time, his men had been the most feared in all of Mexico. None of the other cartels dared challenge their supremacy. But he had been a fool to believe Grover had ever truly worked for him. He was a parasite. Like one of those wasps who laid their eggs inside a live animal, feeding off its flesh before finally breaking free from a dying husk.

But he had gambled big. And now his bet was hanging in the balance.

"So what do you want from me?" Carreon asked, relaxing now that he better understood the lay of the land. "Don't you have a war to fight?"

Grover grimaced, radiating a volcanic energy.

"Ramon has called his men to war, and they've answered, haven't they? But mine haven't. They want to hear from me, not you."

"I kept you for a reason," Grover growled in response. "I need you to film a message. It's in both of our interests. If – *your* – men don't fight, then we'll both lose everything. And what use would you be to me then?"

Carreon paused before he spoke, and when he eventually did so, the words came quietly, with precise enunciation. The tone of a man who has accepted his fate. Or, perhaps, one who spies a way out. "Haven't I already lost everything?"

"You're trying my patience," Grover spat, a tic on his cheek twitching several times before becoming quiescent. "Do you want to find out how much more you have to lose?"

"No recording will work," Carreon said confidently. "No

tape, no video. My people will expect me to fight by their side, not hide in a bunker while they risk their lives. What you want is impossible. Unless..."

He fell silent.

Grover grimaced. The twitch returned. "Unless *what?*"

"Let me meet with them. Explain the stakes. Tell them you are to be trusted. To be followed. Without my blessing they will never be yours." He shrugged, his offer made, and fell silent.

The American dismissed the proposition with a curt nod. "Too risky."

"Then we are at an impasse."

"Perhaps we should rectify that. You don't need fingers to film a recording. You don't need kneecaps either. We won't touch your pretty little face," he said contemptuously. "But the rest of you is fair game."

"Look at me, Grover," Carreon said, unmoved. "Look deep into my eyes and ask yourself how far I am willing to go. I won't break. I won't bend. Not for a man like you. If you want my assistance, this is my only offer."

Another rapidfire sequence of twitches erupted on Grover's face, but the American stayed silent, his gaze probing Carreon's face for any hint of a lie. At long last, the man spoke.

"Two of my men will be your shadows. If you take a shit, they'll be watching. If you attempt to pass a message, you will die. So will your unfortunate penpal. We clear?"

Elated, Carreon battled not to show it. This was scarcely less forlorn a hope than his present predicament. But there was at least a glimmer of light. He could make it work. He had to.

"How will you explain that?" he asked.

Grover smiled, a cold, dead expression that didn't reach his eyes. "This is war. Our enemies are everywhere."

"Then we have a deal."

30

T rapp and Ikeda traveled light and quiet, catching a commercial flight down to California and crossing the southern border by car under assumed names. There was no reason to suppose that anyone was even aware of their little off-books investigation, let alone had any reason to flag their arrival in-country, but why take the chance?

Despite the day's intense heat at their current elevation, the nearby volcano that towered over the city of Toluca still wore its snow cap.

Trapp glanced up from a guidebook placed ostentatiously on the café table between them. "It used to be almost 3000 feet taller, you believe that?"

Ikeda was reclined in her chair, rangy legs stretched out onto the sidewalk, forcing her to retract them on occasion to avoid overly obstructing the passing pedestrians. A pair of ridiculous sunglasses was perched on top of her head. They had a cheap, already scratched Gucci logo, but since they'd been purchased from a nearby street vendor, they didn't command designer label prices.

"What did, honey?"

"The volcano," Trapp said, gesturing down the street, toward where the hulking monolith rose from the earth. "Kinda hard to miss."

"I had other things on my mind," Ikeda said pointedly. She stiffened, though had he not been quite so intimately attuned to her body language, Trapp might never have noticed.

"That him?" he murmured without visibly looking up from his coffee. The café's glass window was suitably reflective and allowed him to observe the street with almost perfect clarity.

"Think so."

"Real All-American, huh?"

"Says you." Ikeda grinned.

Trapp gestured at the waiter, a diminutive man with strangely delicate features, and left a couple of banknotes underneath his now empty coffee cup. The man bustled over with a tray as they stood to leave.

They were dressed like typical tourists. *American* tourists. Which, as the rest of the world understood, meant not very well. Trapp came complete with baggy khaki cargo shorts tucked over a white polo shirt and accented with a camera on a strap around his neck. Ikeda was somewhat better put together, with her dark black hair pulled back in a neat ponytail, but mainly carried off the look as a result of her superior beauty.

DEA agent Raymond Burke was a tall man. Despite the heat, he was wearing a navy blazer and dark pants. He had no luggage and was not visibly armed, though his frame was sufficiently broad to allow for the possibility that a weapon could be concealed from sight somewhere on his body.

They trailed behind him without making any attempt to disguise their presence, relying on their dress and appearance to evade any watching eyes. Overhead, a messy warren of telephone cables crisscrossed the street, swaying gently in the breeze. Gnarled, leafy trees studded the streets at regular intervals. The center of the city was a contradiction of beautiful

Spanish colonial architecture and staid, functional sixties brutalism. Wide-open plazas disappeared into tangles of narrow alleyways without warning.

"I think we're clear," Ikeda said after they paused for a few seconds not far from the cathedral, apparently to consult the guidebook. "No tail."

"I agree."

They resumed their own chase, walking casually through a covered market as hawkers offered them tacos and cold drinks with lazy insouciance. They turned around the corner which Burke's dark head had passed a few seconds earlier – and ran directly into him.

His eyes flashed with suppressed anger, and he spoke quietly yet with evident menace. "Why are you following me?"

"I think we're neighbors," Trapp said, casually scanning the street before he extended his hand. "From Fairfax."

Burke shook it warily, evidently off-balance. "You got any ID you can show me?"

"Don't usually carry any."

"Then I hope you'll understand," Burke said, turning away, "but I don't *usually* trust strangers."

Trapp glanced around the street and spotted a bar that was opening up for the morning. The proprietor was setting up an arrangement of white plastic tables and chairs on the street outside, but the interior was pleasingly gloomy. "Maybe we can take this somewhere private while we establish our bona fides."

"Don't think so, buddy," Burke grunted. He took a step back, and his hand drifted to his belt loop, where his fingers rested before inching backwards.

He's armed, then, Trapp thought to himself. He opened his mouth to reply, but Ikeda got there first.

"Easy, tiger." She smiled disarmingly as she produced a business card from inside an astonishingly large purse, which

Trapp knew contained almost nothing. She flashed it in front of the agent's face. "Recognize the name?"

"So what?" Burke shrugged. "Anyone could get one of those printed. It means nothing."

"I'm not asking you to take my word for it," she said. "Dial the number. Or better yet, dial your own switchboard and ask them to put you through. We can wait. But you know, my colleague's right. We might want to do this out of sight."

Burke's indecision was written on his face. He snatched the card with two fingers and gestured at the bar across the street. "Go get a beer. If this checks out, I'll join you."

"Sounds like a fair trade." Eliza smiled. "See you in a sec."

She indicated for Trapp to join her, and he followed like a meek child. Once they were out of earshot, he grunted: "Colleague?"

"Dos cervezas, por favor," she drawled in deliberately broken Spanish tinged with a distinctive Valley twang as they entered the bar. The owner nodded and gestured to the outdoor seating. Ikeda mimed that she wanted to get out of the heat and selected the furthest table from the entrance.

Once they were seated, both in chairs that offered them a good view of anyone approaching, she said, "If you want to tell him we're screwing, be my guest. I just didn't think it sounded pertinent."

"Pertinent," Trapp grumbled. "You and your big words."

Burke joined them about ninety seconds later, his concerns obviously allayed. He slid Director of Central Intelligence Lawrence's card back across the surface of the table, and Ikeda magicked it back into her purse.

"So I guess you guys are big shots, huh." He glanced over his shoulder and stuck three fingers up. The bartender already had two bottles of beer on the counter and was in the process of removing their caps. He crouched down and procured a third.

"That's the problem with this line of work," Trapp said.

"The more people who know about a thing, the more chance it gets blown to hell. Unfortunately that leads to inefficiencies."

Burke gave a short laugh. "Like needing the director of the CIA to vouch that you're on the up and up. I hear that. So how can I help my beloved cousins from Virginia?"

"We were thinking that maybe we could help each other. Give a little, get a little. That kind of thing."

"Depends what you have for me," Burke said bluntly.

"How well do you know Leo Conway, Agent Burke?" Ikeda asked.

Burke visibly stiffened. He glanced at them in turn, clearly measuring his words. "He's Engel's guy, right?" he said, buying time. "Was, anyway."

Ikeda nodded.

She really could be cold, Trapp reflected. Not to him. Not usually, anyway. Though he would have to make up for the camping trip at some point, that much was clear. But she was good at this line of work.

"He placed a call to you several days ago," she said, revealing that they had been listening.

"I thought you said you wanted to work together?" Burke growled. "Because this don't feel too simpatico right now, if you know what I'm saying."

Trapp glanced at Ikeda, wondering whether to intervene. Burke wasn't too dissimilar a man to him. Was this the correct way to handle him? Evidently sensing that he was wavering, she cut off his train of thought with an almost imperceptible shake of her head.

Okay then.

"I'm not accusing you of anything, Ray," she said. "Can I call you that?"

"My friends do," he replied without warmth.

"Let's see what we can do about that." Ikeda smiled. "Like I said, we're not coming after you."

Burke kinked his eyebrow with interest. "Then Conway?"

She nodded. "Maybe."

"I thought there was something weird about that phone call. The guy sounded spooked."

"We know."

His eyes widened. "You were listening?"

Ikeda inclined her head. "Don't tell anyone."

"I'm not sure I like that," he grumbled to himself, shaking his head. "Big Brother listening in to my phone calls."

"Not yours," she pointed out.

"Still…"

"You said you thought he sounded spooked. Why?"

Burke looked suddenly uneasy. He clenched his jaw, then scanned the bar. The bartender had disappeared into the back, and there were no other customers. "Listen, I don't know you guys from Adam. You've got important friends, I get that. But so did Conway. And now my boss is dead, and no one seems real interested in finding out why. Except you guys, and you just showed up out of the blue."

A trickle of sweat ran down the back of Trapp's neck, and he glanced up at the dark, dusty blades of a criminally underpowered ceiling fan ambling in gentle sweeps above his head with genuine disappointment. He dropped his gaze back down with resignation and said, "You knew Engel?"

Burke took a swig of his beer before replying. "Not socially. He was a nice guy and good at what he did. But that's not the point."

"I know," Trapp replied. He silently measured his next steps and decided to take the plunge. "Conway's a gambling addict. He was selling classified information to dig himself out."

"That's why Engel died? For money?" His expression turned more thoughtful, and he leaned toward them, resting on his elbows. "Who knows this?"

"For now just us three, and a few friends back in Washington. We're keeping the circle tight."

"Why?" Burke frowned. "Can't you just bring him in?"

"We could," Trapp agreed. "But there's another player. His handler. Conway's just a pawn. I'm guessing even he doesn't know why he's digging for what he's selling. We want the guy above him in the chain. Because right now we don't have a clue what's really happening."

"Makes two of us," Burke muttered. His expression cleared. "Fine, I'll bite. You were listening in anyway, so I guess you know what he wanted. The call logs between Salazar and Abalos."

"That's right." Trapp nodded. "Look, this is your beat. Who the hell are these guys?"

"Senator Josefina Salazar is a real piece of work," Burke said, ostentatiously wrinkling his nose. "She's running for the presidency here. Heavily funded, and it looks clean, but so does a lot of the cartel cash. She came out of nowhere, and all of a sudden she has a real shot at winning, too. You know the type: can't just let a hot button issue pass her by without sticking her nose in for the headlines. It looks like she's graduated to generating them, too."

Trapp squinted. "What do you mean?"

Burke glanced around the bar again, confirming that it was still empty. A droplet of condensation on the side of his bottle of beer tumbled into another, creating a chain reaction that dripped onto the table. "You're not listening to Conway, right? Not officially."

"I guess not," Trapp agreed.

"Well, we don't listen to Mexican government types. Not officially."

"But it happens?" Trapp asked with a raised eyebrow.

"The Mexicans let us fly surveillance planes from time to time. Just Cessna Citations fitted out with listening gear and high-resolution cameras. They don't look like nothing from the outside, but they suck in all kinds of data. Mainly cell phone: who's talking to who, and where from. We're not really supposed to listen in to conversations. We're sure as shit not supposed to record them."

"Not officially," Trapp remarked dryly.

"You got it." Burke grinned. "So anyway, a couple days ago one of the surveillance techs called me up. Said he had something hot. Didn't want any part of it. Well, it wasn't just hot. It was dynamite. You guys heard the name Hector León?"

They shook their heads.

"He's a Mexican. Captain in their Marines. Good guy. He was in command of the quick reaction force that went to that prison break last week. Well, Abalos wanted him to take the heat for the screw-up. Not just that – he wanted him out of the picture, so there wouldn't be any unpleasant questions. And Salazar was only too happy to oblige. This is her issue to ride all the way to the presidential mansion. But the thing is –"

"Go on..." Trapp murmured.

"Well, Abalos is on the cartel payroll. We know that. But from what I heard, it sounds like so is she."

Trapp leaned back in his chair. The plastic creaked underneath his weight. "Damn. *Damn.*"

"You got that right," Burke agreed. "Now you see why I didn't want to say anything over the phone to Conway. It wasn't just that I didn't trust him. I didn't, but that's only half of it. It's that if what we overheard got out, the military down here would be in a whole heap of shit. And that's not the half of it: it could blow up the whole Mexican election if somebody leaked that the leading candidate was on the cartel payroll."

"Sounds like that's no bad thing," Trapp said.

"Look, I agree with you, all right?" Burke nodded. "But we ain't got a good reputation down here. We've done some real janky things in these parts, and they won't forget that anytime soon whatever happens. If we start messing with their elections, hell... I don't know. But it wouldn't be good."

"There's one thing I don't understand," Ikeda remarked, frowning. "It's a heck of a story. But why would Conway's handler care about any of that?"

Trapp bit his lip. "That's the question, right? I'm guessing we figure that out, and we crack this whole thing."

31

The car was a battered soccer mom mobile with an ingrained cigarette funk. It wasn't exactly a style to which Fernando Carreon was ordinarily accustomed, but then again, there was a lot about the last few days which was new to him.

And besides, in that moment his mind was otherwise occupied, wrestling with a problem that exercised it more than any he could remember. The plain facts of the matter were that he was in deep peril. Grover had spent two years with him, turning the Federación Cartel into a mean, professional outfit, well-armed and equipped with the latest surveillance tools. He had turned what was essentially a vicious street mob into something more akin to a multinational corporation with its own special forces arm.

And where his predecessors – and hitherto Carreon himself – had largely eschewed the complex, skilled world of professional espionage, Grover had instead embraced it, recruiting reliable sources even in the belly of the beast: Washington DC.

It had always been possible to recruit informants in Mexico, of course. Sometimes it seemed like half the payroll of any given police force supplemented their incomes by judiciously sharing information. After all, when the stick was the threat of death at any moment, the carrot of a comfortable life was far more appealing.

But in recent years, the Americans had changed tack, presumably recognizing the fruitlessness of their prior course. Where once they had been happy to let the Mexican government clean house – which was a threat only of a short incarceration inside a prison where it was possible to procure women, narcotics, alcohol, and satellite television – now they wanted heads.

More precisely, they wanted the leaders of all the major cartels to serve long sentences inside high-security federal Supermax jails. Small, featureless boxes with immovable concrete furniture, bare light bulbs that never turned off, exercise yards where you never even saw the sky. Places in which a man might go mad years before he ever saw freedom. If that was even on offer.

And that was the task he had given Grover: to prevent at all costs his own extradition to the United States.

Unfortunately, it was now clear that Grover had had other intentions all along. Like a parasite, the man had burrowed his way into the Federación and subverted its activities to his benefit. He'd built himself an army in plain sight.

And then he'd seized control.

"You guys plan on telling me where we're going?" Carreon asked, peering out of the darkened rear window into a vast, featureless emptiness of desert. Stars twinkled in the skies overhead, an effervescent glow against the velvet quilt of night.

As expected, he received no reply. Only a strained groan from the car itself as the elderly vehicle jolted over a pothole in the dirt road.

There were four other men in the vehicle with him, all

Grover's. His one-time security chief – now the arbiter of his incarceration – was not with them.

That was a problem. And, doubtless, it was intentional.

If Grover was smart, which was not in doubt, then he would never allow himself to be present in the same place as both Carreon and the cartel's sicarios at the same time.

He switched tack. "What's the plan?"

"You have your instructions," one of his guards replied shortly.

"And you have yours," Carreon murmured softly, slowly switching his gaze over each in turn as they stared resolutely ahead, some clutching on to their weapons, others still with them holstered in plain sight.

Their task was simple: If he showed any sign of disloyalty, any evidence that he was attempting to communicate with his men, then they were to terminate the meeting immediately and allow no survivors. They would probably let him live, but even that was not assured. He gave it maybe a one in two chance, which was a risk not worth countenancing.

The minivan's headlights bounced over the uneven, dusty terrain before the vehicle began to slow, turning left without indicating. Five minutes later, they reached what he presumed was their ultimate destination: a drab wooden farmhouse in the middle of nowhere, electric light leaking through a spiderweb of cracks between the building's wooden slats.

There were no other vehicles, something he found curious.

"Out," one of the guards grunted, jabbing Carreon in his side.

A gentle, backseat swell of car sickness began to fade as he stepped back onto solid ground. It was an unmanly affliction, he'd often thought. He was wearing light blue jeans over tan boots, a white T-shirt, and a faded blue work jacket zipped halfway to his neck. Despite the darkness, he looked like any laborer in the country.

Carreon rubbed his torso, wincing with frustration. As a younger man, he might have taken the blow as a mortal insult and reacted accordingly. He itched to return the favor but held himself back. His time would come.

"You could have just asked," he groaned.

The guard glanced at the shack, apparently determining whether they were being watched before returning his attention to Carreon once he was satisfied they were not. He gripped his upper arm tightly, leather-gloved fingers biting into the soft flesh.

"You do anything I don't like, say anything I don't like, it'll be the last thing you do. You're here for one purpose. If you have other ideas, then you're no use to me – and my instructions are to get rid of you. Understand?"

"Perfectly," Carreon said through gritted teeth. "You need me, and I need you. Message received."

You'll be the first to die, he didn't add.

The walk to the farmhouse was short, punctuated by the crunch of boots against stony desert earth. Carreon kicked up a thin sheen of dust as he walked, two guards ahead and two behind, which coated his lower legs like a mountain's snow line.

The five men paused outside the ramshackle building, and the last, unspoken reminder passed between Carreon and the masked guard who appeared to be in charge. They never shared their names, these people. The message was clear: *Don't screw around*.

The front door was pulled open, hard enough to slam against the opposite wall, and the two guards in front made an ostentatious show of entering first and checking that the room was safe. Only a couple of seconds later was Fernando Carreon allowed to enter.

"Boss!" one of the capos said, jumping to his feet and leaping forward before arresting his momentum, giving the masked guards a strange look. "You're safe. Thank God. We didn't know for sure what happened to you."

Carreon surveyed the squalid, drab room, a far cry from the luxurious accommodation he was used to, and realized he'd sacrifice all of the material comforts of the existence he'd enjoyed for the past two decades for just one more drink at the teat of the most intoxicating narcotic known to man: *power*.

It wasn't a lifestyle that Grover had stolen from him. It was his only reason for existence. A man could live on after being stripped of power, but some inherent part of him would forever be lost.

"Iker..." Carreon murmured, remembering the capo's name.

Until recently, the short, bespectacled man had been a relatively low-level functionary, in charge of some regional security outfit or other. He had a fearsome reputation that belied his bookish appearance, he remembered. A man who was always marked for higher things.

Things had apparently changed since he went to jail. Grover had hidden things from him. Promotions, obviously, and no doubt also the quiet removal of intransigent elements: those who would not acquiesce to his wishes.

Iker squinted curiously. "Jefe?"

"It's been a long day," Carreon said, glancing up and noticing that the guards had filed out so that each was stationed in one corner of the rectangular room. There would be no inch that their eyesight did not cover. Not that he'd expected any different. "A long fucking week."

That prompted a laugh.

"Where have you been?" Iker said, still standing opposite him, glancing over his shoulder at the guards. Carreon suspected that his underling guessed that something was amiss, and the knowledge of his impotence burned within him. The agents of his salvation could as easily be the deliverance of his destruction, and presently the latter was more likely than not.

"Busy," Carreon grunted to buy time. A heavy, rough-hewn wood table sat in the center of the farmhouse, which was lit by a single bare bulb in the center of the room. Somewhere outside, out of sight, he heard the low chugging of a diesel generator powering it. On the surface of the table were half a dozen dusty glasses, messily ringing a bottle that was half-full of amber liquid.

"What are you drinking?" he asked, seating himself at the head.

"Tequila," Iker replied, reaching for the bottle and pouring another round of drinks. He pushed one toward his boss. "My mother's recipe. It's fierce."

"Good, it's been a long drive," Carreon replied.

He reached for the glass, lifted it to his lips, and drained it with his eyes closed. The liquid was fierce. So fierce it burned the back of his throat and stung his eyes, though he was careful not to make a show of it when he opened them. He grinned. "You weren't kidding. That would put hairs on the balls of a 10-year-old."

"Worked for me," Iker replied.

"What's the latest?" Carreon said as the warmth flowed into his gut. He flicked his wrist and sent the glass skating back toward Iker, who dutifully filled it and topped up his own. The capo sat down, taking the seat at Carreon's right, and the other half dozen of his lieutenants – or less senior than Iker himself – followed suit.

Iker looked surprised and barely concealed a glance at the nearest of the masked guards in his eye line. "You don't know?"

"They don't tell me much," Carreon said, accepting a refilled glass of homebrew, which he sniffed appreciatively. This drink, this place, it all reminded him of his childhood. Of pulling himself up from the dirt and grime and hopelessness of poverty. Of becoming one of the most powerful men in all of Mexico.

Grover had tried to steal that from him. But he would not succeed. Not now he remembered why he wanted it in the first place.

"I'm kidding," he said at the look of concern on Iker's face. "We've had to move around. Security concerns. Reyes' men have been everywhere."

"That's true," Iker agreed. "The whole top rank of the organization is gone. Everyone."

Carreon thought about it for a few seconds. The loss of some of his oldest friends pained him. But unlike him, they were weak. They were not leaders. They had allowed themselves to be deceived and decapitated.

He lifted his glass and held it out in front of him expectantly. The legs of the alcohol swirled around the scratched drinking vessel. As it settled, he watched as the other men slowly understood what he was asking of them and raised their own glasses in turn.

"To the next generation, then. You six will be my right hands. You will fight by my side. And you will get the rewards for doing so, you understand?"

They shared looks, all of them except Iker, who held his gaze without blinking. He liked that about the man. He looked like an accountant but had steel in his spine. And he wasn't afraid of violence, either. Was steady in a fight, they said.

He will need to be.

The others, though, shared a variety of expressions. Some were fearful. Others wore a glint of hope or avarice or disbelief – or all of the above. But that was war. The strong would survive, and the weak would be culled, and it would all be worth it so long as they took a few of the enemy down with them.

"What do you want from us?" Iker asked, the alcohol in his hand perfectly steady.

Carreon liked that also. He had his eyes on the prize, this one. "They hit us by surprise," he lied. "Planned to kill me in that fucking jail. That's why I had to get out at such short notice. That's why I've been missing the past few days."

"They've killed too many of us already, those Crusader scum," Iker spat. "They fight like rats in a sack, without honor."

That's because they know what's at stake, Carreon thought. *Not riches or power or fame. Just survival.*

"And so must we," he said. He met eyes with each of the capos in turn, holding his gaze until he saw indecision shift to belief. "We need to kill these assholes. We need to go into their homes and dump their bodies in the streets. We will show them who runs this country."

He paused and sniffed the alcohol. It was coarse, impure stuff and stung his nose hairs. It brought tears to his eyes. But this fight would not be easy. And maybe this was the reminder he needed.

"Are you with me?" Carreon growled.

A roar of affirmation grew in the space, filling his heart with pride. He still had it, after all, whatever it was: the power to inspire men into battle. Perhaps he would have been a warrior in days gone past. Perhaps. But this was his battlefield, and he still had what it took.

They all cheered their belief in him. All but Iker.

The space fell silent. Carreon locked eyes with him. "And you?"

The fighter held the silence for long enough that Carreon began to wonder whether he knew precisely how much power he presently held. But after a long, seemingly interminable wait, he nodded. "To the death, jefe."

Carreon thumped the table. "Then let's drink."

Each man drained his glass in one and set it back on the

table. There was a palpable air of anticipation in the room, a rush of conspiracy that bonded each man to the one at his side. Carreon knew that they would fight for him. Even those with doubts would look to the man on their left, and then the man on their right, and see only shame in refusing to fight. It was what had carried men into battle for thousands of years, and it wasn't changing now.

That some, probably many, would die because of this decision did not trouble him. No one entered this line of business with a lily-white heart. Doubtless each of the men seated around this table had blood on their hands.

And besides, he reasoned, Grover had left him with precious little choice. If he didn't go to war with Reyes' cartel, then the men from Culiacán would wipe his own organization out. There was no retirement for men like him. The only way to survive this fight was to win it.

That meant Grover as well.

He surveyed the four guards – or at least, the two he could see from his current vantage point – shielding his burning distaste for them from his expression.

"Iker," he said loudly so that Grover's lapdogs would hear. "I want you by my side at all times. Spread the word: I'll pay $1000 bounty for the life of every one of Reyes' men. No questions asked. Understood?"

His new right-hand man inclined his head, but Carreon wasn't watching Iker. Instead, his attention was focused on his newly acquired shadows. One of them – he thought it was the man who'd warned him earlier – stepped forward.

"That won't be possible," he said curtly. "For your safety, sir –"

Carreon cut him off brutally. "I make the goddamn rules," he yelled. "It's my life on the line. Do you understand? We can't win this fight without taking a little bit of risk."

He couldn't see the expression on the guard's face, but he

had a good idea. The man was in an impossible position. Either he fell afoul of Grover's instruction to keep him separated from his men or he embarrassed Carreon in front of them. Both outcomes had obvious risks.

But as he knew he would, the masked guard bowed his head and stepped back. "As you wish, jefe."

After all, Carreon knew that he had not technically over-stepped Grover's red line. He hadn't – yet – attempted to warn his people of the trouble he was in. And the guard must have known that to kneecap his charge now, in front of these men, would destroy Carreon's authority and risk dooming the already flailing operation.

"Good. Let's get moving. We have a busy few days in front of us."

32

Ramon Reyes grinned at Mendoza. "Makes you feel a decade younger, doesn't it?"

"What does?"

He clapped his friend on the shoulder. "Come on, don't tell me you don't feel it. The adrenaline. The *rush*. I forgot how good it tasted."

"Let's hope it doesn't get us killed," came the reply.

Reyes checked his weapon for perhaps the hundredth time. "We'll be fine."

"Let's hope you're right."

They were seated with six other men in the back of a minivan. The others wore military-style black Kevlar helmets, but not Reyes or Mendoza. It wasn't because he was unafraid of dying. That was decidedly not the case. But there were worse fates than death.

And besides, he could not run. Not forever. Either he made a stand or he would die. It was a clarifying realization — one he'd shied away from at first. But no longer.

Reyes leaned toward his old friend so that the others would be unable to hear. "You ever wonder why he started this –

Carreon, I mean? Peace was just as profitable for him as it was for us. And war's expensive. How many shipments have we lost? How many men? It'll take us years to rebuild our operations north of the border. Longer if the federales take advantage of our weakness."

Mendoza shrugged. "I guess he wanted the whole pie. Some people just don't like sharing."

"Hell of a risk. And he never struck me as the gambling type. Safe. Fat. But not a risk taker. And why now, after all this time?"

"I don't have the answers you're looking for." Mendoza grinned.

"I know," Reyes said wryly. "Nervous, I guess. It's been a long time."

"We'll be fine," Mendoza replied, gripping his friend by the forearm. "And if not, we'll be dead, and then it won't matter either way."

"An optimist."

"You know me."

The back of the van was dark, and the courtesy lights had their bulbs removed to avoid even the faintest possibility of a screwup. Reyes could picture it now: the door opening, the whole operation being painted in bright white electric light. Someone pulling a gun, and the whole thing going sideways.

The van turned right, drove for several more minutes, and went left. From up at the front, someone barked, "Sixty seconds!"

"This is it," Reyes murmured, fingering his rifle anxiously. "We'll be fine."

The time seemed to flow, not drain, away, and before he'd even blinked twice, the vehicle's rear doors were swinging open, and they were pouring out, all of them. Their boots started against the crumbling sidewalk, and someone started shooting. In the moment, he wasn't even sure whether it was his men or theirs, and then he opened up as well, bringing his rifle to his shoulder and firing round after round at the Federación safe house. In the darkness, it was hard to see whether he was hitting anything or just blazing away at walls.

The magazine ran dry, and with trembling fingers he ejected it and clicked in a new one.

Around him, he was faintly aware that his men had formed a protective bubble. He wasn't wearing a helmet, but whether consciously or not, his sicarios were arrayed to take a bullet for him. One of them in the rear didn't have a gun, just a camera, which was pointed at both him and Mendoza, never wavering.

Or occasionally wavering, anyway, as an errant round from inside the Federación safe house zipped just a few inches from the cameraman's ear, prompting him to dive onto the deck.

Reyes reacted first. He felt somehow aroused by the proximity of death. Turning, he grabbed the cameraman by the webbing on his back, hauled the man bodily into an upright squat, and hissed, "Don't drop that, you fool."

The man, a boy, really, his fatigues and body armor hanging off an undernourished frame, nodded a hasty apology and brought the lens back up. Reyes studied it with conscious disinterest of the chaos around him, even as chips of concrete exploded in every direction.

"You're supposed to get the action as well," he added, grabbing the boy's arm and pointing it toward the safe house's front door, where a sicario was packing strips of plastic explosive to the frame and wiring it.

Another nod. More nervous this time as the kid recognized that he was screwing up, without recognizing that the demands being placed upon him were insane in the first place.

Reyes imposed them without conscious thought. This was a dangerous business, after all, and even more troublesome when your own people had enough time to think. Because when they could think, they could plan, and when they planned, they sometimes chose courses of action that did not fully align with your own.

The sicario at the door yelled, "Duck!"

Unfortunately, he didn't combine the warning with enough time to react to it, as his fingers reflexively clutched the detonator switch. The force of the explosion was bone-crushing. One moment the door was there, whole and intact, and gunfire was cracking in every direction, and the next it was simply gone, replaced by an eruption of dust.

A wave of heat and chemical stink burned Reyes' nostril hairs, and he choked on the cloud of filth. "Keep that lens clean, boy," he muttered. "And stay close."

They can edit the audio out later, he thought.

He was careful not to be the first through the space that had once been occupied by the door, but he was equally careful not to be the last. Image mattered, more so now than ever, and this was the whole reason he was here.

The safe house was a drab, derelict kind of place in a drab, derelict part of town. His own cartel operated many like it, requiring only that they be situated near a major logistics route, and in neighborhoods that knew better than to report nefarious business in their vicinity.

Its interior was a maelstrom of chaos. White, plastic-wrapped bricks of cocaine were stacked against every wall, in every closet, on every table. No stranger to the stuff, even Reyes' eyes bulged when he saw how much there was.

A crackle of gunfire sounded only a few feet away, and a cloud of white powder exploded to his right, causing him to crouch down and bring his rifle to his shoulder. He returned fire without knowing what he was aiming at and whether it was having any effect.

"Hell, Milo," he yelled, his voice coupled with an almost manic laugh. "Why the hell did we ever give this up?"

It was not rational to relish this proximity to danger, he

knew. And for many years, he had allowed himself to forget just how intoxicating it was. But right now, in this moment, he would not trade it for anything in the world.

He squeezed the trigger again, pumping half a dozen more rounds into the next room. They scythed through the plasterboard wall, joining a growing collection of holes in the fragile surface. Huge chunks of it began to chip away and rain in a waterfall of dust and debris against the floor as a renewed, deafening round of gunfire joined in all around him.

"Cease fire!" Reyes yelled after ten or twenty seconds of this madness. He repeated the call, and still it took until his men's guns ran dry before they all stopped firing.

He cupped a hand to his ear and listened. Mendoza shot him a curious look but said nothing, though the ringing in Reyes' ears was so intense that he might not have heard it anyway.

"Any of you fuckers left?" Reyes called out, his voice cold and hard and mean and mocking. He repeated a line he'd heard in some horror film. It seemed fitting. "Come out, come out, wherever you are..."

There was no response. Not a conscious one, anyway. Just a low, guttural moan.

Mendoza snapped his fingers and pointed at one of the sicarios, crouched like the rest of the insertion team near a wall of cocaine bales stacked like sandbags on top of each other. "You – take two men, go see if anyone's out there."

Expressionless, the man nodded and grabbed a shooter from either side. They moved like gangsters, not soldiers, charging forward on adrenaline, not tactics.

Reyes waited, watching to see whether they were about to be cut down by a hail of renewed gunfire.

"Only two of them left," came the cry. "It's clear."

He grinned and bounded to his feet, charging through the chipped doorway into the next room, where he found half a dozen of Carreon's men. Four of them were obviously, visibly dead. One was wearing a white string vest and Lakers basketball shorts and looked perfectly fine – if a little hung over – as long as you didn't look at the back of his head.

Which was entirely missing.

The cause of death for the rest was more immediately obvious. Overwhelming gunfire had ripped their bodies apart. One, a lanky skinhead with a strangely potbellied gut, still had a cigarette behind his left ear. Reyes surreptitiously glanced to see whether the camera was still following him, then leaned over and plucked it free. He placed it between his lips and rummaged in his pockets for a lighter.

Now that the combat was over, he was suddenly jittery. He tasted copper at the back of his tongue and had the sudden, almost overwhelming urge to be sick.

Pull yourself together, he thought angrily. *Not now.*

Concealing the trembling in his fingers, he conjured fire from the flint and sucked in a deep, healing drag of nicotine and tar, which helped settle his nerves. He took another, then turned to the main event.

His remaining sicarios – who seemed to be at least two lighter – were arrayed in a loose semicircle around a pair of captives, who had their hands bound behind their backs with plastic flex cuffs. One was dressed in a full tracksuit that seemed straight out of a 1980s boxing movie, and the other was naked to his waist, blood oozing from a deep, scarring wound to his cheek that was flowing onto his shoulder and then down, staining his torso into a vivid piece of surrealist art.

He pointed at the one on the left. "You – what's your name?"

The man seemed stunned to be asked. The acrylic material of his tracksuit rippled like waves on the empty ocean as he quivered, searching his mind for a response. "I –"

Reyes dragged in another breath of nicotine. In one fluid

motion, he drew his side-arm and fired. "Too slow," he grunted. "What about you?"

It took the guy in the tracksuit a couple of seconds to realize that he was dead. Or at least, that long to topple to the ground, an open hole in the center of his forehead. Reyes figured that was sufficient evidence of his untimely passing for even the most stringent coroner to accept.

The kneeling man gaped at him with all the comprehension of a lobotomized goldfish. Reyes stared, transfixed, as a particularly luminescent droplet of already thickening blood rolled down his taut frame. "I have one piece of advice for you, and you can choose whether or not to take it. Don't keep me waiting."

A glimmer of understanding glinted in the man's eye. "Oscar," he choked, his Adam's apple bobbing manically. "My name is Oscar."

"Thank you, Oscar." Reyes smiled bloodlessly. "Did you see what happened to your friend?"

He took another drag of the cigarette, which by now was over halfway burned. He could feel the heat of the ember against his knuckles.

Oscar nodded, not daring to trust his vocal cords. They rarely did.

"Good. Let's see if we can avoid the same happening to you, shall we?"

Another nod. A little shakier this time.

"Your boss tried to kill me. Did you know that?"

"My... my boss?" Oscar stammered, unconsciously glancing toward the body of one of the men lying crumpled on the ground, and in the process displaying his own shattered ear lobe to Reyes.

"Carreon, you idiot," Reyes snarled. He took one final drag of the cigarette, then stepped forward, placed it between the tip of his forefinger and thumb, and grabbed the back of Oscar's head. "You know the consequences of playing dumb, don't you, Oscar?"

Without giving the captured sicario a chance to reply, he manipulated his head into a jerking nod, yanking at the man's vertebrae and sinews until he moaned with pain.

"Excellent," Reyes said, raising his voice over the unwanted sound. He placed his lips near Oscar's ears and hissed, "Tell me what you want, and I will let you live. I'm a man of my word, Oscar. You know that, don't you?"

"Yes," the man gasped. "I'll help you. I just don't know what you want."

Reyes took a step back. He pointed at two of his men and grunted, "Hold him."

"Please..." Oscar begged.

To no avail.

Reyes violently pushed Oscar's head to one side so that his undamaged ear was pressed against his shoulder, and the broken one was wide open. He pressed the lit cigarette into the seeping wound and twisted it between his fingertips until the ember sizzled in Oscar's flesh. The sound of the bubbling screen was only audible for a fraction of a second before it was replaced by a raw howl that burst from the lips of the man in front of him.

Like a wounded animal, Oscar attempted to lunge in any direction so long as it was away from the pain and the men who were hurting him. His sinews strained, his muscles bulged, and droplets of loose blood splattered around the room.

But he was unsuccessful. Reyes' men restrained him, holding him upright as he sagged, all energy drained.

"Fernando Carreon. You do know the name of your boss, don't you?" Reyes snapped.

"Of course, of course," Oscar gasped once more. "But I don't know him. I've never even seen him. I'm nobody."

"You understand this is a war, don't you?" Reyes said,

leaning forward once again. He glanced at the destroyed cigarette in his fingers and flicked it contemptuously into Oscar's face. "You must know why we are fighting?"

Oscar squinted with a mix of fear and incomprehension. "I don't, I swear."

Reyes took a step back, understanding that he would get nowhere with this man. He drew his side-arm for a second time. "Obviously not."

He pulled the trigger.

He didn't expect to feel anything when Oscar slumped to the floor, and he did not. Reyes holstered the weapon and kicked the body to check that he was dead.

"Make sure you've got all the footage you need," he told the cameraman.

"What about the rest of this place?" Mendoza asked quietly. "I'm guessing there's at least five tons of product here. We could use it."

"Pick five of the men," Reyes said, walking back through the destroyed remnants of the Federación safe house. "Tell them to pack as much as they can carry and burn the rest."

33

P ope entered the Bureau safe house carrying two cups of coffee in a cardboard holder balanced precariously over a bag of fast food. He kicked the front door closed behind him, then walked over to where Kelly was sitting in front of a bank of computer screens.

Her hair was pulled back into a ponytail, though it was so short anyway that it was barely necessary, and she had a ballpoint pen behind her left ear. She barely looked up as he entered.

"Figured you might need a pick me up," he said, dropping the food onto the table beside her, and just about managing to avoid spilling one of the coffees all over her right shoulder. "Black or white?"

"Huh?"

"Did you hear any of that?"

Kelly pushed away the laptop, and sank back into her chair, expressing a slight sigh. "Not really."

"You drink your coffee with milk?"

She looked almost affronted at the suggestion. "No."

"Then take this one," he said, twisting it out of the holder and handing it over. "Should still be hot."

"Thanks," she said with a tired smile, perhaps recognizing her earlier reaction could be construed as ungrateful. She put the paper cup on the table and rubbed her eyes.

"You look exhausted," Pope said, sipping his own. "How long you been at this?"

She glanced at her watch. "Oh – well, I guess all night."

"You need to cut yourself a break," he chided. "You won't catch anyone with tired eyes. Believe me, I've been there."

"Yeah. Maybe you're right."

He pushed the bag of breakfast food over to her. "Hungry?"

She opened it up to take a look, but he suspected it was only to be polite. Her nose scrunched up as she pushed it back. "I'm good."

"Suit yourself," he shrugged. "Let me guess – you're a cyclist. Body is a temple, and all that?"

"Runner," she said with half a laugh. "And I'm vegetarian."

"My bad," Pope said with the scarcely concealed glee of a husband noticing his wife's abandoned plate was still laden with scraps. "I'll remember next time."

"No worries."

"So, how you getting on? Anything from Chernobyl?"

"Maybe," she nodded, bringing the coffee back to her lips and draining about half of it in one gulp. "Then again, maybe not. There's a lot of noise. Just not sure how much of it is signal."

"Sounds about right. Why don't you show me? Maybe I can help lighten the load."

She brought her chair over to him, then leaned back to pluck her laptop. The screensaver had initiated, so she wiggled the mouse, and a map of DC flashed up onto the screen.

Pope pointed at it, his finger landing on one of a number of small red dots. "What are these?"

"Pings from SIGMA," Kelly replied, tracing her finger gently around the Beltway. "We've got good coverage everywhere inside here. Usually not more than a couple of blocks between each Geiger counter."

"Okay," Pope said, opening his mouth wide and inhaling about half his bagel in one bite. "So that's twice on H St. – two nights in a row. That's around Chinatown. Picking up take out?"

"That's my guess."

"Then once more across the intersection. Where is that?"

"A Walmart, I think."

"And then a bunch of pings heading up 5th, and one on M Street. You get anything on the cameras?"

"You could say that," Kelly replied with a helpless laugh. She tapped the keyboard and switched tabs, then flicked through what had to be a couple hundred faces, still shots taken from city security cameras.

Pope grabbed a napkin and cleaned the grease off his fingers. "Who are they?"

"I fed our images of Conway's handler into Metro PD's facial recognition algorithm, and tasked it to search for any matches beyond 80% confidence in this search grid," Kelly said, tracing an imaginary circle around the cluster of SIGMA radiation pings. "I think we've got a problem."

"Which is?"

"None of the SIGMA devices have gone off in the last eighteen hours. I'm guessing he's showered, or maybe he just took pictures of the file and dumped it. Either way, looks like this well's about run dry."

"Great," Pope grumbled. "And that's why you're on the cameras?"

"Exactly. It seems pretty likely that our guy either lives or works within this ten block by ten block square. So that's where I'm looking."

"Good job. Still, that's gotta be home to twenty thousand people. Plus everyone who commutes in and out every day."

"Well... That's my problem."

"What are you doing to solve it?"

"The legwork," Kelly shrugged. She tapped the keyboard again, and the image on screen zoomed out. Suddenly, in addition to the half a dozen red dots were tens, perhaps hundreds more blue ones. "Each of these is where the facial recognition algorithm pinged."

She clicked on one of them, and a grainy surveillance shot of a tall blonde man in a raincoat and baseball cap came up. "This is our guy. Problem is, he never leaves the house without either a cap or a hood up. That makes the algo way less accurate. So I've been going through them one by one."

"You need a hand?"

Kelly chuckled forlornly. "I could use a couple dozen rookies to help me sift through all this."

Pope cracked his knuckles and shot her a wicked grin. "Well, you're shit outta luck. I'm all you got."

Six hours later they were both still at the task, and by this point his eyelids were beginning to droop even though it was only an hour past lunch. He looked up from his laptop after dismissing yet another surveillance image as a false positive and groaned. "You were at this all night, too?"

"Yeah," Kelly replied without looking up from her laptop.

"I'm surprised you haven't gone stir crazy. None of these guys look anything like Conway's handler. The last one must have weighed hundred pounds and I'm pretty sure it was a woman. Who wrote this damn code? Metro PD should get their money back."

He idly tapped the right arrow on his keyboard, and another image flashed up. It was taken on a street of townhouses, from a traffic cam. The note on the system said it was mounted on top of a lamppost. "Hey – wait a minute."

That caught Kelly's attention. She glanced up at him. "You got something?"

"Maybe..." He zoomed in, and then again. "Sure looks like him, right?"

She pulled up a photo of the handler on her own computer, and put it side-by-side. The surveillance image on Pope's screen was a profile shot, and taken from high above, but it had the same facial structure. "I think so. Where was it snapped?"

Pope went back to the map, and hovered the mouse cursor over the spot. "Here."

Kelly squinted, then peered so closely at the screen her nose almost collided with it. "That's M Street!"

"So?"

She stood up sharply, her chair toppling away from behind her, and held her laptop up like it was a trophy. "Don't you remember?"

"Refresh my memory."

With an exasperated expression on her face, Kelly put the laptop back down on the table. She pulled up the original map with the SIGMA pings on it. "Here, you see. That's the first time the system picked him up."

She traced her finger right, along the notation for the road. "And your image was taken at the corner of Brown Court and M. Does it look like he's turning to you?"

Pope peered at his own screen. The figure of Conway's handler did indeed look like he was turning toward one of the houses on the opposite side of the street from the lamppost camera. It was the way his body was angled, his shoulders starting to turn slightly. In fact, the movement was why the traffic camera had caught such a clear shot.

"You might be right," he murmured.

"It's him – I know it is!"

"Well, there's only one way to find out. Let's go take a look."

34

They made the journey at night, in the back of a transit van. It was already dark by the time they entered, though after almost half an hour inside with no signal from the driver as to how close they were, Trapp was beginning to wonder whether it would be light by the time they got out.

"You know where we're going?" Trapp asked Burke after yet another turn rolled them across the vehicle's cargo section. He wedged himself into a corner for support and watched as the DEA agent and Ikeda did the same.

Burke shook his head. "Not a clue."

Trapp cocked his head. "Would you tell me if you did?"

"Not a chance." Burke grinned broadly. "Question of honor, you know? I made a promise, and I intend to keep it."

"Good."

Trapp nodded his head thoughtfully but said no more, and the trio settled into a period of silence that lasted another fifteen minutes or so, during which time the ride became significantly less comfortable as the quality of the road underfoot deteriorated ever further.

Ikeda banged her head against the van's metal chassis as they bounced over a particularly egregious pothole and rubbed it ruefully. "That'll teach me, I guess."

At long last, the engine noise began to quiet, and Trapp sensed that they were finally nearing their destination. Unfortunately, *nearing* appeared to be a relative term, and the ordeal dragged on ten minutes longer as the vehicle rocked from side to side along an abomination of a road.

The motion ceased, and the engine died, and Trapp clenched his fist with quiet satisfaction. There was no air conditioning in the cargo compartment, and between the worn-out suspension and the evening's lingering heat, he was beginning to feel decidedly unwell.

"What now?"

"I guess we wait."

As instructed, none of the three was carrying any form of electric device. No computers, no cell phones, nothing connected to any form of network. It was harder and harder to go off-grid in the US these days, where in many cities it was almost impossible to function without the latest smart phone, or to have your license plate snapped by cameas dozens of times on even a short drive, or to be otherwise caught in the field of the hundreds of surveillance cameras that dotted every storefront and street corner. It was a burden that few disliked as intensely as Jason Trapp – for the constant surveillance threatened the very fabric of his profession.

Rural Mexico, thankfully, was somewhat less advanced. It was an easy place in which to disappear.

The driver's door opened and slammed shut, the force of the act gently rocking the vehicle before the rear doors swung open.

"Out," the driver grunted in Spanish.

Trapp was familiar with the language, though rusty. He trusted himself to understand the best part of what was being said, though speaking it was an entirely separate challenge. As the gloom of the evening began to resolve in his vision, he shrugged and did as instructed.

The van was parked at the edge of a cornfield, and the tall stalks rustled in a gentle wind. The ground underneath was baked hard as concrete, and his boots crunched against the desiccated soil as he jumped lightly to the ground before turning and offering his arm to Ikeda.

As he expected she would, she ignored his offer.

"Kinda cloak and dagger, no?" Trapp murmured to Burke.

"I'm guessing you'd do the same if someone was planning to kill you, your wife and your daughter," the DEA agent said.

"I don't have a wife or daughter."

"Use your imagination, big guy," Burke replied.

The driver, who Trapp now noticed in greater detail was a heavily muscled if not overly tall man, closed the van's rear doors. He pointed at the vehicle, then mimed at Burke to place his palms flat on the doors and separate his rear legs.

Kinda handsy, too, Trapp thought, deciding rightly to keep that observation to himself.

He watched without comment as the driver performed a short but thorough search of the agent's pockets, starting at his right ankle, going up and then down again, and then dealing with his heart. He found nothing more concerning than a leather wallet and an old toothpick.

Trapp was up next. The search didn't go quite as easy this time. The right ankle was clean, so was the left, and the groin, and even both his pants pockets.

The Glock tucked into the small of his back, however, was difficult to conceal. The driver froze as his fingers met the bulge that could only mean one thing and took an anxious step back, drawing his own weapon and pointing it at the back of Trapp's head.

For his part, Trapp didn't move. He listened to an anxious

rattle of Spanish and mostly derived from it that the guy had rightly deduced he was packing heat. Slowly, he looked over his shoulder. Ikeda hadn't moved, though he noticed she was tense.

Burke looked at him in disbelief. "You brought a gun?"

Trapp frowned. "You didn't?"

The DEA agent spoke to the driver in calm, reassuring Spanish, which he then repeated in English for Trapp's benefit. "You're going to reach behind yourself, pull the weapon out, and place it on the ground. Okay? Try not to get shot when you do it."

"You sure he's not going to pull that trigger?" he murmured.

"Don't give him a reason to have to find out," Burke replied, sounding entirely exasperated.

Trapp did as he was instructed, slowly reaching behind himself and lifting up the back of his denim jacket. Next, moving with deliberate exactitude, he inched toward the pistol grip with his index and forefingers and bracketed it before closing them in a pincer and gently teasing the weapon free. A little later, it was lying at his feet.

"Any more weapons?" the driver barked, this time in heavily accented but perfectly understandable English. Trapp suspected it would be better than his own Spanish.

He shook his head. "Just the crossbow in the shoulder holster," he said.

"Qué?"

"Never mind."

The driver kicked the gun aside and proceeded to frisk the rest of Trapp's torso.

When he turned around, Burke was eyeing him with irritation. "You didn't plan on telling me you were carrying?"

Genuinely surprised by the reaction – and a little annoyed himself – Trapp grunted, "Do you need telling that the sky is blue or that water is wet? Come on, you know who we are."

Ikeda turned to the driver with an apologetic expression on

her face. Though an excellent linguist, her skills didn't extend to any working knowledge of Spanish beyond the ability to order a beer in a Cabo beach bar.

"Listen," she said, opening her own jacket and displaying the grip of her own weapon poking out of the holster underneath her left armpit. "We didn't get the memo, okay?"

The driver stared furiously at Burke but said nothing.

Ikeda followed Trapp's lead and dropped her weapon. An equally thorough search followed before she too was pronounced clean.

"So," Trapp murmured quietly to Burke after the driver stepped away to place a call. "When do we get to the main course?"

"Who says we get to, after that stunt?" the DEA man said through gritted teeth.

"Hey!" Trapp protested. "Like I told you, we aren't cops. Down here the only backup we have is each other. So you better believe I'm making sure I'm protected."

Burke's expression softened, though he said nothing. The driver walked over and gestured at them to follow. He left the two pistols on the ground, and Trapp knew better than to attempt to retrieve them.

They walked for about ten minutes down the potholed track. It was bone dry at the moment, but he guessed that a few months from now it would be a morass of churned-up mud every bit as sticky as the Somme.

They had to be at least half an hour away from any major settlement, which meant that though the glow of what he presumed was Toluca was definitely visible on the horizon, little light pollution fouled the night sky. Between that and the endless rows of cornstalks to either side, it was difficult to make out any information that might allow him to work out where he was.

That, of course, was the point.

Throughout the walk, Trapp was confronted with the distinct impression that they were being watched. He suspected that someone was following the small procession from the field to his left. There must have been a tractor track just inside the first row of corn. He didn't glance at the source of the slight but distinct sound or give any impression that he had noticed anything amiss.

They turned a corner, and the dim shape of a building loomed out of the darkness. It was a large farmhouse, and though from this point he could see only two sides, he guessed it was a rectangular shaped courtyard. A little farther away, a large barn dominated the skyline, blocking out the stars.

Three figures were waiting for them out front. All men, each standing at one point of a triangle. They wore pistols on their hips, though none were drawn.

"Hector!" Burke said with quiet but evident satisfaction. "Good to see you're safe."

The man at the front nodded. "Thank you for your warning. I'm in your debt."

"You'd do the same for me," Burke said. "Though let's hope you don't have to, huh?"

"These are the two you mentioned?" Hector said.

He seemed to be studying both Trapp and Ikeda very closely. For his part, Trapp was doing the same. Hector Alvarez León was a striking man, even in the gloom. He was lithe, and in a way that reminded Trapp of Ikeda – the way she moved with a dancer's grace.

He suspected that on this matter, too, he should keep his mouth shut. It was unlikely that she would either understand or appreciate the compliment. Which probably meant it was nothing of the sort.

"They are," Burke confirmed. "You can trust them."

"Can we trust him?" Trapp remarked.

Burke turned with undisguised irritation. "Dammit, Jason.

He's good people –"

"Why do you say that?" Hector interrupted. "You sound unsure of me, my friend."

"I don't like people pointing guns at me," Trapp said baldly.

"I am not."

"I didn't say you were," Trapp said.

He extended his arm and pointed at Hector's chest, holding the limb outstretched for a couple of increasingly uncomfortable seconds before raising it and pointing at the top of the farmhouse, near the corner where the two walls joined.

"But he is," Trapp said, rotating his body and shifting his attention to the fields just behind them. He located the point at which he figured the unseen watcher must be standing. "And him."

He returned his attention to Hector, curious as to the man's response.

The Mexican Marine stood silently for a few seconds, as if considering what to say. Trapp liked that about a man. It was never good to rush into a situation half-cocked, and yet too many did.

"You have good eyes," León remarked. "Not many men can identify Espinoza in the darkness. He's one of my best."

"Let's hope he's not watching your back if someone ever sends me to kill you," Trapp grunted. "You mind?"

Again, a short silence before Hector put two fingers between his lips and let out a loud whistle. Behind Trapp, a figure ghosted out of the darkness, and above, a small chip of terra-cotta roof tiling shattered against the concrete farmyard.

"As I said, you have good eyes. I'll let him know."

Turning to Ikeda, he said, "And you, Madam? What should I call you?"

"Liz will do. Nice to meet you, Hector. I can call you that, right?"

"I have no other name," he said, smiling for the first time

and gesturing behind him. "Please, come inside."

Trapp followed the trim young Mexican officer into the farmhouse. He was right, he saw – the building was a rectangle, built around a small courtyard, which, quite unlike the remainder of the farmyard, contained a beautifully manicured garden. Ikeda walked alongside him and Burke a pace behind, his nose apparently still out of joint. It would pass, he knew. The DEA was the same as the FBI was the same as the CIA was the same as the Army; everyone had their territory and their ways of doing things and didn't take too kindly to someone with different ideas.

They always got over it.

Inside, the farmhouse was dimly lit, mostly with candles, along with a few wall-bracketed electric lamps. The furniture was rustic but solid, and probably hadn't changed much in the last fifty years. Perhaps longer. The walls were solid brick and whitewashed. It was surprisingly cool, a refreshing change from the warmth of the night.

To Trapp's surprise, he found a woman inside cradling a young, sleeping dark-haired child. She was seated in front of a large dining table – grand enough for a dozen places – in an alcove near the kitchen. There were a few more men inside, two of them playing cards on a coffee table between two old, frayed sofas. They glanced up without surprise, then returned to their game.

All were young, in that surprising way of military men. Some looked barely older than boys, and yet Trapp knew without doubt that they could not be further from the life they'd once known.

"This is my wife, María," Hector said, a strange expression passing over his face in the candlelight – at once exhausted, tense, and tender. "And my daughter, Gabriella."

The front door closed behind the last of Hector's men. Trapp counted about ten of them in total.

"You brought them here?" he remarked without either surprise or reproach in his voice.

"Where else would you have me take them?" Hector shrugged tightly. He leaned forward and kissed his wife on the cheek, murmuring something into her ear. She nodded and rose to her feet as a murmur of confusion passed through the daughter's lips. María mimed that she was putting the girl to bed.

Though it was late, the table was still strewn with the remnants of a meal: black beans, spiced rice, tortillas, a simple salad.

Hector sat, the weight escaping with a grunt. "Are you hungry?"

"We ate already," Ikeda replied quickly.

Trapp shrugged. "I could eat."

He earned a sharp elbow in the ribs. "Jason!"

"What? I'm a growing guy, all right?"

That earned him a laugh and seemed to relax the rest of Hector's men, which was his intention all along. He joined the Mexican captain and reached for a plate, which he stacked with a generous selection of the delicacies on offer.

"Did your wife make all this?" Ikeda asked, joining him. She stole a mouthful from the side of his plate. He'd expected that, too.

"I did," Hector said, leaning back and rolling his neck. "It helps me think."

"That can be a dangerous business," Trapp remarked. "But it's good."

"The food – or the thinking?"

"Depends."

"That it does," Hector said with a low rumble that seemed to startle Ikeda before she realized it was a chuckle. He fell silent in a way that indicated Trapp was meant to finish eating before they got to business, which he did with gusto, even helping himself to seconds, much to her dismay and their host's evident amusement.

Hector rose to clear the empty dishes, and one of his men jumped to assist but was waved away with an almost fatherly gesture for a man so young. It was evident that these Marines respected their captain deeply. Then again, they would have to to follow him here.

"What is this place?" Trapp asked once they were seated once more.

Their host gestured at one of the younger men, one of the two who had stood behind him when they'd first arrived. He looked up somewhat uncertainly, then away when it was clear he wasn't needed. "Lieutenant Ramirez over there. It's his family's farm. They've had it in their family for four generations."

"Where are they?"

"Somewhere else."

"That's fair," Trapp agreed as a new thought occurred to him. "What about your men – do they have families as well?"

Hector inclined his head sadly, the gravity of his shared predicament inked in his eyes. "Some. They will be coming here, where we can protect them."

"Why not now?"

"Their houses: are they being watched?"

Trapp frowned. "I don't know."

"Nor do I."

"I see."

"Tell me, Jason, why are you here?" Hector asked after a short pause.

That, Trapp mused, was an exceedingly good question. He didn't *need* to be here. His president had asked, of course, and that was as good a reason as any – as good as any he'd ever needed – but he'd served his time. Nash would have understood if he declined.

Was it an addiction to this life, he wondered? A fear of what came after?

His answer, when it came, was weak and transactional, and it was clear that Hector thought the same, even if he was too polite to say. "Because someone asked me to."

"And that's enough?"

"I'm here, aren't I?" Trapp replied, a bit of bite in his voice now. "Why are *you* here? You could run. Maybe claim asylum up north. You'd get it."

Maybe, he didn't say.

Hector looked toward the closed door behind which his wife and daughter had disappeared. "Do you have any children, Jason?"

He was suddenly conscious of Ikeda's presence by his side. "Never found the time. And my line of work's a little dangerous for that kind of thing."

"So is mine."

Trapp unconsciously glanced around the dimly lit farmhouse, causing Hector to sigh gently.

"Yes, perhaps you're right. And still, if I could go back and do it all again, I would still make the same decision. Can I make a suggestion, Jason?"

Trapp glanced at Ikeda, whose face was inscrutable. When he looked back, he realized that Hector had seen it. And the look of unspoken understanding passed over the young Mexican's face. So he saw that too.

He gestured gruffly. "Go ahead."

"Don't close a door before you've stepped through it. You might like what lies on the other side."

"I'll take that under advisement," Trapp replied shortly. "But what about this present mess? What are you doing to get yourself out of it?"

Hector stood and clapped him gently on the shoulder. "That is a question for tomorrow, perhaps. We'll speak in the morning."

35

L ieutenant Ramirez tossed him the keys underarm.
Trapp snatched them nimbly from the air, determining their position more on instinct than eyesight,
given the darkening gloom of night. They jangled as they disappeared into his callused palms.

Ikeda regarded him with a raised eyebrow. "Sure you don't
want me to come?"

"Need to clear my head, that's all," he replied. "I won't be
long."

"Fine," she sighed. "But damn if I wouldn't kill for a swim
right now."

"What about the river?" Trapp asked, jerking his thumb in a
direction that was vaguely over his shoulder, where the river
Lerma flowed.

"That thing?" she said, wrinkling her nose. "No thank you.
It's more of a drainage ditch than a river. God only knows
what's in it. Fertilizer, human waste, take your pick."

"And here I thought you were tough," Trapp laughed.

"Get out of here before you find out," she said.

He did exactly that. The Jeep Cherokee was parked on the

edge of the property and was unlocked when he reached it. He liked that – it said a lot about a place. It had once been a stone-baked red, though the chassis was so dented, scratched, and aged by the region's relentless sunshine and the vicissitudes of farm life that the original paint job was barely visible. It had to be at least two decades old.

And that was before you saw the thick coat of dried mud and grit that painted most of the rear, including the windows.

Trapp climbed in, adjusted the rear mirror, and started the engine. Old as it was, it turned over without a hitch, and he was rewarded for his effort with a throaty rumble. It was a stick shift, which he preferred. Felt more like driving that way.

He fed the engine a little gas and selected first gear, creeping through the farmyard slowly to avoid accidentally murdering one of the many free-range chickens that treated the place as their own. It wasn't so much that he minded snapping a chicken's neck – he'd grown up in a place not too dissimilar from this – it was just that he preferred his chickens butterflied, not pancaked.

Second gear took him back to the main road, and he started driving nowhere in particular, following a sedan about thirty yards ahead, and in front of an SUV whose headlights looked about twenty behind. With the windows down to allow some of the night air to whistle through the car and some Mexican love ballad blaring on the radio, Trapp felt a tension he didn't know he felt begin to subside.

It was always like this in the days and hours leading up to an operation, he knew. In the moment, when the bullets were flying and grenades began to fly and he didn't have a choice if he wanted to live – then he felt no fear. But the waiting, damn he hated it. Knowing what was to come and knowing there wasn't a damn thing he could do about it.

That's why you had to savor moments like this. Moments where you could forget all of the hell out there in the real world and just remind yourself what you were doing this for in the first place.

He glanced into the rearview mirror as the SUV behind indicated right and executed a messy, slightly too fast turn onto a side road. This far out into the country, though they occasionally passed through sets of traffic lights, the route was not blessed with the glow of streetlights. He didn't really mind. It was easier to lose himself this way.

"I wonder what you're saying, buddy," Trapp murmured as he listened to the radio, tapping against the steering wheel as the singer crooned his lyrics with impossible haste. Even if he could make it through the accent – which he suspected he could not – at this pace he could only make out one word in ten.

Still, it sounded good.

At a crossroad up ahead, he saw the traffic lights dance from green to amber to red and watched as the sedan stepped on the gas, even though it had no chance of making it in time.

"Asshole," Trapp muttered, knowing that a decade before, as a younger, less world-weary man, he would probably have done the same.

And who are you kidding? He grinned to himself. *At his age it's all testosterone.*

By contrast, he stepped on the brake and downshifted through the gears until the Cherokee was stopped at the red light. He briefly toyed with the idea of stepping on the gas on the other side and seeing how far this baby could go but discounted it. No sense getting himself hurt the day before an operation.

It happened more often than you might think. He shook his head. *Testosterone.*

Up ahead, the sedan's taillights winked around the corner, and Trapp found himself entirely alone in the darkness, his own headlights lighting only a small pool of asphalt in front and nothing to the sides. There was no one behind him. Just him, the Jeep, and Casanova on the radio.

The red light didn't linger long. He glanced up, saw it returning back to amber, and fed a little gas into the engine.

He only got a second's warning. Just a flash in the rearview mirror and the rustle of movement closer than it had any right to be.

How–?

It was instinct that fueled his reaction, pitiful as it was, rather than anything more studied. Trapp looked over his shoulder, the muscles on his forehead wrinkling his brow as he tried to work out what the hell was going on.

And then the rope looped around his throat, and whoever was in the back pulled tight, levering their weight against the back of the seat and yanking with all their might. The hard, man-made fibers dug into his skin with terrible force, the ligature forming deep, dark, bruised welts that began to bloom almost instantly.

Trapp understood his predicament in an instant. And just as quickly, the horrific reality dawned on him that if he did not do something fast, then the decision would be taken out of his hands. Whoever was attempting to kill him was good. That much was made perfectly clear by the fact that he hadn't detected their presence this entire drive.

In the background, the singer crooned his lullaby, a discordant, almost satirical soundtrack to the life or death struggle taking place inside the Jeep's cab. The engine – on the verge of stalling – started making its displeasure known.

What the fuck do I do?

Trapp knew that the only thing that had saved him so far was that last second turn of the head. It meant the rope was biting into the side of his neck rather than his windpipe. But it would only buy him a couple more seconds of inaction.

Trapp tried forcing his torso forward, stiffening his core and attempting to lever his way out of the problem. The motion caused him to step a little on the gas pedal, trickling a few droplets into the combustion chamber, where it ignited and jerked the Cherokee forward a few feet.

But that was all it got him.

Behind him, his unseen assailant applied even more pressure on the rope, enough that the nerve endings on Trapp's neck were beginning to cry out in agony. His fingers scrabbled around the side of the seat, but to no avail. He couldn't pry his way out of the problem. He couldn't turn. He couldn't push himself forward – there was *nothing* he could do.

Panic invaded his brainstem. Inside his chest, his heart worked overtime, sending adrenaline pumping through his system as a veil of darkness began falling over his eyes.

"Not today!" he choked – at least he meant to. Whether the words came out or not he didn't know. But that wasn't the point.

Trapp stepped on the gas, reaching blindly for the stick shift's gear lever and somehow putting it into third. The engine squealed in protest, but there was enough gas flowing through the system for it not to matter. The engine of the Cherokee started picking up speed. It was impossible to say how fast, but probably not very.

Behind him, a man said something like, "Puta!"

Truthfully, that too was impossible to say. He could no longer even hear the soothing sounds of the man lost in the agony of love, or the description he couldn't understand about a woman he'd never met.

The Cherokee kept picking up pace. Trapp forced it through fourth gear, then into fifth, and jammed the gas pedal down. How long had this been going on?

Ten seconds?

Twenty?

It felt like a lifetime. And it would be unless this worked.

Trapp forced his eyes open as the man behind him switched

to desperation, yanking the rope left and right in his attempts to finally end his life, scoring his delicate skin ever deeper.

The mantra repeated over and over in his mind.

Not today.

With hundreds of yards of open road ahead of him as far as he could make out, Trapp gave the gas pedal a little extra attention, coaxing as much speed out of the Cherokee's engine as it had to give.

At his side, his fingers searched for the seat lever. And a horrifying thought hit him.

Please don't be electric.

It wasn't. His fingers clutched around good, cold, old-fashioned steel. And at the precise moment that he found it, he stepped his entire weight onto the brake pedal, just as he yanked the seat lever back.

A lot of things happened all at once.

Instantly, the soothing tunes of the radio were wiped out by the scream of the Cherokee's tires on the road, and a thousand old coins, discarded pens, pieces of rope, and old farm machinery suddenly started flying forward in the car, propelled by their own momentum.

And, of course, the person behind him wasn't left out.

That was the bit that even Trapp's oxygen-starved mind wasn't looking forward to.

He took his foot off the brake just in time for the entire weight of what had to be an adult male – and a large one – to crash into the back of his seat, and without the resistance of the seat mechanism, which collapsed inward like the jaws of a pair of pliers, squashing him against the steering wheel.

The horn let out a long, mournful groan, a plaintive cry for help, and then burned out – leaving a ringing in Trapp's ears.

Without anyone holding the wheel, any gas going into the engine, or pressure on the brake, the Cherokee began to wobble wildly on the road as it surged forward, out of control.

But he didn't have time to focus on that. His hands reversed their earlier motion and went for the rope, tugging it away from his neck with all his might.

Trapp met no resistance. His attacker was still too startled by the sudden change in his relation to gravity. He ducked out of the noose and instantly twisted in his seat, jamming his thigh against the steering wheel and smashing his entire weight into his seat back, forcing it into the other direction.

The man behind – it was a man – loosed a guttural grunt as the plastic collided with his face. His fingers were still wrapped uselessly around the two ends of rope, and it was only now that they gave way. Trapp didn't wait for him to regain his senses. Regardless of the fate of the Cherokee, now quickly careering off the road, his only focus was on the guy behind.

It was difficult to fight inside the confines of the car, but he managed to get one good punch into the man's temple, striking with vicious force for all that he could only draw his elbow back a few inches. His assailant's skull rocked backward, cracking against the rear headrest with a thud that echoed even over the roar of the engine.

Trapp's brain practically began to overheat with all the demands being made upon it. He shifted down a gear, dropping the speed to around forty miles an hour, and twisted the wheel right and left, making sharp turns in the center of the dark, empty road.

"How do you like that?" he yelled through gritted teeth as he clutched the wheel with one hand, peering back over his right shoulder only to see the dark-haired man lunging toward him once again.

"Crap," Trapp muttered, stomping hard on the gas pedal and jerking the steering wheel violently to the right.

The combined effect on the motion of the Cherokee upset his joy rider's balance, and though his outstretched fist still made contact with the side of Trapp's head, it was only a glancing blow as the man was flung across the SUV's rear seats, his shoulder colliding with the rear door.

Trapp spun the wheel to the left this time, sending the man in the other direction. With his free hand, he scrabbled for his seat's lever. It was still unlatched, and the back of the seat had now fallen away from him. He was now only remaining upright by virtue of his grip on the steering wheel and an exertion of core strength that was beginning to test his aging frame.

He leaned sharply forward, using the still-attached seatbelt to pull the seat back with him, and clicked it back into place. The angle wasn't ideal, but then, nothing about the situation was. He glanced up into the rearview mirror, hoping he had half a second while the man recovered.

But already, his unknown passenger was coming for him again, fist clenched, teeth bared in a vicious snarl as he launched himself over the center console.

Trapp howled something inchoate as he stomped on the brakes for a second time, now with all his might. The Cherokee's tires screeched loudly – or perhaps it was the brakes themselves – and the Jeep skidded wildly across a section of road that was scattered with loose stones.

The wheels locked.

Time slowed.

Every fraction of a second felt a minute, every minute an hour.

The edge of the road was approaching fast, and while the vehicle wasn't headed directly for it, it was only a matter of seconds away. Trapp knew that he had to take his foot off the brake, to somehow regain control of this skid, or they would both die.

Just a little longer…

His passenger's frame soared, entirely airborne, through the space between the two front seats. At first, the man's fist was outstretched, his expression almost feral, but that quickly changed. Perhaps it was just Trapp's mind filling in the details as his body's position shifted in midair from something that almost resembled a javelin to one that was entirely comic. Roadrunner flailing off the edge of a cliff.

And then the crown of his skull collided with the windshield with a sickening thud.

Trapp took his foot off the brake just in time.

36

Trapp cast one last glance into the Cherokee's backseats as he spun the truck back into the farm-yard, a trail of dust behind him in the rear lights and pebbles rattling against the chassis. His prisoner was still exactly where he was supposed to be – trussed with his own rope and Trapp's belt.

He was also deeply unconscious, with a trail of blood flowing freely down the side of his face from a wound lost somewhere in the forest of his dark hair.

"Little help, guys?" Trapp murmured under his breath, hammering the horn in the center of the steering wheel and repeatedly flashing his headlights as he closed on the farmhouse.

Almost instantly, he saw three men emerge, all armed. He suspected that the shooter on the roof had had a bead on the vehicle ever since he got within range.

Good. After this, they would need to post double patrols. How this guy had gotten so close, Trapp couldn't understand. And how he'd found the farmhouse in the first place was another question entirely.

He brought the truck skidding to a halt, killed the engine, and opened the driver's door in about half a second flat, sending his boots thudding onto the dusty concrete and absorbing the impact with his knees.

Bad idea.

The force ricocheted up Trapp's spine and caused his exhausted neck muscles to scream out in agony. His hand jumped involuntarily to meet it, and a grimace formed on his face, which took him a little while to force away.

"What's going on?" Ramirez asked, dropping his pistol to his side as he recognized Trapp's face. He was flanked on either side by two more of Hector's men, and the captain himself emerged from the farmhouse shortly after – clothed, but still barefoot.

Trapp jerked his thumb at the truck and opened the rear door. "This guy a friend of yours? Because he just tried to kill me."

Ramirez took a step forward, but Hector pushed him aside before he got a chance to peer into the vehicle.

The second he got a good look, he slammed his palm against the roof of the truck. "Son of a bitch. What happened?"

"He jumped me at a traffic light. Was in the back seat the whole time, I think," Trapp admitted with considerable embarrassment. "I don't know how I didn't realize."

"Is he still alive?"

"Just barely." Trapp shrugged, wincing at the pain this elicited. "Least he was when I tied him up. Sorry about the Jeep."

"Ramirez will get over it. Won't you, Lieutenant?"

Without waiting for a response, Hector started barking orders for his men to get the prisoner inside. A pair of them darted back toward the barn, passing Ikeda on the way. Her hair was dark and wet from the shower, and it had left patches on the shoulder of her T-shirt. Unlike Hector, she was at least wearing shoes, though they remained unlaced.

"Jason..." she said, concern etched onto her face as she got close enough to see the welts on his neck. She reached up to examine it. "What the heck happened?"

Trapp shrugged her ministrations aside, mainly because now even the feel of her breath against his damaged skin was beginning to sting. "Just a scuffle, that's all."

"Hell of a scuffle..." Ikeda replied, a bite in her voice, which soon softened. "I can't let you go anywhere on your own, can I?"

He grinned and felt the adrenaline rushing through his system finally beginning to subside. His attacker was most assuredly unconscious, and Trapp had taken the time to restrain him properly, but even so, the man was a hell of a fighter, and the whole drive back he'd wondered whether it would be enough. Their battle had been a close run thing. He'd won, but he wasn't sure he'd have lasted a second round.

The two Marines returned from the barn carrying a large, wide plank of wood, which they promptly – and not entirely carefully – loaded the man onto. Ramirez supervised the procedure, intervening only to ensure they kept his neck straight.

Trapp took a step forward and stood by Hector's side as they watched the would-be assassin's unconscious body stretchered out of the back of the truck and into the house. "So what's his deal? You look like you know him."

Hector nodded. "Not well. But I've seen him before. Just once."

"He got a name?"

"Come on. Let's get inside," Hector said. "I will explain."

The Mexican Marine officer stopped to issue a string of commands to his men, who quickly filed off in different directions, returning with various pieces of equipment and an array of weapons. Trapp quickly understood that they were forming a perimeter – or at least, reinforcing the one that already existed.

They went inside. The makeshift stretcher was laid out on the dining table, and two of Hector's men were in the process of sliding it out from underneath him as another bound his ankles and wrists to the table legs, leaving him splayed out on top of it.

Now María was issuing her own orders. She looked pale and somewhat shellshocked but had as firm a level of control over Hector's men as her husband did.

"Agua," she snapped, pointing at the stove and snapping her fingers as she crouched down and retrieved a bundle of rags from a wooden drawer. "Make sure it's hot!"

Another Marine exited one of the bedrooms with a large olive green duffel bag, from which he pulled out a medical pack emblazoned with a red and white cross. He put it down on the dining table.

"Sit!"

Trapp's neck snapped to the side – which he swiftly regretted – as he searched for the source of the command. It was Ikeda, and she was pointing at a wooden chair beside the table.

"Huh?"

"You heard me," she said, opening the first-aid kit and pulling out a variety of sachets, bandages, and Lord knows what else.

"I'm fine," he grunted, waving away the offer.

"You've got enough scars on your body, Jason," she snapped. "So sit your ass down and let me make sure you don't get another."

He knew better than to argue. And besides, the last thing he needed was to pick up some sub-tropical skin-eating disease down here. It was bad enough that he had nearly died tonight.

There was no point tempting fate and ending up with necrotizing fasciitis.

"Okay."

Trapp sat back heavily. Beneath him, the chair's feet squeaked as it scraped backward across the flagstone floor. Ikeda tore open a sachet containing a disinfectant wipe. He reached for it, but she batted his attempt aside.

María, in many ways aping Ikeda's mannerisms, pointed at a small flashlight on the table, which her husband handed to her. She stood and leaned over the man's prone, unresponsive form. Trapp noted that Hector was watching his prisoner carefully and didn't doubt that he would leap into action the second he saw something amiss.

Though Trapp suspected that would not be necessary. This guy wouldn't be waking up for a while.

María peeled the unconscious man's eyelids back and manipulated the flashlight in a cross pattern – side to side, then up and down as she observed any response. She did the same with the next eye, then murmured something to her husband.

"His pupils are very dilated," he reported. "Unconscious, for sure."

"Good," Trapp grunted malevolently. "So – you plan on telling me who he is? You said you'd seen him before."

The Mexican stepped toward Trapp so he didn't have to raise his voice to reply, though he always kept a wary eye on what was happening on the table beside him. "Once, I said. At the prison, just a few days ago."

"But you know who he is?"

Hector nodded slowly. "I think so. César Torres. At least, that's the name we have on file. It might be right. Probably not."

"So who is he?"

"A hitman," Hector said, his face scrunching up with disdain. "A cleaner. A psychopath."

"I think you're supposed to call them sociopaths these days," Trapp added mildly. "What's so bad about this one?"

"Call him a serial killer, then. He's a freelancer, mostly. Works for whoever pays him best. Until recently, he was thought to be dead."

"Until the prison?"

"Yes. Or if not dead, then at least retired. Intelligence isn't my department, you understand, but I keep on top of the most wanted list, and I read my briefings. He used to be right at the very top, but he hasn't been seen in a couple of years. Until last week."

"And today."

"Yes," Hector winced. "And today."

THE FIRST OUTBREAK of moaning from the prisoner came about two hours later. Trapp, who had allowed himself to fall into a somewhat meditative state, became instantly alert. He didn't move but focused his attention on the dining table to which César Torres was strapped.

Beside him, Ikeda did the same.

César mumbled something in Spanish, though the words were far from intelligible.

"You think we should wake someone up?" Ikeda mouthed into his ear, keeping her voice intentionally low. "In case he says something useful?"

Trapp considered the question and immediately agreed. Eliza disappeared into the murky gloom of the mostly unlit farmhouse to find help. Only a few candles provided illumination – all of the electric lamps were off.

He grabbed one of the candles and walked quietly over to the table, the flickering flame casting shadows that danced atop the flagstones and whitewashed walls. He stood silently a few feet from César, listening as the man said nothing in particular. It wasn't entirely clear that the sounds he was making were words, even this close.

He set the candle down on the table, ensuring that it was far away from the ropes that bound the prisoner's limbs. Even in the warm glow of the candlelight, the pallid color of César's face was evident. Hundreds of tiny droplets of sweat had bubbled on his skin, and Trapp started to wonder whether they should have found him a doctor after all. He looked like he might die at any moment.

There was a bowl of water not far from César's head and a wet rag beside it. Trapp reached for it and soaked it before lifting it over the man's lips and dribbling a little in. The cool liquid seemed to startle him at first before his mouth and tongue started searching greedily for the cool flow.

"Drink up," Trapp murmured softly. "It'll help."

César's eyes jerked open, startling Trapp, who flinched backward, clenching his palm around the cloth as he did so. A little too much water dribbled into the Mexican hitman's mouth, and he choked.

Trapp grimaced, dropped the cloth, and reached for the back of his head, gently angling it upward so that the water would flow down his throat rather than into his windpipe. He didn't mind if the guy died after all this. But drowning was a hell of a way to go.

"What do you want?" César said, his eyes still rotating wildly in their sockets. He seemed unable to focus on anything in particular.

Trapp said nothing, at least not immediately. He didn't know how to respond. Then he frowned. César had spoken English. Not Spanish. Was there anything strange about that?

"I found León," César said, mumbling, his head now lolling from side to side. "With an American. What do you want me to do with him?"

He doesn't know where he is, was Trapp's immediate thought. The realization opened up a world of possibilities, though the likelihood of any of them coming off seemed faint.

"What do you suggest?" Trapp said softly.

"This was never going to work," César said scornfully, his eyelids now closing. "Americans, you think you know everything. Everything!"

Americans? What the hell is he talking about?

On the other side of the farmhouse, Ikeda emerged from one of the hallways, Hector in close pursuit. Trapp glanced up, holding a finger to his lips, his eyes flashing urgently in warning.

"Grover, you idiot," César crowed, his voice growing fainter and fainter with every word as he dropped back into unconsciousness. "All you have done is construct your own coffin."

Trapp warned the others to remain silent as he leaned over César's once again motionless frame, checking whether he was truly unconscious once more. Satisfied, he beckoned for them to approach.

"Either of you heard that name before?"

Hector shook his head, nonplussed.

"Me neither," Ikeda agreed. "I'll fire it over to Nick. Maybe he can work something up by the time our friend wakes up from his little nap…"

37

"This was planned, Jason," Pope started as soon the secure video line blinked into life. "At least, that's our working assumption."

"Good morning to you too," Trapp said, lifting a steaming cup of coffee to his mouth and taking a large gulp, regardless of the fact that the previous two had already scalded the back of his throat. "Why don't you start from the beginning? What was planned – and who did the planning?"

"Hold on," Pope said, leaning toward the camera and fiddling with his laptop so that the video feed shook uncontrollably. Trapp glanced at Ikeda and Burke, who for all the supposed seriousness of the moment were restraining their shared desire to smile.

Pope cursed and beckoned Kelly over. The younger, savvier agent instantly achieved what he wanted: sharing his laptop screen. On the Mexican end, an image appeared on-screen. It was of a young man in dress greens with lieutenants' bars on his shoulders. He was in his early twenties, but already his hairline was halfway up his skull.

"This," Pope said, looking slightly flustered as he hove back into view, "is Warren Grover. Lieutenant Colonel, U.S. Army. Retired. He mustered out back in 2006. Medical discharge. Bad back."

"Okay..." Trapp murmured. He drank the rest of his cup. "And why am I looking at him?"

"We finally put a face to a name with Conway's handler," Pope said, tapping the computer a couple of times and pulling two new photographs onto the screen: the now-familiar surveillance shot from a few days before, and a similar U.S. Army file photograph, again of a young officer.

"This is Ethan Fitz. Also U.S. Army, Captain, retired. A few years younger than Grover, but he was also discharged in 2006. In October, just like Grover. The day after, in fact."

"Uh huh."

"When we learned Fitz's name, we pulled his army files from the National Personnel Records Center down in Missouri. His and everyone he so much as sneezed on. Grover's file didn't jump out. His jacket is squeaky clean, just like our boy Ethan here. Looking at what their superiors wrote, they were just about model soldiers. But when you flagged up the name Grover, the connection was easy to make."

"What connection?" Trapp asked, naturally enough.

"Well—" Pope grimaced. "That's the problem. We know these guys had very similar careers. They jumped from base to base at roughly the same times. The problem is, their files are clean. Way too clean to be real."

"They've been sanitized," Ikeda deduced.

"Exactly. All these documents tell us is that they both worked in Army intelligence about the same time in about the same places. Their performance evaluations are either missing or written by superior officers who don't seem to exist. Anything about that strike you as unusual?"

Trapp groaned. "Where should I start? These guys have black outfit written all over them. Where did you get with the Army? Any connection with that guy who got himself knifed in the park?"

Pope raised his eyebrows meaningfully. "Stonewalled. These guys were discharged a decade and a half ago. Either someone knows who they are and what they were up to and isn't telling us, or –"

"– Or just as likely it was so long ago that nobody has any idea, and now they've gotten this far, they don't exactly want to go plowing up the field in case they find a body," Trapp finished.

"Precisely."

"I sent a request to the agent in charge at the St. Louis field office to go to the Center in person and pull the paper records, just in case they contain something that didn't make it into the system, but I'm not hopeful. We are further than we were, but it's looking like a dead end."

"What about interviewing everyone connected to Grover and Fitz?" Burke asked. "That has to be better than nothing, right?"

It was an option, Trapp thought, but one that was more understandable for a cop than someone in his own line of work. Pope shortly said the same.

"If that's all we're left with, then we'll do it. But I'm kind of hoping to avoid that. Ex-military is the same as retired law enforcement – close-knit. Who's to say these guys haven't asked their old friends to let them know if anyone comes asking around? Or worse, what if they are still working together?"

Burke nodded but stayed silent, looking a little embarrassed that he hadn't considered that eventuality.

"Nick's right," Ikeda murmured thoughtfully. "If we can, we need to do this quietly."

"You have any suggestions?" Pope groaned, massaging his temples. "Because I have to tell you, Jason – we are all out."

Trapp nodded. "One."

"Care to share?"

"A guy I used to work for in Delta. General Caldwell. If there's something to know about these guys that isn't in the files, I'm guessing either he knows it, or he can tell us who will."

Pope sat up and reached for a pen off-screen, which hovered over a notepad that set just in view. He looked up expectantly. "You got his number?"

"Not that easy, champ." Trapp winced. "He's a... How can I say this? A cantankerous kind of guy. Lives off grid near the Shenandoah National Park."

"Of course he does..." Pope sighed. "Okay then. What about an address?"

THE TWO FBI agents were in the air less than half an hour later. It could have been sooner, but they chose to fly in an unmarked Bureau helicopter, as opposed to choosing one of the more numerous – and conspicuous – units marked with three yellow letters.

"What about that?" Pope called out through the intercom headset, pointing at a small homestead surrounded on three sides by thickets of thickly-hemmed trees and bracketed on the fourth by a narrow dirt track, about wide enough for a 1990s pickup truck.

Kelly craned over him in a fashion that might have caused a couple of raised eyebrows had it occurred back in the office, rather than in the field.

"It's in the right place," she said, her voice raised over the combination of the rotor wash and engine noise.

Pope shrugged and leaned forward to tap the pilot on the

shoulder. He indicated the small clearing in question and asked, "You think you can put us down there without digging a rotor into the dust?"

"Sure thing," came the casual, almost lackadaisical response.

He knew that the FBI pilots were good – mostly former military – but even so, his lunch almost divorced his stomach as the man guided the small aircraft into a steep dive before pirouetting the bird's tail 180° and setting it down on a dime just behind a small, three-sided garage roofed with rusted corrugated iron that had the bed of a pickup poking out.

"Thanks, buddy," Pope said, lifting his headset off his ears and yelling out right over the noise that ensued. "You good to wait here?"

"Ain't got a better offer," the pilot replied with an accompanying thumbs-up. He reached under his seat and pulled out a paperback. "I'll be here when you need me. You go do your secret agent shit."

Pope chuckled. "Thanks, Dick. Be right back."

The engine had powered down by this point, though the rotors were still turning in long, lazy spins overhead. They were visible now, which provided a somewhat more disconcerting reminder of the damage they might do to an unsuspecting passerby. He jumped out and kept his frame hunched over far longer than was probably necessary. They were both dressed in black suits – him wearing a tie and Kelly only an open shirt, which proved to be an advantage when his tie whipped violently in the chopper's wash.

By the time they reached the homestead itself, a wooden cabin with a small covered porch and a tin roof, the sounds and fury had almost completely died away. Pope reflected that a man like the one Jason had described – one so unconvinced by modern society that he'd chosen to remove himself from it – probably had little love for the method of arrival, either.

"What do you figure?" he asked as they made it to the cabin, stopping just short of the porch. "Think anyone's home?"

Kelly took a step back, her short-cut hair bobbing around her chin as she did so. Her eyes passed over the entire cabin, and she took her time before she spoke.

"There's smoke coming out the chimney," was all she said.

Now that she mentioned it, he could smell the wood smoke. It wasn't so different from the smog and vehicle pollution of the streets of DC in chemical terms – worse in the summer, with the heat and humidity.

He took a step up onto the porch and knocked loudly on the wooden door. "General Caldwell – are you in there, sir?"

There was no answer. Not even the creak of movement elsewhere in the building. Pope frowned. Was the guy deaf? Surely he couldn't have missed the sound of a helicopter landing in his front yard. It couldn't exactly be an everyday occurrence.

He tried knocking again.

Again, no answer.

Without turning to face Kelly, he said, "What do you think? Should we go in?"

A gruff voice answered, causing him to jump almost out of his skin and to land back on his leather soles with an audible thud against the wooden floorboards.

"I wouldn't do that if I were you," the voice intoned roughly. "Stay exactly where you are. And don't turn around."

Pope cleared his throat, careful not to make any sudden movements, mindful of Trapp's description of the man's mood. "General –"

"Did I ask you to speak, son? Keep your eyes front and your tongue still till I tell you something different."

Feeling like he hadn't since Parris Island and with his cheeks coloring, Pope grunted, "Yes sir."

"That goes for you as well, young lady."

For her part, Kelly said nothing.

"Are either of you armed?"

They replied in the affirmative.

"Weapons on the ground. Nice and slow. You first, big guy."

Pope did as he was instructed, reaching for his holster and retrieving the pistol with a thumb and forefinger before holding it out and away from his body. He then crouched and placed it gently on the ground.

"Now you."

Kelly followed.

"Good. Now kick them away. Nice and far, now."

He kicked out with the side of his Oxford shoe, sending the pistol skittering across the wood until it toppled off the other end of the porch. He winced, half-expecting a misfire. Now that would be a hell of a way to end a hell of a day.

"Excellent," the voice – he presumed Caldwell – said, seeming more relaxed. "You can turn around now. Both of you."

Pope did as he was told, and to his surprise noted that General Caldwell wasn't even pointing a weapon at him. He was armed with an antique wooden hunting rifle with a lustrous sheen, but the weapon was shouldered.

"You look surprised." Caldwell grinned. "Did no one ever tell you you're only supposed to point these things at somebody if you're prepared to shoot them?"

Well, at least that's promising, he thought.

"Yes, sir. Just wondering why you made us go through that whole charade, that's all."

"I just needed to check you weren't rangers," Caldwell grunted.

Pope frowned with genuine confusion. What the hell was this guy talking about? "Army Rangers?"

"Why the hell would the Army be looking for me?" Caldwell asked, a smile playing on his lips. "I served my time. And then some."

"Then who?" Kelly asked.

The general's expression softened as he looked at her, and Pope wondered whether that was why she'd spoken up.

"Park rangers."

Pope decided he had better things to do than ask why the park rangers might be after Caldwell. "Do they usually send choppers out looking for you?"

The old man shrugged. "First time for everything."

"Sir, we're with the FBI. You mind if I reach into my jacket for my ID?"

"No need, son," Caldwell scoffed. "I knew who you were the second you stepped out of that bird."

"Have we met?"

"Not your name," came the reply with an expression on Caldwell's face that indicated he thought the question was frankly idiotic. "You've got that Bureau scent all over you. Damn suits."

He shook his head wonderingly. "Well – are you going in or what?"

"After you, sir."

"You came this far, didn't you? After you."

Pope pushed the cabin's front door, finding that it was unlocked, and entered. The cabin was small, only a few rooms set over a single floor, but it was neatly arranged. They stepped directly into the living room, which was covered on three walls by floor-to-ceiling bookshelves and a smoldering woodstove on the last.

Caldwell seated them on the only sofa and poured them each a cup of coffee before he was prepared to engage. Pope sensed he'd spent a lot of years giving orders, and then once that life was over, he'd retreated here. It might have been weeks since he'd last spoken to another human.

"Thank you," he said, accepting a steaming cup.

"Now, how can I help?" Caldwell asked.

"Sir, my name's Nick Pope. I work counterintelligence at the Bureau."

"Thought as much."

"Do you know a guy called Jason Trapp?" Pope asked.

"Never heard of him," Caldwell replied without so much as a flicker of recognition passing over his face. "Should I have?"

Pope bowed his head a second before continuing. "General, he's in no trouble. He sent me here. Said you might be able to help with something. Told me to ask about your daughter."

Caldwell took his time before replying. He didn't look even faintly embarrassed. "In that case, I'm at your disposal."

Pope reached into his jacket pocket and pulled out a cell phone. He turned it on and faced the screen at Caldwell, quickly flicking through several file photographs in his phone's album. "Sir, do you recognize any these men?"

This time, the general looked more pensive as he studied the photos of Warren Grover, Ethan Fitz, and the unnamed victim of the stabbing in LBJ Memorial Park. He gave a curt nod. "Unfortunately."

"Why do you say that?"

"What do you know about them?" Caldwell replied.

Which wasn't exactly how Pope had hoped this conversation would go. He didn't have time for a game of twenty questions.

Glancing around the cabin's small, austere living room, Pope asked, "General – have you been following the news from Mexico?"

Caldwell laughed. "Son, do you see a television in here? I spent the better part of my entire life following every news story that bubbled up from some shithole corner of this godforsaken planet. The last five years I've tried to forget about all of it."

"I envy you, sir. Unfortunately, right now I don't have that luxury. Last week, the administrator of the Drug Enforcement

Administration was executed in Houston, along with half a dozen US Attorneys. The two largest Mexican drug cartels are currently engaged in a drag-out fight south of the border, and the violence is spilling over into the US itself."

"What do Grover, Fitz and Spratt have to do with any of that?"

"You know their names, then?" Pope observed, privately elated that they now had a name for the dead man.

"Like I said – *unfortunately*."

"Tell me about them."

Caldwell sighed and suddenly looked several years older. His skin, clean-shaven and scarred by decades of shaving accidents, sagged. "Son, have you ever heard of an organization known as the Apparatus?"

Pope, nonplussed, shook his head.

"I suspected not. Few have. Fewer still have any idea what it is – or I should say *was*."

"I'm all ears," Pope remarked dryly, glancing meaningfully at Kelly to indicate that she should take notes. Unsurprisingly, she was already way ahead of him, a pad balanced on her knees, pen hovering expectantly over the paper.

"It was a relic of the eighties, I suppose," Caldwell said, settling into his chair. "A think tank, for all intents and purposes."

He looked sharply at Kelly. "This is classified, you understand. And it will be long after all of us are dead."

"I can keep a secret," she replied without blinking.

Even Caldwell cracked a smile at that. "I'm sure you can. Okay – where was I?"

"A think tank," she said.

"Yeah. But not the report writing kind. None of that bullshit. The Army has enough of those. It did, anyway, and I don't suppose much has changed. The Apparatus was an informal kind of organization, dreamed up by an officer from Army

Intelligence called Marion Spratt who thought that Big Army was too slow, too hidebound, too stuck in the past.

"The idea was simple. Bad ones usually are. The bad guys get to be creative, you understand. They don't have to play by the rules. The Apparatus didn't, either. Usually we have to wait for the enemy to strike us before Washington loosens up the Rules of Engagement. But that way Americans die. The Apparatus was designed to see crises coming and nip them in the bud—by any means necessary. And that's where things got more than a little unethical."

"I don't understand," Pope said.

"Let's put it this way," Caldwell replied. "Maybe there's an up-and-coming politician in a small South American country who doesn't like Big Sam and isn't afraid to shoot his mouth off about it to his electorate. And maybe that guy gets popular, and then he gets himself elected, and suddenly the US of A gets shut out of a counter-narcotics campaign, or the new government refuses to cooperate on military matters or migrant flows, that kind of thing."

"Uh huh."

"Well wouldn't it be easier if that politician just...disappeared?"

Pope frowned. "You're suggesting that this...Apparatus... was involved in plans to murder a foreign head of state."

"Not quite," General Caldwell said. "Like I said, the idea was to nip the problems in the bud early. Arrange an unfortunate accident for some foreign parliamentarian before he or she became president, that kind of thing. Maybe funnel funds to a more friendly candidate, too."

"Jesus."

"Watch your language," Caldwell snapped.

"Did this ever happen?"

"I don't know. Not for sure. Spratt always countenanced ideas that most of the rest of us thought were beyond the pale.

And I'm no bleeding heart, believe me. I just didn't think they were good concepts. But his job was to think big, to have his head in the clouds just in case one day the country needed a plan from his file closet. You said this thing happened in Mexico?"

"Right."

"I heard whispers of an operational concept that Spratt once dreamed up. I suppose most of us in Delta of a certain vintage did. To be honest, I thought the whole thing was an elaborate fantasy."

"Go on..."

"Spratt always had a hornet up his ass about the southern border. He called it our Achilles heel—a conduit for drugs, migrants, terrorists, you name it. And maybe he wasn't wrong."

"What was the plan?"

"I don't know much about the counter-narcotics fight. But I do know that our problem—America's problem—was getting good intel on our enemy. And Spratt always said that the only way to beat the cartels wasn't just to think like them, but to know what they were thinking. One proposal he came up with was to use American special operations personnel to seize control of one or more major Mexican drug cartels so that we knew what they were planning, who their operatives were, that kind of thing. Cut the head off the snake, then replace it."

"You weren't wrong about him dreaming big," Pope muttered.

"Another idea he had was to stage false flag attacks to provoke rival cartels into a war with one another. A whoever wins, they all lose kind of scenario."

"Do you have any evidence of this? Are any of these plans sitting in a desk drawer in the Pentagon?"

Caldwell shook his head. "The Apparatus was never an officially sanctioned outfit. You could say it was looked on kindly from on high. Spratt certainly never struggled with funding. But I doubt you'll find anything if you search his office."

He tapped his head. "It'll all be up here. You'll have to ask him."

"Unfortunately that won't be possible," Pope said.

"Why not?"

Pope opened his phone and flashed the photo of Ethan Fitz at the general. "We believe this man murdered him."

Caldwell said nothing. "What about Grover. Is he alive?"

"We have no reason to believe otherwise. Why?"

"If anyone was going to take the whole thing too far, it would be Lieutenant Colonel Grover."

"Why do you say that?"

"He always had a problem with cause and effect. Fitz I don't know jack about, but he looks like a trigger-puller, not a planner. But I remember Grover. I remember that he never truly understood escalation risks, which is why he never made full bird. He's the kind of guy who would push the nuclear button because it looked shiny and red without ever stopping to wonder what might happen when the Russians detected the launch. At least Marion Spratt knew there was a line. Grover didn't."

"Comforting," Kelly remarked, lifting her pen from the paper after a burst of furious notetaking.

Caldwell scrunched his nose. "Not so much. Tell me, how exactly do you suspect that Lieutenant Colonel Grover is involved in all this?"

"It's still unclear. We think he's working with one of the cartels. Probably the Crusaders, but that's only a guess. Exactly why is still up in the air. But I'd be interested in your theory."

Caldwell demurred. "I don't have all the details. Only what you told me."

"Humor us."

"In that case, I think he's decided to execute one of Spratt's operational concepts. I don't think he's working for a cartel, I think they're working for *him*. It would fit with what I know of the Apparatus. Seizing control of a cartel, turning it against the rest, it's practically ripped from their playbook."

"To what end?"

"Well, that rather depends, doesn't it? Is Grover working for some black element in the government, or is he just out for himself?"

38

It was amusing, thought Fernando Carreon without displaying any evident sign that he was in fact amused, that a man so arrogant as Warren Grover should make such an elementary mistake.

The cartels had learned – *mostly* – long ago that it was possible to pick a fight with the Mexican government. It was possible to go to war with another cartel. It was possible to draw the wrath of the United States of America.

On occasion, it might even be profitable to pick two.

But going with all three was not just unwise, it was beginning to look downright foolish.

And yet it seemed that picking a fight with all three was exactly what Grover had done. And unfortunately, he hadn't knocked any of them out.

For a time, at least, he had sown enough confusion that they started to maul each other. But even that comfort was fading. Even a cartel as powerful as the Federación could only spend so much blood and life and treasure before the well ran dry.

And the water was most certainly running out.

Carreon had set up his command post in an abandoned warehouse on the outskirts of the city of Monterey, the capital of the northeastern state of Nuevo León. It was a place deep inside his own territory, and yet also one in which his enemies would never think to look. That, at least, was the idea. Whether it would bear out in practice was another matter entirely.

Grover had chosen today to pay him a visit: a reminder of who really held the power in their relationship. And yet nothing about the American's demeanor exuded control, or even basic competence. He was pacing up and down the empty half of the warehouse, nervous energy sizzling off his frame, lashing out with his boots at stray stones that skittered across the concrete.

It had been several days since they made their deal. Carreon had played his part. Every night, his sicarios fanned out across Mexico, butchering, torturing, murdering, fighting, and generally causing chaos. And every night, Reyes' men did the same. On a Tuesday, a safe house would be hit, liberated of cash and product. By Wednesday the loot might already have been taken back. The location of the trenches didn't change, only who was fighting over them that particular day.

Carreon was aware that he was losing. But so was Reyes. And more to the point, so was Grover – or else he would not be here.

The detachments of mercenary storm troopers the American controlled were highly effective, that much was certain. It was clear which was their handiwork when news of the night's slaughter broke on social media or the news networks. Clean kills. Accurate shooting. Explosive entry into target buildings. No evidence left behind.

His own sicarios were markedly less professional. Before a night of slaughter, they usually worked themselves up into a frenzy with drink or drugs or women or all three. They died just as fast as they lived.

Grover spent his men's lives more carefully. But he spent them all the same.

And with the tide of battle turning against him, he no longer had the flow of information that allowed him to pick high-value targets for his special units. Instead, night after night they went to war with boys from the barrios. Men whose lives meant nothing to anyone, least of all themselves.

Carreon watched for a few minutes as Grover paced, clenching and unclenching his fists, until he finally judged that the time was right. He walked over and placed a hand on the man's back, guiding him forcefully behind a pillar, far enough away from where his sicarios were resting and planning their next night's work that they could not be overheard. He turned to face Grover.

"What the hell are you staring at?" Grover snarled, angrily dragging his fingertips across the top of his domed head.

The cartel chief shot him a black look, marveling at the thrill of danger that ignited within him as he did so. It would still be so very easy for Grover to kill him. Not now, but he need only give the word the second he left, and one of the "bodyguards" that clung like limpets to his side at every waking hour of the day would pull the trigger.

And Grover was getting to the point where he might do it, too. Jumpy. Nervous. At the end of his rope.

Without making it too obvious, Carreon scanned the warehouse to ensure that no one was watching. "Quiet," he hissed, enjoying the taste of power, as limited as it was. "Or have you forgotten our bargain?"

Grover's eyes bulged with rage. "Forgotten..." he scoffed. "You better not forget who's in charge here, you understand?"

"I wouldn't dare," Carreon remarked dryly, allowing only enough insolence in his tone that he judged he wouldn't draw another angry response. "But I could not help but notice that you seem on edge, Warren. Is anything wrong?"

He spoke with a honeyed, silver tongue, though in truth he was delighting in his tormentor's discomfort, and they likely both knew it. Still, for now at least their fates were entwined. And Grover knew that also.

"What damn business is it of yours?" Grover muttered.

"We are in this together, are we not?" Carreon shrugged. "Blood brothers, if you will. So you might say I have an interest in seeing that no harm comes to you, Warren. And from where I'm standing, your odds are sinking every single day."

The comment, made casually, plainly rocked Grover to the core. He stood silent, rage draining away from him and being replaced just as quickly with something that smelled like fear.

"You want to know the truth?" he spat, thick, rapid droplets of sweat spewing from his lips. "César's gone. Dead, defected, how the hell should I know? Maybe he switched sides, figuring Reyes is the one who's gonna come out of this with his ass smelling like daisies. Half my men are dead. This whole thing's falling apart."

He blinked, seeming to recognize precisely what he had just said – and to whom. His expression stiffened, and he leaned forward, speaking low enough that Carreon had to strain to hear him. "But don't think they won't kill you the second I give the order."

"What happened to César?" Carreon asked, molding his expression to one of sorrow and regret even as an unbelievable lightness of elation threatened to send him airborne.

He gripped Grover by the shoulder and squeezed hard. "We're in this together now, Warren. You screwed us both with this scheme of yours. And whether you like it or not, we're each other's best chance at getting out of this alive."

Grover glowered up at him, and Carreon started to wonder whether the American would simply order him killed out of spite, figuring that if he could not possess the spoils then no one could. The look lingered, raking Carreon's skin.

And then it faded. Became almost pathetic. Like a child begging for forgiveness and salvation.

"That fucking captain," he moaned. "The Marine. The one the media's turning into a hero. I sent César to kill him. For all I know he enlisted instead."

Carreon still could not believe his luck. César scared him like few men on the planet. And given his line of work, that was saying something. With the psychopath out of the game, maybe he really did have a chance at surviving this.

"So what's your plan?" he asked, calibrating his tone to Grover's neediness. Testing, always testing.

"Plan?" Grover said, his voice a pathetic whimper.

"You still have a card to play, don't you?" Carreon said, comforting now, almost therapizing.

"What you mean?"

"The Reyes bitch," Carreon said dismissively. "You have her, or did you forget?"

"What the hell am I supposed to do with her?" Grover spat, angered once more. "I've made approaches. Offered to send her back in return for the Crusaders putting down their arms. I thought having her would at least bring him to the table. But nothing. No reply. I may as well get rid of her for all the use she's been."

"I wouldn't be so hasty." Carreon shrugged. "Maybe she can be some use to us yet."

And just as suddenly as it started, Grover's meltdown was over. He looked hungry once more. And in his eyes was that same wheedling insincerity that Carreon had first noticed almost two years earlier, when the American came to him looking for a job.

Then he'd dismissed it as nothing more than ambition, which was something to be admired, not feared.

And it surely was ambition, after all. But of a kind that was entirely divorced from reality and an honest appraisal of his own abilities. It was ambition that had brought both of them to the verge of utter disaster.

And even now, at the death, it was threatening to sink them both.

But, Carreon thought, he recognized it now. He saw what drove Warren Grover. And if he played his cards right, he could use it.

Grover looked at him sharply. "How?"

"You need Reyes off the board, correct?"

"Of course," he snapped. "If it was that easy I wouldn't need you."

You didn't say you did, Carreon thought. *But it's good to know.*

"Ramon is a proud man," he remarked. "And losing his wife is an extraordinarily careless thing to do. But as long as nobody knows about it, she's no risk to him. He can always find another."

"So we let the world know – then what?"

"We lay down a gauntlet. Draw him to a time and a place of our choosing. And then we'll see if your men really are as good as you once claimed to me they would be. If they can lop the head off the snake, then we can end this fight."

"He'll never fall for it," Grover scoffed. "Don't you think I've thought of that already?"

"He will if he thinks I'm going to be there," Carreon said. "It's a risk, but it's one he has no choice but to take. And I suspect he won't be able to resist the lure of getting rid of me once and for all. He'll think it's a trap, of course. But he'll come."

"What's in it for you?"

Carreon studied the American, gauging how far he could push this. Too little, and he would never be believed. Too far, and the man's pride might cause him to pinch off his only way out.

"I want out," he said. "If you kill Reyes, you create a power vacuum. One that you can fill. My people wouldn't follow you when they didn't know where I was. But if I give you my blessing, maybe things could be different. They love nothing more than winning – and killing Reyes will make you a winner."

"What about you?" Grover asked perceptively. "What's stopping you from trying to fill it?"

"As long as you're around," Carreon scoffed, "there's no future for me here. All I want is to be left alone to drink and screw my way to retirement. Five billion. Enough in cash and diamonds to fill my jet, you can stick the rest in a numbered account."

Grover held out his hand, eyes drunk on ambition and cunning and the tonic of possible salvation. "Deal. You hold up your end, I'll hold up mine."

Carreon exhaled slowly and shook the proffered digits. "You won't regret it."

39

"He is a murderer," Hector said venomously, standing outside the bedroom door along with Trapp and Ikeda. "God only knows how many men, women, and children have died at his hands. And only God can judge him. But I'm happy to speed along the day of that judgment."

"And if he doesn't talk so freely this time?" Trapp asked with a raised eyebrow. "What then?"

Hector shrugged. "You can promise him the world. I might abide by what you agree. Or I might not."

"Fine by me. But," Trapp said, gripping the Mexican captain by the shoulder, "I think you should stay out of the room. He's no fool."

He grimaced, but after a short pause, bowed his head in agreement. "As you wish."

Some hours ago, César had been moved to a bedroom. He was shackled to the bed as before, and the window had been boarded up outside. All items that could be used as either a weapon or to affect an escape had been removed. Two of Hector's men watched the prisoner at all times.

As Trapp entered the makeshift cell, he jerked his head to

the two guards, who filed out of the room. He closed the door after them.

"I heard you were feeling better," he called out loudly, to attract César's attention. "I'm glad."

The Mexican stared directly at the ceiling. The lower half of his body was clothed in loose-fitting cotton joggers, but his torso was bare and covered in a thin sheen of sweat. "Who are you?"

"That is not your concern," Trapp said firmly. "What I can do for you is the more pertinent question."

"Go to hell," César said without any real anger in his tone. It was as though he was going through the motions. "We both know I will get no mercy from you."

"Do we know that?"

"Will you torture me, American?" César asked mockingly, looking at Trapp for the first time. He seemed to take pleasure in this change in attitude, as if deriving some energy from it. "Threaten to break my bones or remove my fingernails?"

Trapp walked over to the bed on which the Mexican hitman was strapped. A single, bare light bulb hung on the ceiling high above. A ring of dust indicated where a lamp had until recently stood on the bedside table. Irritating. He could have used a little extra light.

Still the scars on César's body were obvious even through the gloom. Several puckered, long-healed wounds that looked like bullet holes. There were knife scars. His nose was crooked, indicating that it had healed from some long-ago break.

"I don't think you're motivated by pain," Trapp declared, tracing one of the longer sections of scar tissue that decorated César's slick chest. "We could test that out, of course, but frankly I don't have the time."

César fixed him with his dark eyes. His English was thickly accented, but otherwise perfect. "What the hell do you want?"

"Grover."

The Mexican's gaze narrowed, taking on a cunning, deceptive look, almost as if he was attempting to work out what they already knew. "I hit my head. I was out of my mind."

"We had his name already," Trapp lied. "Lieutenant Colonel Warren Grover, US Army. *Retired*. We know he's had this thing planned out for years. Though I have no idea what precisely took him so long."

César said nothing.

"I don't know what he promised you, but we both know that you aren't going to get it. Not anymore. It's too late for that."

"I was never going to get what he promised me," César snarled. "The man is a fool. A weak, pathetic fool."

Trapp observed him dispassionately, and if anything, the lack of reaction seemed to enrage the Mexican more. It was as though his own mental instability was sated by provoking emotion in others – and when such a reaction was denied him, he couldn't handle it.

It said a lot more about him than he knew.

He took advantage of it. "No, César. It's the chaos you want, isn't it? It's what you can't live without."

The hitman lurched upward, tugging at his chains, searching toward Trapp with the hungered, manic intensity of some B-movie zombie. There wasn't much slack in the lines, but enough for the Mexican to end up, slavering, just a few inches from his face.

Trapp did not flinch.

That was what César wanted, after all. To provoke a response. To elicit fear. It was an unusual, fascinating pathology. And it was one that others had indulged for far too long, whether through fear or through avarice – because they thought they could ride such an elemental force of nature to wherever it was they wanted to go.

But Trapp did not fear this man. In the abstract, César was

terrifying. In the flesh, merely disappointing – no great specimen in a world of such psychopaths.

So he just watched.

When the burst of energy had died away and César was left panting, eyes closed from whatever pain in his skull the effort had provoked, he finally grunted an answer. "What would you give me?"

Trapp leaned forward and whispered his own response quietly into the killer's ear. "I'll give you exactly what you want, César. You tell me where he is, and I'll give you a front row seat as I burn his whole house down."

His eyes snapped open. He was curious, but not convinced. He wanted what Trapp offered but suspected he was being played for a fool.

"You think I care about what happens to this piece of shit country?" Trapp spat roughly, appealing to the basest part of César's personality.

He understood instinctively that the Mexican would only trust someone he believed to be as depraved and amoral as he was. It was no good aiming for the angels in César's nature. If there even were any. It was the demons that were in control of the man's reins. It was they who needed to not just hear his argument – but believe it.

"No," he continued. "All I care about is killing Grover and making sure no one finds out that the US had anything to do with this mess. Beyond that, for all I care Mexico can burn to the ground. I'll give you the can of gasoline, if that's what you want. A signed immunity agreement, too."

César stared up greedily. "You mean that?"

Trapp nodded. "Absolutely."

"Then I'll give you what you want."

40

"You never saw this, understood?" Burke said firmly as he set a ruggedized laptop down on the coffee table in the farmhouse's living room. "As far as your government is concerned, we don't do anything without proper signoff."

"Consider this permission granted," Hector replied, a dry smile on his lips. "I suspect that once we're done, either the president will owe me his personal thanks, or we'll all be in jail."

"Speak for yourself," Burke replied, seasoning the joke with a lusty wink. "If this goes south, I'm on the first plane out of here."

"I wouldn't blame you. If it wasn't my country..." Hector spread his hands wide expressively. "But of course it is. And so I cannot."

That bought him a nod of acknowledgment from the DEA agent. A reminder that even though this was deadly serious to all of them clustered around the small table, it just meant more to Hector and his men. Patriots, in a country that sometimes didn't seem to value them.

Hell, Trapp thought. *That's all of them, sometimes.*

Burke opened the laptop's clamshell and hunched over it as he shielded the entry of his password. The surveillance program was already loaded, a clunky-looking thing which probably cost the government a pretty penny and still looked like it was right out of 1984.

The video feed, however, was clear. It was an aerial shot, taken from at least ten thousand feet up, from a plane circling high over Mexico City. The precise details of latitude and longitude, range and elevation were all detailed in a small grayscale panel in the bottom left of the screen.

"This was shot about three hours ago," Burke explained. "At the location Jason pulled out of César. There's something there all right. He wasn't lying."

"About that, anyway," Trapp remarked.

But he didn't really believe that César was playing them. Not about this, at least. There was probably a sting in the tail somewhere, but he knew his read of the Mexican hitman was correct. The man had a pathological hunger for chaos, the way others did for bread, or comfort, or power. It was an addiction, and in its own way every bit as compelling as that to the white powder trafficked so freely in this part of the world.

"Hold up," Burke said, fast-forwarding through the video. "It's the raw feed. I didn't get a chance to have it processed, and besides – I figured that it was probably best to keep this one close to the vest. Loose lips sink ships, you know?"

Judging by the intense expression on Hector's face – and the matching pallor of his men – they had enough experience of that to last them a lifetime.

"Okay, here we go."

The aircraft the camera was attached to performed a banking turn, as dozens of streets disappeared under the bottom bezel of the screen. Then it steadied, settling on a new heading. The camera began to zoom into an industrial section of the northwest suburbs of the city, just above a lake shaped like a jagged, broken throwing star.

"Looks like Grover and his boys are moving out. Maybe thirty of them, give or take half a dozen in either direction."

The video feed went blurry, perhaps as a result of the Cessna hitting a small patch of turbulence before its operator stabilized it. It resolved on an isolated concrete warehouse at the center of a large area of dark asphalt. The whole area was fenced in – tall, opaque walls that looked like they were topped with either barbed or razor wire. They cast long, dark shadows at this angle, spindly fingers that jutted out almost to the warehouse itself.

"Looks like an industrial park, maybe?" Ikeda murmured, leaning forward. "An old one. Abandoned."

"That's right." Burke nodded, fast forwarding a few minutes on the slider at the bottom of the screen. "Keep watching. We got lucky. Another ten minutes either way, we'd probably have missed them."

The aircraft banked again, and the target site disappeared from view for about twenty seconds before the feed zeroed in once more. When it did, something had changed.

"SUV. No, two of them," Ikeda said. "Three."

"Keep counting..." Burke laughed.

By the time the warehouse was done disgorging them, nine vehicles had emerged from inside. It was impossible to see from this angle – over the other side of the building – but Trapp assumed they were emerging from a service entrance. The small convoy was composed of about five SUVs and four long pickup trucks. Trapp guessed Ford F-250s, or something similar. The cargo beds were stacked high with supplies, though it was impossible to make out exactly what.

And even as they watched, the small dark figures of men surrounded them, checking that everything was stowed away correctly before tying light blue tarpaulins over the top.

"They're really loading up for bear," Trapp muttered.

"You can say that again."

"Any idea where they're headed?"

Burke shook his head. "Right now your guess is as good as mine. The Citation followed them as they got on to the highway, headed northwest, but where they'll end up, that's anybody's bet. The plane had to head back to the airfield to refuel and get a fresh pilot."

"You're not telling me you've lost them?" Trapp growled. "After all that?"

"Chill out," Burke said in a mollifying tone. "I've got a CI – someone I trust – following one of the trucks on the ground. He doesn't know why, just that I need a favor. Right now they're about..."

He pulled out a map and set it on the table, tracing a line from Mexico City up a highway before his finger stopped. "Here. Place called Poligoma. Never heard of it. Doesn't matter anyway; the SUV hasn't stopped once."

"What about air cover?"

Burke checked his watch. "Pilot problems. But it'll be back up in about an hour. Factor in another forty-five minutes or so flight time to follow the route, it won't be long. My guy on the ground doesn't need to get too close. And the further north they go, the better for us. The Cessna's got about six hours on station if they push us that far. But we can get air assets in the air up and down the West Coast if we need them."

"Good work, Ray," Trapp muttered, standing. Around him, Hector's men started to do the same.

"Where are you guys going?" Burke asked, frowning.

Trapp shrugged. "No idea yet. But all those guys have got somewhere to be. I figure in a few hours, so will we. And we're already running late."

41

The location was nowhere, and that was the whole point. It was a dried-up lakebed called Laguna de Mancha in the eastern part of the state of Durango. Of all Mexico's 31 states, this one had the second lowest population density.

And in this particular part, thirty miles from the nearest minor settlement, and farther to the nearest town, there wasn't a policeman within an hour's drive.

The greater part of the lakebed measured just under five miles across, and the outline was visible from space, as though this part hadn't seen more than a few drops of rainfall in ten thousand years. The Laguna de Mancha was by contrast positively well-irrigated, though it too had been dry for the best part of the last decade, and was only filled on the rare occasions when a storm broke over the nearby hillsides, causing water to scurry and trickle through hundreds of tiny streams and dried-out riverbeds.

The lakebed was made up of a soft, blindingly white sand, bleached by centuries of scorching sunshine. It went down only a few inches, meaning that an SUV could drive across it with comparative ease.

Presently, it was entirely empty, though it would not stay that way too much longer. The meeting was to take place at the northern end of the lakebed, in the shadow of a bare ridgeline dotted by only a few desiccated shrubs and large brown boulders that were too numerous to count. A two-lane road topped with incongruously black asphalt and fresh white road markings bracketed the top of the lake, carved into the foothills of the ridge. Two pickup trucks had been left to cut off traffic about five miles southeast of the lake, although few travelers were expected.

The better part of Carreon's force of about a hundred sicarios was situated in a large truck stop about a mile shy of the lake, checking their weapons, smoking, and generally sharing the smiles, jokes and silences of men about to enter the crucible of battle. Iker was there, facing away from him, about ten yards up ahead.

Fernando Carreon himself was nervous. But that was not the whole truth. He was also ecstatic. He could barely contain his energy, bouncing from foot to foot as he checked on his fighters, trailed with only a couple of feet of separation by four of Grover's men. They were like his shadows. He couldn't so much as take a shit without them checking the bathroom both before and after, in case he was attempting to leave a message in a bottle.

Or something like that, he thought, lips curling at his own crude humor. He'd stopped flushing, reasoning that they deserved to pay the price of their bad manners.

"You stick with me, you understand?" he growled at Iker, keeping his voice low. "And your men. Where I go, you go. What I do, you do."

His squat, preternaturally unruffled new lieutenant glanced up from a rifle that he was cleaning on the hood of his truck.

Carreon had watched him disassemble, oil, clean, and reassemble the same weapon at least half a dozen times, but Iker was nothing if not meticulous.

Iker set the weapon down, frowning before glancing meaningfully up at the masked men barely a step behind him. "Of course, jefe. But aren't you protected already?"

Carreon beamed, leaning forward and gripping the man's shoulder with a fierce intensity. He squeezed tight and said, "Of course. These men are paid well, and they are the best at what they do. But they are not Mexicans. They are not our people. You understand?"

"Yes, boss. I'll be with you every step of the way."

"I know you will," Carreon said gruffly, pausing before he continued.

This was the moment – he had to make his move now, or he would never get another chance. He was already pushing it, he knew. He had suggested this place in the middle of nowhere because its inaccessibility would force Grover and his lapdogs onto the back foot.

Of course, the problem was shared, but that was a risk that he was willing to take. In his position, it was one he *had* to take.

Leaning forward, he growled, "Whatever I do, I need you to be there for me. Tell your men, you understand?"

"Boss, I—"

"Promise me," Carreon hissed, feeling the heat of his guards' eyes on the back of his neck. "You will know."

Iker nodded, though a blankness in his eyes suggested that he did not yet understand what was being asked of him. That was fine, Carreon thought, drunk on the taste of danger as he held his gaze for a couple of seconds longer.

"I'll do what you ask," his man said, matching his low tone.

"Good."

"And sir, what about the girl – Jennifer Reyes? I don't see her."

"She'll be here shortly," Carreon replied, giving an approving nod. "Don't worry."

He wheeled away, leaving his subordinate with a confused expression. Carreon himself concealed a self-satisfied warmth from his shadows, molding his face into a blank mask as he had done for so many days.

But no longer.

"Sir – a word?" one of his guards said coldly from behind as Carreon strode forward, walking to another gaggle of parked trucks and waiting men. It was a question that was more of a statement.

"There's no time, fool," Carreon spat without turning. "What do you think this is – a picnic? Reyes will be here in under an hour. If you're not ready, then why don't you fuck off before you put the rest of us in danger?"

He kept walking, picking up the pace and daring Grover's man to challenge him. He could sense that the masked guard wanted to do just that. Sensed that he suspected something was wrong. But what could the man do about it in the here and now? He was in an impossible situation. There was nowhere private, not in the middle of the desert, not for tens of miles.

The only way to remonstrate with his supposed boss would be to do so in public, in front of all these men. And that would blow the whole operation before it ever got started. So all he could do was hope and pray that his charge didn't choose this moment to slip his restraints.

Which was precisely what Fernando Carreon intended to do.

The fact that Grover most likely had a sniper's scope trained on him from the ridgeline at this very moment meant nothing. The American couldn't pull the trigger, either, not without blowing his only shot at getting out of this alive and with his future intact.

So although Carreon was risking everything also – perhaps

more than any of them – he was satisfied with the prospect of losing it all.

He turned his head and watched as a single dark SUV drove quickly toward the makeshift parking lot, kicking up a cloud of dust and sand behind it. It contained Jennifer Reyes, he knew. And his ticket out of this mess.

"YOU THINK HE'S WITH THEM?" Trapp grunted, dragging his palm across a mess of stubble that hadn't been hacked back in almost a week. It was reaching that point where it started to itch, and the heat wasn't making things any better.

They had been tracking Warren Grover's men – at least, that's who they presumed they were – for the best part of 24 hours. The target convoy had stopped for a few hours in the middle of the night, in all likelihood to get some rest.

Burke grunted something noncommittal. "The satellite shots don't have the same resolution as the Cessna," he said. "Can't make out the faces. He might be. But then again, maybe not."

Trapp grinned, clapping the DEA man on his shoulder. "Great. Incisive analysis like that is why we keep you around."

"Buzz off," came the good-natured reply.

If Grover's men had gotten some rest, then Trapp and the ragtag crew around him hadn't gotten so lucky. They were always several hours behind their quarry, scrambling to acquire sufficient weapons, gear, equipment, and vehicles to cover all bases without falling too far behind.

Only time would tell whether they had managed to strike the right balance. He desperately hoped they had.

Burke was sitting in the back of a General Motors SUV, with both the rear doors wide open in the hope of coaxing a little breeze, though there was precious little of that. He had his laptop balanced on his knees and was glued to a live satellite feed. He pointed at the screen.

"That's them," he said. "Looks like about half of them are on foot up on the ridgeline. The rest are still in their vehicles."

"What the hell are they doing?" Trapp muttered. He had a creeping suspicion that Grover had somehow learned that he was being watched and that all this was a setup. Why else would the man have come here?

Could be a thousand reasons, he chided himself, wishing his body would one day learn to resist just this type of pre-battle nerves. It was always the same, no matter how much experience he gained.

"Beats me." Burke shrugged. He squinted at the screen, then tapped it. "Hey, look at this."

Trapp leaned over, his sweaty frame squeaking against the leather seats. "What are you showing me?"

"Not exactly sure. This is them, right?" he said, tapping a collection of about five parked SUVs in a line along a road that cut through a hillside leading to a ridge.

"Yeah…"

"Well, look at this vehicle. It broke away from this group a couple of minutes ago. Driving pretty quick, too."

"Going where?"

"Dunno. And remember – the satellite feed's five minutes delayed, for image processing or whatever. So everything we see now happened, oh, about seven and a half minutes ago."

"Zoom out."

Burke did as he was instructed, and a much larger section of the satellite feed came into view on the small computer screen. At the bottom left, an iridescent circular shape reflected the dying rays of the afternoon sun. The map overlay indicated that it was a lake, though Trapp couldn't see any water.

"Hold up," Trapp said, tapping the screen urgently. "What's that?"

The cursor moved rapidly across the screen as Burke rotated the map before zeroing in on the section that Trapp had just pointed out. Almost thirty vehicles came into view, parked at all angles across the road that led to the dried-up lake, about a mile to the north.

"I'm guessing that's the party," Burke said grimly. "Damn, but that's a lot of bad guys."

"You're telling me," Trapp said.

He jumped out of the back of the SUV, put his fingers between his lips, and let out a sharp whistle. Once he'd attracted Hector's attention, as well as the uncomprehending stares of a couple more of the Marines who didn't speak English so well, he yelled: "Listen up, guys – we've got something. Get your shit together. We might have to move out fast."

"You sure that's a good idea?" Burke asked once he climbed back inside.

"Hell no." Trapp grinned. "But unless you got a better idea, I don't see we have any other option. Besides, I'm not suggesting we go toe to toe with these guys, if that's what's happening. Just to get close enough to watch. Maybe we get lucky."

"Better you than me," Burke muttered.

They watched as the breakaway truck closed the distance to the larger collection of vehicles before stopping. All four doors opened, and five distinct figures stepped out. They were just dots on the screen at first before Burke increased the resolution.

"Four men. And maybe a woman. But don't put money on that," he reported.

"Wouldn't dream of it."

"What do you think's going on here?" Burke asked as Trapp looked over the satellite feed one last time.

Trapp scratched his chin, analyzing the situation as best he could. Grover's men had the high ground, though they were far fewer in number than whoever these new guys were. That was interesting and something he couldn't explain. Tactics and training were important, but in his experience, lead had a weight that couldn't be ignored. There had to be at least a hundred shooters in the big group, and only a couple dozen with Grover. If their situations were reversed, Trapp wouldn't like those odds.

"I'm guessing an ambush, but I might be wrong. If I'm right, the real question is: who's about to get a nasty surprise?"

42

W arren Grover had his belly on the dirt, like the grunt infantryman he'd never been. He held a pair of high-power binoculars and studied the still-empty lakebed below.

"Where are they?" he hissed.

The waiting was getting to him. The stress, ever-present since this whole mess started careering off the rails, stalked him every waking moment of every living day, and nightmares haunted his dreams.

Even now, at the culmination of it all, he couldn't stop his mind from conjuring scenarios of how it all might slip away from him.

"Not long, boss," one of the team leaders replied. He didn't know the man's name. In total, he had twenty-nine shooters with him, dug in at the top of the ridgeline, weapons trained on the meeting place a couple of hundred yards below. They wore camouflaged desert-pattern fatigues that blended perfectly into the tan scrubland they lay on and sported a variety of deadly weaponry.

There were seven machine gun nests in total, and the same

number of sniper teams. He'd argued for more of both, but had been overruled by his own men, who responded that the sharp-shooters needed spotters, and the machine gunners needed assistance reloading. Grover seethed at the intervention but was forced to concede the matter.

But if things went wrong, he vowed, they would have to pay.

"Contact Carreon's guards. Get a status report."

"Sir – are you sure that's wise? Wouldn't it be better to wait? The plan is in motion. Anything we do now will only increase the likelihood of something going wrong."

Grover stared venomously at the man. "Are you questioning my judgment?"

The man adopted a deliberate, deferential tone, in what was an obvious attempt to mollify his paymaster. "We get one shot at this, sir. If we blow it, then that's it."

Cracking his knuckles, Grover was forced to concede the point, though he didn't have to like it. He swiveled the binoculars to the left, searching for the point at which Carreon's convoy would emerge in just a few short minutes. He could almost taste victory, but that was part of the problem.

Because just as prominent in the air was the scent of defeat. And only time would tell which would be his fate.

Trapp, Burke, and Ikeda were accompanied by Hector and eight of his men. The small band numbered 12 in total and was split between four vehicles – all personal trucks and SUVs owned by the Mexican Marines. Sprawled across the back seats of the rearmost vehicle as it jolted at sixty miles an hour over the rough desert mud road, Trapp attempted to strap his equipment on as beside him, Burke continued to monitor the rapidly evolving situation.

"Okay," he yelled into a walkie-talkie that was clamped to

his lips. "Looks like we've got a second group approaching from the northwest. About twenty-five vehicles. Everything from an 18-wheeler to a Range Rover. It's a freaking carnival down there."

"This is the most ridiculous thing I've seen in a long time," Trapp said darkly. "What the hell is going on?"

Burke pulled himself away from the screen for a few moments. "Your guess is as good as mine. We've got three different groups spoiling for a fight. And we don't have a clue who any of them are."

"Four," Trapp said.

"How?"

"Four groups," he repeated. "Grover, the two convoys – and us."

"Oh," Burke muttered, looking somewhat startled, as though he appreciated the true gravity of the situation for the first time. "Yeah. I guess you're right."

Trapp grabbed a duffel bag from the trunk, dragging it over the back seat and pulling it onto his lap. He pulled the zipper open roughly and reached inside to retrieve several loaded magazines, which he stuffed into every available pouch and pocket before passing them forward to the two Marines in the front seats. He knew that the same scene was being repeated in each of the four vehicles.

"You guys look like you do this every week," he said, grinning at the two Mexicans to bleed off a little of his own building anxiety.

The guy in the passenger seat checked his rifle and shot him a thumbs-up of appreciation for the extra ammunition. His face was as expressive as his reply was short. "This is Mexico."

"I hear that."

"We're about five minutes out," Burke said into the radio, his words tumbling out. "We need to slow down once we hit the dogleg up ahead. About three minutes. Otherwise they'll hear us coming a mile off."

Trapp pointed at the laptop and clicked his fingers urgently, practically dragging it off Burke's lap. The DEA man didn't seem to notice and busied himself stocking up on his own ammunition.

He stared at the screen intently, even as the computer bounced on his lap as the SUV's front wheels hit an enormous pothole, causing the entire vehicle to lurch violently upward.

The three groups that Burke had mentioned were clear in the satellite feed. The group they'd followed all the way from Mexico City – Grover's men – were up on the ridgeline. It was hard to make out exactly how many of them there were, but they were exceedingly well armed. The only consolation was that as far as he could tell, each of their firing positions was pointed down toward the dry lake below.

Still, Trapp's ragtag team was outnumbered by at least two to one, and probably closer to three. However the next few minutes was to proceed, it had every chance of going sideways – and fast.

But then – what choice did they have? If Grover had caused this mess, then the United States had a moral duty to do something about it. And in the absence of the cavalry, Trapp, Burke, and Eliza Ikeda were all the help that Hector's men were going to get.

Still, Trapp thought, not entirely honestly. *I've seen worse odds.*

There was of course a secondary reason. A less honorable one. If the United States really had precipitated this crisis, even indirectly, then the truth could never come out. If it did, then the greatest crisis in US-Mexico relations for decades would be just the starting point. The revelation could feasibly usher in an anti-American government that would cease all co-operation with law enforcement authorities. The southern border would cease to be even a speed bump for terrorists, criminals and the cartels that had turned Mexico into a free-fire zone. The thought of American streets consumed by the same violent spasms that had swallowed Hector's country made Trapp's skin crawl.

"Okay, guys," he said, clearing his head as he spoke into his own lapel mic. "The first group is on the move. I think this thing is about to go down."

CARREON'S SUV was at the head of a long convoy of his men's vehicles as they proceeded to the meeting point. That was potentially unwise, but he couldn't bear the thought of dragging this out a moment longer than was necessary. His stomach was a bubbling cauldron of acid, which wasn't helped by the presence of two of Grover's jackbooted thugs sitting in the back seats.

Not long now...

"Stop here," he said, stabbing the air with a pointed finger to reinforce the point.

Iker did as he was instructed, and one by one, the remaining twenty or thirty trucks, pickups, and sedans coalesced into a loose arrangement around him. He put his fingers on the door handle, but before opening it, he turned to his lieutenant.

"You're a good man, Iker," he said. "Believe me, I won't forget that."

He received a frown in return, then the bobbing of the man's head. "Thank you, boss. I'm here for you, you know me."

"Okay," Carreon said, clapping his hands together. "Time to go."

He pulled the truck's front door open and jumped out, instantly bursting into action, ordering and cajoling his men into position. What was about to happen was akin to a Cold War spy swap – with similar odds of someone getting a twitchy trigger finger and blowing everything to hell.

Especially with what he had planned.

First, he created a defensive circle composed of expensive, tricked-out pickup trucks, complete with alloy wheels and custom entertainment systems. Even now, Grover's guards stayed within a few feet from him, close enough to hear every word that escaped his lips.

"You!" Carreon called out, pointing at one of his men. "Get everyone into a circle. Now!"

The sicario ran off as though he'd been stung to carry out his master's command. Within a minute or so, all one hundred of the fighters that Carreon had brought with him were arrayed in loose ranks. Most wore jeans, T-shirts, even a smattering of soccer shirts. In place of Kevlar helmets, they had reversed baseball caps.

But most had body armor strapped to their chests, sourced from the same suppliers that outfitted soldiers worldwide. That was the good thing about the military-industrial complex, Carreon thought. The only language it cared about was money, and he had plenty of that to go around. The men had webbing around their waists and extra magazines stuffed into pockets and underneath their belts. They were a messy, ragtag bunch, but every man among them was a fighter and a killer. Every single one had fired a weapon in anger, and most armies around the world couldn't say that.

They wouldn't break in a fight.

At least, he thought dryly, *not if things are going well.*

Behind them, Reyes' wife was hemmed in by four of Grover's guards. The men were masked, unreadable, and implacable. They carried their weapons like the professionals they were. The girl's presence had attracted his men's attention, and not just because of her unusual beauty. She was wearing denim shorts and a baggy, block-shaped man's T-shirt which did little to disguise her figure. Unsurprisingly, she was greeted with a regular procession of stolen glances and bawdy comments, to which she did not respond.

Carreon lifted his pistol from the holster at his hip and tapped it gently against the windshield to attract the attention of the gathered crowd, though this was hardly necessary. He waited until he had absolute silence before he began.

"Everybody knows why we are here," he called out in a booming voice, knowing that this was entirely impossible – for even he did not know how the next few minutes would unravel. "Nobody wanted this war, but those pussies from Culiacán started it anyway. They hit us in the night like women. They have no honor. No cojones. Isn't that right?"

A growl of agreement followed.

"So it's time to end this thing. Right here, and right now. Are you with me?"

"Hell yeah!"

The comment roared out of a more general, and now slightly louder, rumble of accord, bringing a smile to Carreon's lips. "Good. Because Reyes didn't count on one thing. He didn't count on us taking his wife."

Pointing at Jennifer Reyes, he allowed his voice to build in both strength and volume. His men, he knew, needed to be excited – but they also needed reassurance. To know that he would do everything he could to preserve their lives. That he was not a capricious general, but a father figure.

"So I expect you to fight. I expect you to *win*. But..." He lowered the volume, leaning forward and adopting an almost conspiratorial tone. "Believe me when I tell you that I will do everything possible to resolve this without bloodshed. I never wanted this war. I hope to end it without spilling blood. But that's in her husband's hands."

He paused, appearing to glance casually out at the horizon.

Instead, he was studying the hillside that towered above him, knowing that somewhere up there, Grover's men were already entrenched, aiming their weapons down.

Hopefully not at me.

This was a huge gamble. There was every chance that even if things went well with Ramon Reyes, and Grover's men cut the rival cartel boss down, his former employee still might break their agreement and the men on the hill would turn their weapons on him too.

But what choice did he have? There was a reason you went for the Hail Mary play, and it wasn't because things were going well. He blinked, realizing that his men were still staring expectantly up at him and beginning to glance uncertainly at each other.

Knowing that he could not afford that, he hefted his pistol above his head and looked each of his men in the eye in turn – or at least, as many as he could manage. "And never forget, I'll be right by your side. Not hiding in a bunker. Not on some beach somewhere. But to your left, and to your right. And if I die today, then so be it. But trust me, I wouldn't be anywhere else."

A shrill, excited voice rang out with warning of Reyes' arrival. "They're coming!"

43

Ramon Reyes stepped out of his car, surrounded by a hundred of his deadliest friends. Mindful of the risk of being hit by a sniper's bullet, he was careful to keep himself low and out of sight. Mendoza handed him a slim black pair of binoculars.

He pressed them to his eyes, steadying himself by placing an arm on a nearby truck, and as he did so, he murmured, "You really think she's there?"

Mendoza shrugged. Reyes couldn't actually see that, but he knew his friend too well, knew what that little exhalation of breath meant.

"Probably," he said. "We know they have her. Why take a bargaining chip if you don't plan on using it?"

Although they had trodden this same ground over and over again these past couple of days, always coming to the same conclusion, Reyes gave voice to his fears. "And what if it's an ambush?"

"It probably is," Mendoza replied offhandedly, not seeming flustered in the slightest. "So it's a fight. It was always going to end this way, right?"

Reyes played the binoculars over the assortment of vehicles across the lakebed from him. His boots sank into the delicate, thin sand underfoot as he examined the opposing force. He saw faces, but no weapons. No visible weapons, anyway. They were doubtless armed as heavily as he and his men were. It would be foolish not to do so, and Fernando Carreon was anything but a foolish man.

Though that was certainly true, Ramon still did not understand why he had started this fight in the first place. It made no sense. Why go to all this effort, expend so much blood and treasure, court media attention and government displeasure in equal measure, only to end up in the exact place you started?

It didn't make sense. Not unless this was Carreon's final move, his checkmate. Maybe then the reward would prove worth the risk. Maybe.

"You're right. I guess we're about to find out."

Mendoza nodded as Reyes dropped the binoculars from his eyes. The picture they painted for him was nothing more than an illusion. Information without illumination.

"Do you see her?" Mendoza murmured.

"No."

His lieutenant reached out and squeezed Reyes' shoulder. It was a comforting gesture, overly familiar, but he did not mind. There were few men in the world who could get away with doing that – fewer still after the losses he'd already sustained in this pitiless war – but Milo was one of them. "We'll know shortly. One way or another."

His eyes narrowed, and he pointed out across the lakebed. "Look. They're giving the signal."

Reyes followed the outstretched arm and saw that Mendoza was right. One of Carreon's men had tied a dirty piece of cloth to a pole, climbed on top of his vehicle, and was waving it back and forth. It wasn't quite a white flag of parley, but it would have to do.

He closed his eyes, steadying himself for his part in this. The agreement had been for both men to meet at a spot in between the two camps, unarmed and without guards. The security would be assured by the fighters at their backs – but in no man's land, they would be forced to trust each other.

It had sounded good in principle. Less so now he had to do it.

"Ramon," Mendoza said in a low voice. "When he walks out, hold back. Just for a couple of seconds."

"Why?"

"I don't trust them. That's all. Perhaps he means to shoot you the second you step out into the open."

Reyes grimaced. "A comforting thought. But someone has to take the first step."

"Just a second. That's all I'm asking. Long enough for me to get a bead on him. Call it mutually assured destruction. Once Carreon's in the open, he won't dare let one of his men take a shot at you. It would be signing his own death certificate."

That sounded right, Reyes thought. It would provide a short measure of comfort for the long walk.

"Okay. One moment, that's all. I can't risk delaying any longer. His conditions were plain, and this thing's precarious enough as it is."

Mendoza nodded. "Thank you."

Now that the moment had finally arrived, Fernando Carreon was no longer nervous. He didn't know when the acid had drained from his stomach, when his palms had dried and saliva had once again started to flow inside his mouth, but he was pleased on all three counts.

He tapped the pistol at his hip.

"You sure about this, boss?" Iker grumbled. He was still a

little stiff in his mannerisms and speech, but Carreon liked that he didn't mince his words. "What if it's a trap?"

It is a trap, he thought. *Just not the way you think.*

But since he could not say as much, he instead replied, "Are you ready?"

Iker nodded. "You know I am."

Carreon nodded cryptically. "Let's hope so. For both our sakes."

The squat lieutenant glanced at the pistol on Carreon's hip but said nothing. He knew that his boss wasn't supposed to wear it to the meeting with Reyes, they had discussed as much, but perhaps he assumed that something had changed. Regardless, he didn't question it.

The cartel chief raised his voice. "Bring the girl."

Jennifer Reyes stumbled forward, pushed by her four guards. Like his own, they were not bodyguards. The welfare of their charge was not the primary concern of the men behind the masks.

Carreon waited until they brought her right to him. He was now surrounded by all eight of Grover's men. They held their rifles expertly, fingers resting only a couple of inches away from their triggers.

He leaned into his act. "Remember, when I call her name, don't hesitate. Send her right out. Any delay and Reyes might think something's gone wrong. All I want tonight is a screw and a drink. The last thing I need is a bullet in my back. Understood?"

"Indeed," one of Grover's men replied.

"Good," he replied curtly.

It was all an act, of course. Grover's thugs knew the plan as well as he did. Reyes was never supposed to make it more than a couple of feet from his convoy. His own role was simply to draw the rival cartel leader into the open. One of Grover's snipers was to finish the job.

That was the plan, as Grover's men knew it.

At least, they *thought* they knew the plan.

He turned away from the masked guards, fixing their positions in his mind. It would only take a few seconds; they could not move very far. Perhaps not at all. He bowed his head, breathing out, then sucked in as much oxygen as his lungs could handle. He steadied himself.

Then he started walking out of the circle of trucks and pickups toward Reyes. His hand rested on his holster.

Iker, conscientious as always, called out, "Boss!"

For an instant, Carreon closed his eyes, grateful that his man had taken the bait. He could have done without it, probably. But it was better for Iker to call for him to stop instead of doing it himself. It would raise fewer suspicions.

He stopped.

Not so fast. Make him work.

He looked over his shoulder and yelled angrily, "What?"

"Jefe – the gun. Aren't you supposed to be unarmed? What if Reyes suspects –"

Carreon raised his arm to forestall the speech. He turned with a smile on his face, moving slowly. All of Grover's men were still in their previous positions. They seemed unsuspecting.

"I guess I'm a little jumpy." He grinned, forcing the expression on to his face and hoping that it wasn't too obviously false. "I haven't done this in a while."

He took a step toward Jennifer Reyes and the gaggle of Grover's men who surrounded her. As far as he could make out, their weapons were still safetied. They had no cover. They were arrogant, assuming they were the ones in control of their destiny.

Carreon unbuttoned his holster. He pulled the weapon free, surreptitiously sliding his thumb across the safety and disguising the click with a cough. He walked right up to Iker, raising his arm as if to hand the weapon over.

Then fired.

He squeezed the trigger three times, shifting the aim fractionally with each pull. Each shot hit its target, and three of Grover's men dropped to the ground before the rest had a chance to even flinch.

"Follow me, Iker," Carreon yelled, pivoting to get a clear shot at the fourth.

For the first time, his new right-hand man seemed actually shocked by the events occurring around them. He was frozen in place.

Carreon couldn't wait. His heart was thundering now, halfway between exploding and seizing up. The adrenaline surging through him choked off his aim and made him snatch at the trigger. He squeezed it again but missed, and the same held true for his next few shots.

As if stumbling out of the paralysis of sleep, all of his sicarios were fumbling for their weapons, but slowly. He couldn't blame them. "Hurry!"

A bullet zipped past his hair. It couldn't have missed him by more than a couple of inches. The thought enraged him.

"You fucking donkey," he yelled, squeezing the trigger over and over until the magazine ran dry, and one more of Grover's men lay dead on the desert sand.

Finally, Iker reacted, understanding that either he did something now, or his new boss – and his ticket to the good life – would die before his eyes. He raised his rifle, an AK-47, to his shoulder, and pumped the entire magazine into a space around Jennifer Reyes.

The air was suddenly filled with hot lead and the deafening rattle of automatic gunfire, as from every angle the Federación's sicarios rushed to protect their leader. Carreon ducked for cover, sheltering behind the bed of a pickup that was instantly turned into a pincushion – though whether from enemy fire or friendly was momentarily unclear.

One by one, caught between a vicious pincer of gunfire, Grover's mercenaries succumbed to the inevitable. They crumpled onto the floor of the desert, their blood staining the precious white sand. And then there was a stunned, horrified silence. Everyone here had come expecting to do violence. But not like this.

"What the hell's going on, boss?" Iker yelled out, his throat strangled from adrenaline or fear or just plain shock. "What did they do?"

Carreon was numbed by the realization that he was somehow, miraculously, still alive. He looked down, searching his body for any evidence that he might have been shot and somehow missed it.

But there was nothing.

He was intact.

He'd done it!

"Boss?" Iker said, his voice returning but uncertain. "Shit, boss, the Reyes girl. She's been shot."

Carreon swore and dived toward the body of Jennifer Reyes, who collapsed in slow motion to the desert floor, surrounded by a charnel house of blood and death and gore.

And as he did so, gunfire crackled from the ridge line above.

"RAMON – GET DOWN!"

Acting on instinct and buoyed by not just the rattle of gunfire, but also a lifetime's worth of trust in his friend, Ramon Reyes fell to the deck. He hadn't even made it a foot out of the ring of vehicles before the gunfire started within Fernando Carreon's camp.

He scrambled desperately back, into safety, and sheltered

half-crouched beneath the hood of his Range Rover. "What the fuck was that?"

Mendoza didn't reply immediately. He was barking orders to the men around him, who were all training their weapons on the rival force seventy yards distant. He watched as work parties of sicarios ran to the back of the 18-wheeler, right at the center of their encampment, and retrieved the heavy weaponry that they had brought as a last resort.

Reyes brought the binoculars back to his eyes. "Were they shooting at us?"

"I don't think so," Mendoza replied, dropping to the sand by his boss' side. The butt of his rifle was pressed into the crook of his shoulder, and his eyes never stopped roving. "Maybe one of them went for him."

"Let's hope they did our dirty work for us," Reyes said doubtfully.

He looked around, checking that none of his men were shooting. If this was just a mistake, someone with a twitchy finger on the trigger, then he didn't want to blow the whole thing up while his wife was still in play. Luckily, they were not. As so often, he silently thanked the quick thinking of his oldest friend. While he had been cowering in the dirt, Mendoza had jumped into action.

"Hell," Reyes yelped, concern spiking within him as his brain finally processed a new – and infinitely more troubling – source of information. He pointed upward, careful not to reveal himself. "Look, up in the hills."

Mendoza looked up.

"What the fuck is going on?"

Reyes could only lie there and shrugged helplessly. The term *fog of war* had never seemed more appropriate. Gunfire was crackling all around them, like a sudden hailstorm impacting a tin roof, and yet somehow they were the only actors in this macabre play not currently being shot at.

It didn't make a lick of sense. What the hell kind of plan was to coax someone into an ambush, and then not even bother taking your shot?

No, it was apparent that there was something here that he was missing.

"What do you want us to do?" Mendoza said, his voice strangely distant as he looked up at the ridge line. Reyes' gaze was drawn to the same spot. The gunfire was coming from a section a few hundred feet above and peppering Carreon's position mercilessly.

"Shit," Reyes swore. "What if he thinks it's us?"

He suddenly felt fear for his wife's life as he never had before. Perhaps it wasn't even fear, just the jealousy of a man not used to losing control. But whatever the course, he knew he couldn't let her die.

"We need to make a move while he's distracted," he decided. "We'll use the truck as cover. If it makes it that far, use it to force a gap in his lines. We'll go through that."

"You sure about this, boss? We'll take a hell of a beating. Especially if those guys in the hills decide to make us a target. They can pick us off from up there and we won't be able to do a damn thing about it."

Reyes grimaced, knowing that it was true. And yet what else could he do? To lose his wife once was careless. To allow it to happen twice would be a disaster. One that his enemies wouldn't soon allow him to forget. In his weakened condition, that might prove fatal.

"Let's get moving."

44

"Get them on the radio, now!" Grover screamed at the nearest of his men. "What the hell is going on? I want him dead. I don't care what it costs."

"It's no good, sir," the nearest radio operator reported. "I can't raise them. Any of them."

Grover pushed the hapless man aside and grabbed a tan-colored scope that lay just inside the lip of the ridge. He pushed it to his eye and trained the viewfinder on the unruly gaggle of vehicles that that fool Carreon had brought with him.

He should never have allowed this. Carreon had turned on him. That much was clear. He swore again, sensing that events were slipping from his grasp.

"What should we do?"

The question hung in the air without answer as he lay against the dirt, fruitlessly searching the scene below him for any hint of meaning. Carreon's men were sheltering from the gunfire behind their vehicles. In the center of the circle, half a dozen or more bodies lay still, blood watering the sand around them.

His men, Grover knew. The ones he'd sent to watch Carreon

and the Reyes girl. They were irreplaceable. All he had left were the twenty-nine with him now, all mercenaries. They would not linger long once they understood that all hope of victory was gone. And that fact could surely not remain lost on them for very much longer.

"Did I tell you to stop shooting?" Grover said, both to fill the silence and to push back on his rising anxiety. "I want every last one of them dead."

"What about Reyes?" the team leader questioned.

Grover jerked the scope toward the other assortment of vehicles. "Do you see him?"

"No..."

He tore his eye away from the viewfinder and tossed the scope back at the speaker. "Find him!"

He received no reply, though around him men jumped into action. The machine gun nests still concentrated their fire on Carreon's men, sweeping from vehicle to vehicle and leaving them smoldering wrecks. But the snipers, working in tandem with the spotters beside them, shifted their focus to Reyes' small force. Steady voices called out elevation and windage, confirmed among each other that they were focusing on unique targets, and then fired.

"They're moving," one of them reported calmly. "Three, now four of the trucks. No – all of them."

"Retreating?" Grover asked.

There was a short pause before the reply. "The opposite."

Grover closed his eyes. It was apparent now that he'd lost control, if he'd ever had it at all. The men around him must have reached the same conclusion. What were his options? Whatever he decided, he needed to pick quickly. If he was trying to figure out what came next, those around him would be doing the same, deciding whether their futures would be better served by acting with him – or against.

He could run now and leave the two combatants were

beating seven shades out of each other on the lakebed below. There was money secreted away in Cayman Islands accounts and Dominican Republic vaults. He had prepared passports and bolt holes ahead of time for just this eventuality.

It was still possible for him to escape this mess and live free the rest of his life as an extremely wealthy man. Not a billionaire—too much money had been expended on this operation, and he'd only had full command of El Federación for a couple of weeks. Not long enough to prepare a real retirement, but enough to be extremely comfortable.

But perhaps there was still a chance to salvage this. Reyes needed to die. Or Carreon. Ideally both. Either death would bring chaos, and chaos pulled opportunity in its wake. He still had Abalos on his side. And Salazar. There was still a path.

Whether the glimmer of light he saw was real or not, Grover didn't know. But he saw a way out, a way to not just escape this calamity with his dignity intact, but also a path to the goal he had sought all along. And like a drowning man clutches a rope, he reached for it with single-minded focus.

"Sir –?"

"What?" he snapped, pushing himself back as though dodging a splash of hot oil as a volley of bullets impacted the ridgeline, sparking off boulders just a few feet away.

His interlocutor was now looking down at him from above, and Grover sensed the man's scorn, even if he maintained a studiously polite tone. "I asked if you wanted us to pull back. It looks like they're ranging us now. One of my men spotted a heavy machine gun."

"We have the high ground, do we not?" Grover said, his mind now closing with rage at what he perceived as the man's fear – not recognizing that it was in truth a lack of faith.

"We do. But they have the numbers. This wasn't supposed to turn into a pitched battle."

"Well, now it is. So do your damn job. You think you'll find another gig that pays you as well as this one?"

He received a silent shake of the head in return.

"Then we have an understanding. Do you have eyes on Ramon Reyes?"

Grover watched as the mercenary relayed the question to his men and waited for the response. He was careful to position himself a few feet back from the lip of the ridge, conscious that gunfire and shrapnel was now zipping over his head with increasing regularity.

It wouldn't do to die, not now that he'd come so far.

As he waited, he surveyed his men, who were scattered in line across a section of the hillside about ninety feet across. There were fourteen two-man teams in total, a few feet separated from each other, and each dug in behind a small structure built from sandbags. They were flimsy defenses, really. They'd argued for more, but he hadn't seen the point.

He ground his teeth, frustrated at how long it was taking to get an answer. It was a simple enough question, wasn't it? Either they saw him or they didn't. "Well –?"

Reyes flinched as a whip cracked nearby, again and again, beating down from above with furious intensity. Something scored his face, leaving it stinging with heat and pain. It took him a couple of seconds to realize that it was incoming fire, mostly passing just overhead, and he sighed with relief.

But his mercenaries didn't all get so lucky. Grover watched as one of the sniper teams was eviscerated by incoming machine gun fire. One moment they were there, the next both their heads seemed simply to disappear in a spray of red as the heavy rounds passed through the earth at the top of the ridgeline and into flesh.

There was a moment of stunned silence as all around on the ridge, Grover's men ceased firing and turned to gaze at the bodies of their fallen comrades. The clamor of the violence in the valley below was still clearly audible, if anything growing in intensity as Reyes' men joined the fight.

The tenor of it had changed, and the tempo, and almost instantly the volume of gunfire concentrated on their stronghold on the ridgeline faded as Carreon's men were forced to confront the more immediate threat headed right for them. The two rival cartel mobs were finally confronting each other, as he had hoped they would.

But up on the hillside, Grover's men were no longer joined in battle. He saw one of the machine gun teams scramble backward a few feet, ducking behind cover and leaving their weapons where they were.

He watched, open-mouthed, as both to their right and left others did the same. The trickle became a flow, and before long almost every post was unmanned and men were streaming down the hill on either side of them.

"What the hell are you doing, you idiots?" he screamed. "Keep shooting. You think I'm paying you to fucking run?"

There was no reply other than the clatter of a rifle being tossed onto the stones at his feet as one of the mercenaries ran past. Grover thought about picking it up and firing at the deserters, but as another passed by, he froze.

All that Grover could see of this man was his lips, which were white with fury. Not just fury – rage. And so he froze, correctly suspecting that the anger was directed not at the nameless man who had just killed his friend, but *him*.

It was over.

Rounds were still chewing into the ridgeline up above, but only because the men pulling the triggers didn't know they were shooting at ghosts.

Grover stared at the man dumbly, communicating an unrequited message with his eyes. *It's done.*

And even if his mind had not yet fully come to terms with this new reality, his body did. His foot moved, then his knee, and then he broke into a run, thoughtless, heedless as fear and panic overtook him. He hared after his former men, jinking slightly to the left so that he was heading for a different gully than most as his brain started whirring once again.

His men – *the deserters* – would soon realize that he had value. They would come after him, and by then he had to be long gone. If Fernando Carreon was still alive, he would pay anything for one Warren Grover. And that prospect was too horrifying to even imagine.

And so he too ran.

45

"What the hell –?" Trapp muttered.

A thin rock fall from the slope above first caught his attention. His fist flashed upward, and the men – and one woman – surrounding him instantly dropped to their knees, each with a weapon at the ready. His eyes darted left and right, every sense on edge as he tried to work out what had triggered the sensation of danger in his mind.

They were in a gully on the backside of the hill that led up to the ridge. It was about forty feet wide and a little more forested than the rest of the area, though the foliage competed with large boulders the size of men. Most of the bushes and trees were dried-out husks, but their branches were sturdy and tangled and provided excellent cover. It was now late in the afternoon, and the sun had dropped out of sight. The terrain reminded him of the mountains of Afghanistan – only a lot warmer.

The official warning came a couple seconds later.

"Looks like the bad guys are coming your way," Burke

reported over the radio network from his makeshift command post back in the truck. He repeated the warning in Spanish.

"How many?" Trapp murmured as quietly as he could manage.

"Just about all of them. Moving fast. I'd say maybe thirty? Hard to be sure. And...it looks like they're coming right for you."

Trapp took in the intel without reacting. "Okay. Get yourself somewhere safe. We'll handle it from here."

Burke replied tersely, a rattle over Trapp's radio headset indicating that he was already on the move. "Copy."

They split into two teams of about six apiece and scrambled behind cover on opposite sides of the narrow valley. Trapp scrambled over a large boulder, pausing on the top to give Ikeda a hoist up after him. She patted him on the back in thanks and rolled silently down onto the other side. Both took up firing positions that afforded them a view of the gully.

What now? Trapp wondered.

The prime question was whether they had been spotted. If so, then their small force of a dozen was about to be pitted against one almost three times its size. Hector's men were excellent fighters – but from everything they knew, so was the enemy.

The movement of men was evident to the naked ear by now, which pulled Trapp back to the present. He heard boots thumping against stone and dirt, the heavy breath of bodies under strain, and the same tumbling of debris that had first alerted him to the enemy's movement. He glanced at the boulder to his left, which he was leaning on for support, and cursed the way it blocked his view.

"They're coming into the open now," Hector reported, his voice barely audible in Trapp's ear. "I see them. At least five. More."

Trapp double-tapped the transmit button in acknowledgment.

"Definitely running," came an update only seconds afterward, then, "Gun, gun, gun!"

The warning was appreciated, if not in the slightest surprising. For a second time, Trapp cursed the boulder that was curtailing his field of vision. He looked to his right and left, searching for a better spot, only to realize that he was stuck where he was, at least if he wanted to avoid signposting his presence.

The first of Grover's men crossed the approximately fifteen-yard section of the gully that he had in sight. He almost did a doubletake. They weren't attacking – they were quite clearly retreating in panic.

From what?

He looked again as another runner almost tripped, so careless was his flight. This one was dressed the same as the rest: black boots, dark navy fatigues, and the regulation black balaclava. As far as Trapp could tell, he wasn't armed.

That made the decision for him. Only an idiot ran into a fight without a weapon – an idiot or a fanatic. And Trapp suspected that Grover's men were not the latter. They were mercenaries. Individuals who were capable of fighting hard when offered the right level of compensation – but equally liable to break and run. Which was exactly what they were doing.

"We can take them," Trapp said rapidly into his radio. "They have no idea we're here."

"I concur," Hector agreed. "Ten seconds. Warning shots."

The warning rattled over the radio net a second time in Spanish, for Hector's men's benefit, though Trapp suspected that most understood enough English that it wasn't necessary. Not for the first time in the last few days, he felt a twinge of embarrassment that he'd come to this country and expected everyone else to adapt to his presence, not the other way around.

Hell, ain't that the American way.

He grinned, pushing it from his mind, and turned to Ikeda. Her index finger was tapping against her rifle, but she was otherwise steady. "You ready?"

"Like the day I was born," she replied.

"Not sure if that's a good thing or not," Trapp remarked as the last couple of seconds on his internal stopwatch burned away and the alarm rang out. "Let's go."

Trapp leapt onto the boulder. He brought his rifle to his shoulder and fired three bursts of three rounds, allowing a couple of seconds in between each. A little further up the gorge on his side, four of Hector's men did the same – though one blasted his weapon on full automatic.

He said a prayer of thanks to whoever was watching over them from up above that this part of the country was almost uninhabited. That lead had to come down somewhere, and it was better that it met desert dirt than someone's home.

On the other side of the gully, Hector and five of his men appeared from behind a thick section of foliage and copied the maneuver.

All told, the gunfire lasted a full ten seconds, and even as those at the back continued piling forward, some of Grover's men were so stunned by the sudden appearance of men with guns that they tripped and bit the dirt. Trapp winced as one of them appeared to knock himself out.

Still, it saves having to shoot the guy.

"Down!" Trapp yelled as soon as the gunfire faded away, leaving only the muffled sound of battle on the other side of the ridge. Some of Grover's men were still running down the mountain, though even those seemed to be moving through molasses.

Hector's men repeated the cry over and over in Spanish as

Trapp fell silent. He pressed the stock of his rifle into his shoulder and trained it on the gaggle of retreating soldiers in the gully. They were both above and below the ambush point. At least fifteen of them were above him.

The reality of their present tactical position began to dawn on him. Grover's men might be retreating, but they were still a formidable force – and they had the weight of numbers on their side. It would only take one misstep to turn this into a bloodbath.

"Don't do that, asshole," he grunted, watching as a tall mercenary, his rifle still shouldered, unlike many of the rest, started tugging on its strap. He aimed carefully at a spot just a few inches from the man's boots and fired a single round.

The slug sparked off a stone and ricocheted in the opposite direction, landing somewhere up the hillside with a dull thud. The target of his gentle ministrations reacted in slow motion – jumping in almost comical fashion before falling backward onto his ass. Trapp kept his rifle trained on the man, who divested himself of his own weapon with startling alacrity, throwing it down the hillside and scrambling back.

"Good move."

Trapp glanced over his right shoulder, down the hillside, where almost a dozen of the retreating mercenaries were still picking their way out of the gully. They had a head start of at least eighty yards already, which he suspected was insurmountable. They had to deal with the ones they had in front of them first. He just had to hope that Grover wasn't with the first group.

"Tell them to put their guns down," Trapp called out. "One by one. No one wants to be a hero today, all right?"

As Hector translated the message, Trapp jumped down from the boulder. His partner landed by his side with leonine grace. "Not my first rodeo."

"Never said it was."

They worked as a pair, Ikeda stepping back and providing

cover as Trapp encountered the mercenaries directly, taking weapons from them and patting them down before roughly manhandling them onto the dirt.

He turned to Ikeda and said, "You got any flex cuffs?"

She grimaced. "Nope."

"Okay. Be careful."

The guy on the ground in front of him was only armed with a pistol, holstered at his hip. Trapp reached down, removed the weapon, and ejected the round from the chamber before tossing it in one direction, the magazine in another, and the weapon itself in a third entirely.

He repeated the same with the next, and the next. All over the hillside, Hector's men were copying the maneuver. At least some of them had cuffs with them, and they were none too gentle when affixing them.

Trapp made his way up the hill, leading with his rifle. Half a dozen of the masked fighters were still yet to be apprehended. Two of them, at the front, already had their fingers interlaced behind their heads. He indicated to them to get down, and they did without protest.

He almost missed the movement. Almost.

"Don't do it, jackass!"

Trapp snapped the barrel of his rifle up, aiming it directly at the offending fighter's chest. His finger was already grazing the trigger, applying a couple pounds of pressure. Not enough to fire a round, but sufficient to speed the process in the event he needed to.

Now was one of those times. The shooter at the back had his fingers on his pistol's grip and looked like he planned to draw it at any moment.

"I'm warning you," Trapp growled. "Do not touch that weapon. Drop it, now!"

The man made his decision. His hand clutched the weapon,

elbow already drawing back as he attempted to withdraw it from its holster.

Trapp squeezed the trigger. Three rounds exploded from the barrel and hurtled up the hillside, landing directly in the center of the shooter's chest. He quickly readjusted his aim and fired three more at something more solid, aware that the mercenaries were all wearing armor plates.

He felt no remorse. At least not in that moment. The man had made his decision, and he had to live with the consequences.

Or in this case, not.

"Cover me," he muttered, moving up the hill with his rifle packed to his shoulder.

"You got it," Ikeda replied, her voice level. She barely sounded ruffled by the sudden burst of gunfire.

His own heart was thundering in his chest, and he dropped his trigger hand to his pants to wipe off the sweat as he climbed. As he reached the fallen body of the man he'd just shot, he kicked the pistol from a set of splayed, unmoving fingers.

There was no need.

Now why did you have to go and do that, asshole?

Trapp stood over him for a few seconds, coming to terms with the suddenness of what had just happened. He breathed out, blinking hard, and then got back to work.

Around him, the three other mercenaries were frozen in place, as shocked by the sudden outbreak of violence as he was. As Ikeda held her weapon over them, Hector's men moved up the hillside with professional ease, frisking and securing them.

Only when Trapp was absolutely certain that the scene was secure did he drop his weapon. And even then, he brought his eye to the scope first and scanned every inch of hillside within sight, just in case.

He let the gun fall into its strap and dropped heavily onto

his haunches, boots scraping on the rocky soil below. A wave of exhaustion overcame him, to the point that he didn't even look up when someone joined him.

"Suicide by cop," Ikeda murmured. "You okay?"

"It was a stupid thing to do," he grunted, voice flat. "So what was the point?"

She shrugged. "Only he knows. Maybe he didn't want to spend the rest of his life behind bars. Or maybe he just panicked. Thought he might be able to run."

"Then he was an idiot."

"No one's disputing that," Ikeda replied as lightly as the situation allowed.

"What the hell are we doing here?" Trapp asked at last, watching through clouded eyes as Hector's men started frog marching the bound mercenaries into one central location before frisking them more thoroughly for cell phones, communications devices, anything they could strip for intelligence.

"Our jobs."

"I guess," he said humorlessly. "Sometimes it seems like all we do is clear up messes that people just like us started in the first place."

"Sure." Ikeda shrugged. "But someone's got to do it, right?"

He sighed, climbing to his feet and offering her his hand. She accepted it, and he hauled her upright after him. "You're probably right. It's just – this one seems so..."

"Sordid?" she offered. "I don't think anyone's denying that. This is a messy, horrible freaking situation. It's a war, I guess, but not an honorable one. How many poor bastards have to die just so that kids back home can snort white powder up their noses?"

"You think we caught him? Grover, I mean."

She tapped him gently on the hand. "Let's go find out."

They walked down the hillside in silence, toward where Hector's men had a little over a dozen prisoners lying flat on the ground, hands tied behind their backs and under constant armed guard. Trapp thought over what Ikeda had just said. Maybe it wasn't an honorable war. But did such a thing truly exist? At the end of the day it was still shooting and killing and dying – and did it really matter whether it was a soldier or a criminal on the other end of a bullet?

Sometimes it really didn't feel that way. But as he looked out at the professionalism – and more importantly, *determination* – of Hector's men, he realized that he had it all wrong. Maybe they were fighting criminals. But that didn't make the battle any less just. It didn't make his presence here any less valuable.

If anything, it was the exact opposite. Ikeda was right that the problem started back home when rich kids paid forty bucks for a baggie of coke, and their broke neighbors paid half that for hits of twice-cut meth. That was a chronic disease that was bigger than him, bigger than her, bigger than anything they could do.

But what Warren Grover had started here was worse still. He'd ignited a battle because of some toxic combination of misplaced vanity and unbridled greed. He'd started something he couldn't finish, but someone had to. Maybe that someone was Hector León.

But it was just as likely that it was him.

"He's not here," Hector reported the moment they arrived. "The man you are looking for."

"Okay," Trapp said, ejecting the half-spent magazine from his rifle and replacing it with a fresh one. "Then let's go find him."

46

F ernando Carreon watched in horror as the semitruck began building up steam. In the soft sand of the long-dried lakebed, it took longer than it might have on tarmac.

But not much.

And as he watched, he saw all of his hopes slipping away. There was no way of stopping what was about to happen. That much was painfully clear. And after his men and Reyes' fought hand to hand and slaughtered one another at close range, there would be no stepping back from the abyss.

Perhaps that had always been an impossible dream. It was about to become a hard, unyielding reality.

"You!" he yelled at a nearby sicario who was reaching into a cigarette pack instead of doing something useful. "We need to tighten up this wall. Now!"

Carreon pointed at the makeshift fortification of parked trucks that formed a circle around his temporary encampment. They'd been arranged like that to provide cover from small-arms fire, not withstand the impact of an eighteen-wheeler barreling toward them. But it was all there was.

Iker instantly picked up on the same thread as his master. He directed several men to start moving trucks to reinforce the boundary and climbed into one himself as Carreon stripped a rifle from the body of one of Grover's men. The weapon was still slick with blood, which he wiped on the corpse's pants leg before he hoisted it.

"Everyone," Carreon called out frantically. "Fire on the semi. We need to stop it or we're fucked."

He ran to the wall of trucks, grabbing his men by their shoulders and arms and torsos and pushing them toward the fight. He rested the rifle barrel on the bed of a dented red Silverado and found his aim.

The speeding semi was a hard target to miss, but when he squeezed the trigger he did just that. The stock bucked powerfully against his shoulder, and the first three rounds went wide. As if the sound of gunfire broke a spell, all around him his men got the message and started firing.

The remainder of Reyes' men were climbing into their trucks in the distance before charging across the lakebed toward his already beleaguered circle of men, mostly taking advantage of the cover offered by the much larger semi. The plan was evident – if simple. They intended to use the larger truck as a battering ram to breach the makeshift fortification's walls and let the men in the SUVs and pickups into his lines.

"Come on," Carreon muttered, steadying his aim as the profile of the oncoming semi grew and grew in size. The clattering of gunfire from all around him was incessant now, and the big truck's windshield a patchwork of bullet holes, and yet still it kept coming.

He squeezed the trigger, aiming for the engine block. Three round bursts with a tiny gap between each round to allow him to wrestle the gun back under control. He thought he hit with the last burst, but it was impossible to say. He fired again. Again. The weapon clicked dry.

With numb fingers, he ejected the spent magazine and jacked a new one in. He brought the rifle back to his shoulder and trained it once more on the semi. He fired.

But it was only thirty yards away and closing fast.

It was truly impossible to miss now, and the combined impacts of dozens of men firing at a single target began to show. The windshield, now almost opaque from the combined effect of hundreds of impacts, cracked out of its frame. Half fell inside the cabin, and half came loose and shattered against the ground.

And still it kept closing.

"Keep shooting!" he yelled, an evident note of panic in his voice now. Only a fool would not feel that way, and yet that didn't make it any less shameful. But no one around was listening. The scene was an ecstasy of gunfire and violence. Contorted, rictus faces screaming into the abyss. Brass casings flying everywhere, painting the desert floor gold. Men starting to look over their shoulders. Taking a hesitant half-step back.

Dropping their guns.

The semi's engine buckled under the weight of perhaps a thousand individual bullet impacts. By now it had to be half a ton heavier. A giant geyser of steam erupted out of one side, bursting out in a single giant gush. The beleaguered, broken vehicle resembled a cavalry horse charging into battle, mortally wounded, smoke erupting like frantic exhalations into cold air.

A horrible, mechanical grinding filled the air, drowning out even the loudest of the gunfire, and the semi started listing to its left, threatening to topple over at any moment.

But now it was only a few feet away. A zombie. Dead, but still propelled by its own momentum.

"Jefe," Iker hissed, his lips a few inches away from Carreon's ear and squeezing his shoulder hard. "We have to move. Now!"

Carreon tried to resist, but not particularly hard. He knew that this fight was futile. Probably had known it right from the start. And yet what other choice had he had? He allowed himself to be pulled backward by the right shoulder, the rifle dropping to his side.

Iker yanked him hard, and as he did, the semi impacted the outer boundary of parked trucks. They posed no more resistance as it careered through them than skin does to a bullet. The cabin rocked from left to right, and the trailer skidded out to one side, but still it came forward, still-spinning wheels kicking up great gusts of sand as it pushed seemingly weightless trucks out in front.

"Boss, come on," Iker yelled, having by now abandoned any pretense of decorum. "We have to get the hell out of here."

Carreon shook his head as he surveyed the damage. He watched as the semi finally came to a stop, accompanied by the scream of metal scraping against metal. He watched as one of his men, entirely overtaken by battle lust, clambered onto the hood of the tractor, submachine gun in hand, and wildly sprayed rounds into the cabin.

He shook his head, still stunned by the abject devastation all around him. "It's too late. We're done..."

"We have to go. We've lost this fight. That doesn't mean we've lost everything," Iker said desperately, still tugging at his arm. "Let's get the girl and get out of here. Maybe we have a chance."

Jennifer.

Maybe there was a way out after all. Though in reality it must by now be hopeless, Carreon's mind clutched on to this faint prospect of salvation. They still had the girl. Maybe she would at least buy them their freedom, if nothing else.

He spun, forced to shout over the sound of battle as a retreating sicario sprinted past him, dropping his pistol in his haste to escape. Carreon grimaced at the man's cowardice, not recognizing he was doing exactly the same. "Where is she?"

They ran toward where they'd last seen her – surrounded

by the bodies of Grover's fallen prison guards. She was still there, abandoned by whoever was supposed to be caring for her. Iker covered his boss as Carreon dropped to the ground, bringing his rifle up and firing several bursts toward the column of enemy vehicles hurtling toward them.

"How is she?" he said roughly, the words punctuated by heavy breaths and gunfire.

Carreon's fingers probed the wound. Her dark brown hair was splayed out across the light sand, her denim jeans now stained with blood, which was still trickling out from a wound around her groin. She was barely breathing.

He sank backward onto his haunches. Another blow. He wasn't sure how many more he could take. He wasn't sure if it was worth bothering. "She's nearly dead."

"Then she's still alive," Iker said, emptying his magazine and shouldering the rifle once more. "Come on, help me."

His lieutenant grabbed Ramon Reyes' wife by one shoulder and prompted him to do the same. They dragged her back over the soft sand, leaving a thin trail of blood as they went. By this point, Carreon was simply going through the motions, stumbling over the sand as they moved. Iker was driving this now, somehow still believing that they might survive when every omen told a different story.

Jennifer coughed, and her light top was suddenly sprinkled by a spray of red. Carreon's foreboding only grew at the sight. It was internal bleeding. What hope was there for her now?

He dropped her.

For a moment, his lieutenant didn't appear to notice, though he grunted a little heavier as he kept dragging. But after a few steps, he turned, noticing that Fernando was no longer by his side.

Carreon's exhausted eyes met his searching gaze. "It's too late," he said softly, shaking his head. "We can't get out. We may as well die like men."

His attention was briefly stolen by another riot of noise in the distance as several of Reyes' vehicles impacted the broken outer wall like a line of cavalry falling on a Napoleonic square. They drove ten, fifteen, twenty feet inside before eventually coming to a halt, all the while firing manically from inside. Most of the gunshots went wild, but enough found their targets to turn the tide of battle.

A few of his own men were still in the fight, but many more lay dead in the sand or were retreating in headlong panic. One sprinted right past where he and Iker had stopped, only for a stray round to take off the top-most part of his skull like a vengeful native. His torso kept moving forward longer than his legs did, but a second later the body lay still on the dirt.

Reyes' men kept pouring through the gap created by the semi. One by one, the few remaining sicarios defending it fell, chewed up by a weight of incoming fire that was increasingly relentless. Carreon watched in stunned horror as several enemy shooters clambered up onto the toppled trailer, spewing covering fire in every direction as behind them a pair of fighters set up a heavy machine gun.

The chatter a moment later when that opened up like a demonic chainsaw was what broke the camel's back.

The few of Carreon's men who were left fighting abandoned their positions as one. It didn't save them. The heavy gun bore down on them one after another, cutting two of them apart with impossible ease. One moment they were there, running, the next what was left of them was face down on the sand, in the center of a rapidly enlarging concentric circle of blood.

Almost numbed by the violence, Carreon looked down and was surprised to see that the rifle was still in his hands. He reached slowly for a fresh magazine and reloaded it.

Turning to his side he murmured, "It was good to meet you, my friend."

Iker nodded. His voice was quiet against the din of battle,

but Carreon had known him long enough to understand. "We go out fighting?"

Carreon shrugged. "Better than the alternative."

Iker nodded. He shuffled forward so that he was by his boss's side and raised the rifle to his shoulder. He nestled his chin against it and aimed but did not fire. There was no point – not yet. The battle was long over. Reyes' Crusaders were now engaged in a mopping-up operation, even if they were somehow the last to realize it. They charged forward with blood-lust on their faces and met with no resistance.

The Federación gunmen had simply given up. And those few that were left died, one by one, occasionally lifting a pistol or rifle or carbine or knife in a last-ditch act of desperation.

Most often not.

Slowly, Carreon brought his own weapon up. His finger rested gently on the trigger.

"Cease fire," a commanding voice called out. The gunfire didn't immediately die away, but the call was picked up and echoed all over the now-bloody lakebed. "Cease fire!"

"Ramon," Iker murmured.

Carreon nodded but said nothing.

"What does he want with us, I wonder?"

He glanced down at Jennifer Reyes' broken body and saw that she was still. Too still for there to be any other explanation for her fate. He placed his left hand on her chest and felt for life.

There was none.

"Gone," he whispered.

Reyes approached at the head of a phalanx of his men.

El Toro, Carreon remembered.

That was what they called him. He looked like a bull, too. Squat and muscular, with stocky legs and an animal rage in his eyes. Or perhaps not even true rage, but just the madness of battle. Carreon had felt the same at the start of the fight. The capacity for such delusion was present in every man. It was perhaps what made mankind such a warlike species. As danger approached, you could convince yourself of anything. That you were ten feet tall. The death would not come for you.

How petty such delusions were in the cold light of defeat.

They circled him and Iker. Two dozen men, and those were just in the first ring. All were armed. All wore vicious snarls on their faces, still hopped up on the most potent narcotic known to man.

They would rip him apart, Fernando knew. Give them only an instant, and they would rip him apart.

"Ramon," he murmured, his throat now desperately dry. He cleared it and tried again, but only to elicit the same result. "You came."

Ramon Reyes grinned wide as he saw who was before him. "Fernando – I"

His eyes dropped to the sorry sight at his enemy's feet. Carreon followed the man's gaze down.

She was beautiful even in death, he thought. So young. She looked too innocent to have been caught up in a world like this. She could have been anything. A singer, a dancer, a teacher, but just like him, she had chosen this life. A different path, perhaps, but one that led to the same destination.

And just like him, it would prove the cause of her demise.

"I'm sorry." Carreon shrugged. And he truly was. He had, after all, not started this fight. He had hoped to end it on his own terms, of course. But that was a very different thing.

"You bastard," Reyes spat, lunging forward, only to be stopped by a grunt of warning from Iker, who brandished his rifle without flinching.

"It wasn't me," Carreon said, offering up only the truth and nothing more. There was no bargaining his way out of the fate that lay in store for him. It was better to take it like a man.

"You caused it," Reyes stated, anger swirling in his eyes, though he had begun to reassert control over his emotions.

"Someone else did."

"Liar!"

"What have I got to lose?" he asked, reasonably enough. "I never wanted this fight, Ramon. Believe me when I tell you that. We both got played."

Reyes looked at him disbelievingly. "By who?"

"An American. His name was –"

But Reyes was already turning away. He waited until he was screened by the bodies of several of his men before he gave the command. "Kill them both."

Iker, his finger on a hair trigger, opened fire before anyone else. His rifle was on full automatic, and he chewed through the entire magazine in a matter of a couple of seconds.

There was a stunned silence, punctuated only by the scream of a mortally wounded man.

And then all of Reyes' sicarios opened fire as one.

47

"Hell, you don't see that every day," Trapp muttered, genuinely stunned by what he was watching through a spotter's scope that had been abandoned on the ridgeline. Half a dozen men, maybe more, had just died in the last act of a brutal battle.

"That one was Fernando Carreon," Hector said from beside him. "And one of his capos."

"Then the man he was talking to was Reyes?" Trapp asked.

He pulled himself away from the scope. He didn't need to see what was happening down there. It was an orgy of bloodlust. A gunshot echoed up the hillside every few seconds as the remaining gangsters executed wounded men and even pumped rounds into bodies that seemed most assuredly dead.

"That's right," Hector murmured, his eyes still pressed to the optical sight of one of the discarded sniper rifles. "I don't see him anymore. Damn. We should have taken the shot."

Already, some of Reyes' men were climbing into their vehicles. With their brutal work done, it seemed as though they had little desire to savor the consequences. Trapp wondered what would happen to the bodies. Would they just be left here until someone found them a day, a week, even a month from now?

"You sure that's a good idea?" Trapp asked.

Hector pulled himself away from the gunsight, handing the weapon to another of his men and issuing a sharp command before he returned his attention to his American colleague. "Why would it not be?"

Trapp grimaced. "Look, this is your country – and you know it better than me. But it seems to me that this place is already a tinderbox. And now Carreon's dead, his cartel's as likely as not to fall apart. You better believe there will be a dozen other jumped-up pricks falling over themselves to take his place."

"What's your point?"

"You sure it's a good idea to knock Reyes off, too? It'll feel good in the moment, you better believe I know it, but it'll cause a wave of violence in your country like you haven't ever seen."

Hector glanced down into the valley, his fingers drumming unconsciously on the pistol at his hip. His lips were tight, nostrils slightly flared, a hungry expression on his face that Trapp knew well.

"I don't see how it could get any worse," he stated, not unreasonably.

"You kill Reyes right now, you'll be throwing gasoline on the fire. Every thug in the country will look to make himself king. Anyone who can pull a couple of guys together will call themselves jefe, and you'll spend the next decade mopping them up."

"That'll happen anyway. And what am I supposed to do, just let Reyes walk after everything he's done?"

"For now... Yes." Trapp punctuated the comment by slapping the ground. "It'll feel like shit, I know that. But if you pull the trigger on this guy right now, thousands more innocent people will die. Every town will turn into a battleground for the next few months as a dozen different factions scrap for control.

And look, I don't really care if these psychopaths kill each other. But it's not just them who die."

Hector roughly grabbed the sniper rifle off his man, lay on his belly, and pressed his eye to the sight. In Spanish, he muttered, "Do you see him?"

"Maybe, sir," the Marine replied, sounding uncertain. Trapp strained to translate the words, but kept his mouth shut. This was Hector's country, Hector's command, and Hector's fight. He was only here to help.

"Where?"

"By the red Silverado. I think. Just up from the semi."

"I see it," Hector said softly, slowing his breathing and visibly acquiring his target. He reached up and adjusted something on the gunsight. "It's him."

Trapp thought about doing something to stop him but decided against it.

Maybe he was wrong, and Hector was right. It was entirely possible that getting rid of Ramon Reyes was a net good, even if his death unleashed a wave of violence. It was weighing these countervailing demands that made a soldier's job such a difficult one. The soul they watched through the gunsight was never just a single life.

He knew the pressure well.

Hector cursed and set the rifle down on its side. "A lot of people are going to die anyway," he growled.

Nodding with genuine sorrow, Trapp said, "I'm sure they are. But some won't. And you'll be the one who saved them."

"That's not why," Hector said, gritting his teeth with frustration.

"I know," Trapp murmured, understanding what the Mexican officer meant. He was a rare breed. Not out for himself, or plaudits or medals or acclaim. Just looking to do the best by his countrymen. For his family. For his men.

"This isn't over," Hector replied, crawling backward until

enough of the ridgeline blocked him so that he could stand without attracting attention from the lakebed below.

"No," Trapp agreed. "But it's a start."

WARREN GROVER PULLED up at a gas station outside a town called Fresnillo, about a four-hour drive away from the lakebed in which his dreams had turned to dust. It was the first moment he'd taken his foot off the gas that whole way. When he pulled his fingers off the steering wheel, his knuckles ached.

He sat by the gas pump for a couple of minutes without moving as the reality of what had happened to him that day washed over him. All his hopes, all his ambitions, they were gone. That was the reality. No denying it, no changing it.

The town was a small one, a couple of thousand souls in the middle of the desert. He didn't know what the people who lived here grew or built or otherwise did for a living. But it was quiet, and the only other car at the gas station was pulled up in front. Maybe the owner's. The lights of the convenience store attached glowed brightly against the darkness.

Grover beat his open palm against the dash. "Fuck!"

The curse echoed in the cramped confines of the truck's cabin. He repeated the gesture once more, hitting the dashboard so hard his palms stung, but this time he did it in silence. It seemed even more childish that way, though he couldn't help himself.

With the worst of the frustration over he settled back into his seat and played his eyes around the station, checking to see if anyone was watching. They were not, mostly because there was no *they* to watch him. The cashier had his back to the store glass and seemed to be playing on his phone. There was no one else in sight. His was the only car that had passed by in the last two minutes. He kept looking.

At the front of the gas station store was a selection of clear-fronted newspaper boxes and a rack stacked with the kind of items you find in a place like that. Firewood, engine oil, and a messy selection of gas cans.

He climbed out of the car and retrieved one of the cans from the front of the store. He walked back to the car, wrapped his fingers around the pump handle, and filled first the truck's gas tank, then the can, though he intended only to make use of one.

Grover spilled a little gasoline onto his hands as he filled up the can and wiped it against his pants, savoring the way the chemical burned his nostrils before it finally evaporated away into nothingness. He wondered whether it was an accurate metaphor for what was to happen to him.

With the task done, he returned the pump and walked inside to pay.

"Una lata de gas, por favor," he said, brandishing the newly heavy can. "And pump two."

If the cashier was surprised to see an American out here in the middle of nowhere, he didn't show it. In fact, his face displayed no emotion whatsoever. It was probably easier that way, Grover thought, shivering at the prospect of wasting a life in this way. Had this boy ever even left his hometown?

Did he have dreams – or was he satisfied to live out his life in a place like this?

Grover wasn't sure which answer he would find more troubling. Better not to know.

The cashier rang up the purchase and said blankly, "Todo?"

"Yes. No – wait."

The kid frowned. Finally, some emotion. Grover pointed at a cell phone box stacked on a rack behind him, then told him to add a Sim card and some credit to the total on the register. Again, he displayed no evident interest as to why a stranger would need such an item.

"Thanks, kid," Grover muttered as he paid and left. He received no response.

He climbed back into the truck and drove to a spot in the desert about a mile from town, shielded from view by a sandy mound, where he opened all four doors and dumped the contents of the gas can inside, before creating a short trail of fuel that led a safe distance away. He pulled a lighter from his pocket, struck a flame and tossed it onto the wet ground. The spilled gasoline ignited immediately and a line of fire raced toward the vehicle. It jumped the last few feet as the reaction ate hungrily into the cloud of fumes that hung in the air, before consuming the vehicle whole.

The heat of the initial eruption died away, and for a few moments the only sign that anything was amiss was a faint chemical stink on the air.

And then, split in half by the initial shockwave, the SUV's fuel tank ignited. It didn't happen with explosive force, but rather in a raging inferno that swallowed the vehicle from the rear end and raced forward with terrifying speed.

Grover watched the blaze consume the vehicle for about half a minute, seeing in the reflection of the flames years of planning and months of toil disappearing in seconds.

And then he started walking.

48

The suspect exited his Washington townhouse, dragging behind him a small, hard-sided piece of carry-on luggage. He was wearing a dark blue baseball cap without a logo and made a beeline for the sedan car parked on the street out front. He looked neither left nor right as he walked toward it.

Nick Pope cleared his throat and stepped out of the darkness of a nearby alleyway. "Mr. Fitz?"

Fitz froze. It wasn't entirely true to say that his foot hung momentarily in midair before setting back down on the sidewalk, but it wasn't far off. It was therefore a much more conscious act when his leather soles finally settled on the pavement and then drove forcefully off.

He didn't stop nor look at Pope. "Sorry, buddy, you got the wrong guy," he said as he tapped the button on his key fob.

Surely he doesn't think that'll work? Pope thought.

But then, in his experience, criminals rarely acted rationally once they realized they had been caught. It was difficult for a mind to comprehend the dreadful reality of the state's might until the law actually caught up with it. And by then, it was too late.

"Ethan Fitz, right?" Pope insisted. "I'm sure I recognize you."

"Listen, buddy," Fitz growled, opening the rear door of the sedan and shoving his case inside. "I'm in a rush."

"I'm sure you are." Pope grinned. He reached inside his jacket and pulled out his credentials. "Special Agent Pope with the FBI. You're under arrest, Mr. Fitz, for the murder of Marion Spratt, as an accessory to the murder of Mark Engel, multiple further counts of conspiracy to commit murder, conspiracy to murder a federal official, and activities related to domestic terrorism. Buddy, you're going away for a very long time."

Fitz froze with his fingers resting on the driver's door handle. "I told you, asshole, you got the wrong guy."

"I don't think so," Pope said, pocketing his badge. "Ethan Fitz, US Army retired. We know exactly who you are."

"I've done nothing," Fitz said, abandoning his initial gambit.

"Then you won't mind coming with us."

"I can't."

"Why, going somewhere?"

Fitz didn't answer but glanced left and right down the empty street, his mind so obviously running the percentages that Pope could practically see the cogs whirring through the bone, flesh and skin that made up his forehead. It took him about three seconds to make the decision that was always on the cards.

He sprinted.

Pope didn't bother going after him. He thrust his fingers into his pants pockets and waited for the inevitable.

It didn't take long. Fitz made it about ten yards down the street, arms pumping hard by his sides, when a car door opened, and a man spear tackled him from the side. The suspect went down with a cry of pain that translated into a grunt as the oxygen was squashed from his lungs.

All around, agents appeared from the darkness, screaming, "FBI!" and brandishing pistols with unrestrained glee. As the first agent rested his knee on Fitz' lower back, another grabbed his wrists and put them into cuffs before doing the same with his ankles and dragging him upright. The suspect didn't say a word throughout, though whether because he couldn't or he knew better was unclear.

That was enough for Pope.

"Make sure you read him his rights," he called out before climbing back into his car. The agents present would search Fitz' townhouse, but he suspected they wouldn't find much. Nothing incriminating, anyway.

But then, they had everything they needed on that front.

The Bureau had borrowed a couple of rooms at a local Metro PD precinct, so the drive was only five minutes. Fitz was in an interrogation room five minutes after that. Pope didn't hang around. He needed the guy off balance. He was smart, and that meant if he had too long to prepare himself, then he would simply clam up.

"I want a lawyer" was the first thing Fitz said as Pope entered the room. He'd eschewed the cliché of bringing the guy a cup of coffee, though he had one for himself. This wasn't going to be a good cop/bad cop kind of situation.

Pope didn't sit. He lifted the cup to his lips and drank deeply, letting the silence – and Fitz' anticipation of his answer – drag out before he spoke. "That's your right."

"Damn right it is. You've got nothing on me. I'm innocent."

"Uh huh," Pope said dryly, making a face at the quality of the coffee. "You guys usually are."

"You recording this?"

"You know the deal. No cameras until you get your lawyer."

"Then where the hell is he?"

"You don't want a lawyer," Pope said.

Fitz screwed up his face with sarcastic incomprehension. "Yeah – and you know that how?"

"It's obvious. If I walk back out that door and get you one, you're setting yourself on a path that has only one destination."

"And I'm betting you're going to tell me."

"That's right. You get your lawyer, you go to court, and the US Attorney for the District of Columbia will string you up. You can get the death penalty for drug trafficking, you know, not just murder. Espionage, too. And then there's seven counts of accessory to murder. Hell, we can probably throw sedition in there for good measure. Maybe we'll let you do twenty behind, and *then* we'll execute you. Really get the juices going."

Fitz thumped the table with his fist. "Lawyer."

Pope leaned forward and reached for his coffee. The cup was already lukewarm. He lifted it back to his lips, then thought better of it.

"I hear she's a real hard bitch," he commented, in a practiced offhand manner. "You think she's going to show you any leniency after you sent five of her friends to die? I'm guessing not, but maybe you know her better."

Fitz said nothing.

Pope let the silence between them stretch out, noting knowingly – if without showing so on his face – that the suspect was no longer demanding his lawyer. His chickens were coming home to roost, just like they always did. It had something to do with the bare concrete walls of these interrogation rooms, he thought, wondering if they were an intentional design feature, or just a happy coincidence. Either way, they had an uncanny resemblance to a prison cell.

He checked his watch when it hit sixty seconds and turned to leave, scraping the floor with the sole of his shoe as he spun.

"Wait," Fitz said.

Pope didn't turn. Neither did he reach for the door.

Another short pause as Fitz toyed with his options. Then he spoke. "What's your offer?"

Bingo.

He turned back, speaking as casually as if relaying the baseball scores. "Twenty years. At a medium security penitentiary. Somewhere reasonably pleasant. Mendota, maybe. Or Phoenix."

Fitz shook his head scornfully. "No deal."

Pope shrugged. "There's always Florence," he said. "Supermax, you know. I hear it gets down to 10° in winter. Twenty-three hours a day in a cell with no windows, waiting out all the appeals until they finally lead you to the chair. It'll take twice as long, and you'll fry at the end anyway. Why not take the deal? It's the only one you'll get."

Now ashen-faced, Fitz choked over the words. "The feds don't use the chair."

Pope grinned. Discussing the method of his own execution probably wasn't how Fitz had foreseen this day going when it started.

"I'm sure they'll bring it back for you," he said. "But lethal injection ain't much more fun. Especially these days."

"Why?"

"The drugs come from Europe. The good ones, anyway. The ones that take away the pain. But I guess those cheese-eating surrender monkeys think the whole practice of execution is barbaric. So they don't sell them to us anymore. We have to make do."

"With what?"

"I'm not a pharmacist," Pope replied, flicking his fingers absentmindedly. "I hear the painkiller's no good. But I'm sure all that will be ironed out by the time they strap you down."

In truth, he didn't much like the death penalty either. It wasn't really a moral thing, he just preferred the idea that the men and women he put behind bars had to stay there until they served their time. Going to sleep seemed like the easy way out. But today, as so often, it served as a useful pressure point. Most men will do just about anything to avoid facing death.

And so it proved.

When Fitz next spoke, his voice was quiet. Broken. "What do you want?"

"You'll take the deal?"

"Seven years."

Pope shook his head. "Twenty. That's the only offer. You don't want to take it, I walk right out that room, and you can take your chances with the US Attorney. But like I told you, she's in a real bad mood."

"Okay!" Fitz yelled, attempting to stand before he was yanked back down by his chains. "Twenty. Whatever."

"You'll sign a national security agreement requiring your silence both during and after incarceration," Pope said, quickly ticking off the terms on his fingers. "Twenty years in general population, but you'll get a new name. You can go into witness protection when you get out. But I doubt anyone will bother to come looking for you."

Fitz stared forward at the wall, his body trembling slightly as if he finally understood what lay before him. His defenses were broken. Pope took the opportunity to indulge his own curiosity. "Can I ask you something?"

"What?" His prisoner asked dully.

"Why did you do it?"

There was a flash in Fitz's eyes now, as if the memory of who he had been briefly reasserted its strength. "I was empty after I left the Army. Nothing compares. Not in civilian life. Grover offered me the opportunity to be who I was supposed to be again. So I took it."

Pope nodded. "I'm glad you brought him up."

"Who?"

"Warren Grover."

49

P ope nervously smoothed his suit as he waited. This wasn't his first meeting with President Nash, but it was the only one in which he had been forced to take center stage.

"Relax," FBI Director Rutger murmured, subtly motioning toward the ground. "He's all bark."

Pope frowned. "Is that a good thing?"

"Sir, arms up please."

The Secret Service agent – he hadn't given a name – blandly brandished a magnetic wand, and Pope acquiesced, taking half a step out and lifting both his arms. Since he'd thought better than to bring a weapon into the White House, the check was cursory, except for a moment's consternation as his belt buckle made the device squeal.

"Thank you. If you'll follow me."

Pope did as requested, walking slightly behind the director, and they proceeded through the last few yards of the tunnel from the Treasury Building to the East Wing.

"Thanks, Jake," came a voice as they turned the corner. "I'll take them from here."

It belonged to the familiar face of Emma Martinez, the president's chief of staff. Familiar only to Pope from the media rather than any previous personal interaction. She looked tired and a little older than she had upon entering the White House a couple years earlier. Still, her posture was upright and her intention serious. They stopped in front of her, and the Secret Service agent made himself scarce.

Martinez nodded expressionlessly at the director. "Vince."

"Ms. Martinez."

"Care to tell me what you're doing here?"

"Truth be told," Rutger chuckled, "I don't exactly know myself."

"I don't believe that."

"I'm not asking you to believe it, Emma. The president can choose to loop you in on this or not, but that's not my decision to make."

Nash's chief of staff pursed her lips and said nothing as she spun on her heel. Rutger followed after her easily, but it took Pope a couple of seconds to catch up. They followed her through the East Wing for about a minute before stopping in front of an elevator. Pope noticed that in all that time, they didn't encounter anyone else. He suspected that wasn't unintentional.

The elevator arrived a couple of moments later, prompting an almost farcical situation as the three of them squeezed themselves into a tiny box that looked barely designed to accommodate one. The combination of the tension between his boss and Martinez and their present situation made Pope want to laugh out loud, but he instead steeled his features, reasoning it wouldn't make him popular.

The elevator took them three floors up and opened onto a hallway. Another Secret Service greeted them upon arrival but maintained his post once he saw who was leading the small procession. As they left him behind, Pope thought he heard the man murmuring something into a radio.

What a life this would be, he thought. President Nash wouldn't be able to visit the toilet without an entire chain of command knowing about it.

With a start, Pope realized that Martinez had led them into the White House Executive Residence. The president's home.

"Dear God," he murmured his breath.

"You say something, Nick?" Rutger said, turning.

"No, sir."

"I'll bet."

Martinez led them to a large office and bid them inside. "Wait here. I'll be back shortly."

"Yes, ma'am," Rutger replied easily.

Pope said nothing.

"Vince," a male voice boomed moments later. "Sorry for keeping you."

"Not at all, Mr. President," Director Rutger said as Pope turned back to the open doorway. "I serve at your pleasure."

"And don't forget that," President Nash chuckled. "Agent Pope."

Nick inclined his head, wondering if he was supposed to curtsy or something. He would probably have been given an etiquette briefing before an ordinary visit to this place, but today had been anything but ordinary. "Mr. President."

"Come on, sit," Nash said, gesturing at the armchairs. He walked over to the desk and dragged an upholstered conference chair from in front of it over to the fireplace. Pope tried intercepting him halfway, only to be brushed off.

The president plunked himself on the least comfortable of the three chairs in the room, much to Pope's consternation. He glanced at the director, wondering if he should offer to trade, but the amused look on his boss's face suggested not.

"I said sit," Nash repeated.

The door clicked shut, catching Pope's attention. He saw that Emma Martinez was inside the now-sealed room. He was caught between wanting to offer her the sole remaining armchair and protesting her presence. In the end, he said nothing.

The expression on his face, however, must have been obvious. Nash snorted. "Emma prefers standing. She says sitting encourages lazy thinking, would you believe it? Maybe she's right. But she hears what I hear, and if one of us has to think properly then I'd rather it was her."

"Yes, sir," Pope muttered, chastened by the implicit – if mild – rebuke. He sat.

Nash looked expectantly at Rutger. "Now, Vince, I expect you're about to tell me what's so damn important I had to interrupt my supper?"

"I'll leave that to Nick here," Rutger replied with a broad smile. "I'm just the tour guide."

The president's attention shifted in turn, and he leaned forward, pushing his elbows on his knees.

Thanks a lot, Pope thought, suddenly wishing that he had brought with him a sheaf of notes to fiddle with, or even a damn pen. It wasn't that he thought he needed the information – in fact, as little of the present crisis was being committed to paper as possible, given the potential geopolitical ramifications of a leak – he just wanted a shield. There was something strangely disconcerting about Nash's gaze, as though the man could read him like a book.

That, of course, would be a useful talent to possess in his position.

Pope cleared his throat and looked up at Martinez one last time before beginning. "Mr. President."

Nash leapt up and held a finger in the air. "Hold that thought!"

He crouched down on hands and knees in front of the fireplace and fished for a box of matches. The kindling was already arranged, and he struck the match and held it into its midst. It didn't take long before a low flame was crackling.

"You know, every other year the cleaning company sweeps the chimneys for free," he remarked, dusting the soot off his fingers as he resumed his seat. "A gift to lower the budget deficit. Every chimney in this damn place. It takes them six days, crew of ten, and they do it for free!"

Nash shook his head. "If you think about it too hard, the guy just volunteered to pay more in federal taxes. And it doesn't do a damn thing for the deficit. But it's a nice gesture, don't you think?"

"Yes, sir."

"I light it, and I clean out the ashes after I'm done," Nash continued. "It's one of the few jobs around here the staff allows me to get on with."

"I'm sure they're only trying to help," Pope remarked, wondering what the hell he was supposed to say to that.

"And they are," Nash said, brandishing his fingers. "But sometimes you put to use these things for more than signing legislation. And besides, it helps me clear my head."

"Yes, sir."

Rutger coughed politely and said, "I think Agent Pope here had something important that you needed to know."

It struck Pope in that moment that Nash wasn't making small talk – he was procrastinating. Engaging in avoidant behavior. And it was obvious why.

Nash gestured impatiently. "Go on, then."

"Sir, have you ever heard of an organization called The Apparatus?"

"Should I have?"

"In an ideal world," Pope remarked dryly, momentarily forgetting himself. "But probably not."

"Okay. Enlighten me."

"Sir, it's – I should say, it *was* – an ad hoc intelligence unit under the auspices of the Army. It dates back at least 30 or 40 years, and for most of that time was a think tank for kind of out-there ideas. Kind of the brainiac twin of the military's least known intelligence unit, The Activity. Otherwise known as Task Force Orange."

"You talking MK Ultra, or something even more bananas?" Nash grunted, looking around for something, Pope wasn't sure what.

"Probably less crazy than staring at goats. More crazy than invading Panama."

"Great. So what was it?"

"Mainly an off-the-wall think tank. A military talk shop for generating low-cost, higher-impact solutions."

"I don't like the sound of that," Nash remarked. He stood abruptly and walked toward the lacquered cabinet. "Either of you want a drink?"

"You know me, sir," Rutger said. Pope shook his head, though in truth a little alcohol would have done a world of good.

Undeterred, Nash opened the cabinet and took out a bottle of scotch. He poured a generous measure into each of four tumblers before carrying two of them in either hand. He handed one to Martinez, then sat back down.

"Don't be polite," he said gruffly as he pressed one into Pope's unresisting fingers. "That's an order. This sounds like one of those conversations it's best not to have when you're entirely sober."

"Yes, sir," Pope said, taking a sip.

"Carry on."

"Though the Apparatus more or less dissolved naturally several years ago, we've uncovered evidence that one of the ideas its members tossed around was a hostile takeover of a Mexican drug cartel with a view to seizing control of the entire

South-North narcotics trade and thus blocking flows into the continental United States."

Nash groaned. "Agent Pope, please tell me that what you just said is only for color."

"I'm afraid not, Mr. President. It appears that several former members of the unit have taken the plan freelance, and that this is the cause of the recent uptick in violence in Mexico."

"Dammit," Nash hissed. He sank half the whiskey tumbler in one gulp, then set it onto the floor. "Is that all?"

"No, sir."

"Of course not..."

"Part of the plan – or at least the revised plan that was put into practice – was aimed to engineer the election of a friendly face into the office of the Mexican Presidency."

"Neto's up for election now, isn't he, Emma?"

"That's right, sir."

"So what you're telling me, Agent Pope, is that American intelligence officers in this day and age have attempted to affect the results of free and fair elections of one of our closest allies?"

Pope nodded.

"You planning on bringing me any good news?" Nash muttered irritably.

"Kind of, Mr. President. The man behind this is Warren Grover. We have him under surveillance as we speak."

"Why haven't you brought him in already?" Nash snapped. "Or better yet, killed him."

Pope glanced anxiously at Rutger, who thankfully intervened in his typically booming voice. "Because, Mr. President, this is one of those decisions that guys like me don't get to make."

The president's expression softened, taking on an almost apologetic bent. "This one's on me, huh? Then tell me – what are my options?"

"The problem we have, sir, is that Grover's plan called for

the installation of a new individual as president of Mexico. Someone with whom he could do business."

A deposit of resin inside one of the logs on the fireplace sizzled then popped as Nash glanced sharply up. "Who?"

"Senator Josefina Salazar."

"You've got to be kidding me."

"No sir. The analysis we've done lines up with Fitz's allegations. Salazar's campaign was on life support six months ago, just a few days away from going broke. All of a sudden her campaign was inundated with small dollar donations that looked legit—"

"But weren't," Nash said dryly. "And this was all Grover's work?"

"Yes sir, using laundered cartel funds. Plus a handful of judicious opposition research leaks on her rivals."

The president cut him off. "This isn't an intelligence issue anymore. It's a diplomatic one. God – you're telling me that we nearly mounted a coup on the Mexican government?"

Pope nodded his agreement.

"And it's not over, is it?"

"Not even close. We have one of Grover's associates in custody, a man called Ethan Fitz. He's talking, and he says that Grover has pivoted in order to save his own skin. I've seen messages between the two men indicating he plans to travel to Mexico City to attempt to engineer Salazar's election, using the current chaos in Mexico as pretext. He doubtless has leverage over both the senator and a senior officer in the Mexican Armed Forces, a man called Abalos. All three are too deep in this to simply back out. So they are going to raise the stakes."

"What are my options?"

Pope looked over at Director Rutger, but Nash slapped his thigh to attract his attention. "I'm asking you, Agent Pope. You're the one working this case. What do you suggest?"

"Sir, this is a tricky situation. But that's kind of the CIA's core competency. If you order it, they can clean this up."

"Clean this up?" Nash frowned. "You mean kill them. All three of the plotters."

"Yes, sir."

"Then say that. I don't like euphemisms." Nash paused, studying Pope. "You don't look like you like that option."

"No, Mr. President. But it's not like I have a better one."

"I think you do."

Pope hesitated, wondering how Nash knew, and fearing he was about to be labeled as a Pollyanna. "Sir, my opinion is that you don't fix one cover-up by starting another. I would come clean."

"Thankfully in this situation the right choice is also the only viable one," Nash mused. "You're right. This won't leak from our side. But if we try and hush things up, and the Mexican government ever finds out – which they will – then not to put too fine a point on it, but we're fucked."

The president rose to his feet, looking equal parts determined and uncertain. "Emma, get me President Neto on the phone immediately. And tell the Air Force to fire up the big bird. I'm guessing this one will require a personal touch."

50

The first words out of Ethan Fitz' mouth as Grover approached were, "Are you alone?"

Leo Conway's former handler was now sitting under a café awning on the corner of Calle de Tacuba, in the historic center of Mexico City. It was the appointed place at the appointed time. He had a rolled-up newspaper on the seat next to him, the agreed signal that they were not being watched.

That, of course, was a lie. In truth, Fitz was here to sell a story. A story that would save his life.

"What the hell are you doing here?" Grover snapped, not standing on either ceremony or any conception of loyalty to a friend. "I saw your mark. I'm here. So this better be good."

"What am I doing here?" Fitz spluttered with disbelief. "What do you think? You screwed me."

"How?" Grover asked coldly.

"The feds are looking for me," Fitz replied, starting to pace. "They were at my front door, Warren. You understand what that means? They know who I am!"

"How is that my problem?"

"You think I didn't keep records, you asshole?" Fitz replied.

He looked around to see if anyone had noticed, seemingly aware that he was losing control. He reached for the coffee cup in front of him and wrapped his fingers around it. He leaned forward. "I'm not an idiot, Warren. I knew what we were doing was dangerous."

Grover signaled for a waiter and ordered a cup of his own. Both men waited until the man departed before they resumed conversation. "I repeat: how is that my problem?"

"I can screw you," Fitz snarled. "Just like you did me."

"Don't blame me for your own inadequacies, Ethan," Grover said with an affected calmness. "If the FBI are after you, it's because you failed. Not me."

"Hell, maybe it was, but it doesn't make a blind bit of difference. Like they say in the movies, Warren, I've got receipts."

"And how do you think that helps you?"

Fitz squinted in confusion. "I need money. More than we agreed. A lot more. I got you what you wanted; I didn't know what you were planning to do with it. You killed five US Attorneys, Warren. And the administrator of the DEA. Are you insane?"

"You never asked why I needed it. I might have told you. Besides, you didn't have any problem taking out Spratt. Why the attack of conscience over some underpaid lawyers?"

"Because they are looking for me. I can't go home. I've lost everything."

The waiter brought the espresso and set it in front of Grover. Once again, the two men briefly lapsed into silence. Grover reached for the coffee, but Fitz locked his wrist to the table, wrapping his fingers around it until his nails dug into the skin. "Money, Warren. That's all I need. You owe me."

"I don't owe you a damn thing," Grover hissed. He tore his hand away from the restraint, and more casually lifted the espresso to his lips.

"Then I'll release everything."

Grove shrugged. "Do it. They're after me too."

"They don't know your name. They can't. That's the difference, don't you understand?"

"I've got bigger problems to worry about than the Bureau," Grover said somewhat self-importantly. "The cartels don't fuck around. I crossed them, and now they're coming after me. So you'll forgive me for not caring too much about your legal issues."

"What if I had something? Something you could use."

"It would depend on what exactly you had. I'm going to need more than that."

Fitz rocked back and forth as if coming to a decision. He leaned forward, and his voice adopted a wheedling tone. "What are you doing? You're working an angle, I know you. You're too calm."

Grover prepared to leave. "What do you have, Ethan? You're running out of time."

"I want in," Fitz announced, with the determination of a man who'd made his bed. "Whatever it is. I don't care about the money. We both know you're my best shot at surviving this."

"Show me your cards, and maybe I'll show you mine."

Fitz didn't want to talk, that much was evident. But by now, Grover was intrigued. The truth was that his own position was much less secure than he was making out. He could use an edge. Perhaps this was it. Either way, it was clear that his former comrade in arms wasn't going to give up the goods without an extra push.

Grover stood and tossed a couple of peso notes onto the table. "It was nice to see you, Ethan. But this is all you're getting from me."

"Wait. Okay. Nash is coming."

"Coming where?" Grover asked, his voice hardening.

Fitz screwed up his face, seemingly with disbelief. "Don't you get it? Here!"

51

The Marriott Hotel in Mexico City was located just opposite the famous Campo Marte – the parade ground owned by the Mexican Defense Ministry. An enormous flag mounted on a pole a hundred meters tall occasionally roused itself to flutter in a soporific breeze. It was a beautiful counterpoint to the most obvious example of American power in view – the Starbucks which Trapp was standing in front of.

Ikeda was just barely in his line of sight, waiting at a bus stop. That was one good thing about Mexico. People here didn't rush around like they did back home. They didn't always have some place to be. There was a whole lot more sitting around and enjoying life to be done.

Which fact, combined with her tanned skin and naturally dark hair, meant that she didn't stick out among the crowd as she waited.

"I see him," she murmured. "Coming right your way, Jason. Thirty seconds."

"Copy that," Trapp replied. He was wearing the same white wireless Apple headphones that were de rigueur for anyone from teenagers to tech types, which made surreptitious communications a whole lot easier. Gone were the days of whispering into a wrist mic.

Lieutenant Ramirez, who was now seated in a parked car, added, "He's alone. No one following."

Trapp clicked the radio, and caught sight of Ethan Fitz' unmistakable tall, blond frame a moment later. The spy – or whatever he was now – was wearing a light blue suit and a white shirt. He could have been a model or a business traveler instead of what he was.

A traitor.

The fact that he'd sold out his country for cash in service not of another nation, or even an ideology, but for an international criminal organization did not change the raw facts of the matter. What he had done had led to the deaths of Americans. It helped destabilize one of the United States' closest allies. It had caused violence on American streets.

And now he was doing his penance. There would be a lot more making up for the evil he'd helped wrought. Many years of it. But Trapp was here to ensure that he didn't try and wriggle out of the deal he'd made.

He waited for Fitz to cross his path, then walked intention-ally toward him, shouldering him bodily toward the café. It was a glass-fronted modern franchise, just like any back home. Star-bucks really had swallowed the world and cuffed it back out all the same.

"Inside," Trapp hissed. He'd surreptitiously altered the man's direction without Fitz even really realizing what had just happened.

Fitz grunted as the air was driven out of his lungs. "Who –?"

"Don't look at me," Trapp murmured, pushing ahead of his unwitting charge and through the glass doors. "Keep your eyes forward and order a drink."

Trapp did the same and stepped away from the register. Fitz

did as he was told, only a slight tremor in his voice betraying his concern as he ordered an iced coffee. Both men stood side by side as they waited for their drinks to be made.

"You know who I am?"

"I do."

"Good. You're wearing the watch?"

Fitz raised his left arm and ostentatiously scratched his nose. As he did, the cuff of his suit shifted slightly, revealing a silver wristwatch. "I am."

"It'll pick up any conversations within fifteen feet or so. But keep it in line of sight to anyone who is talking."

"We went through this already, back in Washington. Why –"

"I figured you might need a reminder. Remember, we're watching. If you try and renege on our agreement, it will not end well for you."

"I wouldn't!" Fitz protested.

"We both know you would," Trapp remarked derisively. "So consider this the only warning you are going to get."

"I can't be here long," Fitz said. "I'm expected."

The girl at the counter called out the name "Jackson" rather than his own, but Trapp stepped forward to claim it anyway. It was close enough. The ice rattled in the plastic cup. He took a sip. As he turned to leave, he said, "I've said what I came to say. Just remember the deal you made."

Trapp left the Starbucks and walked directly for the road. Leafy green trees swayed overhead. He stuck his arm out, and a taxi veered out of traffic, pulling in to the yellow-painted curb just beside him. He climbed in.

"You think he got the message?" Hector asked from behind the driver's wheel, already stepping on the gas and easing back into traffic.

"I do. He won't screw us over."

"I hope you're right."

"Me too."

THE TAXI only carried him around the block before parking up outside the W Hotel right next to the Marriott itself.

"I'll see you up there in ten," Hector said as Trapp stepped out. He grinned as he saw the jokingly proffered peso notes. "It's on the house, amigo."

Burke was already waiting inside the hotel room on the twelfth floor, seated behind a bank of surveillance equipment. They had pirated the feed from the Marriott's internal security cameras, every single one of which was being saved onto local hard drives. None of these images would ever see either the light of day or the inside of a courtroom.

But that didn't mean they wouldn't be useful.

"Remind me never to get on your bad side," the DEA agent said as Trapp closed the door behind him. "You do a real ominous bad cop bit. Ever thought about Hollywood?"

"I haven't got the looks." Trapp grinned, grabbing a cold soda from the minibar to wash away the taste of the iced coffee.

"I don't know," Burke said mischievously. "I hear Warner Brothers are doing a Frankenstein reboot."

Trapp sat down beside him. "Frankenstein was the doctor."

"I never said he wasn't. Doesn't mean I'm putting you forward for his role."

"Yeah, yeah, wise guy."

Ikeda joined a moment later. "Good job," she said, squeezing his shoulder, then stealing the Coke. "What did you say to him? He looked real shook up."

Trapp rolled his eyes. "Not you too..."

"What?"

"Forget about it." He turned to Burke. "How's the signal?"

"Right now? Dead."

"That a good thing?" Trapp remarked, his tone of voice suggesting that he very much thought it was not.

Burke replayed one of the feeds on the monitor, pointing to a familiar figure in a tan suit. "That's him thirty seconds ago, climbing into the elevator. It's just the concrete shaft, that's all. Kills the signal."

"Yeah, let's hope so."

"And... he's back," Burke said, holding out a set of headphones. "Want to listen?"

"Sure."

Trapp cupped them around his ears. He didn't last a second before he tore them back off, grimacing. "What the hell is that?"

"Just rustling, that's all. Never took you for such a snowflake."

They watched as Fitz walked up to the door to a suite on the top floor. Trapp tugged the headphones away a second time as he knocked. The door opened, and Fitz quickly slipped inside.

"That's Grover," Burke remarked. "Arrived a couple hours ago. Shame we couldn't get a set of eyes inside."

"The other two?"

"Not here yet."

Grover and Fitz sat in stony silence inside the suite. Trapp wished they had gotten a camera inside as well, but the heavy breathing being transmitted through the listening device in Fitz' watch told a story in itself.

Abalos arrived ten minutes later, walking up the emergency stairwell from the floor below. Senator Salazar didn't bother attempting to obfuscate her movements. She rode the elevator up and strolled right to the front door. Trapp couldn't work out whether he was impressed by her arrogance or disgusted by her stupidity.

The door to their own hotel room clicked open a second time, and Hector joined them.

"You got here right in time," Trapp remarked. "We're getting right to the good part."

"You think there's any chance he tries to screw us?" Ikeda asked. "Goes back on the deal he cut with Pope. Maybe he figures a few million bucks from Grover sounds better than a decade behind bars."

"I hope so," Hector growled ominously. "My men are in position in the Marriott. If any of these traitors tries something on, they know what to do."

Strangely, the meeting in Grover's hotel suite began with small talk and pleasantries. Trapp hadn't expected it to sound quite so...

Normal. It was just like any business meeting between mid-level bureaucrats. Except the topic they were discussing was far graver.

"You fucked us," Abalos declared pompously, his voice muffled but perfectly audible. "You said you had a plan, and instead you've led us to the edge. Neto is furious. He is planning an investigation into this whole mess. None of us can survive that."

"We are where we are," Grover replied. "And I suggest that instead of casting blame, we try and do something about it."

"Like what?" Abalos snarled, seeming to stand and pace around the room. It was difficult to make out with just the audio.

"Neto's investigation," Grover said, his voice cracking, "is only a priority so long as he is president. The election is in three weeks. I suspect if Josefina here had the job she so desires, it might even be made to disappear. Am I correct?"

"President Nash is in this city as we speak," Abalos said, cutting across him. "You think Neto is going to slow-play his investigation with that kind of heat on him? Let alone the chaos in the rest of the country."

"Then do something about it," Grover snapped. "You have the men, do you not? The Federación is crying out for a leader. The Crusaders are on the back foot. Reyes is weak. We have an opportunity to get what we always wanted. Don't just sit on your hands and whine to me when the ball is still in play."

"It's too late," a woman's voice interjected curtly. "I'm three points behind in the polls. Too far behind to catch him with so little time. Especially if you hand him a win by crushing what's left of the cartels."

"Let me handle Neto," Grover said dismissively. "I can pin this whole mess on him, given time. It's easy to manufacture doubt. To make it look like he was in bed with Reyes this whole time. But only if the admiral here gives me an opportunity. Hit the Crusaders while they are down. I'll handle the rest. And let me remind you, you're both in too deep to back out now."

There was a pause. A man's laugh – bitter and desperate. "I'll give you what you want. Like I have a choice."

A woman's voice. "Fine."

They kept listening until the meeting ended, recording and transcribing every word. But in truth, the conspirators had implicated themselves in the crime right from the start – probably sealing their fates. They just didn't know it yet.

Burke pulled his headphones off and turned to Hector. "So do we have what you need?"

The Mexican nodded, and though it would have been understandable for him to be elated, his expression was anything but. He looked almost sad. "This is enough to take to President Neto. After that, our next move is up to him."

Trapp shrugged. "Good enough for me."

"I thought you wanted to shoot them all," Ikeda objected.

"I still do." He grinned. "But I'm a soldier. Rules of engagement are there to be followed. And hey, there's a best-case scenario here."

"Which is?"

"Neto takes one good look at all this and orders us to kill them all himself."

52

2 *Days Later*

THE WINNEBAGO RV was parked inside a fenced-off area behind the stage set up for Senator Salazar's rally in Constitution Square. It was about twenty feet long, and at least as old in years. A bodyguard – a plainclothes officer in the Policía Nacional – was posted outside the door that led to the passenger cabin.

Hector León leaned against a section of metal fence, keeping the area under close surveillance. He was wearing light blue denim jeans and a dark jacket and had a lanyard around his neck that advertised that his presence was authorized.

"Who are you?" the officer on duty asked.

Hector flashed his credentials and placed his index finger across his lips. He spoke in a low voice. "I need to speak with the senator."

"I can't let you do that, sir," the officer replied. The tortured expression on his face reflected the fact that he was in an impossible situation. León clearly outranked him – and yet even so, he had a job to do. And Hector respected him for that.

"Your name is Santiago, correct?" Hector asked, still speaking softly.

The officer nodded. His dark hair bounced gently. "Yes, sir. How did you know?"

"Have you ever met the president, Santi?"

Santiago's forehead descended into a mass of wrinkles. "No..."

"You know what he sounds like?"

A shrug. "I guess."

Hector reached into his inside jacket pocket and pulled out a cell phone. The motion made Santiago flinch, but he did not otherwise react. He dialed the last number in his memory and held the phone out.

The officer accepted it, holding it in front of himself for a few moments before pressing it to his ear. A second later, his eyes widened. He nodded awkwardly, even though it was not a video call, and mumbled into the device. "Yes, sir. Yes. Of course. Thank you."

Santiago handed the phone back. He said nothing, though he looked even more uncertain than before. If such a thing was possible.

"So do we have an understanding?" Hector asked, sliding the phone back into his pocket.

"That's... That's not proof," Santiago muttered, though he didn't even seem to believe it himself. "It could've been anyone."

"I think you know who that was, Santi," Hector murmured. "Search me. I won't touch her, you have my word on that. But I need to speak to the senator. In private."

Santiago looked up to the sky as if for reassurance. His head hung there without moving for a few seconds, then dropped back down. "You won't do a thing to her?"

"If I walk out that door and I've touched even a hair on her head," Hector replied with disarming honesty, "then you can put a bullet in me."

The officer grimaced, but his decision was evidently made. "Arms out."

Hector entered the RV a moment later. He still sensed Santiago's nervousness even as he closed the door behind him. The décor was faded but functional. A couch ran along one side of the cabin and a workspace on the other. There was neither a kitchen nor a bedroom. The senator was seated in front of a backlit mirror.

He waited, saying nothing.

Salazar didn't look away from her reflection as she continued wrangling her hair into a semblance of control. "Is it time?"

"That depends entirely on you," Hector replied coldly.

"Who the hell are you?" Salazar snapped. She didn't raise her voice – at least not yet – but her tone was positively Arctic.

"I think you know."

Her hair and makeup now forgotten, the senator stood. Outrage radiated from her, and her fists clenched into little balls. "Don't presume to know me, young man. Now tell me who you are before I call security."

"I'm surprised," Hector replied, "that you don't recognize me. After all, you tried to have me killed."

Salazar was a pro. He had to give her that. She didn't flinch at the accusation. If anything, her sense of injustice only strengthened. "I did no such thing. We've never met."

Hector held out his hand mockingly. "My name is Captain Hector Alvarez León. Perhaps that will brush away a few cobwebs."

Still, the senator did not react. Hector's respect for the woman's skill grew, if only grudgingly.

"I'm here to offer you a choice, Josefina," he said, deliberately failing to use a term of respect that she did not deserve.

"Senator Salazar."

He shook his head. "No."

She didn't contest the point, and he noted that although she was wary, she did not seem scared by his presence.

"I'll humor you," she said eventually. "If only to keep myself alive."

"I haven't threatened you."

Salazar gestured at herself. "You broke into a woman's dressing room. You're half my age and twice my weight. You could do anything to me, and what defense would I have?"

"You could scream." Hector shrugged. "Your bodyguard is right outside. But you don't want to do that, do you, Josefina? Because you're worried about what I know."

Her lips pursed. "What do you want?"

"To give you a choice," he said, spreading his palms wide. "To do the right thing."

"And what is that?" she replied in a mocking lilt. "I suspect something that makes you rich."

"Quite the opposite. Hand yourself in to me now, and you have my word that you will be treated with the... *respect* due your station. If you don't"—he shrugged—"you will have to bear the consequences."

"That sounds like a threat."

"Quite the opposite. As I said, it's a choice."

Her dark eyes tightened. "What do you have?"

"I thought you were just humoring me."

"I am."

In the background, the chants of the crowd on the opposite side of the stage began to build into a crescendo. Even through the Winnebago's chassis, their words were clear and distinct. "JO–SE–FI–NA! JO–SE–FI–NA!"

They called out the mantra over and over, rising in tempo and volume with each rendition so that it became akin to a Benedictine chant. Salazar closed her eyes, seeming to exult in the adulation.

"Do you hear that?" she murmured.

"Hard to miss."

"You think you can threaten me?" she snapped, her eyes opening wide. "You have nothing. If you did, you wouldn't be in here beguiling me with words. So I reject your offer."

Hector thrust his hands into his pockets, not surprised by the outcome and not entirely disappointed. "Are you sure you want to do this? Remember, you have a choice."

"You have my answer," she snapped. "Now get out."

He didn't linger. On his way out, he shook Santiago's hand.

"She's fine," he said. "You've done a good thing for your country. It won't be forgotten."

53

Warren Grover was seated in the hotel bar in the Four Seasons on Paseo de la Reforma, a stone's throw from Mexico City's enormous and ornate city park. He was wearing a tan suit and an open-collared white shirt, and sat in a plush turquoise armchair, he could easily have been lost in a crowd of similarly-attired international travelers.

A waitress passed by his table and was momentarily painted in the bright midday sunlight now streaming through the large glass windows.

"Can I get you a drink?"

He nodded, not particularly paying attention as he pulled a laptop out of a travel case by his side. "A scotch. Something peaty, with two cubes of ice. And the Wi-Fi code."

"Are you staying with us?"

"I'll pay cash."

"I'll be right back."

She was as good as her word, and after returning with a crystal tumbler filled with amber liquid, she slid a thick business card onto the table in front of him. It was cream-colored, reassuringly hefty, and had the code printed on it.

Grover punched it into his computer and pulled up the website of a local cable news channel. He took a sip of the whisky as the feed buffered, his cheeks puckering slightly as the warmth made its way down his chest. The ice clinked against the glass as he set the whisky back down.

The laptop's tinny speakers started blaring as the video feed began to play. Grover received a couple of irritated looks and tapped the mute button. He didn't want to listen to the inane nonsense the news anchors spouted in order to fill the airwaves either.

The picture on the screen was of the crowd streaming into the Plaza del Zócalo, formally known as Constitution Square. It was a place that had hosted celebrations and demonstrations and festivals and massacres ever since Aztec times. Today, it was home to a political rally.

Senator Salazar was not yet on stage, and so the camera played out over the crowd. The square wasn't yet even a fifth full, though that wasn't an enormous surprise, since it was so enormous that several hundred thousand could fill it comfortably. Nor were the demonstrators assembled like sardines, but instead spread out. Still, they seemed lively, and flags and banners fluttered on a light breeze.

Grover accepted that there was little he could do but sit and wait. And since there was little enough happening in Constitution Square, his eyes wandered across the bar. He'd chosen it precisely because it was the type of location that was frequented by business travelers and tourists rather than cartel types. It was one of Mexico City's most glamorous destinations, and both management and the security services were anxious to keep it that way. It was for that reason that he felt comfortable relaxing. There was little danger to him here.

He spotted a dark-haired woman sitting near the window.

She had a bottle of local beer on the table in front of her, resting on a square white napkin. She had the frame of an athlete, rather than a model, but clearly didn't have an ounce of unwanted fat on her. She could be a local, but Grover thought not. She looked to be of Asian descent. Maybe half and half, resulting in a caramel tan and thick, dark hair.

Attractive, Grover judged.

She was probably about thirty. Maybe a couple of years older, but in sufficiently excellent physical condition that she could have passed for a decade younger with enough makeup. Not that she was wearing any.

He looked away, conscious of the risk of her noticing his attention. Besides, there would be time for women later. He returned his focus to the laptop screen.

Something was happening in the Plaza, he saw. The crowd was chanting something. He plugged in a pair of headphones and listened. They were calling for Salazar. Over and over again, chanting her name, imploring her to come out.

And after a couple of minutes of this, she emerged. As always, she was wearing heels and a tight skirt that ended a few inches below her knees. Two enormous screens on the stage behind her blew her up in size a dozen times as cameras at the event focused on her for the benefit of those at the back of the crowd.

As she reached the podium, she held her arms out in front of her beneficently and waited for the crowd to quiet. It took almost a minute, but eventually they did. She leaned forward to the microphones and started to speak.

But no words came out. At least, not through the PA system – and not through the news feed either. Salazar was clearly talking, but the microphones weren't picking up her voice.

Grover cursed the incompetence of the AV technician who had failed to correctly perform his job. Didn't that prick understand how much was riding on this?

Salazar tapped the microphone, but to no avail.

Behind her, the screens went dead. No longer did they display a live image of the woman at the podium. They were just dark. Salazar didn't appear to notice, though she was gesturing at someone off-stage, presumably to sort out the technical issues.

The screens behind her flashed back into life. But instead of displaying the earlier video feed, they were playing something else entirely. It was slickly produced, almost like a campaign ad.

Grover shook his head, mumbling to himself, "What the hell are they doing? It's a fucking clown show."

Sadly for him, that wasn't the end of it. A voice started dispassionately listing payments and dates. "June 5, 2020: $72,000. July 11, 2020: $101,000.59. September 3, 2020: $41,000..."

The voice went on and on, listing exact amounts, then the banks from which the money was transferred. Then the accounts in which it landed. Each blow deepened Grover's unease. He recognized every word of what was being said. Not the precise amounts of the payments, but close enough.

He'd authorized every one.

It was immediately apparent that this was a hit job. Someone knew everything, and whoever that someone was had waited for the precise moment in which they could inflict the greatest damage to him. The video kept playing, the narrator kept talking, and Senator Josefina Salazar, the leading candidate in the Mexican presidential elections, saw her career disappear into smoke.

She gripped the side of the lectern for support, clearly in shock.

The crowd's mood turned. At first, Grover had heard expressions of surprise and confusion. Now it was anger. They had seen the woman before them as a heroine, as the savior of their country.

And now they understood that she was no different from the rest. She too had her snout deep in the trough.

"Fuck," Grover hissed, thumping the table in front of him so hard the whisky tumbler jumped. A dozen pairs of eyes fell on him, all mirroring the same expression of disapproval.

But the dark-haired woman's didn't. She looked for all the world as though she hadn't heard a thing.

It's over, Grover knew. *There's no coming back from this.*

Without Salazar, he had no hope of ever exercising any real measure of power in this country again. If she'd made it to the presidency, maybe. But not now. Far from running for office, she would now be running for her life. It would be exile abroad, or the scarce comfort of a prison cell for her.

One by one, the watching eyes around him returned to their own conversations. Grover quickly packed his laptop away, cutting the news anchor off mid-stream. He zipped up his wheeled carry-on case and left some money on the table for the drink. He walked quickly outside.

He didn't notice the woman following him. She was good at that.

He walked past the hardwood-fronted reception desk, around a circular table topped with half a dozen vases of lilies, and out through the lobby to the hotel's entrance. He raised his arm, gesturing at a row of taxis. A blinking light flickered on, and one pulled toward him. The driver was hefty, wearing a red plaid shirt and a baseball cap over his eyes.

Grover climbed in, shoving the case onto the back seat beside him, and closed the car door. "The airport."

The driver said nothing.

"I'm in a hurry, man."

"Aren't we all," the man replied dryly.

In English.

Grover froze. To his side, the car door opened, and the

woman from the bar climbed in alongside him. The second she was in, the taxi started moving.

Without blinking the woman pulled out a pistol and thrust it into his crotch. "I wouldn't move if I were you," she murmured, digging the muzzle into his right nut hard enough to bring tears to his eyes. "I hear those things are kinda precious to guys like you."

"Who –?" Grover whispered.

Neither man nor woman said another word for the next half hour, despite his protestations. The taxi drove east out of the city and into the country. After a while, they passed fields on either side. Irrigation sprinklers painted a rainbow in the dry air on one side.

The taxi stopped on the side of a dusty road several miles outside of Mexico City. The asphalt had clearly been laid within the past year or so, but was already crumbling at the sides, as was so often the way in this part of the world. Overstrung powerlines hung overhead, dipping so low that a lost semi-truck might easily find itself barbecued after making contact.

The man killed the engine. He twisted in his seat and stared directly into Grover's eyes. Still he said nothing.

"Who are you?" Grover asked, attempting to stop his voice trembling, but mostly failing.

"Trapp." The man smiled mirthlessly. He didn't extend his hand. "You can call me Jason."

"You don't have to do this," Grover whimpered. "I'll give you anything you want. Everything I have."

"And how much is that?"

"Millions," Grover lied. He was congenitally incapable of doing otherwise.

"That's all?" Trapp said, frowning. "I don't believe you."

"Tens. Hundreds. Just let me live, okay? You can have it all. Just don't kill me."

Trapp cocked his head at Ikeda. "What do you think? Should we take the money and run? Spend the rest of our lives on a white sand beach somewhere sipping mojitos and getting fat?"

Ikeda laughed, though to Grover's ears the sound was cold and discordant. "We've never taken the money before, have we?"

"No, I guess not."

"And why's that?"

Any amusement that had previously decorated Trapp's face disappeared. "Because we're not fucking traitors."

"Oh, that's right," Ikeda murmured, as if the reason had only just dawned on her. She jabbed the muzzle of her pistol hard into his crotch once again, causing him to moan out loud. It wasn't really from the pain, just the mounting realization that there was no way out.

"What do you want?" he moaned.

Outside the car, Grover heard the scratching of tires passing over the loose-packed surface of the road. He looked around desperately, forgetting that both his unwanted visitors could see exactly what he was doing as hope filled his breast. There was someone out there.

"Please!" Grover yelled, hopeless. "Help! Help me, please..."

It took another few seconds for the vehicle to come into view. It was a black sedan, several years old, and coated in a thick layer of dust that mostly obscured the license plates. It was moving slowly, just a few miles an hour. Grover tried again, calling out at the top of his lungs as his fingers ineffectually tugged at the handle of the locked car door.

The car slowed and pulled in behind the taxi.

Maybe they think we've broken down, he thought wildly,

losing any connection to rationality he once possessed. *They'll see the gun.*

Grover twisted and stared over his shoulder, willing the driver to get out. He could see two shapes behind the windshield. Both men. Both young. Both about the same age. And both extremely fit.

And in that moment, he understood that all hope was lost.

"They *are* here for you, Warren." Trapp smiled. "Just not the way you hoped."

"Why won't you just take the money?" Grover moaned, his fingers still scrabbling at the door as though a process in his mind had short-circuited. It wasn't about escape anymore. Just something for his brain to cling on to.

"You know the reason," Trapp commented dispassionately. He looked at Ikeda. "Do you want to do it, or shall I?"

"I'm American! You can't just do this to me. I have rights," Grover protested, his voice tight with desperation. His limbs were now leaden with terror. Even if the door had sprung open, he probably wouldn't have been capable of running.

"You had rights," Ikeda replied. "But the president has determined you are a threat to national security. Don't ask me for the legal precedent. I don't know it by heart."

"I'm entitled to a lawyer," Grover mumbled, still battling.

By this point, Ikeda seemed done caring. She looked up at Trapp. "You have a suppressor?"

He nodded.

"Then you do it."

"My pleasure."

A metallic, scratching sound indicated that Trapp was fixing a suppressor to the end of his own weapon, but it was all happening out of Grover's eyesight, hidden by the rear of the taxi's front seats. He tried looking in the mirror but saw nothing.

The scratching stopped.

"Anything you want to say?" Trapp said, jerking his head to the side as he twisted and leveled his pistol at a spot somewhere between Grover's eyes.

They flared wide. "Huh?"

He didn't notice, not immediately, that the pressure on his groin had subsided. A click echoed around the car's interior, which caused Grover to flinch, thinking it was the pistol's hammer. It wasn't. The locks on the doors were now inactive. Ikeda opened hers and began climbing out.

Grover tried to do the same.

He wasn't quick enough. Trapp squeezed the trigger three times, and as many rounds smashed through Grover's body. The first tore through his heart muscle, destabilizing it so that the next contraction ripped it apart. That would've been enough to kill him, but another round to the skull made absolutely sure.

A single spurt of red bloodied the cab's interior clear plastic shield. After that, the heart was in no shape to continue pumping. Grover slumped to one side.

Dead.

54

Culiacán, *Estadio de Sinaloa*
6 Days Later

RAMON REYES STRODE through the busy hallways of the Catedral Basílica de Nuestra Señora del Rosario, better known as Culiacán Cathedral. His leather-soled shoes clapped against the worn marble floors, ceasing only as he stopped occasionally to examine one facet or another of the preparations for his wife's funeral. Mendoza, who had become ever-present these past few days, hung a few paces behind and remained as silent as always.

As he entered the main body of the cathedral, a priest clad in ankle-length robes bowed his head. His expression was studiously neutral. Reyes ignored him. He didn't really care whether the men of God either liked or respected him. Just so long as they knew their place.

It was late, almost nine in the evening, and tomorrow would be an early start, but the importance of this event could not be overstated. After the turbulent events of the past three weeks, the next day would be a chance to reset. To demonstrate to all of Mexico who was now in charge.

Behind the pews, a small platform had been erected from scaffolding bars. It was in the process of being draped with thick white cloth, heavy bales of which lay on the black and white flagstones, arranged like a chessboard. It was to be a platform for the television cameras. One of them was already installed, and a boom was going up for a microphone.

A woman was standing to one side of it. She had shoulder length light brown hair and was wearing a jacket and black jeans, the latter of which accentuated her frame exceedingly well. Reyes took his time studying her, and after a short while the heat of his attention seemed to make itself known. She turned and shot him an uncertain smile.

He vaguely recognized the face. She was a presenter on one of the local news shows. Perhaps twenty-five years old and selected in that particularly antediluvian nature of television news as much for her looks as for her wits. Though both, he recalled, were mightily impressive.

"She's pretty, don't you think?" Reyes murmured to Mendoza, just loud enough for the presenter to hear, but just quiet enough that she could pretend she hadn't.

Mendoza bowed his head. "I hadn't noticed."

"Liar!" Reyes laughed, the booming sound echoing around the cathedral's long, rectangular name. The sound attracted attention from many of the workers preparing for the following day's events, who just as quickly looked away. "Perhaps you could arrange a private meeting between us."

"Tomorrow?" His lieutenant asked without judgment.

Reyes shook his head. "I'm burying my wife tomorrow. It will be hard enough already. Perhaps next Thursday."

"Consider it done, jefe."

He walked up to the chancel and stared silently at the altar.

Memories of Jennifer ran through his mind. In truth, he hadn't known the girl for very long, but what little time they'd shared together had made both happy. He'd felt that way, anyway. And he'd treated her right. Given her everything she ever asked for.

And in any case, Jennifer Reyes would have the respect of a fine sending off. The whole of Mexico would see his grief, filmed for the television cameras, and cut in time for the 6 o'clock news.

"Ramon," an elderly voice wheezed from behind him, disturbing his train of thought. "I trust that everything is in order?"

"Bishop," Reyes said, recognizing the voice before he turned. It belonged to Bishop Alphonso de Riviera. He swiveled and reached for the bishop's hand. "Thank you, my friend. You've done everything I asked for."

The old man winced, waving absently at the platform on the construction. "The cameras..."

"Are entirely necessary," Reyes finished for him, his tone making clear that on this topic he would brook no argument. "It is important to show strength at a time like this, don't you think?"

"Of course, of course. But is there no other way?"

"There is not," Reyes replied firmly, smoothly moving on to what he suspected was the true cause of the bishop's concern. "Perhaps there's something I can help the church with? Something to make life a little easier, perhaps?"

"You've done so much for us already," de Riviera replied, smoothing his cassock and clutching nervously at the cloth. "I couldn't –"

"Nonsense," Reyes replied, providing the fig leaf that the man needed. "The Cathedral roof needs new tiles, does it not?"

"It does..."

"Then consider it done."

The bishop bowed his head. "Thank you, Ramon."

The use of his name irked Reyes, but he chose to ignore it. "And something to make your life more comfortable perhaps, Bishop? Your robes are so thin."

"I cannot. The church compensates me well enough. And I will have my reward in Heaven. I do not ask for earthly recompense."

"Nevertheless, it would not do for God's work to go unrewarded. How can you save the souls of the city's people if you yourself go to bed hungry at night?"

"That is true, I suppose," Bishop de Riviera murmured, anxiously fingering his cassock's lapels once more. They draped over a frame that gave the lie to the notion that he had ever gone to sleep with an empty belly.

"Then consider it done," Reyes said firmly, glancing at Iker to make sure his man knew what to do. "You will get my friend the correct account details?"

"Thank you, Ramon," de Riviera said once again. "You do so much for the poor of the city. And ask for so little in return. Perhaps that is why they adore you so."

"Perhaps," Reyes replied drily. He was not so arrogant to believe that the poor of either his city or any other saw him as anything but a threat and an opportunity. How much of each depended on the day.

He begged his leave of the bishop and walked into the square outside. The fronds of a palm tree rocked gently from side to side in a humid breeze which carried the smell of roasting chicken. He wrinkled his nose.

"Make sure that restaurant is closed tomorrow," he said, pointing at the offending establishment. "And take down that damn sign. It's unsightly."

"Of course, boss," Mendoza replied quickly, making a note of the task. "Is there anything else?"

Reyes rotated on the spot, testing his eyes over the backlit cathedral. It had a pinkish paint around the base, and accenting the doors and windows, then a light yellow. Two spires rose up into the night sky, their bells invisible against the inky backdrop. It was where he and Jennifer had married. It was fitting that it would also be the place that they formally dissolved their bond.

He stopped turning as he saw two cops strolling down the street by a row of stalls selling vegetables and hot snacks that usually did a roaring trade at this time of night but which were now being broken down by workmen so that they would not muddy the view tomorrow. The two men stared studiously ahead as they walked, ignoring the dozens of armed sicarios scattered all around the square in front of the cathedral and making no attempt to hide their presence.

"That's all. Get my car."

"Yes, jefe."

Reyes rode alone in the back of one of three Range Rover SUVs. They drove only a short distance to the local university's soccer stadium. Though there was no game that evening, the spotlights brightly illuminated the soccer field, which was a luminous green in some places, but speckled with patches of dark brown.

His helicopter was waiting in the circle at the center of the field, rotors already spinning. He climbed in the back without acknowledging the pilot and left the ear defenders draped over his neck as the engine whine grew in intensity before liftoff.

It was a cloudy night, but it was the humidity in the air which really diminished the view. The haze hung heavy over the city of Culiacán, thick and foreboding. Reyes gazed absently out of the windows as the chopper reached cruising altitude, never really registering what was happening below.

It was only five minutes later that he noticed that, instead of roughly following the path of the Culiacán River to the Gulf of California, the chopper was instead traveling on a slightly southerly heading.

He donned the intercom headset and roughly demanded to know where they were going. "Roberto – what the hell is going on? Where are you taking me?"

There was no answer.

Nor did any answer come the next five times he asked, tension growing in his gut with every repetition. Suddenly any thought of the view passing underneath the helicopter was entirely forgotten as his attention became consumed entirely by fears of his impending demise.

Reyes beat against the partition that separated the helicopter's passenger cabin from the controls, knowing even as he did so that it was fruitless. Between a mild turbulence in the air, Roberto's own headset, and the rotor noise that drowned out all other sound, he had no way of being heard.

All that was left to him was to sit and wait.

"To hell with that," he hissed, unbuckling his safety restraints and searching the small cabin for a weapon of any kind. He found no knives, no guns, only a Scotch glass in the chopper's small bar that he put underneath his heel and stomped on hard. He picked up the longest piece of shattered glass and pocketed it, not daring to lift his fingers away.

He tried the headset once again. "Roberto, you fool. Where the hell are we going?"

A blinding flash outside caused him to flinch. Something had crackled out of the night's sky, ripping across the horizon. For one seemingly unending, tortured moment, he thought it was a missile, coming to deliver his judgment.

Lightning. It was only lightning.

Reyes sagged back into his padded leather seat as he at last understood the cause for the flightpath alteration, watching as an almighty squall broke a few miles to the north of the chopper's path. Chain lightning painted the horizon a deep, regal purple and lit giant, swelling storm clouds.

The chopper's heading altered two minutes later, shifting

back to the north, toward his yacht, anchored just off Mazatlán. It touched down ten minutes after that, and as Reyes stepped off onto the familiar deck, he breathed a sigh of relief. Instead of heading toward the crewmember, who was holding a silver tray on which sat a single glass of champagne, he yanked open the pilot's door and gripped Roberto by the chest.

The man stared at him with wild, surprised eyes. "Boss –?"

"What the hell was that about?" Reyes snarled.

"What?" came the stammered response.

"Why didn't you answer me?"

"You didn't say anything."

Reyes' fingers closed into a fist, and he was sorely tempted to punch his pilot in the face. He restrained himself. "There must be an electrical fault. Make sure it's fixed before tomorrow."

"Of course, jefe. At once."

～

TRAPP MOMENTARILY STOPPED KICKING his legs as he checked his dive chronometer once again. The watch face was illuminated by the gentle glow of radium paint and was clearly visible through the dark nighttime waters of the Gulf of California. He was suspended about ten feet below the surface, deep enough that only a powerful searchlight would have any chance at revealing his presence – and then only if it was trained directly on him.

His dive partner, Ikeda, was right alongside him. As a habitual long-distance open water swimmer, the mere twelve hundred yards they'd traveled from the dive boat was nothing to her. She slowed in the water and fell in alongside, grabbing a strap on his breathing apparatus mounted on his back so that they floated in the same patch of water.

Under the surface, using borrowed Mexican Marine diving

gear, it wasn't possible to use anything other than hand signals to communicate. As was practiced in many underwater special forces units across the world, such as the British Special Boat Service and the U.S. Navy Seals, divers typically worked in pairs. One team member carried a compass, the other a depth gauge.

Back home, the Navy SEALs had long since upgraded to more modern technology – the Advanced Diver Mask Mounted Display – a heads up display integrated into their dive mask which showed not just depth but heading and time.

Still, this was how Trapp had learned to swim.

This time, he was carrying the depth gauge. This close to shore, with the bright lights of Mazatlán polluting the night sky, he might have dispensed with it. It was just about possible to work out how far he was from the surface using feel alone.

But diving, especially at night, could be a dangerous business. It was easy to get disoriented in the water, and this only worsened in darkness. So even though he was certain he was in the right spot, he checked the display regardless.

Eleven feet down. Not bad.

He communicated the information to Ikeda, who patted him twice on the shoulder to indicate that she understood. Even with years of experience under his belt, he was glad to have her by his side. Not just because she was a strong swimmer, and just as capable a fighter, but because swimming in the dark wasn't much different from doing so blindfolded.

No matter how much practice you got, it had a way of awakening long-forgotten childhood fears.

Ikeda indicated they needed to shift a couple of degrees to the northwest. They started swimming again, using gentle, measured strokes.

They'd been underwater for eighteen minutes.

55

R eyes emerged from the shower, toweled himself down, then strapped his wristwatch back on.

He grabbed a fresh towel from the stack at the foot of his bed and ran it over his dark hair one last time before critically examining his naked frame in a full-length mirror. Though he was now pushing his mid-forties, he wasn't in bad shape. Stocky, but with precious little extra fat around his midriff. Especially given the temptations he was exposed to on a daily basis. When you could have everything, it was difficult not to indulge.

That did not, however, mean that he was an advocate of fasting. A man still had to eat, and his stomach was reminding him of that fact presently. He glanced at his watch. It was about half past ten, but that wasn't outlandishly late for a meal in this part of the world. He went over the options in his mind.

Perhaps Japanese. Sushi. Good for the waistline, and the new chef was an expert.

He sprayed a little aftershave on his wrist, then dabbed the drying skin on either side of his neck, remembering how the news anchor had looked at him earlier that evening. He'd seen an intrigue in her eyes. A hunger. He liked that.

Jennifer was like that once, he remembered, the memory of his late wife already fading in his mind as he moved on to new pastures. They always worked hardest before they landed their catch.

"Carlos!" Reyes yelled, calling for his steward. "Get in here."

In his mid-twenties, Carlos handled all of his master's desires while on board. If Reyes wanted women flown in from shore, he handled it. If he fancied a wagyu steak, Carlos massaged the damn sirloin himself. And he was usually waiting right outside to instantly attend to even the most fleeting of Reyes' wishes.

"Where the fuck are you?" he groused.

He waited for a few seconds longer in the center of his opulent stateroom, still stark naked, before finally realizing that no one was coming. He dressed quickly, prickling with irritation, and stormed out of the cabin. The warm salt air was a dramatic change from the cool, hermetically sealed environment of the yacht's interior, but wasn't unpleasant.

He called out again. "Carlos!"

Though frustrated, no sense of foreboding imposed on Reyes' thoughts. He was surprised when none of the other crewmembers sprinted to him. Besides the captain and the navigator, there were at least a dozen other crewmembers on board whose sole purpose in life was to make sure that he was never put in precisely this position.

And that was ignoring the dozen armed guards who shadowed him at all times.

Although, as was swiftly becoming apparent – not tonight.

Barefoot, Reyes padded aft along the open passageway that led to the stern. It was made of polished teak, and he presumed it was only this expensive because orangutans swung off its branches and had to be clubbed to death before it could be chopped down. Or something like that.

"Carlos, you piece of shit – what the fuck are you doing?"

Still nothing.

And now, for the second time in one evening, Ramon Reyes truly began to worry. Where the hell was everyone? There were over twenty people on this boat. At least, there was supposed to be. What were the odds that none of them could hear him?

Not good.

He stopped and looked out to sea. There were three smaller yachts around his mother ship, each at one point of a triangle of which he was the center. His sicarios were stationed on each of them, with orders not to let a soul through without clearing it by him.

It was difficult to make out in the darkness, but he thought he saw movement on the one to the yacht's port side, and he relaxed slightly. There had to be an innocent explanation for all this. Maybe a technical fault that required all hands. Yes, that made sense.

Someone was about to get chewed out regardless, but at least there was a reason.

He moved lighter on his feet now, already halfway down the side of the yacht. The passageway kinked right slightly before moving left, and as he passed through, he almost slipped on a puddle of water.

"The hell?"

Reyes looked down and was transfixed by what he saw.

Not water. Blood.

All his earlier fears rushed back to him in an instant, and the wave of nausea that rose inside him was equal to the worst seasickness. His right foot was in the center of a large, circular puddle of blood. The yacht's walls were a dark, glossy blue, but even in the dim safety lighting, glowing splashes were evident.

Dear God.

Reyes thought about turning back, but as he looked over his shoulder, he thought – or imagined – he saw a dark shadow behind him, and an animal terror drove him forward. His bloodied right foot left a trail of single footprints running forward along the deck.

There was an armory on the deck below, he remembered. Even if all of his sicarios were dead – a possibility he still couldn't truly bring himself to believe – then he would be able to arm himself there.

The idea gave him a goal, and he sprinted forward with little regard for the sound he was making. It wasn't a rational decision, for he was presently guided only by animal panic.

In any case, it did not matter.

He exploded onto the yacht's unlit rear deck, pulling up only once he noticed a dark shape emerge by his feet. He backpedaled but was unable to stop in time and tripped over it. The shape was fleshy.

It was warm.

It had once been a man.

Acid rose in Reyes' throat, singeing his esophagus. He swallowed it back and attempted to wrestle control back from his panicked breathing. There was still a way out, but not if he fell apart like some helpless woman. He reminded himself that he'd been in worse scrapes.

He knelt by the body, his hands now as slick with blood as his right foot, and searched it quickly for a weapon. There was none, but he found that the sicario's throat had been expertly cut, and even in the dull gleam of light visible from shore, he could see exposed white sinews deep inside the wound.

The nausea rose once more.

The armory.

He stood, the imagined prospect of safety driving him onward. He took two more steps toward the stairwell that led to the lower deck and tripped over another body. This one too was lying in a pool of his own lifeblood.

Reyes could scarcely believe that this wasn't some terrible nightmare. It was as though demons had somehow gained access to his boat under the cover of darkness and wreaked the most terrible of revenge.

But who – and *why?* Fernando Carreon was dead. What was left of his organization was either pledging their lives to his own cartel or were running for their lives. There was simply no way that any of them could have organized so bold an attack as this.

It didn't matter. There was a way off this boat. The jet ski, mounted by the prow. He needed a gun first, then he could tackle that goal. But only when he had a weapon. In truth, maybe going for the armory wasn't an optimal strategy for survival. But he couldn't face the terror of this yacht without one.

Reyes skirted the second body and climbed down the steps to the lower deck without further incident. It was even darker down here. Even the safety lights were turned off. He was forced to navigate by feel and memory alone. He made his way through the darkness step by step, reaching blindly out with one hand as another gripped the wall.

The searching fingers touched another shape in the darkness. Not cold, or hard, but warm. Reyes froze. Whatever and whoever this was – he was alive.

The shape spoke English. It said, "Going somewhere?"

Trapp, his eyes long since accustomed to the darkness after the underwater swim and another ten minutes crouching next to her bulkhead waiting for this prick to emerge, smiled wide.

The man – by process of elimination he could only be Ramon Reyes – was breathing hard, almost hyperventilating.

He balled his fingers into a fist, drew his elbow back just barely enough to make it hurt, and drove the weapon into Reyes' stomach. The cartel boss went down like a sack of potatoes, grunting once, then moaning as he clutched his belly in agony.

"I thought it would take more than that," Trapp observed as he carefully frisked the Mexican, only to learn that he was unarmed. "Shame. I was looking forward to a fight."

Reyes said nothing, just clutched his belly and gasped as he attempted to suck air into his stunned lungs.

Trapp hauled him upright and dragged him along the deck before entering a hatchway about halfway down the boat. Reyes hardly bothered to resist. He tried pulling himself away once, but the attempted bravery was quickly dispelled by a sharp blow of the head against the nearest bulkhead. That too elicited a dull groan, and after that, just silence.

"Better," Trapp muttered.

With the prisoner secured, Trapp now flicked the nearest light switch, blinking as the yacht's interior lighting flickered into view. He worked his way to the boat's main living space, where Hector and half a dozen of his Marines were waiting. He thrust Reyes to the floor, and the pitiful excuse for a man just lay there, not daring to look up at his captors.

"The crew?" Trapp asked.

"In their quarters. They're secured. I've got two men watching over them. They don't want any trouble. All his guards are dead."

"Good." He gestured at Reyes. "I brought you a gift."

"So I see."

Reyes moaned with fear and started to crawl backwards, stopping only when he was pulled up short by coming into contact with a plush sofa. He flinched as he touched it, eyes snapping over his shoulder in panic, then visibly relaxing as he learned the precise nature of the obstacle.

"Please..." he whispered. "I don't know who you people are. Just let me live."

Trapp glanced at Hector for permission to speak. He didn't want to step on the Mexican officer's toes, and they hadn't exactly rehearsed this part. It was entirely possible that Reyes might have been caught in the crossfire in the initial assault. Not optimal, but always a possibility.

His capture, though, was what they'd hoped for. Hector seemed to consider the request for a couple of seconds, then nodded curtly. Trapp smiled his thanks.

"That's up to you, Ramon."

Reyes squinted up at him. "Who are you?"

Trapp gestured at the sofa that Reyes was sheltering beside. "Go on, sit. I'm getting a neck ache looking at you down there."

He waited for the cartel boss to climb laboriously up onto the piece of furniture, moving so slowly it looked as though his muscles must have turned to jelly. He continued the second Reyes was upright, not giving him a chance to reset. "I guess you could call me a concerned citizen, Ramon."

"Concerned about what?"

"The arrangements for tomorrow. By the way, I don't think I passed along my condolences about your wife's passing. I was there when it happened."

Reyes' face wrinkled with incomprehension. "You –?"

"You guys aren't as subtle as you think you are."

"Who the hell are you?" Reyes snarled, his fear at least momentarily forgotten. "I have rights."

"That's actually a really fascinating point, Ramon," Trapp said, not bothering to disguise the mocking tone in his voice. "I'm glad you made it. But this is the thing: depending on how you read the law, you might be classed as an enemy combatant.

I would be perfectly justified in snapping your neck right here, right now."

"You can't!" Reyes said, attempting to scramble back before realizing he was unable. He jabbed his finger at Hector's men, seeming to recognize that they were compatriots. "They won't let you."

"Who?"

"Them!" Reyes squawked, his voice strangled with panic as he gestured wildly at the Marines.

Trapp looked over his shoulder with exaggerated confusion. "I see no one."

"You can't do this," Reyes moaned.

"Can I be honest with you, Ramon?"

The Mexican waved his hand, barely able to lift it off the sofa cushion. He couldn't look at Trapp.

"I've never liked addicts. My daddy was a drinker. He would come home and beat me. Maybe it's the reason I am the way I am."

"That's nothing to do with me."

"I never said it was. But you see, I can't bust down the door of the Jack Daniels distillery and start taking names. But I *can* do something about you. And these men here, I don't think they are going to stop me."

"So you do see them..." Reyes whimpered, like a child waking from a nightmare.

"There won't be any news cameras at the funeral tomorrow, Ramon," Trapp said, switching tack. "I'm afraid we've reviewed the arrangements, and the guest list doesn't work for us."

"What the hell are you talking about?"

"Wake up, Ramon," Trapp snapped. "I'm offering you a way out. Do you want it or not?"

"What offer?"

Trapp listed the conditions on his fingers. "No cameras. No

guests. No security from your organization. My friends here will be on hand to ensure everything goes to plan."

"I can't agree to this," Reyes grumbled, a sullen expression on his squat face. "Tomorrow is –"

"I know what tomorrow was supposed to be. But I told you, it doesn't work for us."

Reyes cocked his head, seeming to consider the offer, then shook it. He stood, lifted his arms, put his wrists together, and walked toward Hector. "No deal. Arrest me. I'll take my chances in court."

Trapp burst forward, closing the distance in a fraction of a second. He grabbed Reyes by the throat and slammed him down onto the deck. "Listen up, fuckface. This isn't a negotiation. You'll do what I tell you, or I'll put a bullet between your eyes, drive this boat five miles out to sea, and dump your body deep enough that the only creatures who get to see it have gills for lungs. You understand?"

The Mexican's eyes bulged as Trapp's fingers closed around his Adam's apple, squeezing. He opened his mouth, patently attempting to speak, but Trapp only pressed harder. He raised his fingers, attempting to push his attacker off, but Trapp resisted that too, batting them aside as though he were no stronger than a child.

Finally, Reyes nodded, desperation in his eyes. Trapp released the hold and stood off him.

"Good. Now, are you ready for part two?"

Reyes lay back numbly, as though he had simply accepted whatever fate had in store for him.

"I'll take that as a yes. You see, it hasn't escaped my friends' attention that you're planning to expand your organization's activities over the next few weeks and months. We can't have that. At least, not the way you planned. No more violence. No more public executions. No innocents catching a stray bullet. I don't care if you psychopaths kill each other, but the rest of it has to stop. Do we have a deal?"

He received a sullen nod.

"And you will be working closely with my friends here. If they ask you for something, you'll do it. No questions asked. Names, places, shipments, I don't care if Hector here wants you to wipe his ass."

"For how long?" Reyes mumbled, trying hard to locate his spine, but not quite succeeding.

"Forever." Trapp shrugged.

"No."

His eyebrow kinking upward, Trapp said, "No?"

"You heard me."

"I don't think you're a stupid man, Ramon. Would you agree?"

A nod.

"Then I'm guessing you have an idea who I work for."

Another, more grudging one.

"Now, I'm no one. The chain of command is about a million feet long, and I'm right here at the bottom. But the guy at the top lost his son to an overdose, and that's a thing you just don't forget. I can be your worst nightmare. Maybe I won't kill you. Maybe I'll let you go to sleep every night wondering if it'll be your last. And I'm guessing the president won't mind stumping up for my plane ride down here."

"That had nothing to do with me. It was years ago," Reyes protested.

"Like I said." Trapp shrugged. "The kind of thing you just don't forget. So what's it going to be, Ramon? A life of luxury, occasionally jumping as high as we tell you, or no life at all?"

Reyes glowered back, but in the end he only had one road left open to him.

He nodded.

ALSO BY JACK SLATER

Sometimes it's easier to ask for forgiveness than permission.

Siberia in April isn't in any tourist guidebook. But that is where Trapp finds himself. It's cold, dark, and the vodka tastes like gasoline.

After brawling with half a dozen corrupt Russian cops, he's taken to the infamous penal colony marked on maps as IK-29, but known to inmates as the Black Eagle. The guards are brutes, their prisoners little better than animals. It's hell on earth.

And this time, he's on his own. The Agency has no knowledge of his mission. They wouldn't back him if they did. Because men like Trapp are tools. They aren't supposed to get ideas of their own.

It's dangerous when they do.

Head to the Amazon Kindle store to read Black Eagle, book six in the *Jason Trapp* thriller series.

FOR ALL THE LATEST NEWS

I hope you enjoyed The Apparatus. If you did, and don't fancy sifting through thousands of books on Amazon and leaving your next great read to chance, then sign up to my mailing list and be the first to hear when I release a new book.

Visit jack-slater.com/updates to sign up and receive a FREE ebook!

And keep reading if you want to learn more about the real-life inspiration that led me to write *The Apparatus*...

Thanks so much for reading!

Jack.

AUTHOR'S NOTE

Dear Reader,

Thank you so much for making it to the end of *The Apparatus*! I hope you enjoyed the read.

I first wrote this message at the very start of 2021, at which point the past 12 months had been as strange for me as I'm sure it has been for all of you. Except any of you lucky suckers living in New Zealand or Taiwan! I get the odd email from that side of the world, and it recently tempted me to take a trip across the Pacific. I've spent the last few months in tropical paradises (and urban jungles!) galore, and I've returned fresh and ready to put pen back to paper with plenty of ideas for Jason's next cameo role... He normally sniffs out danger one way or another.

The idea for the Apparatus – the organization, rather than the book title – came when I was reading the Wikipedia page for the real life intelligence group known as "The Activity"...

Otherwise known as the Intelligence Support Activity.

Or Mission Support Activity.

Or the Army of Northern Virginia.

Or Task Force Orange.

Or the Field Operations Group.

I could go on...

For a thriller author, there's probably nothing more interesting than coming across a real-life secret organization like this. And it set a spark in my mind that ended in this book.

My personal favorite of those names is the Army of Northern Virginia. Sounds like something right out of the Civil War!

The Activity, as General Caldwell explains in the book, was founded in order to provide intelligence for US Special Forces. It was created just after the disaster of Operation Eagle Claw – the failed attempt to retake the US Embassy in Tehran – so that such a catastrophe could never happen again. It's probably one of the most secretive, least known, and consequential intelligence organization in the whole alphabet soup.

And it got me thinking. Let's be honest, the US has a reputation for half-baked military and intelligence schemes. Whether it's Iran-Contra, adventures in the Middle East or attempted coups in South America, American fingerprints are all over it. That's kind of the price of being a global superpower.

But what if there was one organization whose sole responsibility was to dream up these crackpot schemes?

And that was the genesis for the Apparatus. What if instead of building fences on the border and searching every ship, truck and submarine that tries to make it into the US for cocaine, we just went right to the source instead, and seized control of the drug cartels? Since our approach for the last 50 years to the War on Drugs hasn't really worked, it sounded like as good an idea as any.

And what if the very person who was tasked to dream up the plan decided to take it freelance when his superiors in the military failed to go through with it?

Well, it would probably end in disaster. Sometimes out-of-the-box ideas are best packed away for good. And that's what Warren Grover never understood.

Thank you as always for reading, and until next time.

Jack.